A Woman Perfected by Richard Marsh

Richard Bernard Heldmann was born on 12th October 1857, in St Johns Wood, North London.

By his early 20's Heldmann began publishing fiction for the myriad magazine publications that had sprung up and were eager for good well-written content.

In October 1882, Heldmann was promoted to co-editor of Union Jack, a popular magazine, but his association with the publication ended suddenly in June 1883. It appears Heldman was prone to issuing forged cheques to finance his lifestyle. In April 1884 He was sentenced to 18 months hard labour.

In order to be well away from the scandal and damage this had caused to his reputation Heldmann adopted a pseudonym on his release from jail. Shortly thereafter the name 'Richard Marsh' began to appear in the literary periodicals. The use of his mother's maiden name as part of it seems both a release and a lifeline.

A stroke of very good fortune arrived with his novel The Beetle published in 1897. This would turn out to be his greatest commercial success and added some much-needed gravitas to his literary reputation.

Marsh was a prolific writer and wrote almost 80 volumes of fiction as well as many short stories, across many genres from horror and crime to romance and humour.

Index of Contents

CHAPTER I

STRICKEN

Donald Lindsay was prostrated by a stroke of apoplexy on Thursday, April 3. It was surmised that the immediate cause was mental. He arrived home apparently physically well, but in a state of what, for him, was a state of unusual agitation. As a rule he was a dour man; much given to silence; self-contained. At that time there was staying at Cloverlea, with his daughter Nora, a school-friend, Elaine Harding. During lunch both girls were struck by his unusual talkativeness. Often during a meal he would hardly open his lips for any other purpose except eating and drinking. That morning he talked volubly to both girls on all sorts of subjects. After lunch Nora said laughingly to Elaine—

"I wonder what's the matter with papa. I don't know when I remember him so conversational."

He put in no appearance at tea; but as that was a common occurrence his absence went unnoticed. When, however, the gong having sounded for dinner, the girls were waiting for him in the drawing-room, and still he did not come, Nora sent a servant to his dressing-room to inquire if he would be long. The man returned to say that his master was neither in his dressing-room nor his bedroom; that he had spent the afternoon in his study, from which no one had seen him issue; that the study door was locked, and knockings went unheeded. Nora, opening a French window in the drawing-room, went along the terrace towards the study.

The study opened on to the terrace. It had two long windows. At neither of them were the blinds down or the curtains drawn. It was elicited afterwards that the servant whose duty it was to attend to such matters had knocked at the door when the shadows lowered. On turning the handle, he found that it was locked; Mr. Lindsay informed him from within that he would draw the blinds himself. It seemed that he had not done so. The room was in darkness, with the exception of the flicker of the firelight. Nora said to Miss Harding, who had followed at her heels—

"Whatever does papa want with a fire on a day like this?" All that week the weather had been not only warm, but positively hot. There had been one of those hot spells which we sometimes get in April; and, as frequently, have to do without in August. Save in the evenings and early mornings fires had remained unlit in all the living rooms. That Thursday had been the hottest day of all. Mr. Lindsay was one of those persons who seldom felt the cold, but quickly suffered from the heat. He preferred to be without a fire in his own apartments when the rest of the establishment was glad enough to be within reach of a cheerful blaze. That there should be one in his study on such a day as that struck his daughter as strange. She stood close up to the window, her friend at her side. "The room seems empty."

"It is empty," said Miss Harding. Nora knocked, without result. "What's the use of knocking? There's no one there." Nora tried the handle first of one window, then of the other; both were fastened. "What's the use?" asked Miss Harding. "Any one can see that the room is empty. There's light enough for that."

At that moment the fire flared up in such a way that all the room within was lit by its radiance; so clearly lit as to make it plain that it had no occupant.

"But," observed Nora, "if it's empty why should the door be locked? Papa never leaves it locked when he's not inside."

Two figures approached through the darkness. In front was the housekeeper, Mrs. Steele.

"Miss Nora," she began, "you'd better go indoors. I'm afraid there's something wrong."

"Why should I go indoors?" the girl demanded. "And what can be wrong? We can see all over the room; we saw plainly just now, didn't we, Elaine? There's no one there."

"Your father's there," said Mrs. Steele.

Her tone was grim. Before Nora could ask how she knew that, there was a crash of glass. Looking round with a start she found that Stephen Morgan, the butler, had broken a pane in the other window.

"Morgan," she cried, "what are you doing?"

"This is the shortest way in," he answered.

He thrust his arm through the broken pane; lifted the hasp; the window was open. He went through it. Nora was following when she was checked by Mrs. Steele.

"Miss Nora," she persisted, "you had better go indoors."

"I am going indoors; isn't this indoors? If, as you put it, there is something wrong, who is more concerned than I?" All four entered. Morgan, who had passed round to the other side of the large writing-table, which was in the centre of the room, gave a sudden exclamation. Nora hurried round to where he was. Some one was lying huddled up on the floor; as if, slipping awkwardly out of his chair, he had lain helplessly where he had fallen. Nora dropped on her knees by his side. "Papa!" she cried. "Father!"

No one answered. Morgan lit the lamp which always stood on Mr. Lindsay's writing-table. In the days which followed Nora often had occasion to ask herself what, exactly, happened next. She was conscious that in the room there was a strong smell of burnt paper; always, afterwards, when her nostrils were visited by the odour of charred paper that scene came back to her. The cause of the smell was not far to seek; the hearth was full of ashes. Evidently Mr. Lindsay had been burning papers on a wholesale scale; apparently for that reason he had had a fire; Nora had a vague impression—which recurred to her, later, again and again—that many of the papers were only partially consumed. The room was littered with papers; they were all over the table; on chairs, on the floor; drawers stood open, papers peeped out of them; which was the more remarkable since Mr. Lindsay was the soul of neatness. Plainly the finger of God had touched him when he was still in the midst of the task which he had set himself. There came a time when Nora had reason to wish that she had retained her self-possession sufficiently to give instructions that all papers, both burnt and unburnt, were to be left exactly as they were; and had taken steps to ensure those instructions being carried out. But at the moment all she thought of was her father. He was not dead; his stertorous breathing was proof of that. They carried him up-stairs; undressed him, put him to bed, who an hour or two before had been the hale, strong man; who had never known what it was to be sick; who had so loved to do everything for himself.

Apoplexy was Dr. Banyard's pronouncement, when he appeared upon the scene; though there were features about the case which induced him to fall in readily with Nora's suggestion that a specialist should be sent for from town. The great man arrived in the middle of the night. When he saw Nora he was sententious but vague, as great doctors are apt to be; the girl gathered from his manner that the worst was to be feared.

On the following day, the Friday, towards evening, Mr. Lindsay partially regained consciousness—that is, he opened his eyes, and when his child leaned over him it was plain he knew her, though he got no further than the mere recognition. He could neither speak, nor move, nor do anything for himself at all. That night Nora dreamed a dream. She dreamed that her father came into her room in his night-shirt, and leaned over her, and whispered that he had something to say to her—which he must say to her; but which was for her ear alone—he was just about to tell her what it was when she woke up. So strong had the conviction of his actual presence been that for some moments she could not believe that it was a dream; she started up in bed fully expecting to find him standing by her side. When she found that he was not close enough to touch she leaned out of bed, murmuring—

"Father! father!"

It was only after she had lit a candle that she was constrained to the belief that it was a dream. Even then she was incredulous. She actually carried her candle to the door, and looked out into the passage, half expecting to see him passing along it. When she returned into her room she was in a curious condition, both mentally and bodily. She trembled so that she had to sink on to a chair. Then she did what she had not done for years—she cried. If she had had to say what prompted her tears, her explanation would have been a curious one; she would have had to say that she cried because of her father's grief; that it was his anguish which moved her to tears. Dream or no dream, what had struck her about him, as he leaned over her as she lay in bed, was his agony. In all the years she had known him she had never known him show signs of emotion; yet, as he leant over her she had felt, even in her sleep, that he was under the stress of some terrible trouble; that he wished to say to her what he had to say so much that his anxiety to say it was tearing at the very roots of his being. It was some minutes before she regained her self-control; when she did she slipped on a dressing-gown and went to her father's room. The night nurse answered her unspoken question by informing her that no change had taken place; that the sick man was just as he had been. Nora moved to his bed. There he lay, on his back, exactly as before. She had the feeling strong upon her that he had heard her coming; that, in some strange fashion, he was glad to see her; though, when she stood beside him, he looked up at her with such agony in his eyes that the sight of it brought tears to hers. Again there came to her that odd conviction which had possessed her when she woke out of sleep, that there was something which he strenuously wished to say to her; that he was torn by the desire to relieve himself of a burden which was on his mind.

On the Saturday his condition remained the same; he was conscious but motionless, helpless, and, above all, speechless. So convinced was she that if he could only speak, if only some means could be found by which he could convey his thoughts to her, that he would be more at his ease, that she appealed to Dr. Banyard.

"Can nothing be done to restore to him the power of speech, if only for a few minutes?"

"I believe that I am doing all that medicine can do; you heard Sir Masterman say that he could do no more."

"Can you think of no way in which he can convey to us his meaning? I believe that he has something which he wishes very much to say—something on his mind; and that if he could only say it—get it off his mind—he would at least be happier."

The doctor eyed her shrewdly.

"Have you any notion what it is?"

"Not the slightest. If I had I might prompt him, and get at it that way. But my father has never been very communicative with me; I know nothing of his private affairs—absolutely nothing; I only know that he is my father."

"Have you any other relations?"

"So far as I know only an aunt, his sister. I have never seen her—I don't think they have been on good terms; I don't know her address; I believe she lives abroad."

"Had your mother no relations?"

"I cannot tell you; I know nothing of my mother—she died when I was born. I have been wondering if what he wishes to say is that, if—if the worst comes, he would like to be buried in her grave. I don't know where her grave is; he has never spoken of her to me."

The doctor continued to eye her intently. He had a clever face, with a whimsical mouth, which seemed to be a little on one side; his eyes were deep-set, and were surrounded by a thick thatch of iron-grey hair.

"How old are you?"

"I shall be twenty in June."

"That's a ripe age."

She sighed.

"I feel as if I were a hundred."

"You don't look it; however, that's by the way. At such a time as this, Miss Lindsay, you ought not to be alone in this great house, with all the weight upon your shoulders."

"I'm not alone; Elaine is with me."

"Yes; and she—is even older than you."

"Elaine is twenty-four."

"I don't doubt it. If you're a hundred I should say that she is a thousand."

"What do you mean?"

"Nothing." But she felt that he had meant something; she wondered what. He went on. "What I intended to remark was that I think you ought to have some one with you who would give proper attention to your interests. As it is, you are practically at the mercy of a lot of servants and—and others. Hasn't your father an old friend, in whom you yourself have confidence—a business friend? By the way, who is his man of business—his lawyer?"

She shook her head.

"If father has any friends I don't know them. He has never been very sociable with anybody about here; I can't say what old acquaintances he may have had elsewhere. As you are probably aware, he was frequently away."

"Did you never go with him?"

"Never—never once. I have never been with my father anywhere out of this immediate neighbourhood, except when I first went to school, when he escorted me."

"But you always knew where he was?"

"Sometimes; not always."

"Had he an address in town?"

"Only his club, so far as I know."

"Which was his club?"

"The Carlton."

"That sounds good enough. Did you use to write to him there?"

"Not often; he only liked me to write to him when I had something of importance to say. He cared neither for reading nor for writing letters. He once told me that there were a lot of women who seemed to have nothing better to do than waste their own and other people's time by scribbling a lot of nonsense, which they cut up into lengths, sent through the post, and called letters. He hoped I should never become one of them. I remembered what he said, and never troubled him with one of the 'lengths' called letters if I could help it."

Both of them smiled; only the doctor's was a whimsical smile, and hers was hardly suggestive of mirth.

"You haven't told me who his lawyer is."

"The only lawyer I ever heard him mention was Mr. Nash."

"Nash? He only employed him in little local jobs; in no sense was he his man of business; I've reasons for knowing that his opinion of Herbert Nash's legal ability is not an unduly high one."

As before, Nora shook her head.

"He is the only lawyer I ever heard papa mention."

"But, my dear Miss Lindsay, your father is a man of affairs—of wealth; he lives here at the rate of I don't know how many thousand pounds a year, and has never owed a man a penny; you must know something of his affairs."

"All I know is that he has always given me all the money I wanted, and not seldom more than I wanted; I have never had to ask him for any; but beyond that I know nothing."

When Dr. Banyard got home he said to his wife—

"Helen, if I had to define a male criminal lunatic, I am inclined to think that I should say it was a man who brought up his women-folk in the lap of luxury without giving them the faintest inkling as to where the wherewithal to pay for that luxury came from."

His wife said mischievously—

"It is at least something for women-folk, as you so gracefully describe the salt of the earth, to be brought up in the lap of luxury; please remember that, sir. And pray what prompts this last illustration of the wisdom of the modern Solomon?"

"That man Lindsay; you know how he's been a mystery to all the country-side; the hints which have been dropped; the guesses which have been made; the clues which the curious have followed, ending in nothing; the positive libels which have been uttered. It turns out that he's as much a mystery to his own daughter as he is to anybody else; I've just had it from her own lips. The man lies dying, leaving her in complete ignorance of everything she ought to know—at the mercy, not impossibly, of those who do know. Just as God is calling him home he wants to tell her; I can see it in his eyes, and so can she; but he is dumb. Unless a miracle is worked he'll die silent, longing to tell her what he ought to have told her years ago."

CHAPTER II

THE OPEN WINDOW

On the Sunday Donald Lindsay died, in the afternoon, about half-past four; probably about the time, Dr. Banyard said, when he had first been stricken. Although, apparently, conscious to the last, he died speechless, without being able to do anything to relieve himself of the burden which lay upon his mind; a burden which, it seemed not improbable, had been the first cause of the fate which had so suddenly overtaken him. To Nora the blow was, of course, a bad one; when she realized that her father was dead it seemed as if all the light had gone out of the world for her. And yet, in the nature of things, it was impossible that she should feel for him the affection which sometimes associates the parent with the child. He himself had scoffed at love; sentiment, he had repeatedly told her, was the thing in life which was to be most avoided; he had illustrated his meaning in his own practice. He had never been unkind, but he had certainly never been tender; so far as she was aware he had never kissed her in his life; on those rare occasions on which she had ventured to kiss him he had brushed her aside as if she had been guilty of some folly. His attitude towards her was one of more or less genial indifference. He had provided her with a beautiful home; he had bought Cloverlea, as he was careful to inform her, for her, and in it he left her very much alone. He supplied her liberally with money, and there he seemed to think his duty towards her ended. She was welcome to have any companions she chose; he asked no questions about her comings and her goings; took no sort of interest in the young women of her own age whom, at rare intervals, she induced to stay with her. He made no attempt whatever to find for her a place in local, or any other, society; yet, unaided, she began, by degrees, to occupy a somewhat prominent place on the local horizon.

Living in one of the finest places in the neighbourhood, with horses and carriages at her disposal, and even, latterly, motor cars; possessed of a sufficiency of ready money, it was hardly likely that she should remain unnoticed; her father's peculiarities threw her, if anything, into bolder relief. There was not a house for miles in which she was not a welcome visitor, and for this she had, largely, to thank herself. Not only was she good to look at, she was good to be with; she had that indefinable thing, charm. Not all the pens which ever wrote could make clear to Us the secret of a young girl's charm. Whilst she was still the mistress of Cloverlea her father seemed to be the only living creature who remained impervious to its magic influence; afterwards—that influence waned. On the Sunday on which her father died she was left alone with her grief; but on the Monday morning Dr. Banyard called and insisted on her seeing him. His manner, while it was brusque, was sympathetic.

"Now, my dear young lady," he began, almost as soon as she was in the room, "what you have first of all to remember is that you, at any rate, are still alive, and likely, in all human probability, to remain so for some considerable time to come; your first duty therefore, towards yourself, and towards your father, is to see that your interests are properly safeguarded."

"I don't know what you mean."

"Then I will endeavour to make myself clear. I believe you are engaged to be married."

"You know I am."

"Where, at the present moment, is Mr. Spencer?"

"He is on his way home from Cairo, where he has been staying with his aunt, Lady Jane Carruthers, who is ill."

"Does he know what has happened?"

"I don't quite know where he is. When he last wrote he told me that he was going to take what he called an 'after-cure' in Italy "—she smiled, as if at some thought of her own—"but he entered into no particulars, and until I hear from him again I don't quite know where he's to be found; all I do know is that he's to be home before the first of May."

"As things stand, that's some distance ahead. I believe that his father and mother, the Earl and Countess, are also absent." She nodded. "You say you don't know who was your father's man of business; then who is there to whom you feel yourself entitled to turn for the kind of assistance of which you stand in such imperative need, at once; certainly in the course of to-day?"

"There's Elaine."

"You mean Miss Harding?" It was his turn to smile. "I'm afraid she's not the kind of person I'm thinking of; though I do not for a moment doubt her cleverness. She suffers from one disqualification; she's not a man. What you want is a dependable, and thoroughly capable lawyer."

"There's Mr. Nash."

"Mr. Nash is, again, hardly the sort of person you're in want of. To begin with, he's too young, has too little experience; it was only the other day he qualified—with difficulty."

"He has been qualified more than three years; he did a good many things for papa."

"Yes, but what kind of things? Not the kind which will have to be done for you; and I happen to know that what he did he bungled."

"I believe he's coming here to-day."

"Have you sent for him?"

"I haven't; but Elaine came into my room this morning and asked if she should, and I believe she has."

"Miss Harding sent for him?" The doctor eyed her intently for a moment; then, turning, he went to the window and looked out; presently he spoke to her from there. "And do you propose to give Herbert Nash the run of your father's papers?"

"I don't know what I propose to do; I haven't thought about it at all; I want him to do what he can to help me; I don't feel as if I could do very much to help myself."

"Is it any use my saying that I can give you the name of a well-known firm of family lawyers; and that you have only to send them a wire, and before the day is over you'll have one of the best men in England—in every sense—on the premises, making your interests his own?"

"Elaine seemed to think that Mr. Nash has only to glance through some of my father's papers to discover who my father's man of business really was, and that then all we shall have to do will be to communicate with him."

"I see; there's something in that—Miss Harding has her wits about her. Do you know what time Mr. Nash is coming?"

"I don't—Elaine sent the message, if one was sent, and of that I'm not certain; anyhow I don't know what arrangements she has made."

"Would you mind inquiring?"

"I'll ask her to come here, then you can inquire yourself."

The bell was rung, and presently Miss Harding appeared. She was short and slight; with dark hair, big dark eyes, a dainty little mouth, and very red lips. She made at once for Nora, ignoring the doctor, who was still standing by the window.

"They tell me that you want me."

"It isn't I, it's Dr. Banyard; he wants to know if you have sent to Mr. Nash; and, if so, at what time he's coming."

Miss Harding opened her big eyes wider, which was a trick she had.

"Dr. Banyard wants to know?—why does Dr. Banyard want to know?"

"That I cannot tell you; you had better ask him; here he is. Is Mr. Nash coming?"

"Of course he's coming, but he doesn't seem to know quite when; it seems he has some sort of case on at the police court."

"I know; he's defending that young scoundrel, Gus Peters, who's been robbing his master."

This was the doctor; Miss Harding turned to him.

"Is the gentleman you call Gus Peters a scoundrel?"

"Isn't a fellow who robs his master a scoundrel?"

"Has it been proved that he robbed his master?"

"It's a matter of common notoriety."

"Common notoriety is not infrequently a liar. However, that's not the point; I suppose Mr. Nash will do his duty to his client in any case, and he'll come here as soon as he's done it."

"I'd wait for him if I could, but I have to go my round; I'll look in afterwards on the off-chance of finding him; there's something I particularly wish to say to him. I fancy the magistrates, in spite of Mr. Nash, will make short work of Mr. Peters."

After the doctor had gone Miss Harding said to Miss Lindsay,

"Nora, dear, don't you think that Dr. Banyard is inclined to be a little interfering?"

"It has never struck me that he was."

"It has struck me, more than once. But then I think that G.P.s are apt to be interfering; they hope, by having a finger in everybody's pie, to get a plum out of each. Dr. Banyard doesn't like Mr. Nash, does he?"

"He has never told me that he doesn't."

"Has he never breathed words to the same effect?"

"He has certainly hinted that he doesn't think much of Mr. Nash's legal abilities; but then who does?"

"I do."

"Really, Elaine?"

"Really, Nora. I believe that if he's truly interested in a person he can do as much for that person as anybody else—perhaps more."

"Possibly; but is he ever truly interested in anybody but himself?"

Miss Harding was silent for an instant; then she smiled rather oddly.

"Entirely between ourselves, Nora, that's what I wonder."

She had cause to.

It happened on the Thursday evening on which Mr. Lindsay was taken ill, that Elaine Harding was left with nothing to do, and no one to do it with. It is true that, had she insisted, she might have made herself of use in some way; but, as she herself admitted, she was no good when there was illness about. Indeed, she was one of those persons—though this she kept to herself—who shrunk from suffering in any form with a sort of instinctive physical repugnance. She only needed half-a-hint to the effect that her services were not required, and she was ready to give the sick-room as wide a berth as any one could possibly require. To be plain, she was disposed to regard Mr. Lindsay's attack almost as if it had been an injury to herself. Had she been perfectly free, she would have packed up her boxes and left the house within the hour; it would have been better for her if she had. The idea of having to remain under the same roof with a man who was suffering from an apoplectic stroke was horrid; but, at the same time, there were reasons, of divers sorts, why she should not flee from the dearest friend she had in the world at the first sign of trouble.

Instead of packing up her boxes she dined alone, off food which had been ruined by being kept waiting. That was another grievance. She did like good food, perfectly cooked. She was conscious that the servants were regarding her askance, as if they were surprised that she should dine at all; that also was annoying. When she rose from table she was in quite a bad temper—what Mr. Lindsay meant by falling ill when she was in the house she could not imagine. The solitude of the empty drawing-room was appalling. The French window still stood open; better the solitude of the grounds than that great bare chamber. She went out on to the terrace. It was a lovely night, warmer than many nights in June. There was not a cloud in the sky. A moon, almost at the full, lighted the world with her silver glory. She looked about her. Suddenly she perceived that a light was shining out upon the terrace from what was evidently an uncurtained window. She remembered; no doubt it was the lamp in Mr. Lindsay's study, the lamp which Morgan had lit; in that case the window must still be open. She went to see; her slight form moved along the terrace with something stealthy in its movements, as if she was ashamed of what she was doing. She reached the study; it was as she supposed; the lamp was lit, the window was open, the room was empty. She was seized by what she would afterwards have described as a sudden access of curiosity. She glanced over her shoulder, to left and right; there was no one in sight; not a sound. She put her dainty head inside the window, to indulge herself with just one peep; after all, there is very little harm in innocent peeping; then she passed into the room.

CHAPTER III

LITTLE BY LITTLE

It was just as it was when its owner had been stricken down; in the same state of disorder. Cupboards yawned; drawers were open; letters and papers were everywhere; a fire still smouldered in the grate; the hearth was littered with the ashes of burned and half-burned papers; everywhere were indications that Mr. Lindsay had been interrupted, possibly just as he was setting his house in order. Glancing round her Elaine perceived that the door which led into the passage was open, though only an inch or two; probably it had been left unlatched when they bore the master through it. Moving lightly, on tiptoe, she shut it, noiselessly; but she made sure she had shut it fast. She even laid her small fingers about the handle of the key, seeming to hesitate whether or not to turn it; then, smiling, as if at the absurdity of the notion, she returned towards the centre of the room; standing for some seconds glancing about her in all directions, as if in search of something which it might be worth her while to look at; a pretty, dainty, girlish figure, herself the one thing in the whole room which was best worth looking at.

By degrees her quick, bright eyes, roving hither and thither, reached the writing-table in the centre, by which its owner had been sitting when he had slipped from off his chair; instantly they noted something which gleamed amid the litter of papers with which it was covered. Moving a little towards it she saw that there were coins on a little oasis about the centre; quite a heap of them—gold coins. On the top of them was half-a-sheet of note-paper. Going close to the table she picked this half-sheet up, gingerly, as if it were dangerous to touch. As a matter of fact to her, at that moment, a dynamite bomb could not have been more charged with peril. On the piece of paper were some figures—"£127"—nothing more. She knew that the writing was Mr. Lindsay's. Evidently he had been counting the coins, and had made a note upon that slip of paper of the value they represented; there were one hundred and twenty-seven pounds in gold.

Elaine Harding was poor. Her father was the vicar of a parish in the West of England. His parish was large; his family was large; but his income was small. His wife had died some three years ago, worn out by her efforts to make a pound do the work of at least thirty shillings. Elaine had been sent to an expensive school by a relation; there she had met Nora Lindsay. Just as the time came for her to be leaving school the relation died. It had been expected that he would have done something to establish her in life; had he lived he probably would have done; as it was he left her nothing. So he had done her harm instead of good; that expensive school filled her with notions which might never have got into her head had it not been for him; a fashionable boarding-school is a bad school for a poor man's daughter. Ever since she had left it she had been discontented, inwardly if not outwardly, for nature had made her one of those persons who always, if they can, show a smiling face to the world. Nora Lindsay had been her chief solace. She never refused Nora's invitations to pay her a visit, and when at Cloverlea stayed as long as she could; indeed, she had been there so much just lately, during Mr. Lindsay's almost continual absences, that she knew the people round about almost as well as Nora did herself. She allowed Nora to make her presents; she would have been hard put to it if Nora had not had promptings in that direction. And then the girl had such a pretty way of giving, as if she were receiving a favour instead of bestowing one, that Elaine had no difficulty in preserving her dignity in face of the most delicate donations. Yet in spite of Nora's generosity she was always in need of money; there were special reasons why she was very much in need of it just now. Only the night before she had spent nearly an hour on her knees praying to God to show her some way to the cash she stood so much in want of; and now here were one hundred and twenty-seven pounds in gold at her finger-tips.

It could hardly be called an answer to her prayer. It is said that prayers are heard in two places, in heaven and in hell; Elaine realized with a sudden, shrinking terror that this answer must have come from hell. The owner of that money was up-stairs, dying; she believed that he was dying, speechless; she thought it possible that he might never be able to speak again, this side the grave. The chances were that he was the only person living who knew that that money was where it was. It was hardly likely that he would ever again be able to refer to its existence; she might, therefore, safely regard it as—what? Say, treasure-trove; it was a convenient word, treasure-trove; especially as she was placed. One hundred and twenty-seven pounds! in gold! no one would ever be able to trace it! ever!

Her eyes, which had opened wider and wider, having in them a very singular look, a look which would have startled her had they suddenly glared back at her from a mirror, wandered from the heap of gold coins to a bag, a canvas bag—a good-sized canvas bag, stuffed, apparently, to repletion, tied round the top with red tape; the kind of bag, she was aware, which is used by bankers to contain coin. She touched it, lightly, with her finger-tips; there were coins inside, undoubtedly; she could see them bulging through the canvas. She picked it up, again gingerly, as if, if she did not observe great care, it might explode in her hand; it had been better for her, perhaps, if it had. It was heavy, heavier than she had expected; wedged full of money. Beneath it there was another half-sheet of writing-paper; on it, in Donald Lindsay's writing, was what was probably a statement of what the bag contained—"£500." Five hundred pounds! obviously again in gold! She could feel the sovereigns! and the one person who knew of its existence dumb and dying!

What was the matter with Elaine? The sheet of paper fell from her hand. She reeled as if attacked by sudden vertigo; she leaned against the table as if to save herself from falling; she went quite white; she stared about her as if afraid. Six hundred and twenty-seven pounds in gold! ownerless! practically ownerless, for how could it be said to have an owner when the only creature who knew of its existence was dumb and dying? Six hundred and twenty-seven pounds! what might not that money mean to her?—and—and to some one else who had grown of late to be almost more to her than herself? She turned again to clutch at it; when she saw that on the writing-table there still was something else; a roll of notes, enclosed in a rubber band; banknotes, if she could believe her eyes. She picked them up, to make sure; heedlessly, fearlessly this time; the other things had proved so innocuous that, already, she had grown careless. They were bank-notes, unmistakably; and beneath them, was the inevitable half-sheet of paper. This time it was covered with quite an array of figures, in Donald Lindsay's neat handwriting. Seemingly, according to those figures, the roll of notes contained forty at £5, fifty at £10, twenty-five at £20, six at £50, ten at £100; in all one hundred and twenty-one notes of the value of £2500. The numbers were given of every note of each denomination; Elaine's quick eyes perceived that the numbers were by no means consecutive, from which she deduced that they had not been issued from a bank all at one time, but had come together at different dates, from various quarters.

She perceived on the instant that the discovery of that roll gave the situation quite a different character; she herself was conscious of being surprised at the rapidity with which her brain was working. One hundred and twenty pounds, even six hundred and twenty pounds in gold, was one thing; two thousand five hundred pounds in notes was quite another; the one might provide for her immediate necessities, with the other she might be secure for life. Properly invested the whole sum ought to bring her in three pounds a week—for ever; she believed she knew of an investment in which it might bring her more than that; much more. The point was, would it be safe to treat that as—treasure-trove? She was inclined to think it would. Probably the existence of the entire amount was known only to the dying man, if he was dying. There was, of course, the risk that he might come back to life again, in which case it might be awkward. But some ghoul-like intuition told her that she might dismiss that possibility from her mind; some dreadful voice within proclaimed that he was as good as dead already; in some horrible way she was sure of it. It was a heterogeneous gathering, that roll of notes; probably their owner himself could not have told how most of them came into his possession. The only record of their identity was on that sheet of paper; if that vanished there was nothing by which they could be identified; that seemed pretty obvious. The devil whispered that it would be just as safe to take the notes as to take the gold; and she knew that she would run no risk by taking that.

There was still one point to be considered; she was clear-sighted and logical enough to be aware of that. If Donald Lindsay was dying then this money was, in all human probability, his child's, who was the dearest friend she had in the world, Nora. She loved Nora, really loved her; she was always telling herself that she really loved her. Then Nora had done her nothing but kindnesses; how great some of those kindnesses were only she and Nora knew. The idea that she would allow any one to rob Nora was monstrous; that she should rob her herself was inconceivable. Had any one accused her of being capable of such base ingratitude even then she would have repudiated the charge with honest indignation; nothing would ever induce her to do anything which could injure Nora. She knew herself well enough to be assured of that. And then she glozed the thing over with one of those patent glosses which the devil provides when the occasion needs them.

She argued this way; if her father died then Nora would be a rich woman, immensely rich; rich, possibly, beyond the dreams of avarice. She would never miss such a detail as, say, three thousand pounds; such a sum would be a trifle to her, a nothing; especially if she never knew that the sum had ever existed. There was that to be borne in mind; we do not miss what we never had, especially if we do not know it ever was. And in the case of a rich woman like Nora, with twenty, thirty, forty, perhaps fifty thousand pounds a year, perhaps even more, in such an income there were bound to be leakages; through one of them such a drop in the ocean as three thousand pounds might easily slip, and no one even be aware of it, least of all would the knowledge ever come to Nora, or touch her in any way. No; certainly darling Nora would suffer no injury if what was on the writing-table was regarded as treasure-trove.

At the same time far be it from her—Elaine—to do anything which could be regarded by any one as in the slightest degree unworthy. She was seized with a sudden access of virtue. Take the money—she! Sully her fingers by even touching it! who dare hint that she could do a thing like that! The idea was really too ridiculous; it was not to be taken seriously. It only showed what notions came to people when money was left about. She had always maintained that it was wrong to leave money about. Mr. Lindsay ought to have known better, putting temptation in some weak-minded person's way; she did not stop to consider that for that he could hardly be held responsible. What she had to do was to see that temptation was removed; some servant might stray into the room, and then what might not happen? The least she could do was to see that the money was put out of sight, in a drawer, or anywhere. She glanced about her, and was struck by a rather curious notion. The door of a bookcase stood wide open. A book had obviously been taken down from one of the shelves; a large volume, one of a set; there it lay by her elbow on the table. She looked at it, without clearly apprehending what the title was; she had a vague idea that in it was something about law. Here was the very hiding-place she wanted; no thief would be tempted to take money which was snugly hidden behind a great book like that, if only for the simple reason that he would never know that it was there. She slipped the loose gold into a big blue envelope; then she placed it, and the canvas bag, and the roll of notes, on that shelf in the bookcase. It so chanced that while the backs of the set of books were plumb with the front of the shelf they did not go right against the wall, so that there was space enough behind them to enable her, after a little manipulation, to do what she desired. When the volume had been returned to its place there was nothing whatever to show that behind it were more than three thousand pounds in notes and gold. She surveyed this result with satisfaction.

"Now," she told herself, "I've removed temptation from everybody's way."

The three half-sheets of paper on which Mr. Lindsay had noted the several amounts she folded up together and thrust into the bodice of her dress; possibly she thought that they would be out of harm's way there. She had just done this, and had shut the bookcase door, when, in the silence which prevailed, she distinctly heard the footsteps of some one moving in the grounds without. Instantly she blew the lamp out, and went fluttering through the open window. So soon as she was on the terrace she stood still to listen. Her ear had not deceived her. Some one, not far off, was moving along a gravel path; apparently the sound proceeded from the other side of the house. Either her perceptions must have been very keen, or there was something unusual about the step; though it is strange how quick the ear is to recognize a step with which one is familiar.

"I do believe," she told herself, "that it's his step." She ran along to the end of the terrace; then stopped again. "It is!" she said. With lifted skirts she tiptoed round the side of the house till she came to where a path branched off among the trees, then, drawing herself under their shadow, she stood and waited, smiling. The steps came nearer, close to where she was. She moved out from under the shadow. "Herbert!" she said.

The man—it was a man—was evidently taken by surprise; he stepped back so quickly that he almost stumbled.

"By George!" he exclaimed, "what a start you gave me!"

She laughed, half to herself.

"Did she frighten him, the poor thing! I heard you coming ever so far off; I knew it was you. And pray what are you doing here at this time of night?"

"I came upon the off-chance of getting a word with you."

"With me—at this hour!"

"Well, I've found you, and that's what I wanted."

"Herbert!" She went still closer, almost as if expecting a caress; but when he showed no inclination to take advantage of his opportunities, she saw from his face, in the moonlight, that there was something wrong. "My lord, what ails you?"

"Everything; I've come up to tell you that what we were talking about yesterday is clean off."

"And of what were we talking—yesterday?"

"Why, about our marriage, and all that kind of thing. I can't marry; I don't suppose I ever shall be able to; you'd better give me the mitten right away. To begin with, I've found out—or, rather, I've had the fact forced upon me, that I'm in a mess."

"What kind of mess?"

"Money, of course; what else counts?"

"How much?"

"If I don't get two hundred pounds—and where am I going to get two hundred pounds? why, I haven't as many shillings—and get it pretty soon, I shall have to—"

"What?"

He had left his sentence unfinished; he gave it a conclusion which one felt had not been originally intended.

"Well, I shall be in Queer Street."

He paused, and she was silent; she was thinking.

CHAPTER IV

THE AVERNIAN SLOPE

When she spoke again a quick observer might have noticed that in her voice there was a new intonation.

"Two hundred pounds is not such a very large sum."

"Isn't it? I'm glad you think so. It's a large sum to me; a lot too large. I've about as much chance of getting it as I have of getting the moon. And if I did get it I shouldn't be much forwarder so far as marriage is concerned. What's the use of my talking of marrying when I hardly earn enough to buy myself bread and cheese? and it's as certain as anything can be that in this place I never shall earn enough."

"Why not?"

"For one reason, if for no other, because in this place there's only room for one solicitor; and old Dawson's that one. He's got all the business that's worth having; and, what's more, he'll keep it. Now if I could buy old Dawson out—I happen to know that he's made what he considers pile enough for him, and would be quite willing to retire; or even if I could buy a share in his business, he might be willing to sell that; then it might be a case of talking; but as it is, so far as I'm concerned, marriage is off."

"How much would be wanted?"

"If I could lay my hands on a thousand, or fifteen hundred pounds in cash, then I might go to Dawson and make a proposal; but as I never shall be able to lay my hands on it, it would be better for both of us if we talked sense; that's what I've come for, to talk sense."

"Does all this mean that you've found out that you made a mistake when you told me that you loved me?"

"It means the exact opposite; I've found out that I love you a good deal more than I thought I did. If I didn't love you I might be disposed to behave like a cad, and marry you out of hand; but as I do love you I'm not taking any chances."

"I don't quite follow your reasoning."

"Don't you? It's clear enough to me. I'm in a hole, and because I love you I'm not going to drag you in as well."

"But suppose I should like to be dragged?"

"You don't understand, or you wouldn't talk like that."

"Shouldn't I? Don't be too certain. You are sure you love me?"

"I love you more than I thought I could love any one, and that's the mischief."

"Is it? I don't agree; because, you see, I love you."

"It's no good; I wish you didn't."

"Do you? Then I don't. If you wanted me to, I'd marry you to-morrow."

"Elaine!" Then he did take her in his arms, and he kissed her. And she kissed him. Suddenly he put her from him. "Don't! for God's sake, don't! Elaine, don't you tempt me! I'm not much of a chap, and I'm not much of a hand at resisting temptation—there's frankness for you!—and I want to keep straight where you're concerned. I'll make a clean breast of it; the only way I can see out of the mess I'm in is to make a bolt for it, and I'm going to bolt; there you have it. I've come up here to say good-bye."

"Good-bye?"

Her voice was tremulous.

"If ever I come to any good, which isn't very probable, you'll hear from me; you'll never hear from me if I don't; so I'm afraid that this is going to be very near a case of farewell for ever."

"You say two hundred pounds will get you out of that mess you're in?"

"About that; I dare say I could manage with less if it was ready money. But what's the use of talking? I don't propose to rob a bank, and that's the only way I ever could get it."

"And if you had fifteen hundred to offer Mr. Dawson, what then?"

"What then? Elaine, you're hard on me."

"How hard? I don't mean to be."

"To dangle before my face the things which I most want when you know they're not for me! Why, if I had fifteen hundred pounds, and could go to Dawson with a really serious proposition, the world would become another place; I should see my way to some sort of a career. I'd begin by earning a decent living; in no time I'd be getting together a home; in a year we might be married."

"A year? That's a long time."

He laughed.

"If I were Dawson's partner, with a really substantial share, we might be married right away."

"How soon, from now?"

"Elaine, what are you driving at? what is the use of our deceiving ourselves? I shall become Dawson's partner when pigs have wings, not before. What I have to do is bolt, while there still is time."

There was an interval of silence. They were standing very close together; but he kept his hands in his jacket pockets, as if he were resolved that he would not take her in his arms; while she stood, with downcast eyes, picking at the hem of her dress. When she spoke again it was almost in a whisper.

"Suppose I were able to find you the money?"

He smiled a smile of utter incredulity, as if her words were not worth considering.

"Suppose you were able to buy me the earth? Yesterday you told me that you had not enough money to buy yourself a pair of shoes; in fact, you said that your whole worldly wealth was represented by less than five shillings."

Once more she was still—oddly still.

"Herbert!"

The name was rather sighed than spoken. He saw that she was trembling. The appeal was irresistible. Again he put his arms about her and held her fast.

"Little lady, you've troubles enough of your own without worrying yourself about mine. You'll easily find better men than I am who'll be glad enough to worship the ground on which you stand, and then you'll recognize how much you owe me for running away, and leaving you an open field. The best thing that can happen to you is that I should go."

"I don't think so. I—I don't want you to go."

There was a catching in her breath.

"I don't want to go, but—I might find it awkward if I stayed."

"Herbert, I—I want to tell you something."

"What is it? By the sound of you it must be something very tremendous."

Her manner certainly was strange. As a rule she was a most self-possessed young woman; now she seemed to be able to do nothing but shiver and stammer. Not only was she hardly audible, but her words came from her one by one, as if she found it difficult to speak at all.

"What I—said to you—yesterday—wasn't true; I—said it to try you."

"What did you say to try me? Elaine, you're what I never thought you would be—you're mysterious."

"Suppose—you had fifteen hundred pounds—are you sure Mr. Dawson would make you a partner?"

"Well, I've never asked him, but I'm betting twopence."

"What would your income be if he did? You're not to laugh—answer my questions."

"Oh, I'll answer them; although, as I've already remarked, I've not the faintest notion what you're driving at; and that particular question is rather a wide one. If I were to buy a share I should try to do it on the understanding that some day I was to have the lot. I should probably commence with an income of between three and four hundred, which would become more later on; I dare say old Dawson is making a good thousand a year."

"A thousand? We might live on that."

"I should think we might; we might start on three hundred; I should like to have the chance."

"I'd be willing. And how much would it cost to furnish a house?"

"I've a few sticks in those rooms of mine."

"I know; I also know what kind of sticks they are—we shouldn't want them."

"There at last we are agreed. I suppose that to furnish the kind of house we should want to start with would make a hole in a couple of hundred—you probably know more about that sort of thing than I do. But, my dear Elaine, what is the use of our playing at fairy tales? You haven't five shillings in the world, and I've only just enough to take me clear away, and to keep the breath in my body while I have one look round."

Again there was an interval of silence, which was broken by her in a scarcely audible whisper.

"That—that was what I was trying to explain; what—I said to you yesterday was—to prove you."

"What particular thing did you say? I haven't a notion what you mean."

"Every girl likes to be—wooed for herself alone."

"Of course she does, and it's dead certain you'll never be wooed for anything but your own sweet self; I've known you, and all about you, long enough to be aware that you're no heiress."

"That's—that's where you're wrong."

"Wrong! Elaine, where's the joke?"

"I—I am an heiress; of course, in a very moderate way."

"What do you call an heiress? when yesterday you told me that you didn't possess five shillings!"

"That was said to try you."

Raising her eyes she looked him boldly in the face; there in the bright moonlight they could see each other almost as clearly as if it had been high noon.

"To try me? You're beyond me altogether; Elaine, are you pulling my leg?"

"I have about two thousand pounds."

"Two thousand pounds! Great Scott! where did you get it from? I didn't know there was so much money in all your family."

"There, again, you were mistaken. I got it from an aunt who died—not long ago."

"When did she die?"

"Oh, about six months ago."

"What was her name?"

"The same as mine—Harding."

"Was she an aunt by marriage?"

"She was my father's sister."

"A spinster? But I thought you told me that none of your father's relatives had two pennies to rub together."

"So I thought; but I was wrong. At any rate, when she died she left me about two thousand pounds."

"You've kept it pretty dark."

He was staring at her as if altogether amazed; she smiled at him as if amused by his surprise.

"I have; I've told nobody—not even Nora."

"Doesn't Miss Lindsay know?"

"She doesn't. Nobody knows—except you; and I shall be obliged by your respecting my confidence."

"I'll respect your confidence; but—of all the queer starts! What fibs you've told!"

"I know I've told some; in a position like mine, one had to. But I'd made up my mind that you shouldn't know I had money, and—you didn't know."

"I certainly did not; I scarcely realize it now; I wonder if you're joking."

"No, I'm not joking."

She shook her pretty head, with a grave little smile. Her face looked white in the moonshine.

"Can you touch the capital? Is it in the hands of trustees? Or do you only have the income?"

"It is not in the hands of trustees; it is entirely at my own disposal; I can get it when I want."

"All of it?"

"All of it."

He drew a long breath, as if moved by some new and sudden strength of feeling.

"Can you—can you get two hundred pounds before next Tuesday?"

"I can, and I will—if you want it. You are sure you want it?"

"Elaine, if—if you will I'll—I'll never forget it."

"You shall have it on Monday if you like." He covered his face with his hands, seeming to be shaken by the stress of a great emotion. She drew closer to him, as if frightened; her voice trembled. "Herbert, what—what is wrong?"

Uncovering his face, clenching his fists, he stared straight in front of him, resolution in his eyes.

"Nothing now—nothing!—and there never shall be anything again!—thank-God. Thank God! Considering what sort of mess it was that I was in, I didn't dare to ask God to help me out of it; but He's done it without my asking Him. Elaine, upon my word I believe it's true that God moves in a mysterious way." Elaine, hiding her face against his shoulder, burst into tears, which surprised him more than anything which had gone before. She was not a girl who cries easily, yet now she was shaken by her sobs. Putting his arms about her, he strove to comfort her, showering on her endearing epithets. "My sweet, my dear, my darling, what troubles you? Don't you—don't you want me to have the money? You have only to say so; I shan't mind."

"Of course I want you to have it! I only want it for you!—you know I only want it for you! Herbert, are you—are you sure you love me? Tell me—tell me quite truly."

"I am as sure as that there is the moon above us; and now I dare to tell you so; no man ever loved a woman better than I love you. I know I am unworthy; I know how, in all essentials, you are infinitely above me—"

"I'm not—I'm not!"

"But it shall be my constant endeavour to raise myself to your level—"

"Don't!—you don't know what you're saying! Don't!"

"I do know what I'm saying, and I mean it; if God gives me strength I hope, before I've finished, to prove myself worthy of the wife I've won. You hear? Then make a note of it."

Then there were divers passages.

"Herbert, I want you to go to Mr. Dawson tomorrow, and arrange about that partnership. I'll find the fifteen hundred pounds."

"Sweetheart, you've turned all my sorrow into joy."

"And—this, sir, is supposed to be spoken in the faintest whisper—I—I think I'd like to be married pretty soon."

"As soon as it is legally possible, madam, you shall be married, if you choose to say the word."

"I don't want it in quite such a hurry as that; but—you know what I mean!—I don't want to have to wait a horrid year." Presently she asked, "Do you know that Mr. Lindsay's very ill?"

"I heard it as I came along."

"I think he's dying. I suppose Nora'll be very rich if he does."

"Let's hope that he'll not die."

"Not die?"

She looked at him with such a strange expression on her face that he smiled.

"Why, girlie, you don't want the father to die to make the daughter rich!"

"No; of course not."

But, afterwards, she was not the same; it was as if he had struck some jarring note. When they parted she went round to the back of the house, along the terrace, towards the study window, which still stood open. She paused upon the threshold.

"Suppose he were not to die? suppose he doesn't?"

The problem the supposition presented to her mind seemed to cause her no slight disturbance; still she passed into the room.

Which explains why, when Nora said she doubted if Mr. Nash was ever really interested in anybody but himself, Elaine Harding had good cause to wonder if the thing was true.

CHAPTER V

PETER PIPER'S POPULAR PILLS

On the Monday, after Dr. Banyard had been gone perhaps a couple of hours, Mr. Nash drove up to Cloverlea in a dogcart. Miss Harding met him in the drive. At sight of her the gentleman descended; the cart went on up to the house, to wait for him. So soon as it was out of sight the lady, taking a packet from the bodice of her dress, gave it to her lover.

"That's the two hundred; put it in your pocket; I want you to promise that you'll not breathe a word to any one about the money having come from me."

"I promise readily."

"Nor about any other money which—I may find. I want you to keep your own counsel; I want people to suppose that the money is your own; I don't want them to think I'm buying a husband."

"I certainly will neither do nor say anything to make them think so. All the same, darling, I don't know how to thank you; you don't know what this means to me. It seems to be all in gold?"

He was fingering the parcel in his jacket pocket.

"It is; I thought you might find it more convenient."

"I think it's possible you're right; I believe you always are."

As he had been coming along in the dogcart he had not seemed to be in the best of spirits; now he was unmistakably cheerful; that package had made a difference. A question, however, which she asked seemed to annoy him more than, on the surface, it need have done.

"What became of Mr. Peters?"

"They gave him six months—confound the idiots?"

"Why confound them?"

The smile with which he accompanied his reply seemed forced.

"A lawyer likes his client to be acquitted."

"But Dr. Banyard says that he's a scoundrel."

"Dr. Banyard! You can tell Dr. Banyard, with my compliments, that he's a Pharisee."

"I think nothing of the man; I think he's an interfering prig. I don't like him, and he doesn't like me."

"Which shows that he must be all kinds of a fool."

"I don't know about that; but I do know that I don't like him. By the way, I suppose you understand what you're coming for. Everything here is at sixes and sevens. Nora knows absolutely nothing about her father's business affairs; he never told her anything; he kept his own counsel with a vengeance."

"So I gathered from your note."

"She doesn't even know who his man of business was. She wants you to find out; she thinks that if you look through his papers you will."

"There should be no difficulty about that. If I have access to his papers I ought to find that out inside ten minutes."

"I suppose so. But even if you do find out I don't see why you shouldn't keep the conduct of her affairs as much as possible in your hands; I think it might be done; you'll have my influence upon your side. You needn't say anything about there being an understanding between us; we can't keep people from guessing; but don't let them know—till it suits us."

He saw something in her eyes which caused him to pay her what some people would have regarded as an ambiguous compliment.

"By George, you're a clever one; you're the sort of girl I like!"

"I'm glad of that; because you happen to be the sort of man I like."

He laughed.

"I'd like to kiss you!"

"Quite impossible, here. You see, it might be rather a good thing for you to have the management of Nora's estate."

"True, oh queen!"

"Then why shouldn't you have it?"

"I know of no reason."

"There is no reason, if you take proper advantage of the fact that you're first on the field." They had entered the house and were standing outside the study door. She produced a key. "Nora's not appearing; poor dear, she's more distressed than I ever thought she would have been! so, on this occasion only, I am doing the honours. We've kept this room locked up since the day on which Mr. Lindsay was taken ill; no one has crossed the threshold; you'll find everything in the same condition in which he left it." They entered the room. So soon as they were in he kissed her, and she kissed him, though she protested. "Hush! Nora's waiting for me! Remember what I told you; there's no reason why you shouldn't have the management of everything—if you like."

He communed with himself when she had left him.

"I wonder what she means, exactly; she's careful not to dot her i's. She's the dearest girl in the world, even dearer than I thought. This is something like a windfall." He took out the packet, fingering it, smilingly, with the fingers of both hands. Then, replacing it in his pocket, glancing round the room, he was struck by the state of disorder it was in. "It's as well they kept the door locked; everything seems to have been left about for the first comer to admire. Lindsay must have been having a regular turn-out when he was taken ill; I wonder why." On the writing-table the first thing which caught his eye were some slips of blue paper secured by a rubber band. He snatched them up. They were four promissory notes, payable at various dates; they all bore the same signature, Herbert Nash. He chuckled. "We'll consider those as paid, until they prove the contrary; which they'll find it hard to do." He slipped them into his breast pocket. Settling himself on the chair on which Mr. Lindsay had been seated when death first touched him on the shoulder, he began to go methodically through the papers which were about him, practically, on all sides. He came on one, the contents of which seemed to occasion him profound surprise. "What on earth is this? what the dickens does it mean?" There was not a great deal on the paper; what there was he read again and again, as if he found its meaning curiously obscure. "This is queerish; I'd give a trifle to know what it does mean; it might be worth one's while to inquire."

Folding up the paper he placed it in his breast pocket, with the promissory notes. Hardly had he done so than the door was opened, without any warning, and Dr. Banyard came into the room.

"Hallo, Nash! have you found anything? have you found out who his man of business was?"

Mr. Nash glanced up from the papers he was studying; if he was a little startled by the doctor's unheralded appearance he gave no sign of it.

"I haven't discovered his man of business; but I have found something."

"You haven't come upon anything which shows who it was he generally employed; I understand you've been here some time."

Mr. Nash shook his head.

"I don't know how long I have been here, but I've come on nothing which shows that he ever employed any one at all."

"He must have employed some one."

The other shrugged his shoulders.

"I've gone through a good many of his papers; I've not hit on one which suggests it."

"You said you'd found something; what is it?"

"His will; or, rather, a will."

"That is something."

"Especially as, beyond a shadow of doubt, it's the last will he ever made. It was drawn up on the third, last Thursday, probably just before he was taken ill. It's in his own writing, brief, and to the point, and apparently quite in order, since it was witnessed by Morgan, the butler here, and Mrs. Steele the housekeeper."

"Let's have a look at it."

"Here it is, in the envelope in which I found it."

The doctor examined the paper which he took out of the envelope; it seemed that its contents gave him satisfaction.

"I see that, by this, he's left everything to his daughter unconditionally."

"That is so, the intention's unmistakable."

"Then she's safe; that's all right. It ought to be something handsome; I wonder how much it is."

"That's the question."

"I suppose you've come across something which gives you, at any rate, some vague notion."

"I haven't, that's the odd part of it."

"What do you mean?"

"Well, I'm glad you've come."

"Why? what's up? Found the job too big to tackle single-handed? I thought you would."

"You're mistaken; that is not what I mean. I've gone through—hurriedly, but still thoroughly enough to have a pretty good idea of what it is that they contain—all the available books and papers; and, as you see, most of them seem available, everything seems open; and I've not found anything which even hints that he died the possessor of any property at all; with two exceptions. There is his pass-book at the local bank, showing a balance of about a hundred pounds, which may have been drawn on since; and there are the Cloverlea title-deeds, there, in that deed-box."

"That only shows that everything essential is in the hands of his London lawyer."

"You seem to take the existence of such a person very much for granted. He told me himself he hadn't one."

"Told you? when?"

"Not long ago there was a little difficulty about a right of way; I don't know if you heard of it. He came to me about it; I then asked him who acted for him in town; he said no one."

"You are sure?"

"I am; for a man in his position it struck me as odd."

"He must have had a man in town, you misunderstood him. You haven't gone through all the papers?"

"Not all."

"Then we shall come upon it; I'll help you with the rest. There are no doubt papers elsewhere; probably in his bedroom, or at his rooms in town. Have you found out what was his London address?"

"I have found nothing which shows that he had one."

"But he must have had a London address; why, he spent quite a large part of the year in town."

"I happen to know that the only London address Miss Lindsay ever had was the Carlton Club; they may be able to tell us there."

"Of course they'll be able to tell us. Found any cash?"

"Not a penny."

"Anything which stands for cash?"

"Nothing; except what I have told you."

He had said nothing about what was in his breast-pocket.

"Lindsay was a man of secretive habits; if he could help it he never let his left hand know what his right hand was doing. When you come to deal with the affairs of a man like that you're handicapped; but there can be no sort of doubt that he was a man of considerable means. It must have cost him something to live here; where did the money to do that come from? It must have come from somewhere."

"It seems that there are a good many debts; as you are possibly aware, there is a good deal owing round here."

"He was a man who hated paying."

Suddenly the doctor glanced up from the papers he was examining to glare at his companion.

"Look here, Nash, what are you hinting at?"

"I am merely answering your questions."

"Yes, but you're answering them in a way I don't like."

The younger man smiled.

"I am afraid that I didn't realize that my answers had to be to your liking, whatever the facts might be."

The doctor returned to the papers; he looked as if he could have said something vigorous, but refrained. After a while he had to admit that his researches, so far, had been without result.

"Well, there seems to be nothing here, and that's a fact. These papers seem to contain material for a history of the Cloverlea estate since it came into Lindsay's possession; and that's all. Now for the safe."

"I've gone through that."

"I'll go through it also; though from the look of it, it doesn't seem as if there were much to go through." He pulled out one of the small drawers at the bottom. "Hallo, what have we here?" He took out an oblong wooden box. "What's this on the lid? 'Peter Piper's Popular Pills.'"

"What!"

The exclamation came from Nash.

"Here it is, large as life, in good bold letters; there ought to be something valuable in here." He opened the lid. "An envelope with papers in it; what's this writing on it? 'Analyses of the constituent parts of Peter Piper's Popular Pills by leading analytical chemists.' What fools those fellows are! Lindsay's writing; he doesn't seem to have had a high opinion of some one; let's hope there's nothing libellous. What's here besides? A bottle purporting to contain Peter Piper's Popular Pills; the man seems to have had them on the brain. And—other bottles containing the ingredients of which they're made; so it says outside them; as I'm alive! and the man kept this stuff inside his safe! Nash, why are you looking at me like that?"

Mr. Nash was regarding the doctor with a somewhat singular expression on his face; when the doctor put the question to him he started, as if taken by surprise.

"Looking at you? was I looking at you?"

"Glaring was the better word."

"It was unconscious. Are you—are you sure that they are Peter Piper's Popular Pills in that box?"

"Sure? As if I could be sure about a thing like that! what do I know about such filth? look for yourself."

Mr. Nash examined the box with a show of interest which its contents scarcely seemed to warrant.

"How extremely—curious."

"Fancy a man like Lindsay harbouring such stuff as that! I should think it was curious!"

Though both men used the same adjective one felt that each read into it a different meaning.

When Mr. Nash started to leave the house he found that the dogcart, which he supposed was still in waiting, had disappeared. He asked no questions, but drew his own conclusions. As he passed down the avenue, and perceived that Miss Harding was strolling among the trees, he smiled. So soon as the lady saw him she began to ply him with questions.

"Well, what's happened?"

"One thing's happened, you've sent away my dogcart."

She looked at him with mischief in her eyes.

"Walking will do you more good than driving; and it will cost you less. Besides, it will give you an opportunity of exchanging a few words with me. I hope you don't mind."

"On the contrary, I'm delighted."

"What have you found?"

"I've found his will; he's left his daughter everything."

"Everything! How splendid! I'm so glad he's left her everything!"

Miss Harding's face could not have been more radiant had she received a personal benefit.

"I shouldn't be over hasty in offering her your congratulations if I were you; it's quite possible that everything won't amount to very much."

She seemed struck by his tone even more than by his words.

"Herbert! What do you mean?"

Mr. Nash kicked a pebble with his toe; then he whistled to himself; then he said, just as her patience was at an end—

"It's a bit awkward to explain, but it's this way; Banyard and I have been going through his books and papers, and everything there was to go through; and there was a good deal, as you know; and we haven't come on anything which points to money or money's worth. I've been putting two and two together, and I rather think I understand the situation; when all's over and settled I shouldn't be surprised if Miss Lindsay would be very glad indeed to have your little fortune."

"My—my little fortune?"

"I'm alluding to the snug little legacy left you by your venerated aunt."

"It's—it's impossible!"

"More impossible things have happened; and I think I'm almost inclined to bet twopence that her fortune's nearer two thousand shillings than two thousand pounds."

"Herbert! Herbert!"

"What's the matter? Why, little girl, you mustn't take on like that; what a sensitive little thing it is! it'll be through no fault of yours if she's left penniless! She's never been over nice to me, and I'm sure I shan't worry myself into an early grave if she is."

"You don't understand!" she wailed. "You don't understand."

By the domestic hearth that evening Dr. Banyard addressed to his wife some more or less sententious remarks, as he puffed at his pipe.

"There's something wrong up at Cloverlea, confoundedly wrong. I don't understand what it is, and I don't like what I do understand. There's a riddle somewhere, and I'm half afraid we're not going to find the answer. Mind you, I've actually no grounds to go upon, but I don't trust that man, Nash; I've all sorts of doubts about the fellow."

Mrs. Banyard looked up from her sewing, and smiled; as is the way with wives of some years' standing she did not always take her husband so seriously as she might have done.

"Poor Mr. Nash! you never do like good-looking men."

"It isn't only that."

"No; but it's partly that. You funny old man! It doesn't follow because you're ugly yourself that all good-looking men are necessarily worthless."

"Generally speaking, a certain type of good-looking man is worth nothing."

"And Mr. Nash represents the type? And do you represent Christian charity? What do you suspect him of now? of having the answer to that mysterious riddle?"

"I don't know; that's just it, I don't know; but I doubt him all the same."

CHAPTER VI

HER LOVE STORY

That night Nora dreamed again—the same dream. It was more real even than before. She was lying in bed—she knew she was in bed, and her father came in at the door. In some strange fashion she had expected him; it was not that she heard him moving along the passage, yet, somehow, she knew that he was there, that he was coming. And, before he actually appeared, she knew that he was in great trouble; when he opened the door, so noiselessly, and without a sound came in, and closed the door again, also without a sound, she knew it even better than before, and his trouble communicated itself to her. In such trouble was he that he was even afraid of her. He remained close to the door, looking timidly towards her as she lay in bed, not daring to approach. So moved was she by his strange timidity that she sat up, and held out her arms to him, calling—

"Father!" She was sure she called, because she heard her own voice quite clearly; not as it mostly is in dreams, when one hears nothing. But yet he came no closer. Then she saw that he was crying. She called to him again, more eagerly. Then he went, step by step, timidly towards her; until she had her arms about him, and whispered, "Father, tell me what it is that troubles you." And he tried to tell her, but he could not; he was speechless, and to him his speechlessness was agony. If he only could speak she felt that all might be well with him—and with her; but he was tongue-tied. She tried to think of what it could be that he wished to say to her, and to prompt him; whispering into his ear first this, then that; but it was plain that none of her hints had anything to do with what was in his mind, though once she thought that she might not be far off. When she whispered, "Is it about what I am to do in the future?" his face changed; a sort of convulsion passed all over him; he drew himself away from her, and stood up, raising his arms, seeming to make a frenzied effort to achieve articulation; it even seemed that speech had come to him at last, when, just as words were already almost issuing from his lips, he vanished, and she was alone in the darkness.

Not the least strange part of it was that she was wide awake, having no consciousness of being roused out of sleep; she was sitting up in bed, the tears were streaming down her cheeks, her arms were held out, with about them the oddest feeling of somebody having just been in them. Indeed for a moment or two she could not believe that there was not some one in them still. When she did realize that they were empty she threw herself face downwards in the bed, crying as if her heart would break, because of her father's woe.

Donald Lindsay was buried on the Thursday—exactly a week after he had been stricken with his death. On the Tuesday and Wednesday she had variations of the same dream, and on the Thursday, the day of the funeral, it was so terrible a dream that the agony of it remained with her until the morning. For a long time afterwards some form of that dream would come to her at intervals. She said nothing of it to any one, though there was a moment when she was on the point of speaking of it to Elaine Harding; but she had it sometimes even in her waking thoughts. The course of events induced in her a kind of dormant conviction not only that the dream was sent to her for some special purpose, and that it had a meaning; but, also, that some day both the purpose and the meaning would be made clear. She knew that it is written that, of old, God spake to men in dreams; she believed it to be possible that, in a dream, God might speak to her. The dream always ended at the same point: just as her father, after an agonizing effort, seemed to be about to speak. She fancied that, some night, it might go on further, and that he might speak to her in his dream, and that with his speaking the purpose and the meaning of it all would be discovered.

On the morning of the funeral, among the other letters, Mrs. Steele, the housekeeper, called her attention to one in particular. No doubt she was aware that, during the last few days, either letters had been left unopened, or the task of opening them relegated to Elaine Harding, who communicated their contents if she pleased.

"Miss Nora," she said, "this is a letter from Mr. Spencer."

The girl caught eagerly at it; it was the first sign of eagerness she had lately shown. So soon as Mrs. Steele had gone she opened it. It was from her lover, Robert Spencer; a long letter, on three closely written sheets of foreign note-paper. He was in Sicily; had sent her a gossipy narrative of his wanderings among its ancient places, and among its scenes of beauty. It was full of love, and life, and high spirits; the sort of letter which makes a girl's heart beat happily; which she cherishes amid her most precious possessions. He told her how he wished that she was with him; that she at least was close at hand, that they might see and enjoy, together, what was so much worth seeing, and enjoying. In mischievous mood he added that when the great day came, on which the sun would rise in their sky for ever, and they were married, he humbly ventured to suggest that part of their honeymoon might be spent where he was then—"that would be to invest Taormina, which is already nearly all halos, with another, the brightest and the best."

To a girl's thinking there could be no pleasanter reading than such a letter; she could desire nothing better of the future than that its savour might remain unchanged, and that, throughout the years which were to come, the love of which it was a sign might walk always by her side.

So great was its power that, for a moment, it charmed her to forgetfulness. She saw in it her lover's face, and looked into his eyes; his voice spoke to her from the pages, and sounded sweetly in her ears. When he wrote of honeymooning the blood came to her cheeks; her lips were parted by a smile; her heart seemed speaking unto his. Even when she remembered, and recalled what day it was, and what shortly was about to happen, the light did not quite fade from her eyes, and the world was not all darkness. The match had been one of the few things respecting which her father had expressed to her his audible satisfaction. It was tacitly understood that the marriage was to take place during the current year. Both lovers were young—Robert Spencer had only just turned twenty-four. The only thing which could be said against him was his lack of means. He had done well both at school and at the university. Without being the least bit of a prig, he was exempt from those vices which the facile standard of the world in which he lived associates with youth. He was tall and strong and handsome; easy-mannered, more than is apt to be the case with the young Englishman of twenty-four; of fluent speech—he had been, in his time, one of the stars of the Union; there was no apparent reason why he should not make for himself, among the men of his own generation, a great name for good. The chief obstacle with which he would have to contend might be, as has been said, the eternal question of pence.

He was the fourth, and youngest, son of the Earl of Mountdennis. Everybody knows that his lordship had more children than money; four sons and five daughters is a liberal allowance for any man; the Earl and the Countess have that number living, and three of their children are dead. At the period of which we are writing all the five daughters were married, though by no means, from their mother's point of view, all satisfactorily married. The Countess never attempted to conceal the fact that only the first and third had done really well for themselves. According to the same authority, the boys had not done all that they might have done; the heir, Lord Cookham, in particular, had been a bitter disappointment, having been—his mother called it—wicked enough to marry a girl who had no money, and, practically, no family, merely because he loved her. He had been perfectly well aware that, in his case, marriage must mean money; it had been drummed into his ears from his earliest childhood;—family was of no consequence; he had family enough of his own. The one thing wanted was money—sacks full. And the thing was made more cruel by the fact that he might have had any amount of money, had he chosen. He might have had an English girl with a hundred thousand a year, to say nothing of several Americans with a great deal more; instead of which he married a young woman whom he met, as the Countess put it, at "some horrid foreign place," whose only qualification was that she was generally admitted, by some excellent judges, to be delightful. What, as the Countess pungently inquired, was the use of being delightful if she and her husband had not enough money between them to pay off the family debts, to say nothing of keeping up the family seats. And then they actually started by having three children in less than six years—all girls. It was too perfectly ridiculously absurd!

Montagu, the second son, had refused to marry at all, so his mother said; though it was not known that any girls had ever actually asked him. It was understood that he had made money in Africa, though he showed not the slightest inclination to squander it among his relatives; he had even declined to what his mother termed "lend" her five thousand pounds to be spent on "doing up" Holtye, which was the seat the Earl and the Countess principally favoured. Such conduct, she declared, was inhuman, but "so like Montagu." Arthur, the third son, had done best for himself from at least a financial point of view. He had married Mrs. Parkes-Peters, the widow of the contractor who left three millions. It was true that nasty things had been said of some of his most successful contracts; but, after all, the man was dead. It was also true that no one knew who, or what, his widow was before he married her; it was, if possible, even more true that she was older than her second husband. She herself admitted that she was his senior by ten years—the world said it ought to be twenty. But as she proved to be an ideal wife from the point of view of the man who marries for money, such trifles could hardly be said to count. Their friends asserted that she gave him a thousand pounds every time he kissed her—really no husband could want more.

And yet both his parents were aware that one need not be hypercritical to be able to see objections even against Arthur's wife. There remained, therefore, to them but one hope—their fourth son, Robert.

Theirs must have been a sanguine temperament—when one knew them one felt as if they had only one between them—because, after all their disappointments, they still built on him a castle in Spain, of their own design. It really seemed as if that castle was to be actually reared. Robert had set his affections on Miss Lindsay, and that without the least prompting from either of them; as they knew, from painful experience, in such cases one sometimes had to do such a lot of prompting. They frankly admitted that, looking at the matter as a whole, he could hardly have been expected to do better—to begin with. Cloverlea was quite a nice place, and, as it were, next door to Holtye; there were only nine miles between them. It was kept up in excellent style; the Earl, who was supposed to know something about such things, assured his wife that it probably cost Donald Lindsay at least ten thousand a-year. It was true that its owner was by way of being a curiosity; but then his eccentricities—if they could be called eccentricities—were not of a kind which would be likely to injure his daughter. And she was his only child. In her capacity of young woman nothing whatever could be urged against her; the Earl and Countess were entirely at one in agreeing with Robert that, in that respect, she was all that there was of the most charming. Obviously, when her father died, she would be more than comfortably off. The only thing to be considered was, what would she have until he died—in case she took unto herself a husband. On this point, also, everything was as it should be.

The Earl rode over to Cloverlea one day, when its master happened to be at home, and had a talk with him—than which nothing could be more satisfactory. Lindsay told his visitor, in that plain outspoken way of his, that he was satisfied with the result of inquiries he had been making about the Hon. Robert, and that, in consequence, five thousand a year would be settled on Nora if he married her. Besides this, he would present her, as a wedding gift, with a suitable house in town, and all the furniture. He added, with one of his rare, grim smiles, which the earl interpreted in a fashion of his own, that it was possible that one day she would be much richer than people thought.

The Earl told the Countess, on his return to Holtye, that he should not be surprised if the man was a millionaire. Anyhow his offer was most generous; especially as Robert was the youngest of nine, and had, literally, nothing but himself and his family to bring his wife. The Countess wondered vaguely if, on the strength of the matrimonial alliance which was to unite the two families, Mr. Lindsay might not be induced to advance what she described as "something decent" in order that something might be done to Holtye, which was falling to pieces, and where the furniture was in a scandalous condition. The Earl, who knew that his wife had been searching for years for some one who would play the part of fairy prince towards their family domain, merely remarked that it would be time enough to think of all that kind of thing when the pair were married.

Nora had not been actually informed of the arrangements which had been made for the commercial success of her love-match, but she knew quite well that it never would have entered the domain of practical politics if they had not been satisfactory. Robert was perfectly frank upon the point; he was frank with her about everything; it was his nature to be frank. He told her that he had not a shilling of his own, and never had.

"My aunt paid for me at Eton, and, afterwards, at the 'Varsity; so far as I know, she's paid for me ever since I was born; I believe she's even bought my clothes. I don't know why, because we're not a bit in sympathy; though she's a dear, on lines of her own, which are peculiar. She's only just on speaking terms with my mother, who's her own sister; and the things she says of my father are dreadful—he's really the most inoffensive of men. She has never lived in England since I can remember; she says she can't afford it. The truth is, she's never happy except in pursuit of her health; she passes from one 'cure' place to another, in possession of a number of complaints which nobody understands, but which suit her constitution admirably. She has about two thousand a year of her own, and spends most of it on doctors; though she declares, to their faces, that she never met one yet who knew what he is talking about. Out of what is left after the doctors are paid she is at present allowing me three hundred pounds a year, which is very good of her; especially considering two facts, the one being that I really have no claim on her at all, and the other that the three hundred is sometimes nearly four; for instance, last year she gave me fifty pounds as a birthday present, and twenty-five as a Christmas-box. So you see that I really am a pauper, living upon charity, and that I never ought to have dared to love you at all; only I couldn't help it—who could?"

She had laughed at him.

"Lots of people. Of course, it's very sad that you should be so poor; but I dare say, if we are careful, we can manage; and you know there is such a thing as love in a cottage—would the prospect of such a fate as that seem to you so very frightful?"

"Frightful! I wouldn't mind it a bit; would you?"

"I dare say I could put up with it for a time."

"It should only be for a time, I promise you. I'm handicapped by being who I am, but I don't think I'm an utter fool. I've always taken it for granted that I should have to make my own way, and, to the best of my ability, I've provided myself with the necessary tools; I believe that I could make my own way in the world as well as another man. You have only to say the word, and I'll make it first and woo you afterwards."

"Thank you; I'm content with things as they are; I'm sorry you're not."

This was said with a twinkle in her eyes which was meant to provoke him to warmth, and it did.

"Nora! do you wish me to—shake you?"

"I don't mind."

He did do something to her; but she was not shaken.

CHAPTER VII

THE PUZZLE WHICH DONALD LINDSAY LEFT BEHIND HIM

Donald Lindsay was buried on a glorious afternoon, when all the world seemed at its best and brightest. Carriages from all parts of the district represented their absent owners, but only four mourners were actually present. Nora and Elaine stood together on one side of the grave, confronting Dr. Banyard and Mr. Nash. Afterwards the four were again together in the room at Cloverlea which Nora regarded as in an especial sense her own. The blinds at last were drawn; the windows stood wide open; the April sun, warm enough for June, came streaming in, but it brought no brightness to those within. Each of the quartette seemed to be singularly ill at ease. It was not strange that such should have been the case with Nora; it was her hour of trial. But why Elaine Harding should have been unlike her usual self was not so obvious. An impartial observer, knowing her well, would have said that she had never appeared to such little advantage. Black never became her; either because she was physically unwell, or for some more obscure reason, that afternoon, in her mourning, she looked almost hideous. Had she been at liberty to choose, she would have been present neither at the funeral nor afterwards in Nora's room; but she had not seen her way to refuse compliance with Nora's positive request. Since Mr. Nash had told her of his, and Dr. Banyard's, failure to find among the dead man's papers anything to show that he had left any real provision for his daughter at all, she had been living in what seemed to her to be a continual nightmare. Day and night she was haunted by the three thousand one hundred and twenty-seven pounds which she had regarded as treasure-trove. Had she not taken it for granted that Nora would be a rich woman she would not have touched a farthing; of that she was certain. It was the conviction that such a sum would mean nothing to Nora which had been the irresistible temptation. Had it been in her power she would have replaced the money even then, and would have been only too glad to do it, though it left her penniless. But she had learnt what has to be learnt by all of us, how much easier it is to do than to undo. Any attempt in the direction of restitution would mean not only exposure, but ruin. Herbert Nash had to be considered. He had had two hundred pounds of the money; what he had done with it he alone knew. Then he had swallowed the tale of her aunt's legacy; she was perfectly well aware that if it had not been for that supposititious two thousand pounds she would never have been his promised wife. Was she to tell him now that she had lied? What explanation was she to offer him if she did? Would he not be entitled to regard her as some unspeakable thing? She did not doubt that his love would turn to scorn; that he would cast her from him with loathing and disgust.

No; anything rather than that; for she loved him.

On the other hand, if it was true that Nora had been left a pauper? and she had robbed her of her all! Would that fact not be shouted at her from out of the flaming sky for ever and for aye? would not the face of God be turned from her through all eternity? And how often, and how fervently, she had prayed that God might guide and bless her. She dared not think of the punishment which must inevitably crown so great a sin. She racked her brain to find some way out of the peril which threatened her on every hand; if only she could light on some plausible compromise. And at last she thought—she hoped—that she had discovered something which would relieve the situation at the point of its greatest strain. Three thousand one hundred and twenty-seven pounds she had—found; she had told Mr. Nash that her aunt had left two thousand. Her idea had been that she would have a good, round sum in hand, unknown to him, which, in case of need, would be of service in a tight place. What was to prevent her, should the tale of Nora's impoverishment turn out to be correct, disclosing the existence of that balance of over a thousand pounds; her fertile brain would easily invent some reasonable explanation; though that tale of the legacy would not do for Nora, who knew too much of her family affairs. Then she might insist on Nora accepting it as—what should she call it? a gift? a loan? It did not matter what she called it so long as Nora took the money; and she would have to take it. In that case Nora would regard her as her benefactor, instead of—what she was.

It is wonderful with what ointments we try to salve our consciences. At intervals Elaine was almost pleased with herself as she thought of how, if the worst came to the worst, she was going to present Nora with more than a thousand pounds. Yet that afternoon, in that pleasant room, in which she and her friend had spent so many happy hours, she was as one who knew not peace.

Nor did it seem to be peace with Mr. Nash. If one might judge from his physiognomy he did not appear to be at all inclined to congratulate himself on the position which it seemed likely he would occupy, of administrator of the dead man's estate. Such a position would mean something for him, if it meant nothing for anybody else; in such a case a lawyer always esteems himself worthy of his hire; and he sees that he gets it. Yet he looked as if he would have preferred to have been almost anywhere else rather than where he was.

The same remark applied to Dr. Banyard; though even a superficial observer might have guessed that the two men were troubled because of different things. A keen judge of human nature might have perceived that the doctor was troubled because of Nora; Herbert Nash because of himself.

The order of the proceedings was singular; it required pressure to induce Nora to sit down.

"I would much rather stand," she said. "I don't know what you have to say to me; but I hope that, whatever it is, it won't take long; I feel as if I can't sit; I would much sooner listen standing if you don't mind."

But the doctor did mind; he would not have it; he made her sit. Then nothing would satisfy her but that Elaine should sit by her; which was agony to Miss Harding, who was in the condition which is known as being all over pins and needles; it would have been a relief to have been able to scream.

"Now, Nash," inquired the doctor, when the two young women, looking, in their several ways, pictures of misery, were seated on adjacent chairs, "where are those papers? Let's get to business; and be as brief and as clear as you can."

Nash, with what was almost a hang-dog air, took some papers out of a black leather bag. Untying the tape which bound them together he began. His tale was neither very brief nor very clear; though his meaning was plain enough when it was ended. The dead man had left everything to his daughter; but he had nothing to leave; that was what it came to. There was less than a hundred pounds at the bank; and there was Cloverlea and the contents of the house. On the debit side there were debts amounting, so far as could be ascertained, to several thousand pounds; claims had come in from wholly unexpected quarters for large sums. If they had to be paid at once that would involve a forced sale of Cloverlea, and that would probably mean that very little would be left for Nora.

The faces of the two girls, as this state of affairs was being unfolded, were studies. On Miss Harding's face there came, by degrees, an expression of actual agony, as if her lover was playing the part of a torturer, whose every word was a fresh turn of the rack, or of the thumbscrew. Nora's face, on the other hand, as she began to perceive the point at which Mr. Nash was aiming, suggested anger rather than pain; the same suggestion was in her voice, as she addressed a question to him, so soon as he showed signs of having finished.

"Do you wish me to understand that my father has left no money?"

Mr. Nash looked down, as if unwilling to meet her eyes.

"Neither Dr. Banyard nor I have been able to find anything which points to money, I am sorry to say."

"You needn't be sorry." She turned to Dr. Banyard; with, as she did so, something in her manner which was hardly flattering to Mr. Nash. "If my father has left no money on what have we been living? Does

Mr. Nash mean that my father spent all his money before he died? because, if he does, I tell him, quite plainly, that I don't believe it."

The doctor got up. It was a peculiarity of his that, while he was always anxious that others should sit still, he never could do so himself when he was moved. Thrusting his hands into his trousers pockets he began to fidget about the room.

"That's the point," he exclaimed. "It's a pity, my dear Miss Lindsay, that your father didn't take you more into his confidence."

"He was entitled to do as he pleased."

"Precisely! and he did as he pleased! and this is the result! that you know nothing; that we know nothing; and, apparently, that we can find out nothing. We have been in communication with his London club; they tell us that he was an occasional attendant; that, so far as they know, this was his only address; that sometimes, but not often, letters came for him; but there are none awaiting him at present; they can give us no further information, and we have not the dimmest notion who can. Let me add a sort of postscript to what Mr. Nash has told you, which will shed another sidelight on the position. It is now about five years since your father bought Cloverlea. Ever since he bought it he has paid three thousand pounds into the local bank four times each year, always in notes and gold, which, as you are possibly aware, is not a form in which such payments are usually made. His next payment, if he intended to follow his usual rule, was due last week, to be exact, last Friday; for four years in succession he has paid in three thousand pounds, in notes and gold, on the first Friday in April. He was taken ill, as you know, on Thursday; if he had intended to make his usual payment on the following day the money would have been in his possession; we should have found it; we have found nothing."

Although no one seemed to notice it, Miss Harding looked as if she were trembling on the verge of a serious attack of illness. Her face was white and drawn, her eyes were half closed, her mouth was tightly shut, her hand was pressed against her side, as if compelled to that position by sudden pain. The doctor, oblivious of the fact that it looked as if his services would presently be required, went remorselessly on.

"The only possible alternative is that the money was stolen, and that after he was taken ill; you know what likelihood there is of that. But in order to leave no room for doubt we have questioned every one connected with the household; I am bound to say that we have discovered nothing in the least suspicious."

"Of course not; I wish I had known what you were doing, I would have stopped it. The idea of supposing that any one here would rob me; there is not a creature about the place I would not trust with my life."

This was Nora; her words were like poisoned darts to at least one of her hearers. The doctor continued.

"Just so; but allow me to point out, Miss Lindsay, the inference which may be drawn from what we have been able to learn of your father's methods. He has paid twelve thousand pounds a year into the local bank, invariably in notes and gold, never a cheque among the lot; does not this suggest that he wished to conceal, even from his bankers, the source from which the money came?"

"I don't see why you say that."

"If their ledgers contained the record of his having paid in even so much as a single cheque we might have been able to trace the history of that cheque, and in so doing might have lighted upon something which would have served as the key to the whole puzzle; if, that is, we could discover some one who ever paid him anything we might find out why he paid, and so might chance upon a clue which in the end might show us where his income came from. As it is we have nothing to go upon; and I can't help thinking that he meant his bankers should have nothing to go upon; whether he intended that you should be in the same position is another question. The consequence is, as matters stand, I am bound to say so, my dear Miss Nora, it is no use blinking the truth—"

"Please tell me what you believe to be the truth; pray don't what you call blink it."

"It is a perfectly fair deduction to draw that he had come to the end of his resources, whatever they may have been; quite conceivably the immediate cause of his illness was the consciousness that it was so; I am free to confess that, in this connection, the absence of the three thousand pounds, his usual quarterly payment into the bank, and, indeed, of any cash, is significant. I can only hope, Miss Nora, that you know something which will place the matter in quite a different aspect."

When the doctor ceased there was silence. Mr. Nash, fidgeting with his papers, seemed disposed to let his eyes rest anywhere rather than on the faces of his companions. Miss Harding, judging from her appearance, continually hovered on the verge of collapse; that no one noticed her condition showed how the others were preoccupied. Of the four Nora still bore herself as the one who was most at ease. She sat up straight; well back on her chair; her hands lying idle on her lap; a look upon her face which suggested an assurance which nothing they might say to her could touch; when she spoke she held her head a little back, with, in her wide-open eyes, what was almost the glint of a smile.

"I don't know what you call knowledge. I can only say that I am sure that you have not yet got to the root of the matter; that there is still something to be explained; because I am convinced that my father has left behind him a great deal of money."

"It is more than probable you are right; nothing will surprise me more than to learn that he hasn't; all that is wanted is a clue. Tell us on what you found your conviction."

"It is not altogether easy, but I'll try." The faintest touch of colour tinged her cheeks. "You know I am engaged to be married. My father, in congratulating me, said that the fact that Mr. Spencer had no money wouldn't matter, because I should have enough for both. I am sure he would not have said that had it not been true; I know my father."

"In other words, he practically told you that, after he was gone, he would leave you well provided for."

"That was what it amounted to, yes."

"He said nothing about the quarter from which the provision was to come?"

"He said nothing except what I have told you; but, for me, that is enough."

"No doubt, Miss Nora, but what we want is something which will tell us where the money which he spoke of is to be found."

"It will be found."

"Where? how? when? These questions must be answered."

"They will be answered, in God's good time."

The doctor gave an impatient gesture.

"I wish to say nothing in the least impious; but if it is to be in good time the answer must come now; before Cloverlea is sold, and you are homeless."

"Cloverlea—sold?" The notion seemed to startle her. "Who talks of selling Cloverlea?"

"My dear young lady, here's a creditor for over four thousand pounds, who writes to say that if his claim is not settled at once proceedings will immediately be taken against your father's estate—"

"Four thousand pounds! To whom did my father owe four thousand pounds?"

"That's the worst of it; it's a money-lender."

"A money-lender?"

"The fellow holds your father's paper—promissory notes—to the amount of nearly four thousand five hundred pounds, which is now overdue; and he says he has other paper, which will mature shortly, to the extent of another five thousand pounds. And he is not the only one; claims have been raining in from similar gentry. It actually appears that your father owed them at least thirty thousand pounds."

"I don't believe it."

The doctor shrugged his shoulders.

"I found it hard to credit; but—there are the bills, accepted by your father; what do you suggest? that they are forgeries?"

"At present I suggest nothing; what can I suggest? But I do not believe that my father ever borrowed money from a usurer."

"I am afraid that this is not a matter with which we can deal as a question of belief; do you propose to contest these claims? If so, notice must be given at once; you must clearly understand what that would mean; you would have to prove that the signatures upon these bills, which purport to be your father's, are forgeries; I don't know in which event the consequences would be more serious, if you proved it or if you failed to prove it."

"How do the people who hold these bills pretend they got them?"

"Guldenheim, who is the chief holder, is, in his way, a perfectly respectable man, and enormously rich. I called on him yesterday to put that question. He looked me up and down; and then observed that if payment was not made this week he should commence proceedings, when he would supply the Court with all the necessary information; then he asked his clerk to show me to the door. I am afraid there was something in the manner in which I asked the question which he resented, and perhaps was entitled to resent."

"What will be the result if he does take proceedings?"

"Probably in a short time you'll have the sheriff's officers in the house, and, perhaps before you've had time to turn round, you'll be left without a roof to cover you. Whatever happens we must avoid that."

"How are we going to avoid it? How are we going to find money with which to pay these men?"

"My proposal is that the creditors should be called together all of them; we will explain to them exactly how matters stand; and then I think, for their own sakes, they will join with us in making the best of what your father has left."

"As you say that Cloverlea is all that my father has left I presume that means that, in any case, Cloverlea will have to be sold, that we, my home and I, are at the mercy of a gang of usurers."

"I am afraid I don't see what else is to be done."

"Thank you; that is all I wish to know." She stood up, very erect; on her face there was still no sign of bitterness, only a quiet calmness, which was in strange contrast with the conspicuous lack of ease which marked the bearing of the others. "Do not suppose," she said, in a voice which was very soft and gentle, "that I am not grateful to you both for all that you have done for me. I had thought it possible, Mr. Nash, that the share you were taking in straightening out my small affairs might be of permanent use to you; I hoped you would allow me to retain you as my lawyer; but it seems that's not to be, that I'm not likely to want a lawyer very long. I'm sorry for both our sakes. For the trouble you have taken, doctor, no words of mine can thank you; because you—you're my very dear friend, and I fear you'll insist on making my sorrows your own, and—and that mustn't be." She stopped, as if, for the moment, she was unable to continue; and then added, "I'll think over all that you have said."

Without another word she left the room. The trio neither moved nor spoke some seconds after she had gone. Then Elaine Harding started to her feet with what sounded like a sob of passion.

"It's cruel!" she cried. "Cruel! I don't believe it's so bad as you make it out to be, I won't believe it! If Mr. Lindsay were still alive you wouldn't accuse him of the dreadful things you now pretend he's done, you wouldn't dare to do it!"

She rushed away in what seemed an agony of tears. The doctor stared at the door through which she had vanished; then he turned and stared at Nash; then he laughed queerly.

"Well! who'd have thought she'd such a temper! I like her better for it, the little whirlwind! She might as well have accused us of conspiracy to defraud Miss Lindsay; what do you think of that?"

"Women," observed Mr. Nash, with downcast eyes, and a wry smile, "are capable of anything."

CHAPTER VIII

Nora went to her bedroom. It was a pleasant room; as it was then it was practically her own creation; it represented her ideal of what her sleeping chamber ought to be. She had even invested it with an air of romance, as girls, when they are at the most romantic period of their lives, sometimes will do. There are girls who regard their bedrooms as if they were parts of themselves. Nora was one of them; she regarded her bedroom as if it were part of herself.

As she entered it that afternoon, it seemed to her that there was something strange about it, as if something had come into the atmosphere which was not present when she was in it last. It disturbed her, until she understood that the change was in her; that she had already unconsciously realized that this room, which had meant to her so many things, which she supposed would be hers for ever, might, probably, soon be hers no longer. With that feeling in her mind the room could never again be to her what it had been before; she felt almost as if she were a stranger in it then. Seating herself at her writing-table, she took the Bible which lay on the little shelf in front, and read in it, trying her hardest to concentrate her attention on its pages; but it was not easy, even the sacred words came to her through a mist. But when she closed the book, and went and knelt beside the bed, pillowing her face on the coverlet, as she had done again and again, times without number; alike in her infrequent moments of sorrow—she knew then what pigmy things those sorrows had been! and in her abounding hours of joy;—it was almost with a sense of terror that it was borne in upon her what great happiness she in truth had known—there came to her, as she continued to kneel, that peace which she so earnestly desired; so that she arose from prayer refreshed, and with that courage in her heart which refreshment brings. Placing herself on the armchair which stood by the open window, resting her arms on the sill, looking at the green world, perhaps without seeing how green and beautiful it was, so far as she could, she thought it all out.

And the more she thought the more clearly she apprehended that life for her—life as she hitherto had understood it—was at an end already, before it had scarcely begun, if the things which she had heard were true. She must depart from Cloverlea, and all that it stood for, and go out into a world, of which she knew nothing, to earn her own bread; she wondered, with an odd little smile, how she was going to set about it; if the picture was as black as it had just been painted. But was it? In her heart of hearts she doubted. Although she had been in such slight communion with her father; although his attitude towards her had been, in many respects, so unfatherlike; she believed that she had understood him, and that they had had much more in common than he had chosen to let it appear;—it would require a great deal to convince her that she was wrong.

She was fortified in her belief by a curious idea which, almost in spite of herself, obsessed her more and more; that she understood him better now that he was dead than she had done when he was living; that she was closer to him now than she had been then; that she saw more clearly into his very heart, and knew what manner of man he really was; and she knew that he was not the kind of man he must have been if the things which she had heard were true. He was incapable of falsehood; in small things, as in large, the soul of honour; he had not lied when he had told her that there would be enough for Robert as well as for her. Even then she had gathered more from what he said than his actual words; and she had understood that he had meant that she should gather more. She believed that he had wished her to know that in the future she would be a rich woman, and that his brief speech had been intended to convey that meaning; she was persuaded that he would not have meant it if it had not been true.

Yet, how was she to reconcile these things with the facts as they appeared at present? What explanation would make them harmonize? She did not know; she admitted to herself that she did not know; still she was convinced that, when everything was known, her father's truth would be established.

While Nora thought and thought; in the pretty bedchamber which had been assigned to her as an honoured guest, Elaine Harding was wrestling with troubles of her own, and her troubles were worse than Nora's. In her dressing-case, under a false bottom, were nearly three thousand pounds which did not belong to her; the dressing-case itself had been a gift from Nora, who had shown her the false bottom with glee, pointing out what a safe hiding-place it would be for any special treasures she might desire to keep from prying eyes. Almost the first use she had made of it had been to conceal the huge sum of which she had robbed the giver.

How she hated herself for what she had done! how gladly she would have restored the money to its place upon the dead man's table! She understood now what it had been doing there; doubtless it was the amount which it was his custom to pay into the bank each quarter, which it had been his intention to deliver on the morrow. God had intervened on the one hand, the devil on the other; she had played the devil's game;—fool! idiot! wretch that she had been! She realized quite clearly that that money would never bring any good to her; that it would lie like some obscene incubus on her whole life; even if she bought a husband with the proceeds of her stealing, how could she expect that such a marriage would be blest? The dressing-case itself had become a sort of monomania; not only did she keep it locked, but she hid it in her trunk and kept that locked; even then she was continually haunted by fears that some one was taking liberties with her property, as she had done with that of others. Suppose, by some mischance, the secret of that false bottom was discovered, what would happen then? She did not dare to think. What a fool she had been to tell Herbert Nash that tale about the legacy. It was not only a gratuitous, it was a foolish lie; she had seen that for herself almost as soon as it was told. He had only to make the most superficial inquiries, the falsehood would be discovered. She felt like biting her tongue out every time she thought of it. Her only excuse was that she had done it on the spur of the moment, without thinking; yielding to a temptation which was stronger than her. If only she did not love him! with so strange and violent a love that she had been willing to do what she had done rather than that he should not love her, rather than that she should not win him for her own! If, now, he were to find her out—what she had done—for his sake, what would he think of her then? But he should not find out; she would take care that he did not find out; rather than he should find out she would continue as she had begun, at whatever cost to herself, and to others.

Therefore it seemed to her disordered, tortured, twisted brain, that there was only one thing to be done, to make amends, to wipe off some of the blackness from her sin. She had told him that her aunt had left two thousand pounds. Well, he should have it. He had already had two hundred; there would be fifteen hundred for a share in Mr. Dawson's practice; the rest would be required to furnish a house, so that they might be married at once—on that point she was resolved, that there should be no delay about their being married; after what had happened she would be in constant agony till she had become his wife, and, so far, safe. He could not put his wife from him, even if he did find out. She was inclined to make it a condition that he should marry her before she gave him another farthing; in that way she would make sure of him. Even then, after the whole of the two thousand had been expended, more than a thousand pounds would still remain. It looked as if a thousand pounds would be a fortune to Nora Lindsay; a windfall from the skies; manna from heaven, which would at least preserve her from starvation. Nora should have the superfluous thousand; she would insist on it. It was true that such a sum would be most useful to a young couple, just married; but what did that matter, in face of Nora's pressing need? It was only too probable that they would be occasionally pinched; Herbert had explained that his income from a share of Mr. Dawson's practice would not, at the beginning, be large; there were eventualities for which they ought to be prepared; but such considerations were as nothing when one thought of Nora. She must be considered before anything else; she who had been such a faithful, such a generous friend; the whole of that thousand pounds should be hers.

By the time that Miss Harding had finally decided that this should be so she had nearly worked herself into a consciousness of virtue. When you looked facts in the face, from one point of view, it was generous to give away such a sum as that, especially when you remembered how much she stood in need of it herself; beyond a doubt that was how it would appear to Nora. Nora would appreciate her beneficence; would realize that this was the result of being kind to her humble friend in the days of her prosperity; the knowledge that the bread which she had cast upon the waters had returned to her after many days ought to make her—well, it ought to make her more contented with the measure which had been meted out to her; Elaine felt that it ought.

What Miss Harding had to do next was to invent some plausible explanation of how the money had come into her hands, and she was aware that that was not easy. So hard, indeed, was it to find that explanation that, in her despair, she nearly decided, after all, to relinquish her philanthropic scheme. But she would not do that—she could not do it; she had said that Nora should have the money, and she should. The misfortune was that Nora knew so much about her; it would be impossible to produce an aunt for her; Nora would refuse to swallow that aunt. Being intimately acquainted with the family history, she was pretty well aware that all the members of the Harding family would not be able to produce a thousand pounds between them. And then—there were other things. Only a short time ago Nora had "obliged" her, as Elaine phrased it, with the "loan" of a ten-pound note; if Miss Harding had had a thousand pounds laid by she would hardly have wanted those ten sovereigns.

So elusive did that explanation seem, so persistently did it refuse to come at her bidding, that Elaine brushed back her pretty hair with her pretty hands with what she intended to be a frenzied gesture, which was certainly not unbecoming, and at that moment she formed a resolution. She would go to Nora there and then, straight off, and approach the subject gently, trusting to the inspiration of the moment to provide her with the lie which would sound like truth, which it was so necessary that she should find to aid her in her beneficent purpose. No one knew better than she did how quickly her wits could come to her assistance at a pinch; with characteristic courage she took it for granted that they would not fail her when she was alone with Nora, and heart was speaking unto heart. In so doing she overlooked one factor—the unexpected. Experience had taught her that when she was hard pressed her wits could be relied upon, but hitherto she had always found herself in situations for which she was more or less prepared. The immediate future had something in store for her which was wholly unexpected.

CHAPTER IX

THE BUTLER

Elaine's room was at some distance from Nora's; they were in different wings. Miss Harding, whose habits were, in some respects, peculiar, always preferred that her room should not be too close to her friend's; though Nora herself would have liked to have had her nearer. To reach Miss Lindsay Elaine had to traverse a lengthy passage, which was divided in the centre by a square opening, which was used sometimes as a lounge. As Miss Harding moved along some one came out of this recess, and addressed her. It was Morgan, the butler.

Mr. Morgan was tall and fair—very fair. His face and eyebrows, and eyelashes, and hair were all of the same colour; it had rather an odd effect, which some people thought unpleasant. Many persons have an uncomfortable habit of never looking you in the face; he had what some felt was a nearly equally uncomfortable habit of never looking away from your face; he regarded any one with whom he might be talking with a fixed, impassive stare, which never faltered; there was a quality in his light greyish-blue eyes which, under such circumstances, was occasionally disconcerting. Miss Harding, who, in her way, was shrewd enough, had never known what to make of him; more than once, during her visits to Cloverlea, she had had a vague feeling that his demeanour towards her was not quite all that it ought to have been; the feeling came to her with unpleasant force as he stood before her then. Yet nothing could have been more decorous than his bearing; while he spoke with the softly modulated voice with which a well-trained servant ought to speak.

"I beg your pardon, Miss Harding, but can I speak to you for a moment?"

She said him neither yea nor nay, but put to him a question in return.

"What is it, Morgan?"

"It's about these."

He was extending towards her, on his open palm, what she perceived were three sovereigns. Whose they were, whence they came, what they meant, she had not a notion; but all at once she was conscious, not only of a curious fluttering of the heart, but of a desire to get away from him as quickly as she could.

"I can't stop now; if you have anything you wish to say you must say it later; I'm going to Miss Lindsay, she's waiting for me; and—I'm not feeling very well."

Why she added that last remark she did not know; a second after she wished it had been left unuttered—he fastened on it with such singular eagerness.

"You're not looking well—I've noticed it."

She was just about to hurry on, but there was something about the way in which he spoke which induced her to pause; something impertinent, which stung her, so that she regarded him with angry eyes, and replied to him with scorn.

"It's very good of you."

"I've noticed that you've not been looking well—ever since last Thursday."

This time he spoke with a significance which startled her, though she did not understand.

"Why since last Thursday?"

"I'll tell you. I was in the study when you were. After you had gone I found these three sovereigns. One was lying on the floor, and the other two were lodged on the shelves of the bookcase. And ever since then I've noticed that you've not been looking well."

A great horror was stealing over her, which she tried to get the better of, but failed. He regarded her with that impassive stare of his, which compelled her eyes to be fixed on his, whether they would or they would not.

"I—I don't know what you—what you mean."

It was strange how her voice trembled; his was steady enough, like the voice of doom.

"I'll explain. You remember last Thursday, the day on which the master was taken ill? I don't think you're ever likely to forget it. It occurred to me, after dinner, that the lamp had been left lighted, and the window open; so I went to put out the one and shut the other. When I got into the room, rather to my surprise, I found that the lamp was out, though the window was still open. As I stood there, in the darkness, I heard some one outside, coming along the terrace; presently you appeared at the open window. The moon was shining through the window, and you stood right in the moonshine, so that I saw you as plainly as if it had been daylight. But in the room it was darker; I expect that, coming in out of the moonlight, it seemed darker to you than it did to me. You didn't know I was there; I suppose that, being in a bit of a hurry, and with your thoughts all fixed on one thing, you took it for granted that the room was empty. It was rather funny—that's how it struck me at the time, and that's how it's struck me more than once; but perhaps that's because I've got a very keen eye for anything humorous.

"You went right across the room towards the oak bookcase which stands on the other side of the door, passing so close to me that I felt the wind of your skirts against my trousers as you passed, and I guessed that you knew what you were after before you came there, though I never guessed for a moment what it was. The bookcase was in the shadow, and mine not being cat's eyes, I couldn't see all that you were doing; but I could hear; and there are times when the sense of hearing conveys a good deal of information. I heard you takedown some of the books, then a rustling, then the chink of money. By that time you may be sure that I was all ears, and eyes—mine had almost become cat's eyes before you'd finished. I saw that you had something white in your hand, which I guessed was your pocket-handkerchief; and I partly saw, and partly heard, that you were shovelling coins on it which you were taking from one of the bookcase shelves. Either there were too many coins for such a small handkerchief—those handkerchiefs of yours are pretty, but they're small; I like one which is about the size of a towel—or else you were a little clumsy; you're not, as a rule, I know; I've often been struck by the natty way you have of doing things; but perhaps being in such a hurry made you a trifle nervous. Anyhow, as you're aware, you dropped some of the coins which you were putting into the handkerchief; I heard them fall, and so did you. You stooped to pick them up. I expected every second that you'd strike a match, or get a light somehow; in which case you'd have seen me, and it might have been funnier still. But you didn't. You felt, and felt, and felt; I take it that you thought you'd felt everywhere, and that as you could feel no more of the coins, that you'd picked up all you'd dropped. Presently, whether satisfied or not upon that point, you went out the way that you'd come in."

Mr. Morgan paused, and Miss Harding tried to breathe. It seemed to her that she was choking; that she was bound about as if with bands of iron. If there was anything peculiar in her appearance the butler made no comment; he went on in his easy, softly modulated tones.

"I heard you return along the terrace; I waited till I could hear no more of you; then I shut the window, and drew the curtains; then I lit the lamp, and with its aid I subjected the room to a careful examination, and in less than five seconds I found a sovereign on the floor by the bookcase, and then two more on the shelves. Here they are."

He again extended his hand, with the three shining discs on the open palm. She started back from them, gasping, as if they were dangerous things, of which she stood in physical terror.

"I've marked each coin—see? I want you to notice them carefully, so that you may recognize them, if you see them again." He held up one of the coins between his finger and thumb. "Of course when I found these I knew what had happened; understood it all—better even than you did. I knew some of the governor's little ways, which perhaps you didn't; a man in my position has to keep a sharp look-out; it's part of his duty—to himself. I knew all about the governor's habit of paying into his banking account three thousand pounds every quarter, in notes and gold, which Dr. Banyard has been telling you young ladies about, as if it was news; I'd seen the money on his table, that afternoon when I was helping to carry him away, the next day being his usual one for paying in, I knew what it was there for. He was a man of regular habits, was my late governor; though some of them were queer ones. There wasn't any of it left, except these three sovereigns which, in the dark, had escaped your notice. Because why?—because you'd taken the lot. I consider that a remarkable thing for any one to do, especially for a real young lady. Never before, in my experience, have I known the friend of the house take instant advantage of the host's sudden illness to play a game like that. Remarkable, I call it; most remarkable."

Each time that Mr. Morgan paused the girl before him gasped, as if the mere cessation of his speech removed from her some sense of constriction, which prevented the free play of her lungs.

"Don't suppose," he continued, with what he possibly intended to be affability, "that I am saying this to you in any unfriendly spirit; because I'm not—nothing of the kind. I've always felt that there was in you the makings of something remarkable, though I must admit that you've gone beyond my expectations. I've always liked you, Miss Harding; in fact, I've nearly more than liked you. I want you to understand that you've made of me what you might call an unintentional confidant; so why should there be any barriers between us? Socially there are none to speak of. Your father's a poor country parson, mine was a schoolmaster; there isn't much to choose between them; if I was asked I should say that I don't think much of either. Pecuniarily the advantage is all on my side, as I happen to know; and that in spite of the three thousand pounds you have of somebody else's. Very comfortable I could make a wife, if I had one; she'd be quite the lady. I've no complaint to make about your manner towards me in public; I humbly venture to hope that after this intimation of my friendly feeling towards you, you'll be even affable when we're alone together—if ever we are. It's all up with everything here; from what I happen to know, I shouldn't be surprised if the house, and all that's in it, was sold for what it will fetch in a surprisingly short space of time. Then we shall all be parted. Miss Lindsay will go her way—though I don't know what way that'll be; you'll go yours, and I shall go mine. This will be my last taste of service. When you meet me again afterwards you'll find me a perfect gentleman, whom you won't be a bit ashamed to introduce to your friends; and I assure you I'll do my best to earn their respect and esteem. I won't detain you any longer, Miss Harding—you'll understand that I had to speak to you; and that, situated as I am, I had to take the first chance that offered. Now you can go to Miss Lindsay with a mind at ease. If an opportunity offers you might inform her what a feeling of true sympathy there is for her in the servants' hall. It's very hard for a young lady, who has been brought up in the lap of luxury, to be all at once left with hardly clothes enough to cover her, because, between ourselves, that's what's going to happen to her; and down-stairs we earnestly trust, if I may use the language of metaphor, that her back will be broadened for the burden. There's many a young girl like her who has to earn her bread in ways I shouldn't like to mention; let's hope she won't come to any of those. You might mention, if you have the chance, that we all of us wish her the very best of luck."

With a slight inclination of his head, which might almost have been mistaken for a nod, Mr. Morgan went past her towards the staircase. She remained where he had left her, as if her feet were glued to the carpet. Her inclination would have been to return to her own bedroom; there she would at least be alone, to try to think; but the butler was between it and her. As she glanced in the direction of her room, looking over his shoulder he glanced towards her, and she ran towards Nora's room.

Without knocking she opened the door and entered; but so soon as she had crossed the threshold she stood motionless, as if all her limbs were locked together. Nora, seated on an arm-chair, was leaning on the sill of the open window, trying, in her own fashion, to find light in the darkness which threatened to encompass her round about; when she turned it seemed, from the expression which was on her face, as if she had found it. Certainly a stranger, observing the two girls, would have said that it was Elaine Harding who stood most in need of consolation; and so Nora seemed herself to think. That divine instinct which, in some people, wakes to life in the presence of suffering, was quick to perceive that here was trouble which was greater than hers. She held out her arms, crying—

"You poor child!"

It was enough; Elaine needed no further invitation. With eager, tremulous steps, and a cry which was half gasp, half sob, she went fluttering across the room, sinking in a heap at Nora's feet, pillowing her head upon her lap, crying as if the violence of her grief would tear her asunder. Smoothing her hair with her soft hands, stooping down and kissing her tenderly, using towards her all manner of endearments, Nora strove her utmost to assuage the passion of her woe, in seeming forgetfulness of how much she herself was in need of comfort. But Elaine was not to be consoled.

CHAPTER X

THE EARL AND THE COUNTESS

Events moved quickly; as, at certain crises of our lives, they have a knack of doing. During twenty years very little had really happened to Nora; in a few crowded, bewildering days for her the whole world was turned upside down. On the Friday—the day after the funeral—Nora told Dr. Banyard that she was inclined to be of his opinion, that the creditors had better be called together, and matters left in their hands. She did not tell him that her faith in her father remained unshaken. It was made clear to her that this was a question of hours, possibly even of minutes, if something was not done to appease the creditors at once then the worst would befall; it was no use delivering herself of pious expressions of faith when action was required. So she authorized the doctor to do his best for her, and left everything to his discretion.

Throughout that day she was puzzled by the singularity of Miss Harding's behaviour; she had cares enough of her own to occupy her mind, yet she could not help but notice that there was something very strange the matter with Elaine. The young lady's outburst of the evening before had not been explained. All day long she was in a state of nervous tremor which was almost hysterical; such conduct was unusual in Elaine, who had been wont to laugh at the idea both of nerves and of hysterics. Nora did not know what to make of her. So far as she could gather, from the cryptic utterances which the girl now and then let fall, she was troubled about three things. First, because of the poverty which apparently was in store for Nora; then because of the various amounts, which together did not amount to a very large sum, and most of which, to tell the truth, the creditor had herself forgotten, in which she was indebted to Nora; and, in the third part, because of a nebulous scheme she had for endowing Nora with unnamed, but seemingly immense supplies of ready money. It was this scheme which, apparently, was worrying her more than anything else; though what it really was, was beyond Nora's comprehension. Elaine talked—vaguely, it is true, but passionately, none the less—of being in possession of funds which Nora knew perfectly well she never had had, and probably never would have; and about which she waxed quite warm when Nora smilingly asked if she was quite sure she was not dreaming.

"You're not to laugh!" she cried. "You're not to laugh! You are to have it! you shall have it!"

"I shall have what?"

"The money I'm telling you about!"

"But what money are you telling me about? Elaine, you don't seriously wish me to believe that you have money. Only this week you were crying because of what you said you owed me; though I say you owe me nothing, since all that has been between us has been for love's sake. And only last week you told me that your pockets were empty, and you didn't know where you were going to get something to put in them; don't you remember?"

"But I may know where money is!"

"Yes, and so may I; there's money in the bank, but it's neither yours nor mine; and I'm sure—don't you know I'm sure? you must be a goose if you don't—that you've no more idea how, honestly, it's to be wooed and won than I have; so what's the use of our pretending?"

To the speaker's surprise Miss Harding glared at her for some moments in silence; then, as if in sudden rage, she flung herself out of the room without a word; sounds were audible as if she were sobbing as she went.

"What," inquired Nora of herself, not by any means for the first time that day, "can be the matter with Elaine?"

On the Saturday the storm broke on her from a quarter for which, at the moment, she was unprepared. Word had been brought that the Earl and Countess of Mountdennis were in the drawing-room, waiting to see her. Her first impulse was to send an excuse; the mere announcement of their presence made her conscious of a sinking heart; but it was not her way to excuse herself because she feared unpleasantness; second thoughts prevailed. She recognized that, from their point of view, they were entitled to see her, even in these first days of her bereavement. She needed none to tell her that the purport of their presence was not likely to be an agreeable one; that they probably had not come upon an errand of love; she had too shrewd a notion of their characters. Under the circumstances the last thing she might expect from them was sympathy; she was aware that they had a standard of their own; and that according to that the more a person stood in need of sympathy the less likely they were to vouchsafe it. Still they were Robert's parents; it was for her to consider him rather than herself; so, for the first time since her father was taken ill she ventured into the drawing-room.

The frigidity of the reception which they accorded her was ominous; she knew at once that so far from having deserved their sympathy she had incurred their displeasure. The last time they had met they had both of them taken her, not only metaphorically, but literally, to their bosoms; showering oh her tokens of affection which erred, if anything, on the side of redundance. Now the lady permitted her to touch a fish-like hand, taking care not to allow her to approach too near; while the gentleman merely bowed. It was he who spoke first, as if he were addressing some one whose behaviour had both pained and shocked him.

"We only learnt this morning, actually by the merest accident, that your father was not only dead, but buried."

"Not only dead but buried!"

This was the Countess. It was a standing joke that, if they were both engaged in the same conversation, when he did not echo her she echoed him. If they ever differed it must have been in private; in public their agreement was so complete as sometimes to approach almost to the verge of the exasperating.

"We were not even aware that your father was unwell; we had received positively no information on the subject whatever."

"Positively none whatever!"

"It seems to me—to us—a most extraordinary thing that you should not have apprised us of the condition of your father's health; that you should have given us no intimation of any kind; that you should have kept us in utter ignorance."

"In utter ignorance!"

"May I ask, may we ask, Miss Lindsay, why you have not treated us with at least some approximation to that consideration which our position obviously demanded?"

"Our position obviously demanded!"

"To begin with, it was all very sudden; and then I didn't know where you were.

"But you might have made inquiries, anybody would have told you; almost, one might say, the first person you met in the street. We are not the kind of people who hide ourselves in holes."

"No, not in holes!"

"The moment we learnt what had occurred—learnt, as I have observed, by the sheerest accident,—we rushed back to Holtye, that very moment; though to do so involved us in the most serious inconvenience; but we had no option."

"We had no option."

"Because, not only were we informed, by accident, that your father was dead and buried, but we were also told, at the same time, what struck us as being so surprising as to be almost incredible, that he had not left behind him even so much as a sixpence."

"Not even so much as a sixpence!"

"You will remember, Miss Lindsay—that is, I take it for granted that information was given to you to that effect, that before sanctioning my—our—son Robert's engagement to you I made a special point of calling upon your father, who then and there informed, I may say, assured, me that, on the occasion of your marriage, he would present you with a house and furniture, and settle on you five thousand pounds a year. On the strength of that positive and definite assurance I—we—gave our consent, which, without it, we never should have dreamt of doing. We have our duty to perform, not only to our son, but to ourselves, and I may say, to our family, of which we are the representatives; I therefore offer no excuse for taking advantage of the first opportunity which arises to ask if your father has left his affairs in a condition which will enable you to carry out that assurance. On behalf of the Countess of Mountdennis, and of myself, I beg you, Miss Lindsay, in answering that question, to be perfectly plain and perfectly candid."

"Perfectly plain and perfectly candid!"

The Earl, very tall, very straight, very thin, waved his hard felt hat in one hand, and his gold-knobbed malacca cane in the other, in a manner which was hardly so impressive as he perhaps intended; the Countess, her gloved hands clasped in front of her, wagged not only her head, but her whole body, as if to punctuate, and notify her approval, of his remarks as they fell from him. Nora was silent. At the back of her mind had been the consciousness that, sooner or later, this question would have to be confronted; but she had not anticipated that it would be addressed to her so suddenly, so brusquely, with such a stand-and-deliver air. When she began to speak her lips were tremulous; and, though she might not have been aware of it, her eyes were moist; the feeling was strong upon her how different it all was from what she had expected.

"I—I'm sorry to say that, so far as we have been able to ascertain, the state of my father's affairs is not—not altogether satisfactory."

It was the Countess who took up the running then; the Earl who played the part of echo; but as her volubility was much greater than his she did not give him so many opportunities to shine as he had given her.

"Not altogether satisfactory! my good young woman, what do you mean? I suppose all ideas of a house and furniture and five thousand a year must be given up, though your father led us to expect that there would be much more than that after he was dead; but the Earl has asked you a plain question and what we want is a plain answer; how much has he left you? If you can't give us the exact sum let's have it approximately, in pounds, shillings and pence."

"I'm afraid that I'm not yet in a position which enables me to do that."

"Not in a position? what do you mean, you're not in a position? are you in a position to say that he has left you anything, except debts?"

"I'm certain that when he said he had that money he had it; I believe he was a rich man when he died. Only he was very reserved; and, in consequence, we have not been able to find where the money is."

"Stuff and nonsense! you'd have found the money if there'd been any to find; it's only when there is none that none's found! Have you any sort of solid foundation for thinking that he did leave money?"

"He gave me to understand that I should be left well off; and I can't believe he would have done so if it had not been true."

"Some people can't believe anything; I know a woman who can't believe that her husband committed murder, though he was found guilty on the clearest possible evidence, confessed his guilt, and was hung ten years ago. Husbands and wives can't exist on the incomes they believe they have; tradesmen want coin of the realm. I'm informed that by the time everything's sold, and everything will have to be sold, and the debts paid, there'll be nothing left for you; I want you to tell me, plainly, please, if that's true."

At last the Earl had his chance.

"Yes, plainly, please, if that's true!"

"I am afraid that, as matters stand at present, it does seem as if it were likely to be true."

The Countess, putting up her lorgnettes, surveyed her fixedly, and severely.

"You must allow me to remark, Miss Lindsay, that you have a way of fencing with a plain question which, under the circumstances, seems peculiar, and which compels me to wonder if it can be possible that you knowingly obtained my son's consent to marry you under false pretences."

At this Nora did fire up.

"How dare you say such a thing! I did not obtain his consent, he obtained mine."

"We know very well what that means. I have not arrived at my time of life without understanding what are the wiles with which a young woman of no position lures a handsome young fellow of good family; I have not the slightest doubt that my son would never have asked you to be his wife had you not made it quite clear to him that you wished him to."

Nora stood up; one could see that the colour kept coming and going in her cheeks; that she was trembling; that she seemed to be panting for breath.

"I—I think you'd better go."

The Countess went calmly on; the girl's agitation seemed to make the elder woman calmer, and more corrosive.

"I am going when it suits me; I assure you I have no wish to stay a moment longer in this abode of misrepresentation than I am compelled to. But before I go I wish to appeal to your sense of decency, if you have any sense of decency—"

"How—how dare you! how dare you speak to me like this!"

"I say, if you have any sense of decency, to release him from the most unfortunate position in which your father's misrepresentations, and your own peculiar behaviour, have entangled him."

"Has—has he sent you here?"

"If you persist in putting such a question I shall understand that you have no sense of decency; surely any young woman with a spark of honour in her composition, must perceive that in such a situation the man would not be likely to send—that the initiative must come from her, not from him."

"I simply wish to learn if Mr. Robert Spencer knows that you have come to me upon this errand."

"He does not know; which gives you an opportunity to free him gracefully before the true state of affairs does come to his knowledge."

"If he wishes to be what you call 'free,' do you suppose that for one moment I would stand in his way?"

"It is not so much a question of what he wishes, as of what you wish. If you wish, though ever so slightly, to hold him to his bargain, I dare say he'll be held, even to the extent of making you his wife; though he will regret it ever afterwards, and will probably live to curse the day on which you first placed yourself in his path. Young men have married undesirable women, who were in no way fitted to be their wives, and who were thinking only of themselves, before to-day, and will again; I have seen examples of it in my own family, to my great sorrow. I intend, if I can, to save my son Robert from such a fate, whatever you may say or do; the purport of my presence here is merely to learn if you are, or are not, possessed of a shred of principle."

"I cannot conceive why you talk to me like this; what makes you think yourself entitled to take up such an attitude towards me; what I have done which causes you to address me in such a strain."

"That's high-faluting, it's talk of that sort which makes me suspect that you must be even worse than I supposed. Your father held you out to the world as a young woman who was rich already, and who would be still richer later on, and you tacitly endorsed his positive statements; then he dies just in time to save himself from being made a fraudulent bankrupt, leaving you worse than a pauper, and you have the assurance to pretend to wonder why I and the Earl regard you—I will be as civil as I can—askance. Talk sense, Miss Lindsay; don't presume on our simplicity any longer. You are perfectly well aware that, had we been aware of the truth from the first, we should never have countenanced you in any way whatever. Your father's lies, with which you went out of your way to associate yourself—I know!— deceived us; and they deceived my son; there's the truth for you, if you never heard it before."

Nora looked as if she could have said many things; but she only asked a question.

"What, precisely, is it that you wish me to do?"

"I wish you to do something to, at least in part, undo the mischief which you have done already, to atone for the evil of which you have been the cause; I wish you to show by your demeanour your consciousness of the miserably false position in which you have been placed by others, or in which you have placed yourself, it doesn't matter which. In other, and plainer words, I wish you to hand me my son's letters and presents, and to sit down at once and write a letter, which I will hand him, in which you express your appreciation of the fact that he asked you to become his wife under an entire misapprehension, and that now, since circumstances have turned out so wholly different to what they were represented to be, your own self-respect forbids you to allow any association to continue between you; and that, in short, all is over between you, in every possible sense of the phrase. I want you to put that down, as plainly, and as finally, as it can be put, in black and white, because, Miss Lindsay, I wish to save my son Robert, at the earliest possible, from the danger in which he stands, and to do it while he is still absent."

"But, my dear mother," exclaimed the voice of some new-comer, "your son Robert is not still absent, he is here."

Looking round the trio saw that the Honourable Robert Spencer was standing at the open window.

CHAPTER XI

ROBERT

Robert Spencer was not only, as his mother put it, a handsome young fellow; he had more than good looks, he had that air of distinction which goes with character. No one with even a slight knowledge of physiognomy could see him once without perceiving that he was physically, mentally, and probably morally, a strong man, and, what was almost as much, a likable man. As he stood framed in the open window, with the glory of that almost uncannily glorious April sun lighting up the frame, each of those who saw him was conscious of an impulse which, had it been yielded to, would have resulted in a scene of tenderness. He was dear to his parents, and he knew it; they themselves scarcely knew how dear, and that also he suspected. He was dear, with a different sort of dearness, to the girl who moved towards him, as if impelled by a power against which she was helpless; only to start back, shrinking timidly, with frightened, longing eyes, and cheeks on which the crimson faded to pallor. Yet, though he was dear to all of them, there was not one of the three who would not rather he had not appeared upon the scene just then. His mother, with characteristic courage, gave expression to her feeling on the spot.

"Robert! my boy! we don't want you. Where have you come from? and what are you doing here?"

He smiled, and his was such a pleasant smile it did one good to see it.

"Why, mother, I'm sorry to hear that you don't want me. I've rushed from the station to tell Nora, what I've not a doubt she knows already, that I hope she'll find in me some one who'll take the place, at least in part, of him whom she has lost."

When he advanced into the room his mother placed herself in his path.

"Robert, my dear boy, you ought not to be here. Go back to Holtye, and when I return I will explain to your perfect satisfaction why I say it."

"Ought not to be here!—where Nora is! My dear mother! Nora, why do—why don't—Nora, what's the matter?"

He made a sudden forward movement, but once more his mother was too quick for him; again she interposed; if he did not wish to knock her over he had to stand still.

"Robert, I must beg you to do as I desire, and return at once to Holtye."

"My dear mother, I must beg you to stand aside, and let me speak to Nora."

The old woman turned to the girl.

"Miss Lindsay, you perceive how my son treats me; have you nothing which you wish to say?"

"Of course," replied the son in question, "Nora has something which she wishes to say—I'm sure I don't know why you call her Miss Lindsay; she's not likely to say it when addressed like that. I'll make a suggestion, mother; you go back to Holtye, with the dad, and I'll talk to Nora when you're gone, and I'll tell you some of the things she says to me when I return to Holtye."

The old lady stuck to her guns.

"Miss Lindsay, is there nothing that you wish to say?"

"Yes, Mr. Spencer, there is something which I wish to say—your mother is right; you ought not to be here." With a great effort she had brought herself to the sticking-point. She was one of those women who have in them an infinite capacity for suffering, yet who remain unbeaten though they suffer. If she once saw what she believed to be her duty straight in front of her, though her flesh might quail, her soul would not falter; she would do her duty as certainly as any of that great host who have died for duty, smiling as they died. The Countess had not put things pleasantly, but it seemed to Nora that she had put them correctly; she ought not to marry the man she loved, for his own sake; and because she loved him with something of that love which passes understanding, she would not marry him—to his own hurt. She proceeded to make this as clear to him as she could. "There has been a misunderstanding between us from the first; I don't know that the fault has been altogether mine, but there has been. It is necessary that we should understand each other now. When I consented to become your wife it was under a misapprehension; I did not know it then; I know it now. Now that I do know it, it is quite clear to me that it is impossible that I should be your wife, and I never will be. Therefore, since what your mother says is obviously correct, and you ought not to be here, I would join with her in asking you to go."

Robert Spencer stared as if he found it difficult to credit that this formal, cold, somewhat pedantic young woman was the girl whom he had found all love and tenderness; indeed he refused to credit it.

"Nora, you're—not well."

He said this with such a comical twist, and such a sunny smile, that she all but succumbed, she loved him for it so; she was all of a quiver, her heart seemed melting. It was possibly because she perceived the girl's sad plight that the sharp-eyed old woman took another hand in the game.

"Robert, is it necessary that Miss Lindsay and I should retire? I should not have thought that you would have required two women to ask you to go, before you went. I repeat that you shall have all explanations—from Miss Lindsay and from me—when I see you at Holtye."

But Robert still smiled, and he shook the handsome, clever head, which the Countess ought to have known was too clever to be hoodwinked quite so easily.

"It won't do, mother; I'm sorry to seem to run counter to your wishes; but it's clear to my mind that it is I who am entitled to ask you to leave me alone with Nora; it pains me to observe your seeming reluctance to do what you know you ought to do. Dad, you'll understand; won't you take my mother away?"

The Earl, thus appealed to, cleared his throat, and then observed—

"Robert, you're a fool; leave this business to your mother; you come and talk to me."

He moved towards the window, as though inviting his son to accompany him into the grounds, and to have that talk out there and then; but Robert stood still.

"Thank you, dad; it's very good of you, and I'll have all the talk with you you can possibly desire—after I have had a talk with Nora."

All at once the girl solved the question in her own fashion; she spoke tremulously, yet in haste.

"I—I think that if Mr. Spencer won't go, then—then it is better that I should."

And she did go, towards the door, and through it like a flash, before the person principally concerned had a chance to stop her.

"Nora!" he cried, the instant she had gone, and he went rushing towards the door through which she had vanished; but again his mother, showing an agility which, in a person of her years, was remarkable, stood in his way.

"Robert, I insist upon your conducting yourself like a gentleman! If you will not show me the respect which is due to your mother, you at least shall not behave in a stranger's house in a way which is unbecoming to my son."

He looked at the old woman, who had planted herself in front of him, upright and stiff as a post, and he drew back; this time his smile was grave.

"Mother, I trust that you are not forgetting that there is a respect which a mother owes to her son. Why do you object to my having any conversation with my affianced wife?"

"Don't you know that her father is dead?"

"Certainly I know it; just dead, and just buried; it is on that account that I feel so strongly that my place is with her."

"Don't talk nonsense!"

"Mother, when you were alone in the world, didn't you feel that my father's place was with you?"

"Robert, your brothers have behaved like fools, but I hope you won't; you are all the hope I have left; it will break my heart if you do. This girl's father has turned out to be an impostor!"

"An impostor? Mother, in saying what you have to say to me will you please remember you are speaking of the woman who is to be my wife, and your daughter, and so choose language which does not convey more than you intend?"

"Don't presume to lecture me! that is going too far. I say he has turned out to be an impostor—and he has!"

"In what sense?"

"He told your father he was going to give his girl a house and furniture and five thousand a year, besides leaving her a rich woman when he died; and now he hasn't left enough to pay his debts; if that isn't being an impostor I don't know what is!"

"A good deal of water has gone over the mill since he said that; he may have had money then, and yet have lost every penny of it since."

"Then he ought to have told you."

"Why?"

"Why! you know perfectly well why. I believe it is your wish to irritate me, when I'm very far from well, as your father here will tell you. That man knew that you were not in a position to marry a poor woman, and that we should never have given our consent if it had not been for this distinct assurance that his daughter would be amply provided for."

"Well?"

"Well! it's not well; there's nothing well about it! You shan't speak to me like this—I won't have it! Robert, I want you to promise that all shall be at an end between Miss Lindsay and you; she herself sees the matter in the proper light—"

"Does that mean that you have been talking: to her?"

"Certainly I have been talking to her; and I will say this, that she did not take long to see where her duty lay."

"Is it possible that she took it for granted that I should behave like a blackguard—at my mother's bidding?"

"Robert, how dare you!"

"It is not I, mother, who dare; I dare not. I asked Miss Lindsay to be my wife when her father was alive, and a rich man and all was well with her. If, now that all is not well with her, I attempt to repudiate the solemn engagements into which I then entered—"

"Fiddle-de-dee! solemn engagements indeed! You entered into no solemn engagements, and I'll take care you don't. Robert, you are the only creature I have left to love."

"I don't see how that can be, since you have eight other children and a husband."

"My boy, my boy, don't you be so cruel as to pretend that you don't understand! You're my youngest born, the child of my old age, my baby—you're dear to me in a special sense, as you know very well. If you marry this girl, who is not only penniless, but who is in honour bound to pay her father's debts, and who'll drag you down into the gutter, because your aunt will never give you another penny when she knows the facts, on the day of your marriage I'll commit suicide."

"Mother!"

"I will, so now you're warned; and she shall know why I do it. I'll not live to be mocked by all my children; I've had nine of them, as you say, and if not one of them will try to please his mother—then God help us mothers."

The young man turned to the Earl.

"Do you associate yourself, sir, with my mother in this matter?"

"Certainly I do—most distinctly I do; with what she says respecting this young woman most emphatically I do; I can't conceive of a rational creature doing anything else. As matters have turned out the girl's impossible—absolutely out of the question. If you can't see it, Robert, you're a fool."

"Thank you, sir." The young man regarded his plain-speaking sire with a wry little smile. "I think it probable that when you have thought things over, sir, you will modify your views; but while you hold them so warmly, plainly it is desirable that I should restrict myself to a bare announcement of the fact that they are not mine."

He moved towards the window; his mother called out to him.

"Robert, where are you going? You will return with us. We came in the landau; there is plenty of room. I beg you will give us your company; indeed, if it is not sufficient for a mother to beg of her son, then I insist upon your doing so."

"Pardon me, mother, but I am not going to Holtye; I have taken a room at the 'Unicorn.'"

"The 'Unicorn!' Robert! Harold, will you be so good as to ask him what he means?"

The Earl did as he was bid.

"Robert, what do you mean by saying that you have taken a room at the 'Unicorn'?—an inn!—a mere tavern! at the gate of your father's house!"

"The 'Unicorn' can hardly be said to be at the gate of Holtye, since it is at a distance of a good five miles."

"Stuff, sir! Five miles or fifty, what does it matter? Holtye is your home, and you will be so good as to come home; we've been expecting you; we've been looking forward to your return; I trust that the day is far distant on which you will cease to regard Holtye as your home."

"Unless he wishes to break his mother's heart."

The interpolation was the lady's.

"So no nonsense, sir; get into the carriage and we'll drive you home."

"You are very kind; permit me, sir, to finish. It is plain that my mother and you have made up your minds that Miss Lindsay shall not become my wife; you will probably leave no stone unturned which will keep us apart. I appreciate your motives, and though I think them unworthy, I know you think they're for my good; but I have made up my mind that she shall be my wife, and I will stop at nothing which will bring about that desirable consummation. Under these conditions obviously the more we are together the more friction there will be; and therefore, equally obviously, it is desirable that, for the present at least, I should not come to Holtye. But I promise you this, that when she's my wife I'll come—and I'll bring her with me."

"You'll do nothing of the kind; if you ever do marry her you'll never set foot inside the door again."

This, of course, was the Countess; her son laughed.

"You hear my mother, sir! Isn't that conclusive?"

He passed through the window and out of sight, the Earl and the Countess staring at the place where he had been. The Earl was the first to speak.

"Jemima, what on earth was the use of saying a thing like that? Don't you know him better than to threaten?"

"What am I to say? what am I to do? Who'd have children!—they're the cause of suffering and sorrow to their mothers from their cradles to their graves! I wish I'd never had one!"

"My dear Jemima, I dare say, also, you wish you had two heads, but you haven't. For my part, I don't know that I regret the line he's taken up."

"Harold! Do you wish to see him ruined?"

"Not at all; quite the other way; that's exactly it. In cases of this sort, when the man throws over the woman there's a certain amount of odium attached to his conduct—I realize that as clearly as he does; but when she throws him over that's another thing. Robert's pig-headed—"

"Like his father!"

"And his mother! he's no worse on that account, Jemima, not in the sense in which I use the word. You'll not move him, but you will the girl; there's your objective. In her way, unless I'm mistaken, she's as pig-headed as he is. He may use all the eloquence he has at his command, but, after what you said to her, and the way in which you put things, I doubt if she'll marry him though he pleads till he is dumb—they are a pair of Quixotes; when it comes to rank, downright Quixotry, she'll beat him on his own ground."

And the lady considered her lord's words.

"I shouldn't be surprised," she admitted, "if you are right."

"I know I'm right," he said. "I haven't come to my time of life without being a student of human nature."

CHAPTER XII

IN THE WOOD

On the Sunday morning Nora went to church alone. Miss Harding, who did not appear at breakfast, sent word that she had a headache and hoped that Nora would excuse her; which Nora was glad to do; she preferred to go alone.

For the first time for some days the sky was overcast; the sun was hidden, as if the clerk of the weather desired to show that he was in sympathy with the girl's feelings. Certainly the girl's mood was not a sunny one. The church was distant from the house about a mile. The way to it was through the grounds; along a footpath through the wood, across Farmer Snelling's thirty-acre field, into the copse on the other side, where the first daffodils were always found; when you were out of the copse almost in front of you was the Rectory Lane; a hundred yards along the lane, turn sharply to the left, there was the lych-gate under which, aforetime, more parish coffins rested than men had count of. As she went the familiar way, amid the many evidences of the hasting spring, the spirit of the morning seemed to enter into her, so that, as she passed into the church, and knelt where she had knelt so many times in happier days, the peace of God came into her soul and she knew, with an abiding sense of comfort, that indeed all things are in His hands.

She never forgot that morning's service; the last at which she was privileged to be a worshipper in what she had thought would always be, in a special sense, her own church; the memory was with her, as a sweet savour, in the still darker days which were to come. It was Palm Sunday, for Easter was late that year; the hour of the Church's mourning was close at hand; the appointed service for the day seemed to be peculiarly suited to her own case; before it was at an end her thoughts ceased to be centred on herself; her head, and her heart, were both abased before a sorrow that was greater than hers.

When she came out, at the close of service, she was surrounded by people, villagers and others, for there was not a creature in the parish, good or bad, high or low, with whom she was not on terms of intimacy; unconsciously she illustrated the doctrine that—

"He prayeth best who loveth best All things, both great and small; For the dear God who loveth us, He made and loveth all."

They had all a word of sympathy to offer, crude words some of them were, but she knew that all of them were well meant, and that was something; what was hidden from her, and from them, was knowledge of the fact that to most of those who clustered round her, and who waylaid her as she went, the words which were uttered were words of farewell; that before another Sunday came round she was to be parted from them as by a great sea. At the church porch, in the Rectory Lane, in the copse across Farmer Snelling's field, she found some one who had at least a word to say; sometimes it was an ancient, sometimes a toddling child. She had gained the stile which one had to climb to get into the wood before she was able to feel that the last of the interviewers was done with; she did not guess that on the other side of that stile lurked the most irrepressible of them all.

Although there was a right of way through the wood it was one which was seldom used, except by the household at Cloverlea; and how often they went that way was shown by the untrodden moss which almost hid the track. And yet it was a pleasant wood, and an inviting path; it had only to be followed a very little way, there were delicious nooks and dells. Most of the trees were old, and many of them were stately; yet they were excellent company, if one chanced to be alone. As Nora had found, many a time. She loved that wood; it was to her as a dear friend; so often had she come to it to dream, waking dreams, and to be alone in it, with her joys. The season, that year, was early. The chestnuts—there were not many in the wood, only about a dozen, but they were all fine trees—were already nearly in full leaf; the elms were showing green; there was promise of green upon the beeches; only the oaks were still bare; in all the wood, somewhere, was the gleam and glow and glory of that lustrous, delicate, fleeting green which is spring's greatest marvel. And though the sun still was hidden, she felt how beautiful it was, and how good to be in it there alone; until she came upon a man who was leaning against a tree, the finest chestnut in the wood, the splendour of whose leafing branches formed a canopy above him.

The man was Robert Spencer; the tree was just round a bend in the path, so that she was almost up against him before she had the faintest notion that any one was there. To judge from her demeanour the sight of him alarmed her; she drew back with a half-stifled cry, staring at him as if he were some dangerous thing. He, on his side, was all smiles, as if he was very conscious that she was the pleasantest thing he had seen that day. He held out both hands, with his cap in one.

"Nora! at last! I was afraid you were never coming!"

There was no mistake about the joyous ring which was in his voice. On her part she seemed not to know what to say, or do, or make of him, as if his presence there was a possibility of which she had never dreamed.

"Mr. Spencer, you—you ought not to be here; I—I must beg of you to let me pass."

"Why, my dear Nora, of course I'll let you pass; do you suppose I want to block the way? But why do you call me Mr. Spencer? and why do you keep out of kissing distance? Do you know how long it is since I had a kiss? and how often of late I've pictured the delicious moment in which I was to have another? Nora!"

The colours chased each other across her cheeks in rainbow hues; she strove her utmost to look dignified; but, to his thinking, she only looked more delightful; her very severity he thought became her.

"Mr. Spencer, you—you have no right to talk to me like this. You have had my letter—"

"Your letter? what letter?"

"The one I sent you yesterday; it ought to have been delivered this morning."

"It wasn't; I've had no letter of yours which you sent me yesterday; where did you send it? to what address?"

"I addressed it to you at Holtye."

"Then that's why I've not had it; possibly I never shall have it. You rushed off in such a flurry, before I could speak a word to you, that I had no chance to tell you that I wasn't staying at Holtye."

"Not staying at Holtye? then where are you staying?"

"At the 'Unicorn,' I've taken a room there; it's only another illustration of the truth of what I've so often told you, the more haste the worse speed. I can see now that you'd go tearing off if I'd let you; but I won't. I want to explain."

"I—I'd rather you explained through the post."

"Then I wouldn't; and I'm not going to. When people wish to understand each other in matters of real importance I hold that they'd better do so face to face; I've no faith in pen and ink; microbes breed in ink-bottles, which breed all sorts of misconceptions. Now I can see that you're rushing at your fences again. You're taking it for granted that I wish to speak to you on one subject, when I principally wish to speak to you about your father. I want to tell you something about him which you ought to know."

"What is it?"

Her voice was faint, as if she felt that unfair engines of war were being used against her.

"Your father hoped that we should marry; he knew that I loved you, and would always love you; and he thought you loved me, and would always love me; and therefore—"

"What were you going to tell me about my father?"

She perceived that he was trenching on dangerous ground, and tried to get him off it; he came off with much agility.

"I met him on the morning on which I was starting for Cairo—"

"You never told me."

"I had an idea that he didn't wish me to mention that I'd met him, so I didn't. We lunched together; he gave me a most excellent lunch—"

"I'm glad he gave you an excellent lunch."

"There, Nora! that's much more like you! thank you! It was an excellent lunch; it was after lunch he said he hoped that we should marry, because, as I have already observed, he knew that—"

"Yes; we'll take that for granted; please go on."

"I'm going on as fast as ever I can; but it'll only be another case of more haste worse speed if you won't let me tell my tale my own way, because, if I don't, I'm nearly sure to leave out essential details. Among other things he remarked that, one day, you'd be a rich young woman."

"You're sure he said that?"

"Quite; your father could express himself clearly enough if he chose; and he expressed himself clearly then."

"But—I don't understand."

"Wait a bit; I'm going to make you understand, if you'll have a little patience. Later, I cannot say that he said so clearly, but he intimated, that he obtained his income from some business with which he was connected, and which represented to him a large sum of money."

"Business! I didn't know that he had anything to do with any business."

"Mind, he didn't state definitely that he had; and I asked no questions, but that was what he hinted. Then he said something which, in the light of recent events, appears to me to have been rather remarkable. He observed that life was always uncertain; that one could never tell the hour when one would die, and that, therefore, since I was going to be the husband of his only child, he would like to place in my hands directions as to what he would desire to have done, in case death took him unawares; or before he completed certain arrangements which he then had in view."

"What a strange thing for him to say!"

"You see how necessary it was that I should see you face to face, and how difficult it would have been to put this on to paper? Nora, I love you!"

"Are you—are you really telling me what my father said?"

"I'm going to tell you everything he said, if you'll give me time enough; only don't suppose for a moment that you're going to keep me from saying that I love you; especially as it was because he knew I loved you, and believed that you loved me, that he told me what he did."

"I—I wish you'd go on."

"After I'd been a few days in Cairo there came a package in which there was a note from him; a brief and characteristic note, to this effect. 'Dear Robert,' you see he called me Robert." He paused, as if to challenge her. "Nora, I wish you'd call me Robert; it's a stupid, ugly, vulgar, clumsy name, but you don't know how I long to hear it on your lips."

"I—I don't know that it's any of the things you say it is; I—I don't know that there's anything particularly the matter with the name."

"That's very sweet of you."

"But I don't think it's either fair or kind of you to try to take advantage of me like this!"

"Take advantage of you! is your sense of justice so warped that you can say a thing like that! In what sense am I supposed to be trying to take advantage of you, Nora?"

"You're pretending to tell me about my father, and—and you keep trying to tell me about other things instead."

"The only tie which bound me to your father, the only reason he had for placing his confidence in me, was his knowledge of my love for you."

"Very well; if you like we'll take that for granted—"

"I don't like."

"Tell me what was in the note!"

"'Dear Robert, referring to our conversation of' such and such a date; at this moment I can't give it you exactly—"

"It doesn't matter."

"'You will find in envelope enclosed herewith the instructions of which I spoke. It is understood that it is only to be opened in the event of my demise; and that, should I for any reason whatever desire its return, you will at once hand it me intact. In acknowledging kindly state that you understand.—Faithfully yours, DONALD LINDSAY.' That was the note. With it was a sealed envelope, inscribed, 'To ROBERT SPENCER. Not to be opened until after my death.—DONALD LINDSAY.'"

"And have you opened it?"

"That's the gist and point of the whole affair—I haven't it."

"I don't understand; I thought you said—"

"I did say. What's that?"

Mr. Spencer's question referred to a sound like the rustling of bushes.

"It's only a rabbit, or a hare."

"It must be a large specimen of either animal, and an awkward one, to make a noise like that."

"What were you going to say?"

"I placed the sealed envelope in my suit-case, together with my other most valuable possessions; which, with the exception of some of your dear letters, were worth about twopence; at the moment I'd nowhere else to put it. When I left, the suitcase was placed, with my other luggage, on the train, and, I presumed, transferred from the train to the boat; yet, when I went down to my cabin, after the boat was fairly off, the suit-case wasn't there."

"What had become of it?"

"That's the problem which I have still to solve, and which I'm going to solve. Either it was left behind at my aunt's, which she denies, or it was left on the train, which the railway company denies, or it was taken by mistake to somebody else's cabin, which every one denies, or it was stolen, of which I haven't the faintest proof. Anyhow, it was, and, at present, it isn't; as yet that's as far as I've got."

"Then my father's letter to you is lost."

"But it's not going to continue lost; I have lost things before, but I'm not going to lose the only thing I ever had worth losing; I've a ridiculous sort of fatalistic feeling that, as matters have chanced, if I lose that letter—really, and truly, and finally lose it—I may lose you; you don't suppose I'm going to sit down quietly and endure that loss with equanimity? You don't know me, my lady, if you do. What is that? Don't tell me that that's either a rabbit or a hare."

"Perhaps it's a fox."

"Foxes don't set the whole countryside in a clatter when they start moving; they're of much too retiring a nature. It's some one making off through the bushes, that's who it is. Hi! you there, who are you?"

There was no reply to his call.

"Perhaps it was some one who came upon us unexpectedly, and—and didn't wish to disturb us."

"Perhaps so; we're obliged to his taste for self-effacement if it is."

"I suppose you've no idea what was in the envelope."

"I've been putting two and two together, and I've formed a hypothesis which I'm convinced can't be very far out. Your father was not a man to say the thing which is not."

"I'm sure of it."

"I also; he did not say you would be a rich woman without cause. The hypothesis I've deduced is this. Your father was a gentleman of the old school; he didn't like commerce; he didn't wish people to think that he had anything to do with commerce; yet all the while he was drawing his income from a business with which he had probably been associated more or less unwillingly. At the time I saw him he was making arrangements to dispose of it; whether or not they were completed I cannot say; that envelope contains the clue. When he spoke of the suddenness of death he was possibly aware that he had a congenital predisposition towards the end which was actually his; and that envelope contained the secret—which he was even perilously anxious to preserve in life—of what was the source of his income, and of the fortune which he had built up for you."

"All this, of course, is surmise."

"You know it's more than surmise; you know that you're a rich woman, as you stand there."

"I know, from the only facts which as yet are established, that, at present, I'm a pauper."

"Well, we're both of us paupers; all the better."

"I don't agree."

"You're taking your cue from my mother."

"I should prove myself very foolish if I need take such a cue from any one."

"There's a wisdom of the foolish which is sometimes wonderful. If you were to marry me tomorrow—"

"As if I should!"

"You'd make my fortune!"

"When, as you've told me again and again, you live on charity; and directly you married me that charity would stop?"

"I know a way by which I could earn two or three hundred a year right off; before long I'd be earning thousands; I'm not incapable, I only need a spur; to work for the woman I love! I ask for nothing better. If I marry a woman with money the probability is that I should never earn a penny."

"No, but you'd earn a name for yourself instead; one can earn something better than money."

"May be."

"And she'd be proud of you."

"Even supposing that you're not buttering me up—"

"As if I would!"

"As if you would! as if you haven't done it over and over again! I know! I say, even granting I'm a swan of the very finest plumage—"

"Mr. Spencer!"

"Miss Lindsay; since you will interrupt me; and will descend to surnames; though, Nora, you're a darling."

"It's no use our indulging in abstract discussions. I've no doubt you'll be able to clothe charming sentiments in the very best language. I know how clever you are."

"Thanks very much."

"But what's the use, since my mind's made up that I won't marry you while I'm a pauper?"

"Acting on my mother's instructions."

"If you like to put it that way; though I wouldn't even if your mother hadn't interposed; if I'd thought I was going to be a pauper I'd never have said I would."

"Although you love me?"

"Because I love you."

"Nora! You're going to make a mess of things."

"I'm going to try not to make a mess of things."

"You're starting the wrong way."

"Listen. I don't think you've behaved well about that envelope my father sent you."

"Do you imagine that I think I have? do I look it? How my countenance belies me!"

"There appear to have been some letters of mine in that suit-case; I didn't think you'd have left my letters lying about."

"Nora!"

"You seem to have left the suit-case lying about, so I suppose you left my letters too."

"Of all the—of all the—! Well, I deserve it."

"I think you do. When you find that envelope you can come and show me what is in it; until then—good-bye."

"Do you mean that?"

"I hope that I am like my father in not saying what I don't mean; I do mean it."

"I'll find that envelope!"

"And I hope you'll find my letters."

"I'll find them too."

"I hope there was nothing in them very—very amusing; it isn't nice to feel that strangers are reading one's—one's private letters."

"You rub it in."

"That's not my intention; would you like to feel that people you know nothing about were reading some of the letters you wrote to me?'

"I know what you mean; I'll find the letters and the envelope, and the suit-case; and if any one has opened that suit-case I'll—I'll make them smart."

"Good-bye."

Already she was moving off; he exclaimed—"Like that! Nora! won't you even give me your hand?"

She stopped, and turned; with something on her face which, in his eyes, made her very beautiful.

"If you'll promise only to take my hand."

"I promise; I'll take only what you're willing to give." They stood, for some seconds, hand in hand, eyes looking into eyes, as if they found it difficult to speak. Then he said, "Don't suppose I don't think you're right; I know you're doing this for me, and I know you're always right. This good-bye is only the prelude to a time of waiting, and hope, and work. First of all I'll find that envelope, then if there's nothing in it to show that you're a millionaire, I'm going to work and be a millionaire—I'll win you in my own way. I'm not afraid of waiting; you'll not marry any one but me."

"I don't think I shall."

"I don't think you will either."

"There's something I'd like to ask, if you won't misunderstand."

"I'll not misunderstand."

"I'd like to kiss you before I go, only—I don't want you to kiss me."

"Nora!"

She moved closer to him, and, while he stood still, she touched her lips to his, a butterfly kiss, then, turning, went quickly down the path. He stood and watched her as she went.

CHAPTER XIII

Nora had not long been gone to church before Miss Harding became sufficiently cured of her headache to permit of her quitting her own apartment. Perhaps she was of opinion that fresh air would do it good; and, notoriously, fresh air is good for headaches; certainly she looked very far from well. She donned her smartest hat, and one of her prettiest frocks, relinquishing, for the nonce, the black dress she had been wearing for her lately departed host. She attired herself with the greatest care, giving minute attention to those small details which mean so much; possibly she was under the impression that costume might have something to do with a cure—yet all her care could not conceal the fact that she was looking ill. When she saw how white she was, and the black marks under the eyes—and actually wrinkles in the corners, and how thin and worn and pinched her face seemed to have suddenly become, she could have cried, only she was painfully conscious that tears had already had too large a share in bringing her to the state in which she was. If she could she would have "assisted nature," only she had nothing with which to do it. Nora's opinions on the subject of "aids to beauty" were strong; Elaine had frequently declared that hers were even stronger. That was the worst of being in the position of "humble friend"; one had sometimes to pretend that one thought what one really did not think, or so it seemed to her. If she had only had a little "something," in a jar, or in a tube, or a stick, or anything—but she would not have dared to run the risk of allowing Nora to find such a thing in her possession. Moreover, until then she had never wanted it. Still, if she had been left alone—that was how she put it—she might have had it by her. Now that she really wanted something, she had absolutely not a thing—obviously the fault of that was Nora's.

The consequence was that when at last she sallied out into the grounds she was conscious that she was not looking her best, in spite of her hat and frock—she knew that there was nothing amiss with them; and that morning it was so very desirable that she should look even better than her best, because she was going to meet Mr. Herbert Nash, and was particularly anxious to twist him round her finger. Every one knows that, where a man's concerned, the better one looks the easier that operation is apt to be found. Miss Harding made one slight error; she ought to have remembered that when one is not looking one's best matters are not improved by being in a bad temper. Good temper may almost act as an "aid to beauty," bad temper certainly won't; and, unfortunately, Miss Harding was so conscious of her defects that her temper suffered.

Nor was it mended by the fact that the gentleman kept her waiting. Perhaps that headache of hers had had something to do with the accident that she had an appointment to keep. She had asked Mr. Nash to let her see him somewhere on Sunday morning, where they could be alone, and he had told her he would be by the fish-pond at such and such an hour. She herself was a little late at the trysting-place; her toilette had taken longer than she had intended; still she was first. She waited—she had no watch, but it seemed that she waited hours, yet he did not come. By the time he did appear her mood was hardly lover-like; nor, it seemed, was his. He came strolling leisurely through the trees, his hands in his jacket pockets, a cane under his arm, a big cigar in his mouth, his hat at a rakish angle—quite at his ease; there was something in his appearance which would hardly have induced the average client to select him as his legal adviser. Elaine always had a more or less vague feeling that this was so; the feeling was stronger than usual as she watched him coming; yet the man had for her such an intense physical fascination that she deliberately refused to let her eyes see what they would have perceived plainly enough if she had only let them. More or less, it was possibly because she realized that that Sunday morning he did not look quite so desirable an example of his sex as he might have done that her greeting was hardly saccharine.

"You've taken your time in coming."

He planted himself in front of her, without removing his hands from his pockets, his cane from under his arm, his cigar from his mouth, or his hat from his head.

"Well, what's the hurry? I had to see a man."

"You knew I was waiting; you might have let him wait."

"I might; but I didn't. Hello! what's wrong?"

He was looking her up and down in a way which made her tingle.

"What do you mean—what's wrong?"

"You look—no offence intended—but you look as if you'd been up all night—a hot night too."

"I have a headache, and waiting for you hasn't made it any better."

"A headache? My mother used to have headaches, and, my word! when she had them didn't she use to make it warm for us. I used to say—"

He stopped, and laughed.

"What did you use to say?"

"I used to say—again no offence intended—that I'd never marry a woman who had headaches."

"I'm not subject to headaches—don't suppose it; I scarcely ever have them; in fact, I don't ever remember having had one before; only—I've been worried."

"Have you? that's bad. Don't do it; be like me—don't let yourself be worried by anything." He took out his cigar and surveyed the ash. "I read somewhere the other day that it's worry makes people grow old before their time; I don't believe much I read, but I do believe that. No matter what goes wrong, don't worry, it will come right; that's my theory of life."

"It's very easy to talk, it's harder to do. You don't seem very pleased to see me now that you have come."

"Don't I? I am; I'm as pleased as Punch."

"You don't show it."

"How do you expect me to show it? By taking you in my arms and kissing you out here in broad daylight, with you don't know what eyes enjoying the fun? If you'll come over the stile into the wood you shall have all the kissing you want—before lunch."

"I shall do nothing of the kind, and I expect you to do nothing of the kind, as you very well know; only—" She suddenly changed the subject. "Did you see Mr. Dawson yesterday, and arrange about the partnership?"

"I saw him, but I can't say I did much more than see him. He didn't seem to be so enthusiastic about the idea of having me for a partner as I expected, and—I can't say I'm very enthusiastic."

"What do you mean? The other day you said it was just the thing you would like to be."

"Yes, in a sense—in default of something better; but I don't want to be premature; since the other day something has occurred to me which may turn out to be better than a partnership with the venerable Mr. Dawson—who, between ourselves, is as supercilious an old beast as I ever want to meet—a good deal better."

"What is it, Herbert?"

She was observing him with—in her eyes, and on her face—an eagerness, a something strained, of which he seemed unconscious, and of which, no doubt, she was unconscious also.

"Excuse me, but that's exactly what I can't tell you—not at the present moment. It's still, as you may say, in the embryo—in the making; but it's there."

He touched his forehead with his finger, as if to denote that the something in question had a safe location in his brain.

"Can't—can't you give me some idea of what it is?"

"It depends on what you call an idea. I'll tell you this much; I'm meditating a coup—a great coup; if I bring it off it'll mean a really big thing; how big I can't tell you, not just now—I don't know myself; but something altogether beyond anything a partnership with old Dawson would mean.

"Herbert, I hope it's nothing risky."

She had run such a risk herself she wanted him to run none; she had had enough of risks, for ever.

"That depends again on what you mean by risky. I'm not sure that I shall go in for it; I haven't quite finished turning it over in my mind; I don't altogether see my way; but if, by the time I have finished turning it over in my mind, I do see my way, why, there you are; I'm a starter. Of course there's always the risk of my not bringing it off, though you may bet I'll do my best"—he said this with a very curious smile; a smile which, for some reason, seemed to bring a sense of chill to her heart. "But I shall be no worse off if I don't—there's no risk in that sense. Then will be the time to join myself in partnership with dear old Dawson."

She drew a long breath. The position was becoming complicated. She had not dreamed that he would have formed a scheme of his own, which she was to be kept out of, or she would not have gone, the second time, through the study window.

"Will—will any money be wanted for what you're thinking of?"

"No; not, at least, from you; of course, money will be wanted, but—it will come from some one else, if it comes at all; that's the idea; plenty of it too."

Again that curious smile came on his face; that, this time, it positively frightened her, showed what a state her nerves were in.

"Herbert, of what are you thinking?"

"I'm thinking—of a real big thing."

As she watched him some instinct warned her not to push her curiosity too far; yet there were certain things she must know.

"How long—will it take you to make up your mind?"

"That's something else I can't tell you; I never may make it up. You see, I'm only mentioning this so that you can understand why I'm not anxious to press old Dawson, just yet awhile. There's nothing to be lost by waiting; I'm in no hurry."

"How about our marriage?"

"What do you mean—how about our marriage?"

She would have liked to have told him just what she did mean—that she had invented her aunt's legacy simply because she wanted to be married at once. But she could not do that; she had to get to the point some other way.

"You said if you had enough money to buy a partnership in Mr. Dawson's business we might be married at once; that's why I told you about my aunt's legacy."

"That's all right; the legacy'll keep; what's the harm?"

"The harm is—it's not nice of you to make me say so, though—you ought to be—you ought to be flattered."

"I am flattered."

"You're not! I don't believe you care for me one bit, or—or you'd know I want to be married."

"So you shall be."

"When?"

"Oh, when I've had time enough to find out where I'm standing; say in a month or two."

"Herbert, you should never have had that two hundred pounds if you hadn't promised me that we should be married at once."

"What do you call at once?"

"Next week."

"Next week! why, that's Easter!"

"Well, why shouldn't we be married at Easter?"

"Good gracious! Where do you propose to set up housekeeping? in my rooms?"

"Not necessarily in your rooms; but in some rooms—nice rooms, for the present; they needn't be just about here. I've money enough to go on with—plenty of money; and you might think over what you've been talking about, and come to a decision, while—while we're on our honeymoon."

Again he took the cigar out of his mouth, and again he regarded the ash; it was white, and long, and firm; it seemed it was a good cigar; and while he was still regarding the ash, he observed—

"Young woman, there's more in you than meets the eye. There's something in what you say; I admit there's a good deal in what you say. I'll give it my serious attention."

"Your serious attention! Won't you understand? Any day I may have to leave this place."

"That's true enough, unless you propose to remain on the premises while the catalogue s being drawn up, and the lots are being ticketed."

"Herbert! What do you mean?"

"Nothing to speak of; only I happen to know that the principal creditors don't mean to wait for their money a moment longer than they can help. Either the estate will have to be administered in bankruptcy, or Miss Nora Lindsay will have to agree to the whole thing being sold—lock, stock and barrel, for what it will fetch."

"When?"

"As a matter of fact, they want to come into the place and start the catalogue to-morrow."

"But what will become of Nora?"

"Quite so."

"Where will she go?"

"Where will she?"

"Couldn't she—couldn't she come and live with us?"

"What's that?"

"Couldn't she—live with us?"

"Who's us?"

"With you and me—just for a time—when we're married?"

Mr. Nash looked the lady straight in the face, significantly; his tone was as significant as his look.

"My dear, I don't think you care for Miss Nora Lindsay one snap of your fingers, and I'm sure I don't."

"You've no right to say that."

"I fancy that you've a sort of notion that you ought to behave prettily to her because she's let you come and liven her up when she hadn't a soul in the place to speak to. So far as I can see, she's at least as much under an obligation as you are. She'd have been deadly dull without you; she'd have had to pay a companion, and pay her well, if it hadn't been for your society. You got nothing for your services; seems to me she owes you. Don't talk about her living with us! I wouldn't live under the same roof as Miss Nora Lindsay, not for a million a year. I don't like her—never did—never could; she's not the kind of girl I care about. What does it matter to me what becomes of her? Do you think she'd trouble if I came to eternal grief? Very much so! I fancy I see her at it! No, if you're going to take up with Miss Nora Lindsay you've done with me. There never has been any love lost between us, and now if I had my way I'd never see her or speak to her again. So if your sentiments are different I'll hand you back the two hundred pounds you so kindly threw into my face just now, and we'll cry quits. I'm not going to start by letting the girl who's going to be my wife mix herself up with people who are objectionable to me."

The expression which was on the girl's face, as she looked at him, was pitiful; had he been aware of the emotions which seemed to be tearing at her in a dozen different places at once, even he might have been moved to pity. Had his words been lashes they could hardly have hurt her more. She stood trembling, hardly able to speak.

"I—I'd no idea you—you felt like this—about—Nora."

"Hadn't you? Well, you know now; and as perhaps you'd like to have a little time to get the idea well into your head, I'll say good-day."

"Herbert, you—you mustn't go."

"Mustn't go? Why mustn't I go?"

"How about our marriage?"

"How about our marriage?—when just now you were talking about her coming to live with us."

"I—I —was only—suggesting."

"Then let me tell you that the suggestion's made me feel sick. I don't want any words—I hate them; and as I'm not going to be bustled, when I know that I ought not to allow myself to be bustled, as I remarked, I'll return you the money which you threw into my face just now."

"I—I didn't mean to throw it in your face."

"Then what did you mean? You as good as said that I'd been up for sale, and that you'd bought me; but as I didn't understand that I was being bought, I'll hand you back the purchase price, then perhaps I shall be able to call my soul my own."

"I—I—Herbert, don't—don't let's quarrel. I—I—you don't know how I love you."

"Very well, then, and I love you; so that's all right."

"Are you sure you love me? If I were only sure!"

"You may be dead sure; at the same time you must allow me to speak a few plain words. There's something the matter with you, and there has been for some little time; I don't know what it is—it may be a headache, as you say, but if it is it's the kind of headache which, if I were you, I should take something for. You've changed altogether during the last few days; the little girl I used to know wouldn't have tried to bully me into marrying her at a moment's notice, when I told her that I thought it would be better, for both our sakes, that we should wait a little. I promise you that as soon as I see my way I'll come and ask you to name the day, and I hope you'll name an early one. But, in the meantime, where's the hurry? So far as I know you'll get no harm by waiting; it isn't as though I was asking you to wait long—a month or two at most; and it isn't as though you were hard up; you've got the cash, not I. As for leaving the place, I should say the sooner you leave it the better; you've got a home to go to—what's wrong with your home? You can write to me, I can come and see you; or, if I can't manage to come, after a bit you might step over to see me; you might find quarters with a mutual friend—why not? My present advice to you is to take a dose of medicine, that is medicine, and lie down, and sleep it off; then when you're feeling more like yourself you'll see that I'm quite right; and then you might let me know, and we can have another little talk together. In the meantime, as I observed before, I'll say good-day. By the bye, if you do want that money back again, you've only got to let me have a line, and you shall have it."

CHAPTER XIV

THE PARTING OF THE WAYS

Mr. Nash strolled leisurely off, lighting another cigar as he went. Elaine could have done nothing to stop him, had her entire future depended on her making the effort. Indeed she only dimly realized that he was going; something seemed to be pressing on her brain, and numbing it; until all at once the pressure lightened, and, with a start, she perceived that he had gone. For a second or two she stood staring about her on all sides, as if, just roused out of sleep, she was wondering where she was. When she understood that he had left her, and had passed out of sight, and that she was alone, oblivious of her smart hat and pretty frock, she sank down on to the grass, just where she was, and hid her face in her hands.

She stayed like that some time; she herself did not know how long; then, uncovering her face, again she looked about her; and, possibly recognizing that nothing was to be gained by behaving like that, she scrambled to her feet, shaking herself, touching herself here and there, where she thought that her costume might stand in need of a touch, then she started to return to the house.

She had just got on to the path which wound among the trees when she encountered the person she would have most wished to avoid—the butler, Morgan. Elaine had never before seen him attired in anything but what might be described as his official garments; such was her mental confusion that, at her first sight, in his well-cut, neat grey suit, she hardly knew him; it had to be admitted that in it he looked more like a gentleman is supposed to look than Mr. Nash had done. He carried himself with less swagger than Herbert Nash; what was still more marked, he uncovered when he saw Miss Harding, showing all those signs of outward respect which a gentleman is supposed to show in the presence of a lady, but which Mr. Nash had entirely ignored; yet Miss Harding shrank back from Mr. Morgan as if he had been some noxious thing. Nothing could have been more deferential than the air with which he addressed her.

"With your permission, Miss Harding, I should like to speak to you."

She looked as if she was afraid that he would whip her.

"Not—not now; I'm afraid I shall be late for lunch; I—I don't want to keep Miss Lindsay waiting."

"We don't lunch on Sunday; you forget, Miss Harding; we take early dinner; I assure you you shan't be late; they can't begin without me, and I'm always punctual. Pray don't be distressed."

"I—I can't stop now; I—I'm not feeling very well."

"You're not looking very well, I'm sorry to say; as Mr. Nash informed you."

She started.

"Mr.— What do you mean?"

"You were so engrossed with each other that you had no eyes for anything but yourselves; or you would certainly have noticed me. I was so close that I actually heard everything you said."

"Are you always spying?"

"Candidly, I very often am. I regard it as my duty to keep at least one eye on everything that's going on; that's a high ideal, but I do my best to live up to it. When I had that little conversation with you with reference to the three thousand pounds you found, I endeavoured to assure you that you might rely implicitly on my discretion; but, at the same time, I did not bargain that you would throw the money away on such a man as Herbert Nash."

"Morgan! you—you forget yourself."

"Not at all, Miss Harding, not at all. When first I saw you together my feeling was one of resentment; but, when I heard what was said, my resentment grew less; for one reason, because I perceived that I might be able to work with Mr. Nash, as well as with you."

"You might work with Mr. Nash? What do you mean?"

"Is it not obvious? As you are doubtless aware, Mr. Nash is a young man of many possibilities."

"Possibilities?"

"You will remember that I told you that I saw possibilities in you, which have become facts. In the same sense I see possibilities in Herbert Nash, so that I may be able to work with him. We shall be a united trio."

"Do you—do you dare to hint—"

"Yes? do I dare to hint? pray finish."

"Let me pass! I'll have nothing to say to you! Get out of my way!"

"Still one moment, Miss Harding, if you please. I heard you ask Mr. Nash to marry you, which was rather 'coming on,' to use a kitchen phrase, wasn't it? Luckily he declined; the anxiety was plainly all on your side; or I should have objected."

"You would have objected! Do you suppose I should ask your permission?"

"If you didn't, and I did object, on your wedding-day I'd have you arrested at the church door; and if your husband was Herbert Nash that would be the last you'd see of him. When you came out of jail he'd slam the door in your face, unless I mistake the man, and he'd stick up a notice in his front garden, 'No convicted felons need apply.' It's not my wish to be disagreeable, Miss Harding, quite the other way; but I've a feeling that you don't want to treat me fairly; and in matters of this sort both sides expect fair treatment, it's only natural. I can tell you, at this moment, exactly what I propose, as Herbert Nash put it; I want time to find out where I'm standing; as you must see for yourself, everything's at sixes and sevens. But I can tell you what I don't propose; that you should hand over that three thousand pounds to a man who doesn't deserve it. You catch what I mean? I fancy you will if you think it over." He glanced at his watch. "Now I am afraid that I must go; if you go straight home you'll have plenty of time to tittivate; and I do trust, Miss Harding, that, at dinner, you'll be once more the charming, lively, high-spirited young lady I've always loved to rest my eyes upon."

When the gong sounded for dinner Miss Lindsay was informed, by the butler, that although Miss Harding had been out, and had returned, she had sent down word that her headache was still so bad that she wanted nothing to eat, and preferred to remain in her own room. Whereupon Nora went up-stairs to make inquiries on her own account. She found the young lady's door was locked. Having tapped twice without eliciting a response, the third time she knocked more peremptorily, exclaiming—

"Elaine! please let me in! it's Nora."

A shrill voice cried out within.

"I can't let you in! I won't! I only want people to let me alone."

Wondering, Nora let her alone, and went down to a solitary dinner; while Elaine lay face downward on the bed, wildly asking herself if suicide was not the best way out of it.

That night there came to Nora still another variation of the dream which she had dreamed before. Throughout the day she had been conscious of a sense of curious depression; as if she was realizing, for the first time, how wholly alone in the world she was, and was likely to remain. She had said good-bye to the man she loved; Mr. Spencer's story of the envelope which her father had sent him was an odd one; but the envelope was lost. She resented with a bitterness of which she had not imagined herself capable the fact that he had lost it; she had not put her bitterness into words, she had not wished to reproach him; it was contrary to her nature to reproach any one; but it had seemed to her the hardest blow which fate had dealt her yet, and that it should have come from him! If the envelope were found it was possible that it might contain the key to the mystery of Donald Lindsay's money; so that it would be shown that she was, after all, pecuniarily, in the fortunate position her father had led her to suppose she would be. But, to begin with, it had to be found. It seemed that its loser had already been making strenuous efforts to recover it, without success; if it was to be retrieved surely it was most likely to be the case when the scent was hot. What reason was there to suppose that the search which had failed when the conditions were more favourable was likely to have a more satisfactory result now that everything was against it? Even if the envelope was regained there was still the—should she say probability, or possibility?—that its contents might lead to nothing after all. Disappointments had crowded on her so fast lately that it would only be in the natural order of things if she was to be visited by yet another.

Almost worse than all the rest; suppose the envelope was recovered, and it was found that she was indeed an heiress, still to her the world would never again be what it was; in her heart of hearts she knew it; it was that knowledge which, that Sunday, weighed on her so heavily. During the last few days disillusions had come to her from every quarter. Whatever the future might have in store for her the attitude taken up by the Earl and Countess of Mountdennis was one which she never could forget. That her position as an heiress had heightened her charms in their eyes she had known; but she had supposed that they had cared for her a little for herself. That bubble was blown. Common decency, it seemed to her, would have bade them extend to her at least some show of sympathy. Plainly such an idea had not occurred to them. All they had done was to revile her for having lost everything she valued most, father, home, all; as if the fault was hers, and she had been engaged in a conspiracy to bring about her own destruction; they had made it so hideously clear that, from the first, and all along, they had only thought of her as a representative of so many pounds, shillings and pence; not a creature of flesh and blood, who was one day to stand to them in the place of a daughter, to be loved and cherished by their son. Though to-morrow millions were to come tumbling into her lap her lovers' parents could never now be what she had once hoped they would become; with their own hands they had rent into nothing the veil of illusion through which she had seen them.

That Robert was not as they were she admitted, gladly admitted. Yet he was their son; if she became his wife she would be in duty bound to regard his parents, in a sense, as hers; how could she pretend filial attachment and respect for such persons as they had shown themselves to be? Hers was the young girl's high ideal of marriage; husband and wife ought to be one; they ought to have a common community of interest; what was dear to the one should be dear to the other; how would that ideal work out if she were to marry Robert Spencer? Obviously, it would not work at all; he would be on one side; his parents—not improbably all his relatives and friends—would be on the other side, against her. It would begin in dissension, and end—where? Even the discovery that she was rich would make but little difference; she was not going to buy a husband from his father and mother, well knowing that all they wanted for the light of their countenance was their price, and that they would only consent to receive her into the family circle if she came plastered with gold. Rather than become a wife upon those terms she would remain a spinster all her life. She knew her weakness; if she came within reach of Robert her love—his love—might prove greater than her strength; that morning it had been all that she could do to keep herself out of his arms. Next time—and she was pretty sure that if Robert was in the neighbourhood there would be a next time before very long—she might succumb, and regret it ever afterwards. Better that she should leave Cloverlea than run such a risk.

The probability that she would have to go—whether she wanted to go or not—had been continually in her mind since she had heard Dr. Banyard's statement of her affairs; and with it there had been a hazy sort of notion that, when the moment of parting came, she might find temporary refuge in Elaine Harding's home in the west country, as a guest in her father's vicarage. Elaine had asked her often; it was true that the invitations had been coupled with intimations that the vicarage was but a humble one, and would seem but a poor place to the heiress of Cloverlea. But now circumstances had changed; to Nora any place seemed desirable where she would be welcome; especially her dear friend's home, however modest it might be. Although she would not confess it even to herself she had vaguely expected that Elaine would have spoken to her on the subject before now; Elaine had always been so full of protestations of what she would do—of what she would love to do—for Nora, if opportunity ever offered, in return for all that Nora had done for her. But now that opportunity did offer, and Elaine was well aware of the plight which Nora was shortly likely to be in, not a hint had she dropped of a disposition to be of service to her in any way whatever. More, it seemed to Nora that Elaine was avoiding her as if misfortune had made of her a pariah. It was true that she excused herself by alleging illness; and Nora was not prepared to say that her illness was diplomatic. But during all the time they had known each other Elaine had always enjoyed excellent health; so far as Nora knew—and they had been intimate for years—she had not endured an ache or pain until the moment arrived when it seemed likely that she might be able to render some slight services to the friend who had done so much for her.

It was not strange that Nora took it for granted that she need expect nothing from the dearest friend she had in the world; and that that feeling did not tend to lighten the load of depression which, that Sunday, weighed on her so heavily.

In the evening she took stock of such possessions as, in any case, she might be entitled to call her own. She had it strongly in her mind that she and Elaine might soon be parted; just how close the hour of parting was she could not tell, but she felt that, whenever it came, it would be as well that it should find her ready. There had been, she knew, a meeting of the creditors yesterday; exactly what course they had decided to pursue she had not learnt; and, again, that troubled her; she felt that either Dr. Banyard or Mr. Nash might have let her have some sort of intimation. But, anyhow, from what she had gathered it seemed likely that before long there would be strangers at Cloverlea; when they came she must go, practically on the instant. Even if their coming was postponed it appeared to her that she must go. It cost money to keep up Cloverlea; since the little money which her father had left belonged to the creditors, when she came to consider the matter calmly, it seemed to her that she had no real right to remain another hour. Her continued stay in that huge house involved the expenditure of money to which it had not yet been shown that she had any claim; even if money enough had been discovered to keep it going for another week, which she doubted.

No; it seemed to her, from whatever point of view she regarded the position, that the hour was close at hand for the parting of the ways; and that it behoved her to be ready for it when it came.

CHAPTER XV

'SO EARLY IN THE MORNING'

So she took stock of such things as, whatever befell, she felt that she would have a right to take away with her from Cloverlea; it seemed to her that, since God had opened her eyes to her actual situation, He would forgive her for undertaking, on the Sabbath evening, what He had shown her was a work of necessity. A pathetic business that stocktaking was, and a queer one, and not a very heavy one either.

She began with the money. She concluded that such cash as her father had given her for her own separate and private use she might still call her own, and use as her own. Had she been dealing with a sum of any magnitude she would have hesitated; for this young woman was a Don Quixote in petticoats, and would rather starve than eat food which she even fancied belonged to others; but she was not dealing with a sum of any magnitude. Her father had always made her a generous allowance, of which she had always made a generous use; regarding herself as, in a sense, her father's almoner, she used far the larger part of it in works of charity. Since she left school it had been his custom to give her, four times a year, a sum of one hundred and twenty-five pounds, always in gold. It had been one of his peculiarities that he had never given her either cheques or bank-notes, but always sovereigns. One of the quarterly sums had always been handed to her during the first week in April; she had been expecting it when her father had been taken ill. As a matter of fact, it was her hundred and twenty-five sovereigns, plus two more, which had formed that little heap of gold which was on the study table when Elaine Harding first adventured through the window. So, as that little heap had never found its way to her, all she actually possessed was what was left from last quarter—and the first three months of the year always were such expensive months. During the winter there was apt to be so much want and suffering; sometimes she found it hard to make both ends meet, even though she spent scarcely anything on herself at all. However, that winter quarter there had been something over; that something represented her entire fortune, nearly nine pounds; to be exact, eight pounds fourteen and eightpence. Even the most clamorous creditor might have suffered her to go out to face the world with that. Especially as beyond that Nora had very little of a portable nature which she considered she would be justified in regarding as her own, except her clothes.

Among the other things to which he had objected Donald Lindsay included jewellery. He wore none himself; had he had his way he would have called no man an acquaintance who did. He disliked to see jewellery even on a woman. On an elderly woman he esteemed it bad enough; like the cynic he was, he held that the average elderly woman very properly felt that she was only worth the net value of what she had on her. On a girl, to his thinking, it was impossible; if ever he encountered, under his own roof, young women who were, as they fancied, ornamented by products of the jeweller's art, he was apt to make such plain-spoken comments that Nora always endeavoured to warn her girl acquaintances to put aside their ornaments while, at any rate, her father was about. Nora herself had only had four pieces of jewellery in her life. One was a plain gold watch, which her father had given her when she was at school, which she then wore attached to a plain black ribbon; another was a gold locket, in which was her father's portrait, which she had worn on the same black ribbon. The other two articles had been presents from Robert Spencer—her engagement ring, and another locket, in which was his portrait. These she had returned to him on the previous day, together with his letters. So that all the jewellery she now had was the gold watch and the locket with the portrait of her father. These, she decided, came in the same category as the eight pounds fourteen and eightpence; she was entitled to regard them as her very own.

Her wardrobe presented difficulties. She had heaps of pretty dresses; quantities of all sorts of pretty clothes; the puzzle was, what to take and what to leave. She knew, from experience, that if her garments were turned into cash they would not fetch a great deal, however much they might previously have cost, or however little they might have been worn; so that if she took all her clothes she was aware that she would not be depriving her creditors of an appreciable sum of money. It was the difficulty of selection which troubled her. Obviously elaborate and costly evening dresses consorted ill with a fortune of eight pounds fourteen and eightpence, which represented both capital and income; in that sense the daintier and prettier they were, the more undesirable they were. Yet—she loved her pretty frocks; only a woman could understand how hard it seemed to her to have to part from them. With them were entwined so many associations; she wore this one on that never-to-be-forgotten night when Robert first asked her to be his wife; that when he slipped the engagement ring upon her finger; how pretty she had thought it! how she had kissed it when she was alone! She blushed at the memory.

After all, those were sentimental considerations which reached back to the life with which she had done for ever. It was quite another sort of life which was in front of her; she must be equipped for that. Three or four plain, substantial dresses would be sufficient; the rest—those triumphs of the dressmaker's art—she was not likely to require garments of that sort again, ever. So she packed the few clothes she thought she would require into a trunk, together with her Bible, her writing-case, and a few odds and ends; looking round the room, she decided that all her other things, which she had so treasured, must remain behind. She undressed, feeling as if she was undressing in a room peopled with ghosts, all of them memories of the many-sided Nora of the days which were gone; then, all radiant in her white attire, she knelt in prayer; supposing, as she poured forth all the dear, secret things which were in her heart, that she was a woman; but God, who heard her, knew that she was a child; and, as she prayed, He breathed peace into her soul; so that hardly, at last, was she between the sheets when she fell fast asleep.

And in her sleep she dreamed the dream which she had dreamed before; of her father, stealing timidly into her room, filled with a great longing to tell her something, which he would have given much that she should know, yet speechless. And to him the knowledge that he was dumb was agony, and to her; so that she put her arms about him, and whispered in his ear words which were meant to assist him in the efforts he was making to say what he so yearned to tell her. But struggle as he might, speech would not come; until, all at once, in the exceeding bitterness of his grief he made her understand that, because he had been still so long, and so had sinned, God would not let him speak now; He would not forgive him for the opportunities he had wasted. Mingling her anguish with his, she held him closer, crying—

"God will forgive you, father! God will forgive you!" and, with her own crying, she woke herself up, to find herself in the darkness, alone, and the sound of her own voice in her ears.

As before, the delusion of her father's presence was so real that, at first, she could not believe it was delusion. She put out her hands to feel for him; when they found nothing, she whispered—

"Father!"

When none answered she got out of bed, and crossed the room, and stood at the open door, listening for the sound of his retreating footsteps; she had heard them so plainly when he entered. When she remembered that he was dead, and that it must have been a dream, she began to tremble all over; she did not dare to ask herself if this dream had been sent to her of God; she was afraid.

Throughout the remainder of the night she lay awake. Day had scarcely dawned when she rose and dressed. Recollections of the awe which had obsessed her spirit were with her still. She was conscious of an uncomfortable feeling that something unusual was about to happen. So soon as she was dressed she left her own room and went to the bedroom which had been her father's. As she crossed its threshold she had an odd sensation of having come again into his presence. Impelled by she knew not what motive of curiosity, she examined methodically all that the room contained, opening drawers and wardrobes, going through their contents. It seemed to her that they were emptier than they used to be. Her father had accumulated clothes until every store-place he had was filled to over-flowing; she had told him not long ago that if he would keep on getting more, without ridding himself of some of those he had, he would require another room to put them in. She knew he had got rid of nothing, yet drawers and cupboards in bedroom and dressing-room were nearly empty. Certainly more than three-quarters of them were gone; what were left were scarcely more than odds and ends. And not only clothes; as she looked about her she began to miss all sorts of things. Both rooms had been nearly stripped of all her father's personal belongings. By whom had they been taken? who had given the necessary authority?

From the bedroom she passed through the still silent house to the rooms below, and presently to her father's study. Here again was some subtle suggestion of its late owner. He seemed to be standing by her as she touched this and that, moving from one familiar object to another. Nor had she been there very long before she perceived that here also things were missing; and, in this case, they were things which mattered. A pair of bronzes had gone from the mantel, for which her father had paid a large sum, and which he valued highly; some ivory antiques, fine specimens of the carver's art, which he had brought with him from China, had also vanished; a Satsuma vase, two costly examples of powder blue, even prints and pictures from the walls, all kinds of curiosities, the possession of which would gladden a collector's heart, had disappeared. Of course their absence was capable of a natural and legitimate interpretation; they might have been put out of sight for safer keeping. Still—they were there on Saturday; she was sure she had noticed them when she came in a moment for some ink; why should they have been removed during the course of yesterday?

While she stood looking about her, feeling a little bewildered, the door was opened suddenly, and Morgan, the butler, came hastily in. He stared at her as if she was not at all the person he had expected to see; indeed, he said as much.

"I beg your pardon, Miss Lindsay, I thought—" He left his sentence unfinished, and began another. "I heard some one moving about below, and knowing that the household was still upstairs, I thought it might be some one who had no business here, so hurried down to see who it was."

He made as if to withdraw, but Nora stopped him.

"Morgan, who has been interfering with my father's things?"

"I beg your pardon; I don't quite follow."

"Where's the Satsuma vase? and the powder blues? and the bronzes? and all sorts of things?"

"Have they been removed?"

"You can see for yourself that they've been removed; who has taken them? where are they?"

Morgan glanced round the room with, in his air, as it seemed to Nora, almost a suggestion of amusement.

"They do seem to have been removed, don't they? As you say, all sorts of things."

"Didn't you know they had been removed?"

"Perhaps Mr. Nash has had it done; or Dr. Banyard."

"Why should they? Besides, neither of them has been here since Saturday; and the things were here then, because I saw them."

"Ah, if you saw them that doesn't look as if they could have had it done, does it? But—may I ask, Miss Lindsay, how it matters?"

"How it matters, Morgan—the things are worth a great deal of money."

"Isn't that all the more reason why they shouldn't be allowed to fall into the hands of—I don't wish to cause you pain, Miss Lindsay—of those who are coming?"

"What do you mean?"

"Don't you know? Then, in that case, Miss Lindsay, I will have inquiries made, and will inform you, at the earliest possible moment, of the result."

He slipped out of the room so rapidly that she had not a chance to question him further, leaving her more bewildered than he had found her. What did he mean? what could he mean? She did not like to suspect him of impertinence, or even something worse; yet—what had he implied? That it would be just as well that these most valuable possessions of her father should be kept out of the hand—of those who were coming? She did not doubt that the state of affairs was known to the household; could he have been referring to the creditors? was he suggesting that they should be defrauded of what might go some distance towards settling their claims, and that she should connive at such a fraud? If he had not meant that, what had he meant? Her impulse was to call him back, and insist upon an explanation there and then.

But she reflected that, whatever his meaning might have been, she had made herself quite plain; his manner had shown it. His error, perhaps, had been one of over-zeal for her service; though that was not a fault of which she had supposed Morgan would have been likely to be guilty. Still, that was how it might have been. If so, now he understood—that that was not the sort of zeal which she desired. If—as, in spite of his evasions, she thought was possible, he knew where the missing articles were to be found—she gave him an opportunity to restore them, in his own fashion, to their former places, no doubt, when she returned again to the study, she would find them where they had always been. With some vague notion of giving him such an opportunity, there and then, she opened the French window which led into the grounds—through which Elaine Harding had made that entry she was never to forget, which had changed the whole face of the world for her, as well as for others—and, hatless, passed out into the morning air.

Although she did not know it, she was setting out on what was to be her last walk through the familiar places she had known so long, and loved so well.

CHAPTER XVI

GULDENHEIM

It was hardly the morning she would have chosen for such a jaunt. A change was impending in the weather. Fickle April seemed to be of opinion that the world thereabouts had already had too fair a taste of summer, and that the time had come for quite a different sort of thing. Heavy banks of cloud scudded across the sky, blown by a cold north-easterly wind, which at times almost amounted to a gale. But Nora was heedless of the weather; her mood was in tune with the wind, wild and vagrant. The chilly breezes blew her hair this way and that, she cared nothing. Now and then a splash of rain was dashed on her uncovered head; she paid no heed. She walked rapidly, delighting in the sensation of striding swiftly through the open air, careless of all else. How far she walked, or how long, she did not know; she kept no count; one could walk some distance without quitting the grounds of Cloverlea; but even she awoke to the fact, at last, that she had better seek shelter, or else go home. The rain threatened to fall in earnest; without hat or jacket, or protection of any sort, she would soon be soaked to the skin.

She stood up under the shelter of a tree; as much to enable her to take her bearings as for anything else; and had just realized that the road ran on the other side of the hedge which was close at hand, when a trap came bowling along it, whose driver, seeing her peeping out from behind her tree, brought his horse to a sudden standstill. It was Dr. Banyard.

"Why, Miss Nora," he exclaimed, "you're early abroad. And have you joined the anti-hat brigade that you venture so far afield without one on, and in such weather? I'll give you a lift, I'll get you home now before the rain; and if I don't Sam and I between us will find something which will keep you dry. There's a gate a little further on; if you hurry I'll be there to meet you."

She shook her head; and stood closer to the tree.

"You're very good; but I'd sooner walk if you don't mind."

"Walk! but it's going to pour! and you haven't even so much as an umbrella!"

"It's not going to be so much, only a shower; I can see blue sky there."

The doctor looked in the direction to which she pointed, and, seeing the peeping blue, perceived that, probably, after all, it was only going to be an April whimper.

"You're a refractory young person; if you catch a cold don't look for sympathy from me; and, I say, I want to speak to you. In fact, I've been wanting to speak to you since Saturday; but of course the parish chooses the wrong moment to get itself ill, I haven't had a moment to call on you. I've been up practically all night, and when I do get home I expect I'll be dragged out again directly; I know them! But you will have heard from Nash."

"I have heard-nothing from Mr. Nash since I saw you last."

"No? How's that? I told him to communicate with you in case I couldn't, and he said he would."

Again she shook her head. Leaning over the side of the trap he eyed her with his shrewd grey eyes.

"In that case, here, Sam, take the reins, and drive a little way down the road; I'll call you when I want you; I have something which I wish to say to Miss Lindsay, in the rain." As a matter of fact when he alighted, and the trap had gone on, the shower had already nearly died away; she stood close up to the hedge on one side and he on the other. "I am sorry to be the first bearer of the bad news, I had hoped Nash would have broken the ice. I was present on Saturday at the meeting of Guldenheim and his friends." He did not tell her at what inconvenience he had been present, and of how, in consequence, all his work had got into confusion. "I said all we had arranged that I should say; but I am sorry to have to inform you that the only terms on which they would consent not to throw your father's estate into bankruptcy were that everything should be realized at once."

She smiled, a rather wintry smile, but still it was a smile.

"Thank you; it is very kind of you to take so much trouble; but would you mind telling me exactly what that means."

"I'm afraid it means that Guldenheim and his friends, or their representative, may arrive at Cloverlea to-day. They seem to be hot against your father with a heat I confess I don't understand, and declare they won't wait a moment longer for their money than they can help."

"They need not; I am quite ready to go."

Her pale face grew perhaps a little paler, and her lips were closed a little tighter; but the girl still smiled. He seemed to be more moved than she was.

"If you take my advice, my dear young lady, you'll at once get together as much as you possibly can, and have the things removed from the premises before they come; you can have them sent over to us if you like. Anyhow you're entitled to personal belongings; and in a case like yours the law takes a liberal view of what that term covers."

"I think I've packed up everything already, practically."

"I hope you've treated the situation broadly, and have not been unduly generous to persons who you may be quite sure will show no generosity to you." She nodded; she did not care to tell him, in so many words, that what she chose to regard as her personal belongings were all contained in one small trunk. "And of course you'll come over to us till you have had time to look round; things may turn out much better than at present they promise; you never can tell. The wife is taking it for granted that you're coming, you can take that from me; but, if you think it's necessary, so soon as I get home she'll come and fetch you."

Perhaps it was because that was the first offer of real assistance she had received that her voice was tremulous.

"Thank you; you—you know I thank you and Mrs. Banyard; but—I can't come, I've made other arrangements."

He eyed her suspiciously; his tone was brusque.

"What arrangements have you made?"

"Just for a while they're private."

"Are you going to be married? It would be the best thing you could possibly do, to get married out of hand; I hear your young man's back again, and I've no doubt he's willing; Robert Spencer's not a fool."

Her voice sank nearly to a whisper.

"I'm not going to be married."

"Then what are you going to do?"

"If you don't mind, doctor, I prefer to keep my own counsel for a while."

He broke into alliterative violence.

"You're contemplating some feebly foolish female knight-errantry. I know you! But it won't be allowed; directly I get home I'll send my wife to talk to you; she'll do it better than I can. Your best friends are here; it's they who have your best interests at heart; and you're going to consider their feelings whether you like it or not; you're not going to be allowed to ride over them roughshod, young lady. Sam, bring that pony." He discharged a parting shaft at her as he climbed into the trap. "You understand, my wife will come and talk to you as soon as she gets her hat on; or whatever it is she does put on when she goes out visiting. And I hope you'll have the grace to listen to what she says."

Nora re-entered the house through the open study-window. As she passed through the room she saw that the butler had taken her hint; the missing articles had been replaced. As she was sitting at her lonely early breakfast—for it seemed that Elaine Harding had not yet sufficiently recovered to put in an appearance at so matutinal a meal—she commented on the fact to Morgan.

"I am glad to see that the study is again as it always has been. I wish everything, throughout the house, to remain exactly as it was when my father was alive; nothing is to be touched. Let the servants understand that this is my wish."

Morgan slightly inclined his head, as if to express both perfect comprehension and his readiness to carry out her directions. Then, when, feeling that she preferred to be alone, she told him that he need not wait, he returned straight to the study, gathered together the articles which he had only recently replaced, and walked off with them to a hiding-place of which he flattered himself he alone knew the secret.

"She's had her way," he told himself, as he was stowing them in what he hoped was a place of safety. "Always let a woman have her way, if you can, especially if she's young and good to look at; now it's my turn. She's not likely to go back to the study for a bit; it's worth chancing, anyhow, these things mean quite a heap of money; from what I hear others are likely to get here before she does, and they can look after themselves. At a time like we're going to have every one has to look after himself. If the things are missed, why they can be produced, and everything explained; if they're not missed, and I don't see how they're going to be, if there's a little management, there's no reason why I shouldn't have them, instead of that pack of thieves. I have got some artistic taste; it's born in me; I doubt if they've got any."

He grinned, as he wrapped the Satsuma vase carefully in a large white silk handkerchief.

Having finished breakfast Nora went up to her own sitting-room; but had not been there very long before a servant first knocked shakily, then entered hastily.

"If you please, miss, there's a lot of men downstairs; they didn't ask for you, and I don't know what they want, but they've got such a free and easy way about them that I thought I'd better let you know that they were there; Morgan let them in; they came in a wagonette."

Nora went down without a word. In the hall there was quite a little crowd of men; ten or twelve of them there seemed; among them some sufficiently rough-looking customers. None of them had troubled to remove their hats; but at sight of Nora one of them, a big fat man, beautifully dressed, with a red face, a large nose, and curly shining black hair, removing his hat, advanced to meet her.

"Are you Miss Lindsay?"

He spoke with a curious nasal utterance.

"I am."

"I'm Guldenheim, you know all about me; and these are my friends, who are in the same boat with me, you've heard about them; and these are our chaps. I suppose you know we've agreed not to make a fuss on condition that you give us possession of everything, to cut up between us so that we can get a bit of our own back again, what there is of it to cut up."

"I do know."

"Well, we've come into possession." As he looked at the girl and saw, dimly, what manner of girl she was, he seemed to think that he owed her some sort of apology, which he offered in a fashion of his own. "I dare say it seems hard to you, our coming in like this, but you must know that your father had our money, and my friends' money, and we can't afford to lose it, it isn't to be expected that we should; you must understand that."

"I quite understand," said Nora.

"Then that's all right," said Mr. Guldenheim.

About that time some one was rapping at Miss Harding's bedroom door, on the other side of which Miss Harding was completing her toilette.

"Who's there?" she asked.

"It's me, Morgan; here, come closer to the door, I want to speak to you."

She went so close to the door that even a whisper of his would have been audible.

"What is it?"

"The bailiffs are in down-stairs, the whole show's burst up. You'd better pack up—you know what, as soon as you can; and everything else you've got as well; and anything you see lying about worth packing; at a time like this anything's any one's. Only get a move on you; they may be up here directly, there's a lot of them, and there's no telling how they're going to do things, those sort of people can make themselves very nasty if they like; you don't want to have them superintending your packing; don't you let them in, if you can help it, till you've got your boxes locked. I thought I'd just give you a tip, so that you might look lively."

Miss Harding acted on Mr. Morgan's "tip," beginning, so soon as he had gone, to pack everything she had got, and doing it with feverish haste; but had not proceeded far when something came rattling against the window-panes, something which sounded as if it were a handful of gravel. She drew aside the curtain and looked out. Mr. Nash was below, he waved his hand; apparently it was he who had saluted the window. Hurriedly throwing a dressing-jacket over her bare shoulders, she raised the sash sufficiently to enable her to put her head out, apparently oblivious of the fact that her black hair was streaming loose; she had been engaged in "doing" it when Morgan had knocked at the door.

"Herbert! Did you throw those stones at my window? What do you want?"

The reply from below was hardly an answer to her question.

"I say! Now you are worth looking at! Now you're what I call something like a picture!"

Her cheeks were flushed with excitement; there was a light in her eyes; the streaming locks certainly were not unbecoming; nor did the blush with which she received his words detract from the general effect.

"Herbert, you naughty boy, you don't mean to say you nearly broke my window simply to make me put my head out, and I'm in this state!"

"Well, not exactly; though it would have been worth breaking a window for. I chucked that gravel up at your window because I've something to say to you which has got to be said now, if it's to be said at all; only don't shout."

"Am I shouting?"

"I thought I'd just give you the hint in case you felt as if you'd like to. Somehow, do you know, the more I look at you the more I seem to want to; if I could only get at you."

"It's lucky you can't; what do you want to say? Do you know I'm freezing?"

"You remember what we were talking about yesterday?"

"Am I likely to have forgotten?"

"I've been thinking things over, and I've come to the conclusion that if you're game I am."

"Game? game for what? what do you mean?"

Mr. Nash glanced round, as if to ascertain if any one was in sight, then dropped his voice.

"To marry."

"Herbert!"

Her heart seemed to leap into her mouth, as if the word, coming from his lips, touched a spring and made it bound.

"You said you'd like the marriage to be at once; what do you say to our being married to-morrow?"

"Herbert!"

At the moment she could only trust herself to repeat his name, she was in such a curious state of tremblement.

"Do you know that Guldenheim and his crowd are in the house?"

"I've just heard."

"A nice lot they are; you can't stop in the house with them; you'll have to clear."

"I told you I should."

"You'd better pack everything you've got and I'll send a trap for you; they may object to your taking anything out of the stable; it's quite possible that they've laid hands on the lot. Anyhow I'll send something for you; how long'll you be?"

"Half-an-hour."

"Not more?"

"I can't tell you to the exact moment how long I'll be; don't be absurd. You send the trap in half-an-hour, and I'll be as quick as ever I can. Where's it going to take me?"

"To the station; I'll meet you there."

"Why at the station?"

"You poor little thing! we're going off together; it's going to be a regular elopement."

"Herbert! How are we going to get married?"

"How soon can you get some of your aunt's money?"

"I've got enough by me to go on with."

"How much do you call enough?"

"Oh, about ninety pounds."

"You sly little thing! Who'd have thought you were stuffed with money like this? It's not so long ago since I pointed out a big hole in your glove, and you said you had to wear old gloves, because you couldn't afford to buy yourself a pair of new ones."

"I dare say; that was a hint to you."

"Was it? then it was thrown away, because if I possessed the price of a pair of gloves it was as much as I did have; though in the sweet by and by I'm going to be a millionaire."

"You haven't said how we're going to get married."

"I'm going to get the licence the other end, and we're going to be married to-morrow."

"Are you sure we can get married to-morrow?"

"Of course I'm sure."

"In church?"

"In church; in St. Paul's Cathedral if you like; though to arrange that might take a little longer."

"I don't want to be married in St. Paul's Cathedral; I want to be married quietly."

"That's what I want; so there we are agreed; hooray!" This cry of jubilation was uttered in a sepulchral whisper. "Now you quite understand? Trap's coming in half-an-hour; you're to be ready; you're going to meet me at the station; we're going to elope; we're going together to get the licence; and to-morrow we're going to be married together; is that perfectly clear?"

"Don't be silly! Are you glad?"

"What for?"

"That we're going to be married; you know!"

"Of course I'm glad; how do you want me to show it? would you like me to stand on my head and dance?"

"No; I only want to know you're glad."

"You wait; you shall have all the knowledge you feel you stand in need of."

"Herbert!"

CHAPTER XVII

NORA GOES

When Elaine brought back her head into the room, the window was closed, Mr. Nash had vanished; the young lady was in such a state of palpitation, that for some seconds she was incapable of continuing the operation of packing, conscious though she was of how time was pressing. Half-an-hour is not long. She was not yet fully dressed; it seemed that now she was to dress to meet her lover, to elope with him; if she had known that before she would have arrayed herself in some quite different garments. There was no time to change now; it was out of the question. Really, there was not time even to finish packing properly; her things would have to be squashed in anyhow; if she could get them in at all she would have to be content. There was one comfort, she would buy herself an entirely new outfit when she had once got clear away. Herbert need not think—no one need think—that she was going to do without a trousseau; she was not. She was going to have a proper trousseau; a complete trousseau. Only it seemed that in her case the various articles would have to be purchased after marriage instead of before; but she would have them.

While such thoughts chased themselves through her excited little head, she returned to the process of packing with still greater zeal than before. Cherished garments received unceremonious treatment; if they could have felt they would have wondered why their mistress was using them as she had never done before. Rolled up anyhow; squeezed in anywhere; no regard paid to frills or dainty trimmings; plainly Elaine's one and only desire was to get her things in somewhere, somehow. Yet as if it was not enough to have to pack against time, she was not allowed to pack in peace; she was doomed to interruption. Just as the first box seemed full as it could hold, and she was wondering if her weight would be enough to induce the hasp to meet the lock, there came a tapping at the bedroom door. The sound was to her an occasion of irritation; her voice suggested it.

"Now who's that?"

"It is I."

It was a voice she knew—at that moment it seemed to her—too well. So entirely was this young woman a creature of mood that there was only room in her for one mood at a time, and while that possessed her she forgot everything else; before she heard that voice she had forgotten Nora. And it was Nora who stood on the other side of the door. Elaine's selfish little soul shook with fear when the sound of the voice without recalled her friend's existence to her recollection.

"What am I to do?" was the question which instantly sprang up within her. She could scarcely put her off with an excuse now. Nora was probably at her wit's end; all the seas of trouble had been opened on her unprotected head. If ever there was a moment in which she was in need of friendly service it was this; unless some one held out to her a helping hand she might sink in the deep waters, never to rise again. In the box which she had just been packing was the money which Elaine had "found" on the study table; that huge sum which, of course, was Nora's. Here was a chance to show that, after all, she was not altogether the worthless wretch she had seemed to be. Should she?

No, she told herself, Herbert would not like it; then there was Morgan, and the trousseau, and the honeymoon; if she kept all the money she might have the kind of honeymoon of which she had so often dreamed; and—there were other things. All the uses she might have for the money crowded into her brain, treading on each other's heels. She dropped the lid and ran to the door.

"I'm awfully sorry, Nora, to keep you waiting, but—" She stopped, to stare. "Why, you've got your hat on; where are you going?"

Nora was dressed for travelling. It was Elaine's cue to be surprised at everything; she meant to be so surprised that the mere force of her surprise should drive all other things clean out of her. Nora came into the room.

"I see you are packing."

For a second Elaine was slightly embarrassed, but she quickly got over that.

"Yes, I've had a letter from papa this morning."

"A letter from your father?"

The calm eyes looked Elaine straight in the face. The girl turned away; the glib tongue began to reel off lies.

"Just now—I should think I ought to have had it yesterday; I don't know why I only had it to-day. He wants me to come home; of course he feels I'm frightfully in the way; and then it seems Polly has the scarlet fever, and Jennie looks as if she were sickening for it, and there are the other children, and papa has no one to help him—he can't afford a nurse; so you see I must go; the poor man writes as if he were half distracted."

"Of course you must go; and, perhaps, in a way it's as well you must, though I'm so sorry to hear about Polly and Jennie; but I'm afraid that in any case I should have had to ask you to go."

"Nora! Am I so much in the way as that?"

"It is not only you who are in the way; we both of us are, both you and me. Mr. Guldenheim and his friends have come, and, in consequence, I also am leaving Cloverlea."

"Nora! What do you mean?"

Nothing could have been more eloquent than the amazement on Elaine's face.

"You knew that they were going to sell everything to pay what it appears were my father's debts; well, it's come a little sooner than I expected, that's all."

"But where will you go? What will you do?"

"Something; don't fear. 'God's in His heaven, all's well with the world.' I don't doubt there's a place in it somewhere for me."

"Oh, Nora, if I could only take you home with me! But it's such a poor place, and so small; and now it's like a hospital, with all the children ill of that dreadful fever, and papa writing that he's nearly penniless; what do you think yourself?"

It was rather a neat way of passing on the responsibility.

"I think it's out of the question. With that poor father of yours already nearly borne down beneath his troubles, do you think I'd add to them? What I'm wondering is if you've enough money to take you home."

"Papa hasn't sent me any—I'm afraid he's none to send; but I've been reckoning—I've just enough, with a squeeze; but then I'm used to squeezing. Nora, I do hope you've plenty of money."

"I've enough to go on with. Can I help you with your packing?"

"The idea! As if I'd let you, you poor dear!"

"Then, Elaine, if you won't mind very much—"

Nora stopped, as if at a loss to find words with which to clothe her thoughts. Miss Harding was gushing.

"I shan't mind anything, my darling. What is it?"

"It—it's only, if you won't think me very unkind, that I'd—I'd like to catch a train which starts almost at once."

She was thinking, perhaps, of Dr. Banyard's promise to send his wife to talk to her, and desired to avoid that talking. Miss Harding leapt at the hint.

"And you want to get away immediately? And do you think I'd wish to stop you from doing anything you want to do?—you sweet! Good-bye, Nora, my darling! God bless you! I hope everything will turn out all right yet; I feel sure it will; it's bound to. And mind you write!"

"I will—when I am settled."

"And what address will find you?"

"I'll let you know that also, when I'm settled."

So they parted, with fond embraces, many kisses, words of endearment, tears in their eyes. Nora's heart was very full, and Elaine felt hers ought to be. So soon as Nora had left the room Elaine banged her foot against the floor; clapped her hands together with such violence that she actually stung her tender palms, and cried—

"What a little beast I am! what a little beast!"

Then, instantly, she resumed her packing, remembering that the trap was coming in less than half-an-hour, but not with quite so much zest as before. There was a vague consciousness in her somewhere that her conduct had not been—and still was not—altogether without reproach.

When Nora got down-stairs she found the hall door open, a dog-cart without, a footman keeping guard over the single trunk which he had brought from her room, and Morgan, as it were, keeping watch and ward over him; otherwise the hall was deserted. Nora recognized the fact with something like a pang. She knew then that she had hoped that at least some of the servants would have been gathered together to wish her God-speed; then she told herself, with the quick philosophy which was eminently hers, that it did not matter after all.

Morgan greeted her with a question.

"Is there any more luggage?"

"No; none."

"What directions are there as to what is to be done with the contents of your own rooms—your two rooms, bedroom and boudoir? Perhaps I may be allowed to remark, Miss Lindsay, that I believe you've a right to whatever is in your own rooms; no one's a right to touch anything that's in them except you."

"Thank you, Morgan; there are no directions. By the bye, if you like I will write you two or three lines, before I go, which you will be able to use as a reference when you are applying for another situation. I don't wish you to suffer by what has happened."

"Thank you, Miss Lindsay, you are very good; but I don't propose to seek another situation. I am giving up service. I trust, Miss Lindsay, that in the future everything will turn out as you would like it to."

"Thank you, Morgan, I hope it will. Say goodbye to the others for me, and say I wish them all well."

The butler inclined his head with his most deferential air. The trunk had been lifted into its place at the back of the cart, the footman had ascended to the driver's seat, and Nora was climbing up to his side, when a seedy-looking man came shambling along the drive, apparently in a state of some excitement.

"Here, what's all this!" he cried. "This won't do, you know."

"What won't do?" inquired the footman.

"What you're doing of—that won't do. I'm in charge of the stable, and that horse and cart have been took out of it; can't have that; nothing's to be took off the premises without the governor's express permission."

"Isn't it? We'll see about that; and so will you see if you don't watch out."

The footman evinced an inclination to use his whip with some degree of freedom. Nora laid a restraining hand upon his arm. She addressed the seedy-looking man.

"The dog-cart is only going to drive me to the station; it will be returned to the stable, uninjured, probably in less than half-an-hour. You need fear nothing."

There she was mistaken; the man was in imminent peril of being run over. The footman flicked the mare on the shoulder, she gave a startled bound, then went dashing down the drive; if the fellow had not sprung nimbly aside both the mare and the cart might have gone right over him.

And that was how Nora left Cloverlea.

While the vehicle was still in sight Mr. Morgan addressed a few outspoken remarks to the seedy-looking man on his own account.

"You're a fool, my lad, that's what you are; you don't know when you're well off. You and your governor have no more right to be where you are than you have to be in the moon. That young lady's been badly advised. If she'd had your governor, and his friends, thrown out of the house, and dragged down the drive, and deposited in the high road—your governor, for one, wouldn't have wanted much dragging; he knows enough to get in out of the rain—he'd have taken to his heels as fast as ever he could, to save himself from something worse. As for your laying your hand upon her horse, and her cart—because they are hers, and hers only—if she'd had you locked up you'd have got six months, and serve you right. I call you a low down thief, because that's exactly what you are; and I call your governor a low down thief, because that's exactly what he is; and if I have an opportunity so I'll tell him. Taking rascally advantage of a fatherless girl. Poor young lady! it goes to my heart to see the way she's being put upon."

Mr. Morgan ascended the steps with an air of virtuous indignation which caused the other to stare at him open-mouthed, as if an assault from that quarter was the last thing he had expected.

Before many minutes had passed a trap drew up before the hall door, from which Mrs. Banyard alighted. She was received by Morgan; her air was a trifle imperious; she had come, as her husband had promised she should come, to talk to Nora.

"Where is Miss Lindsay? I wish to see her; take me to her at once."

The butler was affable, but unsatisfactory.

"I am afraid I cannot do that."

"What do you mean? Why can't you? Has she given instructions that she doesn't wish to see me?"

"Miss Lindsay has gone."

"Gone! Gone where?"

"I apprehend that Miss Lindsay has left Cloverlea for ever."

"You apprehend! Man, you're dreaming! How long is it since she has been gone?"

She glanced towards the trap, as if she meditated jumping into it, and starting in instant pursuit; but if she entertained such an idea Morgan's answer put an end to it.

"Possibly an hour, possibly not quite so much; I cannot say exactly when she started."

He must have been aware that she had not been gone ten minutes; possibly he wished to spare his late mistress the indignity of being chased—even by a friend.

"Where do you say she's gone?"

"The directions were to drive her to the station."

"To the station? Then what address has she left?"

"None with me."

"She must have left an address with some one."

"Not with any member of the household."

"But where are her letters to be forwarded?"

"That I cannot say."

"Man! why did you let her go?" Probably this time the expression of surprise which was on Morgan's face was genuine. "I'm afraid I don't understand."

"Oh-h-h!"

She clenched her fists, and, so to speak, she ground her teeth; she looked as if she would have liked to have beaten the butler; only just then another dog-cart drew up, from which the Hon. Robert Spencer descended. He hailed the butler.

"Morgan, I want to speak to Miss Lindsay; where is she? I'll show myself in." Then he saw the doctor's wife. "Oh, Mrs. Banyard, how are you? But I needn't ask, you're looking so well." He returned to the butler. "Morgan, where is Miss Lindsay?"

"Miss Lindsay, sir, has gone."

Mr. Spencer did what Mrs. Banyard had done—he echoed the butler.

"Gone! Gone where?"

Mrs. Banyard took it on herself to explain.

"The headstrong girl has gone to the station, and probably to London, and as she's left no address she's gone goodness only knows where. But I know—I understand perfectly well. She's got some Quixotic notion into her head, and because she's got it she's bent on suffering martyrdom, and she will too, if somebody doesn't stop her; though who for, or what for, nobody knows."

Mr. Spencer laughed, as if he thought the doctor's wife was joking; but he seemed to do it with an effort.

"If she's gone we'll find her, wherever she's gone; don't let your imagination paint any very frightful pictures, Mrs. Banyard. I'll undertake to find her, and save her from the martyrdom at which you hint— well, I'll be on the safe side, and say within four-and-twenty hours."

But he was undertaking more than he was able to perform.

CHAPTER XVIII

MISS GIBB

Nora's knowledge of London was as slight as the average young lady's, who has lived mostly in the country, is apt to be; yet, when she left Cloverlea, she went straight to London, with eight pounds, four and twopence in her pocket, intending to live upon that sum until she had discovered some means of earning more. There was some method in her madness. She had been reading a story lately about a young woman who had struggled to make a living in town, and she had had rooms in Newington Butts. Nora had gathered that, while Newington Butts was not an abode of fashion, nor a particularly salubrious neighbourhood, it was within reasonable distance of places where young women could earn money; and, above all, that thereabouts lodgings were both plentiful and cheap.

The train deposited Nora at Paddington. Had she known her way about she would have left her trunk in the cloak-room, and crossed London by one of half-a-dozen different routes, for a few coppers; when she had found lodgings the box would have been delivered at her address for a few more coppers. What she did do was to charter a four-wheeler. It is some distance from Paddington to Newington Butts; to Nora, an unaccustomed traveller, already tired with her journey, hungry and thirsty, the way seemed interminable. She began to wonder if the driver quite knew where he was going; he seemed to go on and on and never get there. At last, a little desperate, she put her head out of the window and asked him—

"Are you sure this is the right way?"

The cab stopped. The driver screwed himself round in his seat, and he observed, in the tone of one who is offended—

"You said Newington Butts, didn't you?"

"Yes."

Hers was the voice of deprecation.

"Very well then; I'm driving you to Newington Butts. If you think you know the way better than I do you can come outside and I'll get inside. I've been driving this cab two and twenty years, and if there's any one who knows the way to Newington Butts better than I do, I should like to know who it is."

She drew her head back and subsided on the seat, doubting no longer. She felt that a man who had been a cabman for two and twenty years ought to know the way to Newington Butts better than she did. The cab went on. There was another period of seemingly interminable jolting; it seemed likely that the springs had been on that cab as long as the driver had. Once more the vehicle stopped. This time the driver asked a question.

"What address?"

As Nora put her head out again hers was the tone of anxiety.

"Is this Newington Butts?"

"It used to be when I was here last, but perhaps it's been and gone and turned itself into something else since; you might ask a policeman if you think it has been up to any game of the kind. There's one standing over there; I'll call him if you like; he might know."

"Thank you; I—I don't think I'll trouble you. The fact is I want lodgings; do you know of any round here?"

"Lodgings? I shouldn't have thought there was any round here to suit you."

"Oh, I'm so sorry; why not?"

"There's about two hundred thousand, I dare say, so perhaps one of them might suit. Anyhow, I'll show you a few samples. Only, mind you, I'm not engaged by the hour, nor yet by the week."

When next the cab stopped the main thoroughfare had been left behind, and they were in a street of private houses.

"Here you are; here's a street pretty nearly full of them; all you've got to do is pick and choose."

Nora, getting out, perceived that in many of the windows there were cards announcing that there were rooms to let. She began her search. At some houses they asked too much; at others they did not take ladies; and there were rooms in which she would not have lived rent-free; perhaps she tried a dozen without success. The cabman, who had followed her from house to house, did not appear to be so disheartened by this result as she did.

"That's nothing," he declared, as she regarded him with doubtful eyes. "Sometimes people go dodging about after rooms the whole day long, and then don't find what they want. There's more round the corner; try them."

Nora went round the corner, the cab moving at a walking pace beside her. The first door at which she knocked was opened by a girl, a small girl, who looked about twelve; but she wore her hair in a knob at the back of her head, and there was something in her manner which seemed intended to inform the world at large that she was to be regarded as a grown woman.

"What rooms have you to let?" asked Nora.

The girl looked at her with sharp, shrewd eyes; her reply was almost aggressive.

"We don't care for ladies, not in the ordinary way we don't."

Nora had been told this before. Though she had not understood why a woman should be objected to merely because she was a woman, she had meekly withdrawn. But there was that about this child—who bore herself as if she were so old—which induced her to persevere.

"I am sorry to hear that. If you were to make an exception in my case I would try not to make myself more objectionable than I could help."

The girl remained unsoftened.

"That may be; but you never can tell. Some give more trouble than they're worth, and some aren't worth anything; this is a respectable house. Still there's no harm in letting you see what we have got."

On the upper floor were a small sitting-room in front and a still smaller bedroom behind; barely, poorly furnished, with many obvious makeshifts, but scrupulously clean.

"What rent are you asking?"

"Ten shillings a week, and not a penny less; it ought to be fourteen."

"I'm afraid I can't pay fourteen shillings a week just yet, but I think I can manage ten; I like the rooms because they seem so clean."

"They are clean; no one can say they're not clean; I defy 'em to."

"Can I see the landlady?"

"My mother's the landlady; she's not very well just now; I can make all arrangements."

"Then in that case don't you think that if I were to take the rooms for a week on trial, at the end of that time we might find out if we were likely to suit each other?"

"We might; there's no knowing. When would you want them?"

"At once; my luggage is at the door."

"Then mind you make the cabman bring it up before you pay him; I know them cabmen."

But the cabman would not be made; he pleaded inability to leave his horse. An individual had appeared who offered to carry up the box for threepence; so Nora let him. After the cabman had been paid there remained of her capital less than eight pounds. When they were again up-stairs she said to the girl—

"What's your name? I'm Miss Lindsay."

"I'm Miss Gibb."

Nora smiled; the child said it as if she wished the fact to be properly appreciated.

"I meant, what is your Christian name?"

"Angelina; though I'm generally known as Angel, you see it's shorter; though I don't pretend that there's anything of the angel about me, because there isn't."

"I fancy I'm tired, my head aches; do you think you could let me have some tea?"

"Course I could; are you going to do for yourself, or are we going to do for you?"

"I'm afraid I don't understand."

"Are we going to do your marketing, or are you going to do it for yourself? If you take my advice you'll do it for yourself; it'll save you trouble in the end, and then there won't be no bother about the bills. The last lodger we had in these rooms he never could be got to see that he'd had what he had had, there was always a rumpus. Quarter of a pound of tea a week he used to have, yet he never could understand how ever it got into his bill. I'll let you have a cup of tea, and some bread and butter, and perhaps an egg; then afterwards I dare say you might like to go out and lay in a few stores for yourself." The girl turned as she was leaving the room to supply the new-comer with a piece of information. "Number 1, Swan Street, Stoke Newington, S.E., that's the address you're now in, in case you might be wanting to tell your friends."

In Swan Street Nora continued to reside, while the days went by, though she never told her friends. From Cloverlea, and the position of a great heiress, with all the world at her feet to pick and choose from, to Swan Street and less than eight pounds between her and beggary, was a change indeed. Used only to a scale of expenditure in which cost was never counted she was incapable of making the best of such resources as she had. Miss Gibb took her to task, on more than one occasion, for what that young woman regarded as her extravagance.

"Don't want it again? What's the matter with the bread? Why, there's the better part of half a loaf here."

"Yes, but I had it the day before yesterday."

Nora spoke with something like an air of timidity, as she stood rather in awe of Miss Gibb when that young person showed a disposition to expand herself on questions of domestic economy.

"Day before yesterday? Let's hope you'll never be wanting bread. I've known the time when I'd have been glad to have the week before last's. Then look at those two rashers of bacon you told me to take away yesterday, what was the matter with them?"

"They weren't—quite nice."

"Not nice?"

"I didn't think they were—quite fresh."

"Not fresh? I know I cooked them for my dinner and there didn't seem to be anything wrong about them to me. Then there was that lump of cheese which you said was all rind, it made me and Eustace a handsome supper. Of course I know it's none of my business, and of course any one can see you're a lady from the clothes you send to the wash; but if there's one thing I can't stand it's waste; perhaps that's because I've known what want is."

Nora had been in the house more than a week without seeing or hearing anything of her landlady, or of any managing person except Miss Gibb. She made constant inquiries, but each time it seemed that Mrs. Gibb was "not very well just now," though what ailed her Miss Gibb did not explain. One afternoon, as she was removing the tea-things, Nora was struck by the look of unusual weariness which was on the preternaturally old young face; something in the look determined her to make an effort to solve the mystery of the invisible and inaudible landlady.

"Angel, whenever I ask you how your mother is you always say she's not very well just now; but the only person I've seen or heard moving about the house is you. I'm beginning to wonder if your mother is a creature of your imagination." Angel said nothing; she continued to scrape the crumbs off the tablecloth with the blunt edge of a knife. "Are you alone in the house?"

"Course I'm not; how about my brother, Eustace? You've seen and heard him, haven't you?"

Eustace, it appeared, was only slightly his sister's senior, and almost as old; though Nora felt that no one could really be as old as Angel seemed; she admitted that she had seen Eustace.

"Very well then; he don't go till after nine and he's back most days before six, so how can I be alone in the house?"

"I know about Eustace; as you say, I've seen him. But I was thinking of your mother. Where is she; or have you reasons why you would rather not tell me?"

"What do you mean by have I reasons?"

The light of battle came into the child's eyes; it was extraordinary how soon it did come there.

"I was wondering if, for any reason, you would prefer to keep your own counsel."

"We don't all of us care to turn ourselves inside out; seems to me you don't for one."

The accusation was so true that Nora was routed.

"I beg your pardon, Angel; I didn't mean to seem to pry."

"No harm done that I know of; bones aren't broke by questions." She folded the tablecloth. As she placed it in its drawer, and her back was turned to Nora, she said, as with an effort, "Mother's paralyzed."

"Paralyzed? Oh, Angel, I'm so sorry; where is she?"

Miss Gibb faced round, again all battle.

"Where is she? This is her own house, isn't it? In whose house do you suppose she'd be if she wasn't in her own? I can't think what you mean by keeping on asking where is she?"

Nora was properly meek.

"You see, I only asked because I never hear her moving about; I never hear any one but you, and Eustace."

"Mean I make a clatter?"

"Angel! you know I don't. You are nearly, as quiet as a mouse; but your mother is so very quiet. I hope the paralysis is only slight."

"That's the trouble, it isn't. It's been coming on for years; during the last three years it's been downright bad; and during the last twelve months she's hardly been able to move so much as a finger."

Nora reflected; how old could the child have been when the mother was taken "downright bad"?

"Can she do nothing for herself?"

"Can't even feed herself."

"But how does she manage?"

"What do you mean, how does she manage?"

"Who does everything for her?"

"I never heard such questions as you do ask! Who do you suppose does everything for her? Isn't there me? and isn't there Eustace? Me and Eustace always have done everything for her; she wouldn't have anybody else do anything for her not if it were ever so."

"Has she any income of her own?"

"I wish she had; that would be heaven below."

"But on what do you live?"

"Don't we let lodgings? What do you think we let 'em for? We live on our lodgings, that's what we live on; leastways mother and me; Eustace keeps himself, and a bit over now that Mr. Hooper's started giving him his old clothes. I only hope he'll keep on giving him them. The way Eustace wears out his clothes is something frightful; it always has been Eustace's weakness, wearing out his clothes."

Later Nora did a sum in arithmetic. Miss Gibb had previously told her that, including rent, rates, and taxes the house cost more than forty pounds a year. Nora paid ten shillings a week; Mr. Carter, on the floor below, paid twelve and six; which meant twenty-two and sixpence a week, or fifty-eight pounds ten shillings a year; so that when rent, rates, and taxes had been paid under eighteen pounds per annum were left for the support of the Gibb family, or less than seven shillings a week. And this when times were flourishing! The rooms Nora had had been vacant more than a month before she came; small wonder Miss Gibb—as she would have put it—had "chanced" a lady.

More than another week elapsed before Nora was permitted to see her landlady. She found her in the front room in the basement, which was used by Miss Gibb as well as herself to live and sleep in. There, also, were performed most of the necessary cooking operations.

"Mother," explained Miss Gibb, "always does feel the cold; we can't have a fire going both in the kitchen and in here, so that's how it is. Besides, mother likes to see what's going on, don't you, mother?"

Mother said she did; for she could talk, and that was the only thing she still could do; it seemed to Nora that even the faculty of speech was threatened. Mrs. Gibb spoke very quietly and very slowly, and sometimes she paused, even in the middle of a word; as she listened Nora wondered how long it would be before that pause remained unbroken. Her landlady lay on a chair bedstead. Miss Gibb and her brother, between them, had contrived a method, of which every one was proud, by means of an arrangement of sloping boards, to raise her head and shoulders, when she desired to be raised. Nora was not surprised to find that, in common with the rest of the house, she was spotlessly neat and clean; but she was conscious of something akin to a feeling of surprise when she observed the expression which was on her face; and the more attentively she observed the more the feeling grew. Although she seemed so old—the cares of this world had pressed heavily on her—still, in a sense, she seemed younger than her daughter; for on her face was a look of peace, as on the face of those who are conscious that they also serve although they only stand and wait.

"I have nothing of which to complain," she told her lodger; "only—it's hard on Angelina." Nora noticed that she always referred to her daughter by her full Christian name. Angelina remonstrated.

"Now, mother, don't you be silly; if you are going to say things like that I shall have to send Miss Lindsay away."

The mother looked at her daughter with a look in her eyes which, when she saw it, brought the tears into Nora's; there was in it an eloquence which she wondered if, with all her wisdom, Angelina comprehended. If she had only been able to take the burden of the mother off the daughter's shoulders, how gladly she would have done it. But the days when she was able to bear the burdens of others were gone; it seemed not unlikely that she would be crushed out of existence by her own.

CHAPTER XIX

A YOUNG LADY IN SEARCH OF A LIVING

The more Nora sought for means to earn her own livelihood, the more they seemed to evade her. In her time she had heard a good deal about how difficult it sometimes is to earn one's own living, but she never realized what that meant until she started to earn hers. To begin with, she had only the very vaguest notions of how to set about it. She could not serve in a shop; at least she did not feel as if she could; she was conscious that she was not qualified to be a governess; she had no leaning towards domestic service, though she would have preferred that to serving in a shop; she had no woman's trade at her fingers' ends, so that she was unfit for a workroom. What remained? It seemed to her very little, except some sort of clerkship; she had heard that thousands of women were employed as clerks; or if she could get a post as secretary. That was the objective she had in her mind when she left Cloverlea, a secretaryship; for that she believed herself to have two necessary qualifications—she wrote a very clear hand, and she had some knowledge of typewriting. She had once started a typewriting class in the village; she had taken lessons herself. She had bought a machine and practised on that, until she gave it away to one of the pupils, who wished to take advantage of the information she had acquired to earn something for herself. That was nearly a year ago; she had not practised since; but she did not doubt that if she came within reach of a machine it would all come back to her; and she had attained to a state of considerable proficiency.

So she bought the daily papers and answered all the advertisements for secretaryships which they contained. There were not as many as she would have wished; some days there were none; and the only answers she received were from agents, who offered to place her name upon their books, in consideration of a fee, which she did not see her way to give them. The way those eight pounds were slipping through her fingers was marvellous; when three weeks had gone she had scarcely thirty shillings left, between her and destitution. Of course, she had been extravagant—monstrously extravagant, as Miss Gibb occasionally told her; but when you have been accustomed all your life to an establishment kept up at the rate of some twelve thousand pounds a year, to say nothing of having five hundred a year for pocket money, it is not easy, all at once, to learn the secret of how to make a shilling do the work of eighteenpence; that is a secret which takes a great deal of learning; by many temperaments it can never be learnt at all.

She had been a month in Swan Street; had paid three weeks' bills; the fourth lay in front of her. It was such a modest bill—Miss Gibb's bills were curiosities; yet when it was paid she would not have six shillings left in the world. It frightened her to think of it; the effort to think seemed to set her head in a whirl; her heart was thumping against her ribs; it made her dizzy. What was she to do? where was she to go? She could not stay in Swan Street; she had not enough to pay next week's rent, to say nothing of food. Yet, what was the alternative? With less than six shillings in the world what could she do?

In a sense, since her coming to Newington Butts she had kept herself to herself. She had this much in common with her father, she could not wear her heart upon her sleeve. She had kept her own counsel; told no one of the straits she was in, of the efforts she was making to find a way to earn her daily bread. But it was plain even to her, as she regarded her few shillings, that the time had come when she must take counsel of some one. If she had to go out into the highways and byways, with her scanty capital, she must learn of some one what highways and byways there were for her to go out into; of herself she knew nothing. As she cast about in her mind for some way out of her trouble, it seemed to her that the only person to whom she could unbosom herself was Miss Gibb.

She rang the bell, paid her bill, and as she watched Angelina, with her tongue out and her head on one side, making magnificent efforts to affix her signature to the receipt, she prepared herself for the ordeal. When the receipt was signed, and Angelina was about to go, Nora stopped her.

"If you have nothing particular to do just now, and you don't mind, there is something which I should like to say to you."

"I don't know that there's anything you might call particular that I've got to do, but there's always something."

Which was true enough; from the first thing in the morning to the last thing at night, Miss Gibb was always doing something; and sometimes also, Nora suspected, in the silent watches of the night. Nora hesitated; she found the subject a difficult one to broach.

"I'm in rather an uncomfortable position; I—I'm afraid I shall have to leave you."

"Why? Aren't we giving satisfaction?"

"If I give you as much satisfaction as you give me there'd be no trouble on that score."

"Oh, you give us satisfaction all right enough; although, of course, any one can see you're several cuts above our place."

"You are likely to be several cuts above me; I am having to leave you because I have not money enough left to pay you next week's rent."

"Not enough money left? How much have you?"

"Five and eightpence halfpenny, to be precise." Miss Gibb changed countenance. "Five and eightpence halfpenny! That's not much."

"No one can appreciate the fact better than I do."

"But however come you to have so little?"

"I hadn't much when I came, and I suppose I've been extravagant."

"You have been that."

"You see,"—despite herself Nora sighed—"I haven't been used to economy."

"Any one could see that with half-an-eye; I shouldn't be surprised to learn that you're one of those who've been used to spend as much as five pounds a week."

"I'm afraid I am.

"Then of course there's excuses. We can't get out of ways like that with a hop, skip and a jump; it's not to be expected. But haven't you got any friends who'd help you?"

"I haven't a friend to whom I can apply for help."

"I should have thought you were the kind who'd have had lots of friends. Have you fell out with them?"

"I thought my father was a rich man; but when he died—it was only a very little while ago—it appeared that he wasn't; so I have to make my own way in the world, and that is how I came to Swan Street."

"I know them fathers; I had one of my own, and he wasn't of any account; though I will say this, I always liked him."

"I have been trying to find something by means of which I could earn enough money to keep me. I hoped to have found it before now, but I haven't, and that's the trouble."

"What sort of work have you been looking for?"

"I've been endeavouring to get a post as secretary, among other things, and I've answered no end of advertisements, but nothing has come of one of them."

"Secretary? what's that? The notices that the water'll be cut off if it's not paid for, they're signed by a secretary; I always took him to be some kind of a bailiff."

Nora endeavoured to explain, but her explanation was not very lucid, and Miss Gibb was not extremely impressed.

"Is that the only kind of work you want?" she asked; "a secretary?"

"Indeed it isn't; I should be glad to do anything."

"Some people, when they say they'd be glad to do anything, mean nothing, which is about all they're good for; I know. How would you like to go out charing?"

"Charing? Well, I may be glad to have an opportunity of doing that."

"Yes, no doubt; I fancy I see you at it! you charing! My word! Strikes me you're the kind who'll find it difficult to get work of any sort."

"You're not very reassuring."

"Facts is facts."

"That's true enough; and it's no use blinking them. I fear you're right; I shall find it hard; anyhow while I'm looking for work it's clear that I can't continue to be your lodger. That's what I wanted to explain."

"And pray why not?"

"Isn't it pretty obvious? With five and eightpence halfpenny, and no prospect of more, how am I to pay you next week's rent?"

"I did think you'd have talked better sense than that."

"Angel!"

"If there's one thing I cannot stand it is to hear people talk right-down silly; I never could stand it, and I never shall. I wouldn't take this week's bill if it wasn't that we were so short; but if that there poor-rate isn't paid next week we shall have the brokers in, so paid it must be; them there poor-rates is demons; they'll turn me grey yet before I've done. But as for your next week's rent—we'll talk about that when it's due."

"Are you proposing that I should run up debts with you, which I may never be able to pay? Do you call that sense?"

"As it happens that's not what I'm proposing; though if I were as sure of most things as I am of that you'll pay me first chance you get, it might be better for me; but you can hardly say you've got no money when you've got plenty of things you can get money on."

"I don't understand."

"Look at your clothes—lovely some of them are; you can get money on them."

"Get money on my clothes? How?"

"Why, bless me, aren't there pawnbrokers? What do you think they're for? Taken to the proper place, by the proper person, you'd get a lot of money on those things of yours; I know. I always say that so long as you've something to pawn it's like having money at the bank."

It was to Nora as though Miss Gibb's words had opened out to her a new world, of which she had not dreamed. In none of the country towns within miles of Cloverlea was there a pawnshop; to her knowledge she had never seen one; there were plenty within an easy stroll of Swan Street; she had passed and re-passed them, but her attention had not been called to what they were; they had escaped her notice. In her mind the word pawnshop stood for almost the lowest word in the scale of degradation; it was the drunkard's last hope; the friend of the felon; the resource of those to whom there was no resource left; that gate into the unthinkable which was associated only with despair. And that it should be suggested to her that she should enter a pawnbroker's den—she had heard it spoken of as a "den"—to "raise" money on the clothes she had worn yesterday, and had hoped to wear again to-morrow—in her blackest hours she had not anticipated such a fate for herself as that. The proposal actually appalled her; filled her with a fear of she knew not what; shamed her; hurled her from a pedestal into a morass. She stammered as she replied, conscious of the crass banality of what she was saying—

"I—I don't think I—I should like to pawn any—any of my things if—if I could help it."

Miss Gibb's scorn was monumental, as if she resented something which the other implied, though it had been left unuttered.

"And who do you think does like to pawn their things if they can help it? Do you suppose people pawn their boots because they've got their pockets full of money? I am surprised to hear you talk, I really am; should have thought at your time of life you'd have known better. Wouldn't you rather pawn your clothes than starve?"

"If you—if you put it in that crude way, I suppose I would."

Nora smiled; a horrible libel on what a smile ought to be. There was no pretence of a smile about Miss Gibb; there never was; she was always like a combatant, who, armed at all points, is ever ready for the fray.

"Very well, then; you say you've got no money, and I say how do you make that out when you have got things that you can pawn? If you like to go hungry rather than put away a lace petticoat—which you can get out again, mind you, whenever you've a chance—all I can say is I don't; I've known what it is to be hungry, I have."

"But I fear that I—I shouldn't know how to set about pawning a lace petticoat even if I wanted to save myself from going hungry."

"Who said you would? Who said anything about your setting about it? Not me; I do hope I have more sense than that. Why, you'd be worse than a baby at the game; it needs some knowing. I'll do all in that way that's wanted; if I don't know pretty well all about pawning that there is to know I ought to, I've been pawning pretty nearly ever since I could walk. What's more, I've pawned pretty nearly every blessed thing that there is to pawn, down to a towel-horse and a kitchen fender. Mother and Eustace and me would have been a case for a coroner's inquest long ago if I hadn't; and I will say this for them there pawnbrokers, that, considering the class they've got to do with, and that they have got to make a living, they've got as much of the milk of human kindness in them as most. You're going to stop here, that's what you're going to do, and mother and Eustace and me will put our heads together to see about finding you some work to do, though I don't know about that there secretary. Only for goodness' sake don't you lose heart; no one ever gained anything by doing that. I've seen as much of the world as most, and I know from my own experience that when things are tightest is just the moment when help comes. Mother says it comes from heaven; but I don't know, it may or it may not; but it comes from somewhere, and that often from where you least expected it. When next week's bill comes due, if nothing's turned up, you give me something, and I'll take it round to Mr. Thompson—he's about as good as any—and I'll get as much on it as ever I can, and you'll be able to pay all right; you see, I'm not concealing from you that we've got to live as well as you, and them poor-rates there's no shirking. But don't you fear; mother and Eustace and me will have found you something to do between us long before you've spent all the money you've got in the bank; but whatever you do do, don't you go losing heart."

So the child taught the woman, who was learning rapidly that age is not measured by the years one has lived; Miss Gibb was a century older than she was, though she was only just in her teens. Two visits were paid to Mr. Thompson, each time with a petticoat. Nora lived on the proceeds of those two petticoats for nearly another month, during which all the members of the establishment were putting their heads together in endeavours to find her something to do. The heart-sickness it meant for her; the consciousness of wasted effort; the sense of shame; the realization of her own futility; she had aged more during the time she had been in Swan Street than in all the preceding years. She had long ceased to confine herself to attempts to find a post as secretary, or as clerk. She tramped half over London in her desire to answer, in person, advertisements of all sorts and kinds, always in vain. Any one but a sheer ignoramus—Miss Gibb's ignorance outside her own sphere of action was colossal—would have told her at a glance that her efforts were foredoomed to failure. And why? The idea of such a one as she was occupying some of the situations for which she applied was in itself an absurdity; her appearance, her bearing, her manners, her dress, all were against her; perhaps her dress handicapped her worst of all. She did not know it; she thought her frocks were as simple as they could be; and so they were, in the sense of the great costumier, with the simplicity which is the hall-mark of the dressmaker's art. There was not one of them which had not cost her ten or fifteen guineas. The would-be employer saw this at once, and decided that the applicant was unsuited, which she was; so Nora was sent sorrowing away.

So with Nora the world went from bad to worse; until, as if to justify Miss Gibb's prophetic instinct, when things seemed really at their "tightest," help came to her from a quarter—as Angelina had foretold—from which she had least expected it.

CHAPTER XX

KING SOLOMON

John Hooper, Esquire, barrister-at-law, of Fountain Court, Inner Temple, was the employer of Mr. Eustace Gibb, who was the brother of Miss Gibb. It is not easy to define the relation which Mr. Gibb occupied with regard to Mr. Hooper. Mr. Hooper, although, presumably, learned in the law, had never held a brief in his life, and, to be frank, did not particularly want one; only his uncle worried. He had a small income of his own, and great expectations from his uncle; as his expenditure always exceeded his income, he regarded it as of the first importance that he should continue to stand in what he called his uncle's "good books," since he looked to that gentleman for sufficient financial assistance to enable him to what he termed "rub along." To please his uncle, who appeared to think he ought, very shortly, to be sitting on the woolsack, since he could get no briefs of his own he worked on those of other people; in other words he devilled for a gentleman who was always promising to do more work than, as he knew very well, he could do, and who, therefore, allowed Mr. Hooper, among others, to do some of the work which he was paid to do, but for which he paid Mr. Hooper nothing; there was not so much of this as Mr. Hooper chose to allow his uncle to imagine; still, from his point of view, there was emphatically enough.

What position Mr. Gibb filled in his chambers he himself occasionally wondered. To those whom he wished to impress with his legal standing he spoke of him as his clerk; to those whom it was impossible to impress, and they were many, as his office boy; while in his own circle of intimates, which was of rather a peculiar kind, he generally referred to him as King Solomon. Mr. Gibb generally referred to himself as Mr. Hooper's right-hand man.

"I'm his right hand man, that's what I am," he was wont to tell any one who showed interest in the subject; whereat the listener whistled, or did worse, and wondered, if he stopped at that. His duties appeared chiefly to consist in sitting, if Mr. Hooper was in his chambers, in a sort of lobby, which opened on to the staircase, which he called his office, and where he did nothing; or if Mr. Hooper was not in his chambers, he went out, as far out as he thought was discreet, and did nothing there. Sometimes when, as was not infrequently the case, both employer and employed had nothing to do, Mr. Hooper would summon Mr. Gibb into his inner room, and would talk to him—and Mr. Gibb would talk to him. It was the words of wisdom which Mr. Gibb would casually let drop in the course of these conversations which induced Mr. Hooper to allude to him, in the privacy of his own circle, as King Solomon; the barrister declared that it was worth his while to pay Mr. Gibb ten shillings a week, which he with difficulty did, merely on account of the benefit which he derived from hearing him talk.

It was during one of these conversations that Mr. Gibb touched on a subject which was foremost both in his heart and head. He had taken a strenuous part in the family endeavours to find for Miss Lindsay some employment by means of which she could at least provide herself with the wherewithal to keep herself alive. He had entered on the search with sanguine zest. Apart from any feeling which he might himself entertain for the lady he felt that his reputation was at stake. He had pledged himself to find for her at least half-a-dozen ways of earning a living in a ridiculously short space of time; and as yet he had not found her one; and she herself still searched. He was aware of the visits to Mr. Thompson; they troubled him nearly as much as they troubled Nora; he felt almost as if he was himself responsible for their continuation. He knew that any day another might have to be paid; the knowledge made him desperate. He had had, for some time, a vague intention of speaking to his employer on the matter; but he was aware that Mr. Hooper did not always take him seriously, and he was curiously unwilling to have Miss Lindsay made the subject of that gentleman's chaff. Yet the thought of that further impending visit pressed heavily on his mind; so that presently the barrister perceived that in his air there was something singular.

"You're not up to your usual mark, Mr. Gibb; those pearls of wisdom which I love to cherish as they drop from your lips don't seem dropping; stock run out?"

Mr. Gibb looked up at the ceiling, then down to Mr. Hooper.

"The fact is, sir, I've got something on my mind."

"Is it possible? My good Mr. Gibb, do I ever allow anything to stop on my mind? Get it off!"

"It's easy to talk, sir, but I don't seem as though I can."

"Perhaps it would do your mind good to tell me what's on it; I have known that prescription work a cure. Give your mind its head, Mr. Gibb, let her go."

Mr. Gibb hesitated; he was trying to find fitting words in which to express what he had to say.

"It's like this, sir; I know somebody who very much wants to find the means of earning a living."

"Not an uncommon character, Mr. Gibb. I suppose there are the usual requirements, large salary wanted, and very little work."

"Not at all, sir, not in this case. The person to whom I'm alluding would be only too glad to do any amount of work, for very little wages."

"That is unusual; I fear an effort has been made to impose upon your innocence. Who's the gentleman?"

"It's not a gentleman, sir, it's a lady."

"A lady? I say, Mr. Gibb! warnings out all along that coast; if at this period of your existence you get yourself mixed up with a lady, especially one who is on the look out for means of earning a living, your whole career may be blighted. She may look upon you as her living, and then where are you?"

"No fear of that, sir; this is a lady born and bred; she's as high as the heavens above me."

"Is she? Then she's tallish. Old?"

"No, sir; in her early prime."

"Meaning?"

"I couldn't say exactly, sir; I should say somewhere about twenty. You could tell better than me.

"What on earth do you mean?"

"If you saw her."

"If I saw her! Look here, Mr. Gibb, have you got anything at the back of your head?" Mr. Gibb sighed. "Is she hideous?"

"No, sir; she's the most beautiful young lady ever I set eyes on; and I've seen a few."

"You have, Mr. Gibb, I admit it; still as I don't know what your type of beauty really is your remark conveys little to me."

"It would convey more, sir, if you were to see her. You wouldn't want to see her twice to know that she's the most beautiful young lady ever you set eyes on. I feel sure of it. I wish you would see her, sir."

"May I ask, Mr. Gibb, what it is you're driving at? Why should I see her?"

"So that you might understand."

"Understand what?"

"How it is."

"How what is? I'll trouble you, Mr. Gibb, to be a trifle more explicit. Where's this lady of birth and breeding, who's as high as the heavens above you, to be found?"

"She's lodging at my mother's. Yes, sir, I don't wonder you look surprised; I know it's no place for a lady, especially one like her; and that's the trouble, she is a lady; I know a lady when I see one as well as I know a gentleman."

"You must forgive me, Mr. Gibb, but I'm wondering if you do; it's not every one who can tell a lady by the look of her."

"Perhaps not, sir; but you can. If you saw her you'd soon tell. She'd have found something long ago she could have turned her hand to if she'd been one of your common sort; but that's the mischief, she's a lady; and I happen to know that she's in a very bad way. She lost her father and her mother, and she doesn't seem to have a friend in the world; if she doesn't find something soon by which she can earn a little money I don't know what will become of her. I wish you would see her, sir."

"What good do you suppose will be gained by my seeing her? What sort of work does she want?"

"She has been trying for a secretaryship; but she's tried, and tried, and nothing's come of it; and now she'd be only too glad to do anything by which she could earn money. You see, sir, you know all kinds of people, and I thought that if you saw her, so that you might know what she's like, and how it is with her, you might think of some one who could give her work; I know you wouldn't regret it if you did."

"Mr. Gibb, you're a—you're a person of a Mephistophelian habit! Mind you, I've no more chance of putting anything in the way of your lady born and bred, who's as high as the heavens above you, than the man in the moon; but I've got plenty of time on my hands; I'm always ready to see any one; and I've no objection to see her."

"Thank you, sir. Will you see her to-morrow morning?"

"Look here, Mr. Gibb, are you trying to bustle me?"

"Well,' sir, you see she's pawning her things—"

"Pawning her things! and you say she's a lady."

"Yes, sir, she is pawning her things, and she is a lady; and it's because I've reason to know that she may have to pawn something else either to-day or to-morrow that I've mentioned her to you at all; because when she's pawned all she's got what will she do?"

"Do you want me to lend her some money? or to give her some?"

Mr. Gibb smiled.

"When you've seen her, sir, you won't need to ask me that. Then you'll see her to-morrow morning?"

"Now don't you go putting any false hopes in her head, you'll only be doing her a disservice if you do; nothing will come of my seeing her, I'm only doing it to oblige you; let that be clearly understood."

"Yes, sir; thank you very much."

When Mr. Gibb got home he rushed straight up to Miss Lindsay, who was commencing the nondescript apology for a meal which served her as tea and supper.

"Miss Lindsay, I believe I've found you something which may lead to something."

"Oh, Eustace! have you? what is it?"

"It's my chief." Mr. Gibb never would refer to him as "governor," as other clerks did; he thought it vulgar. "It's Mr. Hooper!"

"Mr. Hooper?"

"I happened to mention to him to-day that you were looking out for a secretaryship, and he said would you call round and see him to-morrow morning."

"Oh, Eustace! how shall I ever thank you? Is it for himself he wants a secretary?"

"That I can't say; but if you'll take my advice you'll call and see him."

"Of course I'll call and see him; I'm—I'm all trembling! as if I wouldn't call and see him! Do you think I've any chance?"

"That also I can't say; but if you'll allow me to give you what I should describe as a hint—"

"Please do! What is it? You are so clever!"

"If I were you I should put on your prettiest frock, and your prettiest hat, and the prettiest everything you've got."

"Eustace! Why?"

Mr. Gibb put his hand up to his mouth, and coughed discreetly.

"Fact is, Mr. Hooper's more of an eye for female beauty than he thinks, and if you come to him looking as I've seen you look, you'll knock him."

"Knock him?"

Mr. Gibb was apologetic.

"It's not often that I do use words of that kind, but, asking your pardon, this time I mean it."

"But—I don't understand what you do mean. You can't mean that Mr. Hooper would engage me as his secretary merely because I happened to be wearing my prettiest frock?"

"I don't say anything of the kind; not at all. I don't know that he wants a secretary; I only know he told me to ask you to call. You want to make a good impression when you do call, don't you?"

"Of course I do."

"Exactly; of course you do! What I say is don't leave anything undone which will help you to make a good impression; and that's all I do say."

When Mr. Gibb went Nora was left blushing, trembling, excited, and slightly bewildered; she continued her meal without having any clear idea of what it was that she was eating.

"That's a queer boy," she said to herself, more than once.

Mr. Gibb was a queer boy; which was why his "chief" occasionally alluded to him as King Solomon.

CHAPTER XXI

NORA FINDS SOMETHING TO DO

Mr. Hooper had not long arrived at his chambers, on the following morning; he was lounging in his chair, his hat still on the back of his head, his pipe between his lips, studying, in the newspaper which he held out in front of him, reports of cricket, golf, and similar legal matters, when the door was opened and Mr. Gibb came in.

"Lady to see you, sir."

Mr. Hooper started.

"Lady? What lady?"

"Lady you made an appointment with yesterday, sir."

"Lady I made an appointment with yesterday?" Mr. Hooper seemed to be making an effort to collect his wits, which Mr. Gibb's announcement had scattered. "You young scoundrel! I'd forgotten—"

Fortunately he had got no further; because, even as he was speaking, the lady entered; whereupon Mr. Gibb vanished with a degree of haste which was almost suspicious. Mr. Hooper dropped his newspaper, removed his hat with one hand, his pipe with the other, and sprang to his feet, to stare; forgetful altogether, for the moment, of his manners, so completely was he taken by surprise. What he had expected to see he could not have said; what he actually did see, standing

"in his room, Making it rich and like a lily in bloom,"

was the most beautiful girl he ever had seen. She was tall and most divinely fair, perfectly dressed, in a long, trailing black gown, which became her slender form, and a big black hat, which threw into strong relief what seemed to him to be the almost ethereal beauty of her face; and she held herself daintily erect, like the great lady he could have sworn she was. The fact that the bowl of his pipe was burning his hand recalled him to his senses.

"I—I beg your pardon; I'm afraid I've been smoking; if you'll allow me I'll open the windows."

He opened them; the three windows the room contained.

"You are Mr. Hooper?"

Her voice was just the kind of voice it was fitting should be hers, soft, clear, sweet; it was to him like the sound of music which he loved; and, when he heard it, off went his wits again.

"Yes, that—that is my name; yes—exactly—I—I am Mr. Hooper—yes."

"I am Nora Lindsay."

Nora! That was one of his pet names; as she pronounced it it seemed to him to be the sweetest name a woman could have; like everything about her, it became her so.

"May I—may I offer you a seat, Miss Lindsay? I—I am very glad to see you."

She sat down, with what seemed to him almost awful calmness; but she was all tremblement within, a maze of conflicting emotions, for already it was clear to her that this was quite a singular young man; only she was able to exhibit more outward self-control than he was. When she saw that he showed no immediate disposition to touch on the subject on which she had come, but seemed to be able to do nothing but fidget, she began on the theme herself.

"Eustace tells me that he mentioned to you that I am looking for a post as secretary."

"Eustace? Oh, you mean King Solomon—that is, young Gibb. Young Gibb's a curious boy."

"Curious? I think he's delightful."

"Delightful? Yes, so—so he is; a—a most valuable acquisition for a man like me."

"Do you yourself require a secretary, Mr. Hooper.

"Do I—require a secretary—myself? I—I—the fact is—" A wild idea was germinating in the erratic young gentleman's brain. "What are your qualifications, Miss Lindsay?"

"I can work a typewriter."

"Can you? That's splendid."

"At least I could about twelve months ago, and I dare say I could again, after a little practice."

"Of course you could; not a doubt of it. And—and can you write shorthand?"

"No, I can't write shorthand; is that indispensable?"

"No, not—not indispensable."

"I can speak and write French, and I know some German."

"Those—those are decidedly advantages."

"And I write a very clear hand; I don't think any one would have any difficulty in reading what I write; I will show you a specimen if you like."

"There's—there's not the slightest necessity; not the least; I feel sure you write a clear hand. And—when are you disengaged?"

"At once; I should like to begin as soon as I possibly could; I am very anxious to begin." Something which she fancied she saw on his face seemed to trouble her. "Isn't the secretary wanted at once?"

"Well, the fact is, it's this way—"

"I could come for a week on trial, so that you might see if I suited."

The idea of this divine creature coming to his chambers, day after day, for a whole week, made his brain whirl round.

"I'm sure you'd suit; I—I've not the slightest doubt about that."

"You can't be quite sure; but I'd try to please you."

"I—I—I—" He was about to remark that there was not the slightest necessity for her to try, since she could not help but please him, whether she tried or not, when a sudden fear came to him that his remark might be misconstrued; so he pulled himself up in time. "The remark I was about to make is, since—since I desire to be quite plain, in order that we may not commence with—with a misunderstanding; what it is I wish to point out is that the post may be of a purely temporary nature."

"That doesn't matter; it would be something; and that's better than nothing. How long would it be likely to last?"

"That's—that's not easy to determine; the fact is it's really a jobbing secretary that's wanted."

"What is a jobbing secretary?"

"One who works by the job."

"By the job?"

"Let me explain. Say there's a job—that is, a piece of work—wants doing; when that's done there may be an interregnum before more's required."

"I see. And—will the secretary be paid by the job?"

"Paid by the job?"

"Or—by the week—or how?"

"That—that reminds me." It seemed to Nora that Mr. Hooper drew in a long breath, as if he desired to lay in a stock in case of emergency. "What honorarium were you thinking of asking, Miss Lindsay?"

"I was thinking of asking two guineas a week." She fancied his jaw fell; so she hedged, quickly. "But, of course, if that's too much—"

"Not at all; not in the least; practically it's less than I expected." Although he had not the faintest notion where the money was to come from, if it had to come from him, he was thinking that if she proposed to keep herself on two guineas a week it would be some time—slight though his knowledge of such matters was, before she would be able to buy another dress like the one which she had on. "Well, Miss Lindsay, we'll leave it like this; I will think it over and let you know my decision."

"Couldn't you decide now? I've found that when people say they'll let me know their decision they mean no. Please—please give me a trial; do let me try. If—if you'll give me a chance I'll—I'll do my very best, so that you—you shan't regret it."

Unless he was mistaken, something very much like tears stood in her eyes; they affected him in a way nothing ever had done before; he would have liked to have knocked his head against the wall.

"My dear Miss Lindsay, you altogether misunderstand me—entirely misunderstand me; I shall be delighted to offer you the post—delighted."

"Mr. Hooper! Do you mean it? Really?"

It was worth two guineas a week to see the look which came into her face.

"Certainly I mean it."

"But—what did you mean when you said you'd let me know your decision?"

"I meant my decision with—with reference to—to when your duties are to commence."

"Oh! Will it be very long before you want me?"

"Emphatically no. As to wanting you, I—I want you immediately. Shall we say—"

"To-morrow? If you could let me begin tomorrow!"

"Undoubtedly you can begin to-morrow."

"At what time?"

"Shall we put it—at eleven? or would you prefer to make it twelve?"

"Twelve! But Eustace comes at ten."

"Yes, Eustace comes at ten; but I don't want to put you to any inconvenience."

"You don't want to put me to any inconvenience!" She got up from her chair with something in her way of doing it which frightened him. "But I don't want you to study my convenience; in the future it will be my duty to study yours; please understand that, before all else, I wish to do my duty. I want to do a man's work and to earn a man's wage—to deserve a man's wage. Of course I know I shan't deserve it at first; but I'm going to try hard, and if you'll only give me a chance, and treat me as if I were a man, I think you'll admit that I do deserve it before very long. I know that being a woman is against me—"

"Really, Miss Lindsay, I can't admit that."

"But I know it is—I learnt that long ago; and only when I have succeeded in making you forget that I am a woman shall I know that I am beginning to earn my wage—as a man. Then I am to come to-morrow with Eustace, at ten."

"With Eustace? Oh yes; quite so—that is—certainly; that will suit me very well."

She went out of the room without another word; he stood staring at the door through which she had passed.

"This is uncommonly awkward; ought I to have opened the door for her or not? It wouldn't have been treating her like a man, and she might have resented it. She has a way of speaking, to say nothing of looking, which takes the stiffening right out of me. I'd have given anything to have dared to ask her to lunch; but—if I had dared, anything might have happened. One thing's certain, I've been and gone and done it. I've given myself two problems to solve; one thing is, what am I to find for her to do?—for even a jobbing secretary must do something, especially when she's full of enthusiasm to the bursting-point. And the other is, how I am going to find the cash to pay her for doing it; I'll be hanged if I know which of the problems is likely to prove the most insoluble."

When Nora reached the office Mr. Gibb assailed her with questions; her answers seeming to amaze him in an ascending scale.

"Well, what did he say to you?"

"He's engaged me."

"Engaged you? What for?"

"As jobbing secretary."

"As what?"

"As jobbing secretary."

"Who to?"

"Why, to himself, of course."

"He's engaged you as jobbing secretary to himself? What are you going to do?"

"How can I tell? I suppose he has something very important which he wants me to do."

"Has he? Oh! When are you going to start on it?"

"To-morrow!"

"To-morrow? What's he going to pay you?"

"Two guineas a week; isn't it splendid?" The announcement seemed to startle Mr. Gibb out of the faculty of asking further questions. She went on. "And I have to thank you for it! Only think! if it hadn't been for you such luck never would have come my way; you dear, dear boy! I should like to kiss you for it; and I will!" And she did, quite heartily too, though she had to stoop to do it. "And out of my first two guineas I'll buy you something; what shall it be?"

"Nothing you could buy could ever equal what you've given me."

"What I've given you? what have I given you?"

"A kiss; I never shall forget you kissed me as long as I live."

"Eustace, you are—you are a queer boy!"

She went out, all blushes. When she had gone Mr. Gibb did what his employer had done; he stared at the door through which she had passed.

"Well, I call this of the nature of a startler; she must have knocked him. His jobbing secretary! What's he going to find for her to do, when there's nothing for him to do? or, for the matter of that, for me either. And two guineas a week! When the other day he sent me out to change his last fiver, and told me he'd have to make it do till quarter day, and there's still three weeks to that. Looks to me as if he'd rather overdone it."

The door of Mr. Hooper's room was opened; his voice was heard.

"Mr. Gibb, come in here!" Mr. Gibb went in there.

CHAPTER XXII

MASTER AND MAN

When Mr. Gibb entered he found Mr. Hooper in a state of agitation; there was nothing very amazing in that, as he had found him in that condition on previous occasions; but it seemed to Mr. Gibb that, in his agitation then, there was a quality which was new. Mr. Hooper assailed him the moment he was past the door.

"Now, Mr. Gibb, you have been and gone and done it."

"Done what, sir?"

"I think it's extremely possible that you've laid yourself open to an indictment for conspiracy."

"Have I, sir?"

"You brought Miss Lindsay here?"

"Excuse me, sir, but if you'll remember you told me to ask her to come."

"You put me up to it."

"I merely happened to mention that she was looking for something to do, and so she is."

"No she isn't."

"Isn't she, sir?"

"No, she's found it! And that's where I'm in a position to prove conspiracy. Mr. Gibb, do you mean to tell me that Miss Lindsay has been pawning her things?"

"I hope you won't let it go any further, sir."

"Do you think I'm—What do you think I am?"

"I haven't thought, sir; only it happened to come to my knowledge, and it seemed to me to be a sad thing for her to have to do."

"All I can say is that she hasn't pawned all her things."

"No, sir, but she soon would have done."

"Have you any idea of how much that dress cost which she had on? to say nothing of the hat!"

"Not exactly, sir, I haven't; but my sister told me that some of her things must have cost a good bit of money."

"That dress cost every penny of five-and-twenty or thirty pounds, and I dare say the hat cost another tenner; and she's been walking about in those kind of things her whole life long, I'm sure of it."

"I told you, sir, she was a lady born and bred."

"Mr. Gibb, you see advertisements for a lady, as barmaid; when I think of that I don't want to think of Miss Lindsay as a lady; she's on a different plane; she's of heaven, not of earth."

"I told you, sir, she was high as the heavens above me."

"So she is; you were right there; although the construction of your sentence is faulty, Mr. Gibb. She's a divinity among women; a poem among girls; the ideal which a man sets up for himself of what a woman may be when God chooses."

"Is she, sir?"

"Look at her! how she walks, how she moves, how she bears herself! And what a voice! had Orpheus had it he'd have needed no warbling string to aid him to draw 'iron tears down Pluto's cheek!' Then what beauty's in her face; but there's in it what not one beautiful woman in a thousand has, there's a soul! Mr. Gibb, I've only seen Miss Lindsay about twenty minutes, but I regard her as 'a perfect woman, nobly planned'; and I may add 'she was a phantom of delight, when first she gleamed upon my sight,' therefore I say you were guilty of conspiracy in luring me on to ask her to come here; because what has the result been?"

"What has it, sir?"

"The result has been that I've made an idiot of myself; a complete and perfect ass."

"Have you, sir?"

"I don't like your tone, Mr. Gibb, it exacerbates. It is in itself enough to prove your guilt. Had you not been engaged in a conspiracy you would have been surprised beyond measure at the wholly unforeseen result. But, as it is, I put it to you, Mr. Gibb; are you surprised?"

"Well, sir, in a way I can't say I am, not exactly."

"There you are! there you are! Do you know, Mr. Gibb, that I've given Miss Lindsay to understand that I've retained her services as a member of my staff?"

"She told me you'd engaged her, sir."

"Oh, she did, did she? What did she tell you I'd engaged her as?"

"As jobbing secretary, sir."

"And pray what is a jobbing secretary?"

"That's what I was wondering."

"She asked me what a jobbing secretary was; and I explained as clearly as I could under the circumstances, and considering that I don't know myself. When you reflect on the fact that I have engaged her to be something which I never heard of before you will have grasped the initial difficulty of my position; which is complicated by the further fact that she is, what she certainly is, a divinity among women. If she'd come, say, about twelve and leave before one; or if she'd spend a few hours daily in intellectual conversation with me in here; or if she'd come out with me to enjoy the air, say on the top of an omnibus; or even if she'd go out with you, for a little pedestrian exercise, from two to six; the situation might be lightened. But she'll do none of these things; she's as good as said so. She told me, with a delicious seriousness which took all idea of resistance clean out of me, that she meant to do a man's work for a man's wage. Now, Mr. Gibb, in this office I don't see how it's going to be done."

"I'm sure I don't."

"I don't do a man's work."

"No, sir, you don't."

"You do still less."

On this point Mr. Gibb was discreetly silent; he seemed to be turning something over in his mind, of which he presently gave Mr. Hooper the benefit.

"I think, sir, I've got an idea of something you might give Miss Lindsay to do."

"Let's have it; you know, Mr. Gibb, any pearls of wisdom which you may drop are always welcome."

"You remember, sir, when I first came you gave me some papers which you said I might copy when I'd nothing else to do."

"I have some dim recollection of something of the kind. Well, have they been copied?"

"No, sir, they haven't."

"How long have you had them?"

"Oh, rather more than two years."

"Then it's time they were copied. What papers are they?"

"I never could make out, and I don't think you could either; they're counsels' opinions, or judges' rulings, or something like that. I know when I asked you what they were you told me not to ask any questions; so I knew you didn't know."

"Mr. Gibb, you have a way of your own of arriving at conclusions. I think I recall those papers; they were here when I came into possession; they'd been stuffed up the chimney to keep out the draught or something."

"I was thinking, sir, if you could think of nothing else, that you might get Miss Lindsay to copy them."

"There's—there's something in the idea. Could we pass them off as genuine?"

"As how, sir?"

"Are they of an appearance, and character, which would enable us to induce Miss Lindsay to believe that they really are papers of importance?"

"I should think so, sir; I know it took me ever so long before I found them out."

"Ah; then it might take her a week. By that time we may have hit upon something else. Where are those papers?"

"They're in my desk."

"Then get them out of your desk. Have them cleaned, tidied, made presentable; Miss Lindsay shall commence on them as soon as she arrives. And I tell you something else I'll do. Miss Lindsay tells me she can work a typewriter."

"Can she?"

"I'll get her one. I think I should prefer to have good, clear typewritten copies of those papers, Mr. Gibb; they'll be so much more accessible for reference. I—I suppose a typewriter can be hired."

"Oh yes, sir; I believe from about half-a-crown a week."

"That doesn't seem to be a prohibitive figure; I'll hire one; I'll go out this afternoon to see about it. You see, Mr. Gibb, how one thing leads to another. I propose to increase my staff; the mere proposition adds materially to my own labours. I know no more about typewriters than I do about sewing-machines; of which I know nothing; so I foresee that my afternoon will be fully occupied. By the way, Mr. Gibb, a further point; you have found an idea which has been of assistance in one direction, perhaps you might find a second which would be of some service to me in another."

"What is it, sir?"

"As you put it to me, I take it that you will allow it to go no further; but, between ourselves, I have undertaken to pay Miss Lindsay, as jobbing secretary, since she proposes to do a man's work for a man's wage, an honorarium of two guineas a week."

"So she told me, sir."

"So she told you, did she? Oh! Then I suppose she expects to get it."

"I expect she does, sir."

"Then in that case I think that, perhaps, I had better make it perfectly clear to you how, precisely, the land lies." From a drawer which he unlocked in his writing-table Mr. Hooper took three sovereigns and some silver; he displayed the coins to the best advantage on the table. "This choice, but small, collection of bullion has to last me, Mr. Gibb, to quarter day. There are still three clear weeks. I have to pay you thirty shillings; being three weeks' wages at ten shillings a week; out of the balance I have to pay Miss Lindsay six guineas, and keep myself; besides having to meet certain small liabilities which must be met. I should be glad, Mr. Gibb, if you would give me some idea of how it is to be done."

"I think, sir, if I were you, I should let me explain to Miss Lindsay."

"Explain what, Mr. Gibb?"

"What kind of gentleman you are."

"And pray, in your opinion, what kind of gentleman am I?"

"Well, considering how you've gone and done it with Miss Lindsay I shouldn't think you'd want much explaining, sir."

"That's true, Mr. Gibb, most true. Still, I'm curious to hear what you'd tell her."

"I wouldn't give you away, sir."

"Wouldn't you? Oh! What would you do?"

"I should simply tell her, sir, that you'd been thinking things over, and that you'd come to the conclusion that two guineas a week was too much to pay her at the start; and that you thought—should I say fifteen shillings ought to be enough at the beginning, sir?"

"Fifteen shillings! And I promised her two guineas!"

"Yes, sir, you promised her."

"What kind of a person do you suppose she'd think I am?"

"I don't see how it matters, sir."

"You don't see how it matters!"

"Well, sir, you can't pay her two guineas a week, no matter what she thinks of you; and you might manage to pay her fifteen shillings—somehow. I expect you'd find she'd sooner have fifteen shillings in cash than two guineas in promises."

"Mr. Gibb, you appear to have a high opinion of me."

"I have, sir; I couldn't have a higher."

"Couldn't you? you young scoundrel! Pray when did I make a promise to you which I didn't keep, to the letter?"

"When I came, sir, you gave me six shillings a week, now you give me ten; but there's a difference between ten shillings and two guineas."

"Yes, Mr. Gibb, and there's a difference between you and Miss Lindsay."

"Don't I know it, sir? There's all the difference in the world."

"As you say, there's all the difference in the world. Miss Lindsay is a divinity among women."

"That's exactly my opinion, sir; and has been from the first."

"It has been your opinion, has it, Mr. Gibb? Then allow me to inform you that when I enter into an undertaking with—with a divinity among women, to do a certain thing, I do that thing. I have undertaken to pay Miss Lindsay two guineas a week; I will pay her two guineas a week. The money shall be found; I will find it. Be so good, Mr. Gibb, as to look up those papers you spoke about, and see that they are in a presentable condition, so that Miss Lindsay can begin on them directly she arrives."

CHAPTER XXIII

A JOBBING SECRETARY

The next morning Nora did not start for Fountain Court with Mr. Gibb; he positively forbade her, explaining that he had certain duties to perform immediately on his arrival which he preferred, and which Mr. Hooper preferred, that he should perform before anybody else appeared upon the scene; so he started at half-past nine, and she followed thirty minutes later. When she reached Fountain Court the door was promptly opened by Mr. Gibb, who called her attention to a curtained recess, with the remark—

"Please hang your hat and coat up there."

Behind the curtain she found three pegs and a looking-glass; which articles, if she had not been too nervous to observe closely, might have struck her as being even suspiciously new. She had no coat on, but she had a hat, which she hung upon one of the pegs, with a breathless feeling, as if the simple action, in that strange place, stood to her as an emblem of the passage she was about to take from the old world to the new; as she hung up her hat, with Mr. Gibb's stony gaze fixed on her coldly from behind, it almost seemed to her that with it she hung up her freedom, and passed into servitude. Nor was this feeling lessened by the unaccustomed, and unnatural, rigidity of Mr. Gibb's bearing; she being unaware of the fact that Mr. Hooper had informed the young gentleman, not ten minutes before she came, that if he did not treat her with the profound and distant respect with which a divinity ought to be treated, the consequences would be serious for him. While she was still touching her hair with her fingers, as a girl must do when she has just taken her hat off, he inquired, with what he felt to be cutting coldness—

"Have you quite finished?"

"Yes, Eustace, I—I think I have—quite, thank you."

"Then Mr. Hooper is waiting to see you; kindly step this way."

She stepped that way, Mr. Gibb moving as stiffly as if he had a poker down his back. She found Mr. Hooper seated at a table which was littered with a number of papers and documents which were of a most portentous looking nature, over one of which he was bending with an air of earnest preoccupation which, it is to be feared, had been put on about thirty seconds before she had entered the room, and would be taken off in less than thirty seconds after she had left it.

"Miss Lindsay has come, sir." As Mr. Gibb made this announcement Mr. Hooper looked up with a start, which was very well done, as if nothing could have surprised him more; he rose, a little doubtfully, as if the professional cares of this world were almost more than he could bear.

"Miss Lindsay? Yes, yes, quite so; Miss Lindsay, of course. I hope, Miss Lindsay, I see you well."

"Quite well, thank you."

She ignored the hand which he extended, possibly in a moment of absence of mind, in a manner which seemed to him to be marked; he trusted Mr. Gibb had not noticed it before he left the room. He continued to be as professional in his manner as he knew how.

"Miss Lindsay—eh—might I—eh—ask you to take a seat?"

"Thank you, sir, I prefer to stand."

Really this young woman was trying; she was reversing the positions; it was she who was keeping him at a distance, not he her; there was something in the way in which she said "sir" which made him wince; however, he was still professional.

"Quite so, Miss Lindsay, quite so—whichever you prefer. Now, Miss Lindsay, here are some papers of a—of an abstract nature; privacy with regard to them is of the first importance; serious consequences might result were their character to become known outside these chambers." The jobbing secretary inclined her head; he thought she did it very gracefully. "Now, what I require are copies of these papers; you understand, copies—perfectly clean copies. How long do you think it will take you to let me have them?"

"There seem to be a good many."

"There are—oh, there are; quite a number; only they are not all of the same character. Now, for instance, how long will it take you to let me have a perfectly clean copy of that?"

He held out what looked like a musty document, consisting of several foolscap pages, covered with close writing on both sides of each page. She turned it nervously over.

"Is it—is it to be typed?"

"Certainly; oh yes, emphatically."

"What—what machine have you?" He mentioned the maker's name; fortunately it was on one of the same maker's machines she had learnt. "I told you that I had not used a machine recently; I fear, therefore, that I may be rather awkward at first, so that I can hardly tell how long it will take me to let you have a perfectly clean copy of this. There—there appears to be a good deal of it."

"There does—oh yes, I admit it, there does—and of course I shouldn't want an absolutely clean copy." She looked at him; there was something in her look which caused him to look away, with some appearance of confusion; he realized that he had made a mistake. "By that I—I should wish you to understand that—that I shouldn't require you to destroy the entire document merely—merely because of one slight error."

She spoke with what seemed to him to be magisterial severity; he felt that there was more than a touch of that severity in her demeanour.

"You said that you wanted perfectly clean copies, and you shall have perfectly clean copies; I quite understand that only perfectly clean copies will be of the slightest use. I hope you do not think that I wish you to put up with indifferent work. I merely wished to point out that I am afraid that I may be a little clumsy at first."

She turned to go.

"The—the typewriter's in the next room."

"I saw it as I came in."

"Pray—pray allow me to open the door for you." But she would not.

"If you don't mind, sir"—the stress upon that "sir"!—"I would rather open it for myself; and I do hope that you won't allow a difference in sex to alter the relations which ought to exist between employer and employed. You wouldn't open the door for Eustace Gibb; I would like you to regard me in the same light as you do him."

No, he certainly would not open the door for Eustace Gibb, but the idea of regarding her in the same light as Mr. Gibb was preposterous; the trouble was that he could only see her through a golden haze. The typewriter was in the next room to Mr. Hooper's, with beyond it the lobby which Mr. Gibb termed his office; the room was known to Mr. Gibb as the waiting-room, though no one had ever been known to wait in it. It was furnished with an old wooden table, and three older wooden chairs, and nothing else. On the table was the typewriter, and a plentiful supply of paper. After about an hour's interval, Mr. Hooper, who felt as if he were a prisoner in his own rooms, began to find himself in a state of fidgetiness which was beyond endurance. It was ridiculous to suppose that he did not dare to venture into the presence of his own jobbing secretary, yet—he did not dare. What was worse, he found himself incapable of smoking in the room next to her, and that in spite of her expressed desire that he should treat her as he treated Mr. Gibb. When the tension had reached a point at which he could stand it no longer, snatching up his hat, he burst into the room with an air of haste, seeming, when he was in it, to realize her presence there with a touch of surprise.

"Miss Lindsay!—oh yes, yes, quite so. And—and how are we getting on?"

The moment he had asked he saw that he had made another mistake. This time there was something on her face which moved him in a manner which really did surprise him. She looked as if she had at least been near to tears, and still was not far off.

"I—I'm not getting on at all well," she said.

"I've not the slightest doubt, Miss Lindsay, that you are getting on much better than you imagine."

"I—I suppose I ought to know how I am getting on."

"But your—yours is such a strenuously high standard."

"I—I've spoilt I don't know how many sheets of paper."

"What does it matter how many sheets of paper you spoil? The more you spoil the better I'll be pleased."

"Will you? Then all I can say is that if I—I spoil many more I shall know that I'm not fit for the situation which you've been so kind as to offer me, and—I shall go."

"Really you must not talk like that." He picked up one of the ominously numerous sheets of paper which lay at her side, all of which had plainly had at any rate some slight acquaintance with the machine. "Now this is not at all bad."

"There are three errors in the first line."

"Are there? So many as that?"

"And five in the second."

"Indeed! you don't say so!"

"And the third line's wrong altogether."

"That only shows that with a little practice you'll regain all your old facility."

"I'm not sure that I ever had any facility; I can see that now; I'm afraid I only used to play at typing."

"Then in that case you shall copy them by hand; I'm disposed to think that perhaps good clear writing is best after all."

"Copy them by hand?" Suddenly a look came on her face which actually frightened him; his words had evidently been to her an occasion of serious offence. "I applied for your situation, Mr. Hooper, in the belief that I could work a typewriter; you gave it me on that understanding. If, now, it turns out that I cannot work a typewriter it would look as if I had applied for your situation under false pretences; do you suppose that I will continue to hold it knowing that to be the case, and that you are paying me for something which it turns out I cannot do? Either you shall have perfectly clean typewritten copies, Mr. Hooper, or I must resign; I will not go through the farce of pretending to occupy a position for which I have been proved to be unfit."

He could have answered her many things, but he answered her nothing; he was afraid. Instead, he shuffled out of the room, excusing himself.

"I've a most pressing appointment, Miss Lindsay." He was longing for a pipe; the appointment was to smoke, all by himself, in the Temple Gardens. "When I return I've no doubt you'll have advanced beyond your expectations. Rome wasn't built in a day; you must persevere, persevere!" In the office Mr. Hooper, placing his hand on King Solomon's shoulder, whispered in his ear, as if anxious not to be overheard, "Mr. Gibb, I am inclined to the opinion that having a divinity on the premises is not all lavender."

To which Mr. Gibb replied, with a sigh, as if he himself was vaguely conscious of a feeling of being "cribbed, cabined and confined"—

"No, sir; that's what I was thinking."

For two days Nora continued to wrestle with the typewriter, and on the third something happened which ultimately resulted in another upheaval of the world for her. She had found the "document" which she had to copy—it was one of those which Mr. Hooper had discovered stuffed up the chimney—not easy to decipher, which perhaps was not surprising; she was puzzling over a part of it which seemed even worse than usual when the office door was opened, and a masculine person came striding in who had not even troubled to remove his hat. At sight, however, of the girl poring over that refractory passage, with her pretty brows all creased, off came his hat; but no sooner was he uncovered than, with something in his bearing which almost suggested that he was unconscious of what he was doing, he stood and stared. The girl glanced up and looked at him. For some seconds there was silence; then, seeming to come to himself with a start, he ejaculated—.

"I beg your pardon; I—I'd no idea!"

He did not stay to explain what he had no idea of, but passed into Mr. Hooper's room beyond. As he entered Mr. Hooper rose from his chair; then stared in his turn, as if this was not at all the kind of person he had expected to see.

"Frank!" he exclaimed. "What on earth has brought you here?"

The gentleman addressed as Frank replied to the question with a statement which was sufficiently startling.

"Jack, I've seen a ghost!"

Mr. Hooper, as was not unnatural, stared still more.

"You've seen what?"

"Of course I don't mean that I've seen an actual ghost, but I feel as if I had."

"What's given you such a very curious feeling at this hour of the morning? And what's brought you here, anyhow?"

The gentleman addressed seemed genuinely disturbed.

"I'll tell you, what's brought me if you'll give me time; I'm in a frightful mess, that's what's brought me; but before I tell you anything, you tell me who—who's that girl in the next room?"

Mr. Hooper's bearing betrayed annoyance, which was perhaps caused by the singularity of the other's demeanour.

"The lady in the next room, whom you speak of as 'that girl,' is—"

There was a tapping; the door was opened; the girl in question entered, the "document" over which she had been puzzling in her hand. She crossed to Mr. Hooper.

"I beg your pardon if I am interrupting you, but there is something here which I cannot make out; I thought that perhaps you would not mind telling me what it is before you become really engaged."

Mr. Hooper took the paper which she held out to him, with a glance towards the gentleman who had just now entered, in which there was a hint of mischief.

"Will you allow me to present to you my cousin, Mr. Frank Clifford? Frank, this is Miss Lindsay."

"Lindsay!" Mr. Clifford was staring more than ever. "Lindsay! Not—not—I beg your pardon, but—would you mind telling me if you are related to Mr. Donald Lindsay of Cloverlea?"

"I am his daughter."

"His—daughter? Thank you; thank you."

He sank on to a chair as one who had been dealt a crushing blow. Nora's bearing was frigid; the stranger's unexpected question had touched in her a chord of memory which hurt her more than she would have cared to say. She returned to Mr. Hooper.

"Can you tell me what that sentence is? One or two of the words seem quite illegible."

He explained, to the best of his ability, which was not much greater than hers. When she had gone back to her own apartment, Mr. Hooper said to his visitor, with what was possibly meant to be an air of politeness—

"May I venture to inquire if that is how you generally behave when you're introduced to a lady, Frank? because if it is I shall know better than to attempt to introduce you to another."

Mr. Clifford's reply was remarkable.

"I told you that when I first saw her I felt as if I had seen a ghost; now I know my instinct was right; I have seen a ghost. If you knew—what I know, and had had to go through what I've had to go through, and still have to go through, you would understand how meeting Donald Lindsay's daughter like this makes it seem to me as if the hand of God had been stretched out of the skies."

CHAPTER XXIV

MR. MORGAN'S EXPERIENCES OF THE UNEXPECTED

It was a shock to Mr. Morgan when he learnt that Miss Harding had quitted Cloverlea without a word to him. At first he could not believe that she had gone; that she could have gone without his knowledge. When belief was forced on him his language was unbecoming. While he was engaged in little matters of a sort which demanded privacy, and which had to do with the safe storage of certain articles which he had brought himself to believe were his own property, a wagonette arrived at the front door, which, the driver explained to the footman who appeared, had come to fetch Miss Harding. The footman, with the aid of a colleague, had borne the young lady's belongings down the stairs; for which she liberally recompensed them with a sovereign apiece; and she and her possessions were safely away before Mr. Morgan had a notion she was going. Mr. Morgan abused the footmen for not having said a word to him; which abuse they, having no longer the fear of him before their eyes, returned in kind. The butler had to console himself as best he could.

"Given me the slip, have you, Miss Harding?" That was what he said to himself. "Very well, my dear, we'll see; I'm not so easily got rid of as you may perhaps suppose. You're a pretty darling, upon my Sam you are!"

As soon as circumstances permitted—at Cloverlea there were a great many things which he thought it desirable that he should do that day—he went out on a little voyage of discovery. He learnt at the local station that Miss Harding had not taken a ticket for her home in the west country; she had not taken a ticket for herself at all, Mr. Nash had taken one for her, and another for himself; they had gone up to London in the same compartment, and both had luggage. This news added to Mr. Morgan's pleasure.

"Dear me, has she? And I meant her to be Mrs. Morgan, and so she would have been if I'd put on the screw when I'd the chance. As my wife she might have come to something; but as his wife—I'll show her, and I'll show him. If she thinks she's going to hand over to him, by way of a dowry, that nice little lot of money, and leave me out; if that really is her expectation she'll be treated to another illustration of the vanity of human wishes. That sweet young wife will have an interrupted honeymoon."

Mr. Morgan called at an inn which it was his habit to honour with his custom in quest of something to soothe his ruffled feelings. There he met a friend, George Wickham, the Holtye head groom. Mr. Wickham had a grievance, in which respect, if he had only known it, he resembled Mr. Morgan. It seemed that he was the bearer of letters which had been addressed to the Hon. Robert Spencer at Holtye, which he was carrying to that gentleman's actual present address, the Unicorn Hotel, Baltash. It was supposed to be Mr. Wickham's "night out"; he wanted to spend his hours of freedom in one direction while Baltash lay in another.

"Might as well have sent 'em by post, or by one of the other chaps; but no, nothing would please the old woman"—by "old woman" it is to be feared that he meant the Countess of Mountdennis—"but that I should go. I had half a mind to tell her I'd an appointment."

Mr. Morgan was sympathetic; he explained that he was going to Baltash, and even carried his sympathy so far as to offer to take the letters for him. The groom hesitated; then decided to take advantage of his friend's good-nature.

"There's thirteen letters," he pointed out, "five post-cards, four newspapers, eighteen circulars, and these parcels, about enough to fill a carrier's cart."

Mr. Morgan laughed.

"I shall make nothing of that little lot," he said. "And I'll charge nothing for carriage."

On the way to Baltash he leaned against a gate to light a cigar; it was one of his peculiarities to smoke nothing but cigars; he held that a pipe was low. When the cigar was lighted he remained a moment to glance at the letters he was carrying. He noticed that one of them was from the London offices of a steamship company; the name of the company was printed on the envelope. While Miss Lindsay had been talking to Mr. Spencer in the copse on the preceding Sunday morning Mr. Morgan had been quite close at hand; the lady had supposed that the noise he made among the undergrowth was caused by a hare or a rabbit; had Mr. Spencer proceeded to investigate the cause of the noise the butler would have been discovered in a somewhat ignominious position. As it was Mr. Morgan, remaining undetected, heard a good deal that was said; among the things he heard Mr. Spencer's story of the letter which Donald Lindsay had sent to him at Cairo, which was only to be opened after the writer's death, which Mr. Spencer had put in his suit-case, and which suit-case Mr. Spencer had lost, containing not only Mr. Lindsay's letters, but also some more intimate epistles from that gentleman's daughter.

Mr. Morgan remembered the story very well; he had a knack of remembering nearly everything he heard, and he managed to hear a good deal. He was struck by the fact that the letter which he held in his hand was from the steamship company by one of whose boats Mr. Spencer had travelled on his homeward journey; it might contain news of the missing suit-case. On the other hand, emphatically, it might not. Still! It is notorious how carelessly some envelopes are fastened. Here was a case in point; the gummed flap only adhered in one place, and there so slightly that Mr. Morgan had only to slip the blade of a penknife underneath and—it came open. It was as he had guessed. The steamship company wrote to say that the missing suit-case had turned up. It had strayed among the voluminous luggage of an American family, where it remained unnoticed until the luggage had been divided up among the members of the family; the explanation seemed rather lame, but it appeared it was the only one that steamship company had to offer. Now the suit-case was at Mr. Spencer's disposition, and the company would be glad to hear what he wished them to do with it.

As Mr. Morgan enjoyed his cigar, and leaned against the gate, and looked up at the glories of the evening sky, he indulged in some philosophical reflections.

"It's an extraordinary world; extraordinary. To think that George Wickham's burning desire to see that red-headed girl of his at Addlecombe should have thrown a thing like this right into my hands. It's quite possible that that suit-case may turn out to be worth more to me than that nice little sum of money with which Miss Elaine Harding erroneously supposes she's going to set her husband up in life. Beyond a shadow of doubt things are managed in a mysterious way."

Mr. Morgan faithfully delivered those letters at the Unicorn Hotel at Baltash, with the exception of one letter; and on the morrow he treated himself to a trip up to town. He took a bedroom at a quiet hotel in the neighbourhood of the Strand, and he sent a messenger boy to the steamship company's office with an envelope. In the envelope was the Hon. Robert Spencer's visiting card; on the back of which was written—

"Your letter duly received; please give suit-case to bearer."

Some one at the office gave it to the bearer; who took it to the hotel, where it was sent up to Mr. Spencer's room; it happened that Mr. Morgan had registered as Robert Spencer. Mr. Morgan opened it with difficulty; none of his keys fitted the lock, which was of a curious make; but he did open it; he was an ingenious man. And when he had opened the suit-case he found that the letter, for whose sake he had taken so much trouble, was not in it. It was a painful shock; he was loth to believe that a man of the

Hon. Robert Spencer's character could have played him such a trick; to say nothing of the deceit which, in that case, he must have practised on Miss Lindsay. He turned the contents of the case over and over, subjecting each article to a close examination. No, there was nothing there which in any way resembled the letter which he had heard Mr. Spencer describe. What was almost worse, as showing the lover's utter unreliability, there were none of Miss Lindsay's letters either. Mr. Morgan had distinctly heard Mr. Spencer tell Miss Lindsay that in his missing suitcase were not only her father's unopened letter, but also some letters of hers. What confidence could be placed in the man who, at such a sacred moment, made such a gross mis-statement to the woman whom he professed to love? It was dreadful; Mr. Morgan was pained beyond measure. In the future he would never be able to believe anything he overheard; even though his ear was glued to the keyhole. He was a dispirited man.

He did not return at once to Cloverlea. As a matter of fact he had brought with him to town a number of packages of various shapes and sizes. He had some trouble in removing them from Cloverlea; but he had removed them, having dared Mr. Guldenheim and his friends and minions to do anything to try to stop him. He devoted a few days to the bestowal of these trophies in a safe place. When he did return to Cloverlea he put up at the village inn, whence he kept an eye on the doings of the neighbourhood. Having succeeded in screwing out of Mr. Guldenheim more than was due to him for wages, and in lieu of notice, he attended the sale with melancholy feelings, going so far as to purchase some lots for which he felt a sentimental interest, and which he had reasons for knowing were going for much less than they were worth.

It was only after the sale that he ascertained what he thought was likely to be Miss Harding's present address. He had made regular, and persistent, inquiries at Mr. Nash's office; but nothing had been heard of that promising solicitor by his staff, which consisted of a weedy youth of seventeen summers, with whom Mr. Morgan was on terms of the closest intimacy; until there came one morning a curtly worded request to forward any letters which might be awaiting him to Mr. Nash at an address which he gave. Mr. Morgan saw that address; a couple of days after he called there.

The address was at that charming south-coast seaside resort, Littlehampton, 27, Ocean Villas. Ocean Villas proved to be some quite picturesque cottages fronting both the common and the sea; 27 was, perhaps, the most picturesque of them all. The front door was open in the confiding way one finds at seaside resorts, and which saves the trouble of having to open it; Mr. Morgan, entering, rapped on the floor with his stick. A diminutive maid instantly appeared who, without waiting for him to state his business, instantly broke into breathless speech.

"If you've come after the rooms, sir, if you please Mrs. Lorrimer's not in, but if you'll wait half-a-minute I'll fetch her."

Mr. Morgan explained that he had not come after the rooms; he asked if Mrs. Nash was in.

"Mrs. Nash is out, sir, along with Mr. Nash; I did hear them say they were going to Arundel."

"I'll wait till they return; which are their apartments?"

"This is their sitting-room, sir."

She opened the door of what, for a lodging-house, was quite a pleasant room. Mr. Morgan entered; the maid went; the moment he was alone Mr. Morgan did what he always did do when he found himself alone in a strange apartment, he treated everything it contained to a rigorous inspection, and was still engaged in doing so when the diminutive maid reappeared.

"If you please, sir, I'm going out to do some errands, and if there's anything you want would you mind letting me know before I go; though I really shan't hardly be five minutes before I'm back again."

On the visitor assuring her that he was not likely to require her services during the next five minutes she departed to do those errands; scarcely was her back turned than Mr. Morgan started on what might have been a tour of curiosity through the house. He got no further, however, than the room behind the sitting-room, which proved to be a bedroom; unmistakably the sleeping apartment of Mr. and Mrs. Nash. Against the window stood a large trunk, a lady's; Mr. Morgan tried it; it was locked. He surmised as he eyed it.

"What's the betting that in there isn't that nice little sum of money? I wonder if she's told her loving husband that she's got it, and where it is; if she has I wonder how much he's left her. It might be worth my while to look and see; but I think I can manage to get all I want without what would look to the ignorant eye like dabbling in felony. What's that?" "That" was something which lay on the floor just underneath the bed; something which resembled a letter-case. He picked it up. "I rather fancy that this is the property of my friend Nash. Looks as if it had fallen out of his pocket while he was putting on his coat, and that he hadn't noticed it had fallen; extraordinary how careless some people are about things of that kind. It is a letter-case; let's hope there's nothing in it which he would not like to meet the public eye. What have we here? Papers which, apparently, are of value only to the owner. What's in this?" In one of the compartments of the case was a single paper. Mr. Morgan took it out, unfolded it, read it, not once only, but twice, and again a third time. The contents of the paper seemed to puzzle him; he stared at it hard, rubbing his forehead as he did so, as if he hoped by the mere force of vision to get at its meaning. Then he smiled, as if suddenly a light had dawned on him. "So that's it, is it? To think of his leaving a thing like this lying about on the floor! What a foolish man! I never had a high opinion of Herbert Nash; but that he should leave a thing like this for any one to find, and borrow; dear, dear! I never should have thought it. Let's replace these papers which are of no value to any one but the owner. And the case we'll put upon the mantelpiece; so that he'll see it directly he returns, when he'll understand the risk he's run." The letter-case which he had picked up from the floor he put on the mantelpiece, in plain sight; but the paper which he had taken from it he slipped into a case of his own; and that case he placed in his own pocket. When the diminutive maid returned with a basket full of parcels, she found him lounging on the doorstep. His manner to her was affable; as it nearly always was to every one. "You've been rather more than five minutes, haven't you?"

"Yes, sir, I'm afraid I have; but they kept me at the grocer's."

"Did they? Ah! I don't think I shall wait for my friends to return." He grinned as he said "friends." "Tell them that Mr. Morgan called; Mr. Stephen Morgan, of Cloverlea. Do you understand?"

"Yes, sir; Mr. Stephen Morgan, of Cloverlea."

"Exactly. And you can also tell them that I shall call again; I can't say quite when, but I certainly shall call again before they leave Littlehampton. You understand that also?"

"Yes, sir; you'll call again; you can't say quite when, but certainly before they leave Littlehampton."

"That's it; you have it just right. Mind you give them the messages as I gave them you; and here's a shilling for your trouble."

He presented her with a shilling; and left the maid all smiles.

CHAPTER XXV

ON THEIR HONEYMOON

Mr. and Mrs. Nash had been spending the afternoon in Arundel Park. When they returned to their rooms at Littlehampton they were met by the diminutive maid with a message.

"If you please, Mr. Stephen Morgan of Cloverlea called."

"Mr.— who?" asked Mr. Nash. Mrs. Nash changed colour. The maid repeated the visitor's name. "She must mean Morgan the butler; what does he mean by coming here?"

"I—I can't think."

She was conscious of that sudden sickness which she had experienced once before; all at once the room seemed to be whirling round and round. The maid went on.

"He said he'd call again; he couldn't say quite when, but he'd certainly call again before you left Littlehampton."

"Like his impudence! What on earth can the fellow mean? By the way, Louisa, have you seen a letter-case of mine lying about?"

"No, sir, that I haven't."

Mr. Nash went into the next room, hurriedly. So soon as he was through the door he saw the letter-case upon the mantelpiece, where Mr. Morgan had left it. The sight of it seemed to surprise him.

"Who put it there? I'll swear I didn't. Louisa, have you been in here since I went out?"

"No, sir; not once."

"Has Mrs. Lorrimer?"

"I don't think so, sir; she's been out; she only come in just before you did."

He was searching the letter-case, turning it literally inside out. Suddenly he went to the door.

"Louisa, come here!" Louisa came. He spoke to her in lowered tones, as if he did not wish what he said to be heard in the next room, where his wife still was. "Who was in when Mr. Morgan came?"

"If you please, sir, I was; Mrs. Lorrimer, she was out."

"Where you in all the time that he was here?"

"No, sir; I had to go out and do some errands."

"And was he alone in the house while you were gone?"

"Yes, sir; he was outside the front door when I came back; it was then he gave me the message about his calling again."

So surprising a look came on Mr. Nash's face that the girl shrunk back, almost as if she had been afraid that he would strike her. He went back into the bedroom, shutting the door with a bang. He stood glaring about him, as if beside himself with rage. Then, with an effort, he steadied himself. Again he turned the letter-case inside out, going carefully through the papers it contained. Then he searched the room so methodically that even a pin could hardly have escaped his notice, moving every article it contained, his wife's trunks, his own boxes, even turning down the bedclothes and looking under the pillows, going down on his knees to peer under the bed. When all his hunting came to nothing he leaned his elbows on the mantelpiece and shut his eyes, as if suffering physical pain.

In the next room his wife was fighting a fight of her own. So soon as he left her she dropped on to a chair, as if her legs refused her support. A curious change had come over her face, and her lips were twitching; she looked furtively about her, as if she was afraid of she knew not what. When she heard the bedroom door banged, and she knew that her husband had dismissed the maid, she called, "Louisa," softly; so softly that one wondered if she wished to be heard.

But Louisa did hear, appearing with a startled visage in the doorway.

"Who—who did Mr. Morgan ask for?"

The question was put so softly that it was nearly whispered; the speaker's tongue and lips seemed parched.

"Please, ma'am, he asked for you."

"For me? What—what did he say?"

"Please, ma'am, he said 'Is Mrs. Nash in?'"

"Mrs. Nash? You're sure he said Mrs. Nash?"

"Yes, ma'am, quite sure."

"And when you told him I wasn't in, did he ask for Mr. Nash?"

"No, ma'am; he said he'd wait."

"How—how long did he wait?"

"Maybe twenty minutes, maybe half-an-hour; please, ma'am, I couldn't say exactly."

"And did he seem angry?"

"No, ma'am; quite pleasant. He gave me a shilling as he was going."

"A shilling! Oh! Now tell me, exactly, what was the message he left."

"If you please, ma'am, he told me to tell you exactly what he said, so I took particular notice." She repeated word for word what Mr. Morgan had said; Mrs. Nash listening with singular intentness, as if her attention was fixed not so much on the actual words as on what was behind them. When the girl had finished she sat still, as if pondering. Louisa roused her. "If you please, ma'am, can I lay for supper?"

Mrs. Nash rose with a little jump.

"Supper! of course; how silly I am! I was quite forgetting about supper. Certainly, Louisa, you can lay for supper; I—I think I'm quite ready for it." When she went into the bedroom her husband was still standing with his elbows on the mantelpiece and his face to the wall. As she entered he looked round with a start; the pair stood looking at each other as if each was taken aback by something which was on the other's face. She spoke first, in a voice which seemed to tremble. "Herbert, what—what's the matter?"

"The matter?" He laughed, a forced laugh. "Nothing's the matter; why do you ask what's the matter?"

"You're—you're looking so strange."

"That's your imagination, my dear. What is the matter is that I've got a touch of headache—one of my mother's headaches; you remember what I've told you about the headaches she used to have. I fancy the sun was stronger than I thought."

"I didn't notice it; you said nothing about it."

"No; I didn't notice it at the time. I expect that what I want is my supper; it'll be better after I've had something to eat."

"Have you found your letter-case?"

"Oh yes, yes; I've found my letter-case; I must have dropped it out of my pocket as I was putting on my coat—very stupid of me; but I've found it all right. Anyhow there wasn't anything in it of very great consequence, so it wouldn't have mattered much if I hadn't."

It was a curious meal, that supper of theirs. It was as if ghosts sat with them at the table; phantoms of horror; one by his side, and one at hers, whose presence each hoped was hidden from the other. Conversation languished, and they were in general so talkative; the efforts they made to disguise their incapacity for speech were pathetic. Their appetites were as poor as their talking powers, and that although each had professed to be ready to make an excellent meal. He ate little, and what he did eat was with an obvious effort; she ate still less, each mouthful seemed to choke her. When the make-believe repast was at an end Mr. Nash got up.

"I'm afraid my headache isn't much better; I think I'll go for a turn on the front; the night air may do it good."

She also rose.

"It won't take me a minute to put on my hat; I'll come with you."

He was not so pleased at her suggestion as he might have been.

"I think, if you don't mind, I'll go alone; I don't feel as if I were in a mood for company."

She seemed hurt.

"Oh, Herbert, don't leave me behind! I won't keep you waiting; I'll come without my hat."

But he still professed unwillingness for her society, speaking almost roughly.

"Don't I tell you I'd sooner go alone? Can't you take a hint?"

It was the first time he had spoken to her like that since they had been married, which was not so very long ago. Had he struck her he could not have hurt her more. When he had gone, without another word, or a kiss, or a sign of tenderness, she sat staring at the nearly untouched meal, and shivered, although the night was warm. What had happened to Herbert, to have produced such a change in his manner? Could Morgan have left a note for him, or a message for his own private ear; or dropped a hint; or communicated with him without her knowledge? As Louisa cleared away the supper things she cross-examined her. The girl told all that she had to tell again; Elaine could find nothing in her story which would account for the singularity of her husband's demeanour; but on one point she fastened, when the maid told her that she had left the visitor in the house alone.

With Mr. Morgan in sole possession of the premises, Elaine saw instant possibilities. What might he not have been doing while Louisa was out? He might—he certainly might have intruded himself in her bedroom; if he had gone so far he might have gone much farther. At the thought of what he might have done she felt inclined to shake Louisa for giving him the chance of doing it; instead, however, of assaulting the maid she hurried off to learn, if she could, what he had done.

Apparently nothing. So far as she could perceive everything in the bedroom remained untouched, just as she had left it. She opened her trunk, and took out her dressing-case, to make sure; she kept her dressing-case in her locked trunk for greater security. Herbert laughed at her for her caution, but she did not mind; she knew its secret, he did not. After all it was perhaps as well he had left her behind; she never had a chance of peeping at her hidden hoard while he was there. Morgan had not touched that; that was safe enough. She examined it with feverish fingers, fearful every moment of her husband's return. The tale of the money was correct; nothing was missing there.

When she had done counting she hesitated, and thought, a big bundle of notes in her hand. She slipped some of them into the bosom of her dress—notes for a hundred pounds. Now that Morgan had thrust himself again upon the scene they might be wanted; anything might happen; she might not be able to get at her store at a moment's notice, with Herbert always hovering round. She was just as anxious to keep the secret of her hiding-place from her husband as from Morgan, or from any one.

She had not long returned the dressing-case to the trunk, and locked the trunk, and placed the notes representing a hundred pounds in a more convenient spot than her bodice, when her husband returned. As he came bustling into the bedroom she perceived at once that his mood had changed. He put his hands on her shoulders and kissed her, rather boisterously; his breath told her he had been drinking.

"Hello, old girl! that headache's better; the stroll has done it good."

She wondered if it was the stroll or the refreshment he had taken; she had already discovered that stimulants made of him another man; even after one bottle of ale he was not the same man he had been before. Her cue was to ignore the part which alcohol might have played in affecting a cure.

"I am so glad you're better, dear; I know what it is to have a headache; I believe I've got one. Please mayn't I go out on to the common now?"

He laughed at her, lifting her off her feet.

"I'll carry you," he said.

And he did; out of the house, across the road, not putting her down till he had borne her on to the grass; then, running the risk of what eyes there might be about to see, she gave him a kiss to pay for porterage. Presently they were, outwardly, on proper honeymooning terms again, each making a gallant, and not wholly unsuccessful, effort to shut out from actual vision the ghosts which kept step at their sides. When they had retired to rest Herbert Nash said to his wife—

"Do you know, I think I have had about enough of Littlehampton; what do you say?"

"I say what you say; only the question is, wherever shall we go to? and when?"

"There are heaps of places we can go to; and as for when, we can leave this to-morrow. I'll think it over."

He thought it over; all through the night he lay thinking, with wide-open eyes, and so did she. But they did not leave on the morrow, nor the next day. And on the morning of the third day there came a letter addressed to "Mr. and Mrs. Herbert Nash," which Mr. Nash, being first at the breakfast table, opened. It ran—

"DEAR FRIENDS,

"Mrs. Lorrimer's servant will have told you that I called to see you, and also that I propose to call again. Apart from the pleasure which I anticipate from meeting you once more, I have something of the utmost importance which I wish to say to both of you. As I believe you have no pressing engagements, I confidently hope that you will not leave Littlehampton till I have had an opportunity of saying it. I will let you have a wire, advising you of my coming, and shall be glad if you will leave word at the house where, at any moment, you are to be found, as I should not like to miss you a second time.

"Adding my congratulations to the numerous expressions of goodwill which, I do not doubt, you have already received on the auspicious occasion of your marriage, believe me to be,

"Yours most sincerely,

"STEPHEN MORGAN."

Mr. Nash was reading this epistle a second time when his wife came in.

"What have you got there?" she asked.

He looked up with a frown, seeming to hesitate about what to say, then answered—

"It's from that fellow Morgan; the most insolent, presumptuous scrawl. What he's driving at I can't imagine; the fellow must be stark, staring mad."

If Mr. Nash had been in an observant mood he might have noticed that the smile which had been on his wife's face gave way to quite a different expression, and that she shivered, as she always did do when Mr. Morgan's name was mentioned.

"What does he say? Let me look at his letter."

He was folding it up, as with the intention of consigning it to his pocket unseen by his wife; at her point-blank request he seemed to hesitate, then tossed it to her across the table.

"If you can explain what the fellow means by sending a letter like that I can't; it's beyond me altogether." As she read he commented. "Fancy calling us 'Dear friends.'"

"What an extraordinary thing for him to do."

"A butler!"

"It's quite inexplicable."

"What on earth has he to say to us which is of the least importance?"

"That's it; what can he have?"

"He practically orders us not to leave the place till it pleases him to come."

"It does—it does amount to that, doesn't it?"

"Fancy his telling us to let them know in the house where, at any moment, we're to be found, as if the one thing to be considered was his sovereign pleasure!"

"That is really remarkable."

"Remarkable! I should say so; remarkable is a mild way of putting it. I've half-a-mind to pack directly after breakfast and leave the place this morning; the idea of his attempting to dictate to us! As I say, the only explanation I can think of is that the fellow's stark, staring mad."

"That—that must be it."

Mr. Nash continued to comment on Mr. Morgan's insolent epistle while he trifled with his breakfast; but it was noticeable that he only trifled. If he had had an appetite it had vanished; it seemed as if the man's impertinence must have affected him more than he would have cared to own. It was the same with his wife, she had no appetite either. Indeed, when one came to think of it, neither of them had eaten much since they had first heard of Mr. Morgan's call. The fact had even been noticed by the landlady.

"I can't think what's the matter with them all at once," she declared to her diminutive maid, Louisa. "They used to eat heartily enough; as you know, I remarked on it to you."

"Yes, Mrs. Lorrimer, that you did."

"But these last couple of days they've scarcely touched a thing. There's been nothing the matter with the food, and I'm sure there's been nothing the matter with the cooking; it must be them that's wrong."

When breakfast was finished—such a breakfast as it was; even the soles went out practically as they came in—Mrs. Nash went to put on her hat preparatory to going out with her husband on to the front, as she usually did on fine mornings; he with a newspaper, and she with a book. That morning the process was a lengthy one; she seemed preoccupied, as if her mind was so full that there was no room in it for her hat. She moved restlessly about the room, as if her thoughts kept her in motion. All at once it seemed that she arrived at a sudden resolution.

"I know what I'll do; I'll get Herbert to go; we will go, before he comes; we'll go to-day. I'll talk to Herbert directly we get outside. I believe he wants to go as much as I do; though I—I don't know why. And this time we won't stay in England; we'll go abroad, as far away as ever we can; somewhere where that wretch can't get at us; and—and we'll leave no address behind."

While the lady so resolved the gentleman—unconscious of her resolution—waited for her on the doorstep. As he waited he saw, advancing towards the house on a bicycle, a telegraph boy. Some instinct induced him to leave that doorstep and move to meet him.

"Got a telegram for me—Nash?"

"Nash? Yes, sir." The boy jumped off; he produced the familiar yellow envelope. "Herbert Nash."

"That's for me; that's all right. Wait while I see if there's an answer." He tore the envelope open; this was the message it contained: "Coming by the train due 12.28. You had better meet me at the station alone.—STEPHEN MORGAN." "There is no answer," Mr. Nash informed the boy.

The boy got on his machine and rode away. Mr. Nash read that telegram again, then stuffed it into his jacket pocket, swearing beneath his breath. He looked quite ugly when he swore. He glanced at his watch, as if to make sure about the time, then returned to his place upon the doorstep. He said nothing about the telegram to his wife.

CHAPTER XXVI

AN OFFER OF FRIENDSHIP

Mr. Nash was at the station when the 12.28 came in, and alone; it might have been by some sort of coincidence that he happened to be there just then, but Mr. Morgan seemed to take it for granted that he had come to meet him, an inference which Mr. Nash apparently resented. Mr. Morgan came up to him smiling in the most friendly fashion, and with hand held out.

"My dear Nash, how are you?"

There was no smile on Mr. Nash's face, and he ignored the proffered hand.

"Thank you, Mr. Morgan, I am well."

"And my good friend, your dear wife? blooming, eh?"

"I'm not aware that Mrs. Nash ever was a friend of yours."

"No! my dear fellow! when we were so often under the same roof together."

"Do the servants of a house always regard their master's friends as their own?"

"My dear Nash, if you hadn't said that I should have said it was meant to be nasty. I was in the service of the head of the house, and your wife was a sort of attendant of the daughter's.

"Do you dare to say that my wife was ever Miss Lindsay's attendant?"

"Unpaid attendant, my boy, unpaid; sort of hanger-on—poor companion. I received a regular income; she got an occasional frock; some article of clothing; now and then a few pounds; as it were, the crumbs which fell from Miss Lindsay's table. Of course, pecuniarily mine was much the better position of the two; but I always have been one to overlook a mere financial difference, and I hope I always shall be."

"Look here, Morgan, if you're come down with the express intention of being insolent, I'll wring your neck, here, in the station."

Mr. Nash looked as if he were capable of at least trying to perform that operation on Mr. Morgan there and then, but Mr. Morgan only smiled.

"My dear Nash! the idea! Nothing can be further from my wish than to be insolent to you; as I'll show you before I've done. Where can we go where we can be quiet, and have a little chat together? And afterwards if you'll take me to 37, Ocean Villas, and offer me a little lunch, and give me an opportunity of renewing my acquaintance with your charming wife, I think you'll find that we are on better terms than you seem to suppose. Where are you going?"

Mr. Nash was striding out of the station.

"To the golf-links; you say you want to go somewhere where we can be quiet; you'll have the quietude you want there."

"Thank you; I don't think we need go quite so far as the golf-links, really; nor is that exactly the sort of solitude I was thinking of. You come with me; I'll be conductor." He opened the door of a fly which was by the kerb, and stood with the handle in his hand. "Step in."

The two men looked at each other, as if each was measuring the other's strength. Then Mr. Nash said—

"Where do you think you're going?"

Mr. Morgan spoke to the driver.

"Take us to the east end of the promenade, right to the extreme end." Then he turned to Nash. "We shall have all the quietude we want there. After you."

Nash hesitated, then entered the fly; Morgan followed; the fly drove off. As it rumbled along Mr. Morgan beguiled the way by spirited attempts at conversation; but he had all the talking to himself; not once did his companion open his lips. Mr. Nash sat with unbending back, stiff neck, grim face, looking straight in front of him; Mr. Morgan might not have been in the same vehicle for all the notice he took of him. Under the circumstances his unruffled affability did the latter gentleman credit. The vehicle set them down not only at the extreme end of the promenade, but beyond it. When the fly had gone Mr. Morgan called his companion's attention to their surroundings.

"You see! where could we have more privacy, even on the golf-links? Not a creature within many yards of us. We can sit on the beam of this groyne—could it be at a more convenient height?—and talk at our leisure."

Again Mr. Nash seemed to be measuring the other with his eye; his bearing did not point to his being at all in the conversational frame of mind which Mr. Morgan's words suggested; indeed he said as much.

"Now, my man, if you have anything to say, out with it; I've not the dimmest notion what it is you think you've got to say; to be quite frank, your whole conduct looks to me like infernal insolence; but, whatever it is, make it short; and take my advice, and be careful how you say it."

"My dear Nash, I assure you that no one could be more careful than I shall be."

"And don't you call me your dear Nash! you swollen-headed butler! I don't propose to allow a servant to treat me as an equal, nor do I propose to consort with him."

"Don't you? Now that shows how different we are. I don't mind with whom I consort; I'm even willing to consort with a thief."

"What—what the devil do you mean?"

Mr. Nash's eyes blazed; but they blazed out of a face which, consciously to himself or not, had suddenly grown pale. Mr. Morgan smiled as affably as ever; he offered Mr. Nash his cigar-case.

"Try one of my cigars; I think you'll find them something rather exceptional."

"Confound your cigars! I don't want your cigars! What do you mean by what you said just now?"

"You know what I mean as well as I do. There are moments when it's so unpleasant to have to dot one's i's; surely this is one. Then isn't it rather childish to pretend that you don't know what I mean when you do?"

"Are you going to tell me what you mean?"

"Certainly, if you insist; but is it wise?"

"Morgan, am I to knock you down?"

"You can try if you like; I dare say I can put up as good a fight as you can."

Again they seemed to gauge each other, eye to eye; Nash as if half beside himself with rage, Morgan all smiles.

"Will you tell me what you mean?"

Morgan looked away from the other's face, up into the air. He blew a ring of smoke from the cigar which he had lighted, following it with his eyes. Nothing could have been pleasanter than his manner, or more affable than his smile; he spoke as one who meditated.

"I happen to know that you borrowed certain sums of money from the late Mr. Donald Lindsay, for which you gave him notes of hand, amounting altogether to a little over a hundred pounds; a flea-bite to him, but a deal to you. When you were going through Mr. Lindsay's papers, on behalf of his daughter, you came upon those notes of hand; you put them into your pocket; you concealed their existence; in plainer words, you stole them."

"It's—it's an infernal lie!"

"My dear Nash, I saw you do it."

"You saw me!"

"I did. If you like I can describe to you, in detail, how you found them, and where, and how you looked to an unprejudiced observer, and precisely what you did when you had found them; but is it necessary?"

"Why—why don't I knock you down?"

"Because you have more sense. Pray don't indulge in heroics for my benefit, I beg of you; I know! I know! I also saw you steal another paper."

"What other paper?"

"That's what I said to myself; what can that other paper be? I confess that I was gravelled; and I continued gravelled until I called on you the other day at Ocean Villas, and found it in your letter-case."

"You—you scoundrel!"

"That's a hard word, from one who is both a scoundrel and a thief. Don't let us bandy epithets. Here is the paper—gently! I should have said, here is a copy of the paper. You and I know how desirable it is that so important a document should be in safe keeping. I have arranged that if I don't turn up at a certain place, at a certain time, the actual letter—you know it is a letter—will be posted to Dr. Banyard, together with a history of how it came into my possession, and particulars of those notes of hand you stole; so let us hope, for your sake, that no accident will happen to me. I will read you the copy I made of the letter; you will possibly have forgotten the precise wording, and the precise wording is of such importance—

'DEAR SIR,

'Referring to the acceptances of yours which we hold, and which fall due on the 7th inst., they reached us, in the ordinary course, through a client with whom we have done business before; who informed us that they came to him from Mr. Frank Clifford, of Marlborough Buildings, Farringdon Road, E.C., who, we presume, discounted them for you. We do not know that we are called upon to furnish you with this information, and, as your inquiry is an unusual one, we shall be glad to know why you make it.

'Your obedient servants,

'GULDENHEIM AND CO.'

Now that, my dear Nash, is the letter which you found; I don't know if your memory will enable you to recognize the accuracy of the copy." Mr. Nash was silent, presenting a curious picture of indecision; of the man who lets "I dare not" wait upon "I would." Mr. Morgan went affably on, diplomatically ignoring the singularity of the other's attitude. "To the superficial eye there is nothing in that letter; it is a mere routine business communication; in fact, however, as matters were, you could scarcely have found anything more important. I take it that you recognized this, or you would hardly have appropriated it; but I fancy that you only recognized it dimly. Your whole after-behaviour seems to point to it." Mr. Morgan glanced round at the moment, in time to catch the ghost of a smile, which seemed to flicker across Mr. Nash's face; Mr. Morgan's comment on that flickering smile was characteristic. "Perhaps not so dimly as I supposed; the springs of human action do lie so deep. Perhaps, after all, it has occurred to you, as it has to me, that that letter killed Donald Lindsay. You remember where you found it? Lindsay's was a pedestal writing-table; it was on the floor, under one of the pedestals, with one corner of the paper just showing. I think that was the last letter Donald Lindsay ever read. He had read it again and again before, and was re-reading it; but that re-reading was just the one too many. The strain of that cumulative shock was greater than he could bear; something snapped; he fell forward; the letter slipped from his fingers, under one of the pedestals, where it might have remained but for your sharp eyes." Mr. Morgan held the paper out in front of him with the air of one who is explaining something which he desires to make quite plain. "Now what is there in this letter which could have produced so extraordinary an effect upon a person possessed of so much self-restraint as Donald Lindsay undoubtedly was? What does the letter itself tell us? It tells us that Messrs. Guldenheim, as is the custom, I have reason to know, of a certain type of usurer, had written to advise him that certain acceptances of his, which matured at a certain date, had come into their hands. I'll bet sixpence that Lindsay was a man who never in his life put his name on a piece of paper which was likely, in the ordinary course, as they put it, to fall into the hands of carrion like the Guldenheims; that first communication of theirs must in itself have been a shock to him. But he was a cautious man; he liked to move gently; whether he already had suspicions I cannot say; evidently he wrote a non-committal letter, asking them from whom they had obtained acceptances of his. This was their reply; they informed him that originally the acceptances came from Mr. Frank Clifford, of Marlborough Buildings, Farringdon Road, and that information killed him. Is that how it occurred to you?"

"Never mind what occurred to me."

"Quite so, I won't; I'll content myself with telling you what occurred to me. I've only known what was in this letter a couple of days, and, with its aid, I have already learned that, when he died, Donald Lindsay was, probably, one of the richest men in England. Have you learned that?"

"I—I had my doubts."

"But you hadn't verified them? I see. Other matters interfered; for instance, your marriage. Now, my dear Nash, pray understand that I congratulate you, from the bottom of my heart, on what is, in all respects, an auspicious event; but you must forgive my saying that you were one of the last persons I should have associated with a love match. Now I happen to know that neither Miss Harding nor you had money, or prospects. Indeed, I've been wondering how you managed between you to pay the marriage fees, to say nothing of the expenses of your honeymoon. Did a good fairy drop down from the skies?"

"It strikes me, Morgan, that you are constitutionally incapable of seeing how infernally insolent you are."

"Am I? Perhaps; you should be a better judge of insolence than I. And believe me that I quite understand that a man is entitled to keep his own counsel; I don't wish to pry into your secrets; only I was wondering if you had a secret. However, to return to business. Do you know that this letter means a fortune for you, and incidentally, perhaps, also one for me; but certainly a fortune for you. All we have to do is to pull together; treat each other as friends, not enemies; although I say it, you'll find my friendship well worth having, from every point of view. Don't let the accident of my having once been a butler stand in the way; that's nonsense. Let me tell you that the butler at Cloverlea had a better position, in every respect, than the average clerk in a government office; as for your banks, and such dustbins—pah! he was better off than many a solicitor; though I know that's a delicate subject. But don't let's cut each other's throats for the sake of a merely imaginary social distinction; let's be friends, and I'll undertake to make your fortune. That's the proposition I've come down to Littlehampton to make."

CHAPTER XXVII

A ROYAL ROAD TO FORTUNE

Mr. Nash considered. The expression which had been on his face a few minutes ago had nearly vanished. The ex-butler had expressed himself in terms which the solicitor felt might justify him in modifying the attitude he had been disposed to take up. That Morgan had been, and still was, presumptuous went without saying; at the same time, as matters were turning out, it seemed that there were things which might be said on the other side; at least so it appeared to Herbert Nash. On the whole, he was inclined to concede as much. He took a few steps, to and fro, beside the groyne; then planting himself directly in front of Morgan, he told him his mind, rather in sorrow, perhaps, than in anger; indeed his bearing altogether was very different from what it had been.

"I tell you what it is, Morgan, your conduct, from first to last, has been bad."

Mr. Morgan smiled at him, affably.

"Has it? That's good, coming from you."

"That's where you've got the wrong end of the stick; whatever I've done I've done nothing to you."

"No; and therefore you think that I've no right to put a finger in the pie you've found."

"You'd no right to force yourself into my place, and run the rule over my things."

"That was luck, Nash, pure luck. I didn't call intending to run the rule over your things; is it likely? But if you will carry papers in your letter-case, you shouldn't leave your letter-case lying about."

"Idiot that I was! I found what I'd done soon after I'd started, but I was fool enough not to come back for it."

"You weren't an idiot; not at all; it was the best thing that could have happened for both of us—that I should find it."

"I'm afraid I can't agree. To begin with, see how awkward you've made it for me with my wife."

"Have I?"

"She can't understand what I have done which gives you any title to call yourself my friend—you!"

"Can't she?"

"And how am I going to explain? I may only be—as you suggest—a poor brute of a country solicitor; but you forget that she's a lady."

"Not for one moment. Mrs. Nash is a perfect lady; none knows that better than I do. But, if I help you to make your fortune; if we become partners in, say, a mercantile speculation; if I show you how to pour gold, and all the pretty things gold can buy, into her lap, will she require any better explanation? I think not. My dear fellow, you exaggerate the difficulties she will make; believe me.

"You talk very largely, but how are you going to do these things? I had the letter, and I didn't see my way."

"You didn't? Then that shows how fortunate it was that you communicated the contents of the letter to me; because I do. Tell me—now be frank; I'll be perfectly frank with you; it's to our common interest to be frank with each other—how far did you go?"

"I looked up Mr. Frank Clifford."

"And found?"

"That Marlborough Buildings is the head office of Peter Piper's Popular Pills; of which business Clifford's the managing director."

"And what else?"

"That's as far as I got; I meant to go on after—after—"

"After the honeymoon? I see; I've got a great deal further than that, a great deal. I take it you're aware that Peter Piper's Popular Pills is one of the medicines of the hour; the profits are stupendous; sometimes amounting to a hundred thousand pounds in a year, possibly more."

"I dare say; that doesn't want much finding out, everybody knows it; but what's it to do with us?"

"A good deal."

"How?"

"We're going to have a share of the business, and of the profits, and probably of former profits also."

"Are we indeed? How are we going to manage it?"

"Do you know who the proprietor was?"

Again the two men eyed each other; this time as if Nash was trying to read in Morgan's eyes the answer to his question.

"He was Donald Lindsay of Cloverlea."

"You don't mean it?"

"I do."

"Are you sure?"

"Perfectly. He called himself Joseph Oldfield; he was a bachelor; he was a reserved man, standoffish, of secretive habits. He had a flat in Bloomsbury Square, I've seen it, where he was supposed to spend most of his time in thinking out new advertising dodges; the present position of Peter Piper's Popular Pills is principally owing to clever advertising. The proprietor was his own advertising agent, he was a master of the art. He called himself, as I've said, Joseph Oldfield in town, and in the country he was Donald Lindsay of Cloverlea."

"The old fox!"

"I don't think you can exactly call him that; there was nothing in the opprobrious sense foxy about him. He was one of those men who live double lives, owing, one might say, to the pressure of circumstances; there are more of them about than is supposed. He bought the pill business when it was at a very low ebb; he hadn't very much money himself, at that time, and I dare say he got it for a song. Mrs. Lindsay was just dead; his girl was with her nurses, or at school; for business purposes he called himself Oldfield; it isn't every man who cares to have it known that he's associated with a patent medicine; in England it's quite a common custom for a man to carry on a business under an alias, under half-a-dozen aliases sometimes. As time went on I take it that his secretive habit grew stronger; he became less and less disposed to have it known that Donald Lindsay had anything to do with pills, which do rather stink in people's nostrils; and so he drifted into the double life. That's the word, drifted."

"You seem to have got up his history."

"I have a way of finding out things; people have noticed it before. Now take Mr. Frank Clifford; I can tell you something about him. He's a young man, a protégé of Oldfield's—we'll call him Oldfield. Oldfield had faith in him, he'd have trusted him with his immortal soul. That's how it was that it was such a shock to him to learn that he had been taking liberties with his name."

"But had he?"

"Had he what?"

"Been taking liberties with Lindsay's name?"

"He forged those bills which Guldenheim and his friends got hold of."

"That's what I guessed; but guessing's one thing, proof's another."

"Of course it is; I've the proof. I have some of the bills; I got hold of them rather neatly, though, as a matter of abstract right, I've as much title to them as anybody else. When you show Mr. Clifford one of them he won't deny he forged it."

"Yes; when I show it."

"Exactly. I said when you show it to him; and you're going to show it, if necessary, that's part of the scheme; though it mayn't be necessary, since it's quite possible he'll capitulate at once. My dear chap, at the present moment, to all intent's and purposes, Mr. Frank Clifford is the sole proprietor of one of the finest businesses in the world, and one of the largest fortunes in England, while the actual owner is starving in town."

"It's hard upon Miss Lindsay."

"It's the fortune of war. A little starving won't do her any harm; and I dare say she won't starve long. I never liked the girl."

"Nor I."

"Then there you are; why worry? She's too superior for me, too good; knocking about in the gutter may bring her down to your level, and mine; I've known it pan out that way where a young woman's concerned. I don't like any one to be too good, it makes me conscious of my own deficiencies; you see, I'm candid. However, she's a factor with whom we may, or may not, deal later. At present we've to concentrate our attention on Clifford; think of the possibilities for him, and for us. No one knows of the connection between Oldfield and Lindsay; no one even knows that he's dead. Clifford already has powers to draw cheques in the name of the firm, within certain limits; a man capable of committing forgery will soon be able to make those limits wider; there's no reason why he shouldn't appropriate to his own use every penny that comes in; as things stand nobody'll be able to call him to account for it; there's no reason why he should not lay hands on the whole of the old gentleman's investments; and they're—you may take it from me that they're magnificent. We're the only persons on this side of the grave who can stop him, and there's no reason why we should, if he gives us a proper share; in other words, if he takes us in as partners."

"It's playing with fire."

"Not a bit of it; it's playing with nothing that's in the least dangerous, if it's managed as I propose to manage it. You think it over. And now you take me in to lunch, and let me have the pleasure of meeting that charming wife of yours again; I'm starving! And if by the time we've done lunch you haven't formulated a scheme of your own I'll tell you what mine is, and then you'll see that without the slightest danger to either of us, without the shadow of a shade of danger—there's no reason why we shouldn't, within a very short space of time, be worth a quarter of a million apiece."

"A quarter of a million!"

"At least; we're going to deal with big figures, my boy. It'll pay Clifford, pay him handsomely, to split it up into three parts; and let me tell you that a third ought to come out at a good deal more than a quarter of a million."

Herbert Nash hesitated—for his credit's sake let it be written that he did hesitate—but he took Mr. Morgan home with him to lunch. And when his wife saw the visitor coming she would have been almost glad if the earth could have opened to swallow her up; it was as if she beheld avenging fate advancing towards her in the shape of a policeman. Her husband was late; it was long after their usual hour for lunch; he had left no word as to where he had gone; half beside herself with anxiety, she would have liked to send the town crier round in search of him; she had been along the pavement to the corner of this street and the corner of that, to and fro across the common for a glimpse of him along the front; these man[oe]uvres she had repeated again and again, and, standing on the doorstep, was frantically debating within herself as to what could have become of him, as to what she should do, when she saw him coming with Morgan at his side. Then, if she could, she would have run away, but she could not, her feet were as if they had been shod with iron weights, she could not lift them; she could not move; when they came to her she was a white-faced, shivering, terror-stricken little wretch; a poor ghost of the sunny-faced, light-hearted Elaine Harding of such a little while ago.

Mr. Nash offered a pretty lame explanation of his appearance with the man of whose presumption in claiming his acquaintance he had spoken with such scorn in the morning.

"This is Mr. Morgan; he is going to have some lunch with us; we have business to transact together. You remember Mr. Morgan, Elaine?"

As if she ever could forget him! How she would have prayed for the power to forget him if she had dared to hope that such prayers were answered. She hardly heard her husband's words; her white face was turned towards Morgan, as the convicted criminal has eyes only for the judge who is to pronounce his doom. Yet nothing could have been less judge-like than Mr. Morgan's bearing; nothing more affably respectful than the manner of his greeting. He stood before her with uncovered head, without even presuming to offer his hand.

"This is indeed an honour to be permitted to meet you again. May I venture to hope that you will allow me to offer my congratulations on the fortunate event which has occurred since I saw you last?"

She had to moisten her parched lips with her tongue before she could speak at all. Then—

"Thank you," was all she said to him; and to her husband, "I—I was wondering what had become of you."

Nash replied—

"Mr. Morgan had something which he wished to say to me." He led the way into the house; his wife and Morgan followed. He paused at the sitting-room door. "Take Mr. Morgan in there," he said to her. "I will join you in a minute."

Dumbly she obeyed; not realizing that he wanted what she did, a few minutes' solitude to enable him to pull himself together. He meant to have them, she had to do without; so that when she was in the room, and the ex-butler, coming after her, closed the door behind him he had her wholly at his mercy. She was still limp and helpless, having had no chance to recover from the shock and horror of encountering him again; a fact of which he, instantly perceiving, took prompt advantage. As he pulled the door to behind him a subtle change took place in his manner; he still smiled, but neither respectfully nor affably. He addressed the cowering woman in front of him as if she were some base creature.

"A pretty trick you played me, slipping away like that and leaving no address! Sneaking off with the man you'd paid to marry you, when, if it hadn't been for me, you'd have been in jail; and you call yourself a lady! and I'd treated you as one! Never again, my beauty, never again need you expect me to treat you like a lady, because you've shown me what you are. Now you listen to me! You'll give me five hundred pounds before I leave, or to-night you'll sleep in Littlehampton jail; and when your husband's told what kind of a character he's been diddled into marrying by way of a start he'll throw you out into the road. Now then! that five hundred pounds!"

He held out his hand, as if he expected her to give him the money there and then. She presented a pitiable spectacle; being scarcely able to stammer.

"I—I—I can't—can't give it you now."

"No lies! I'm off them! How much have you got in the house?"

"I—I—I might—" Her voice failed her; there was a hiatus in her sentence. "A hundred pounds."

"Then you'll give me a hundred pounds within half-an-hour after lunch, and you'll send another four hundred to an address I'll give you within four-and-twenty hours, or I promise you that, in less than an hour after, the man you've bought shall kick you out of this house into a policeman's arms."

Before he could speak again, or she either, the door opened to admit the diminutive maid; how she managed to open the door, as she apparently had done, was a mystery, since she was carrying a tray which was nearly as big as herself. And Mr. Nash presently appearing, the three sat down to lunch.

CHAPTER XXVIII

TO BE—OR NOT TO BE—POSTPONED

Daisy Ross was annoyed, almost indignant, and with reason. As she said to Mr. Clifford—

"It's really too ridiculous! One's wedding day is an occasion of some importance, even to a man." Mr. Clifford admitted that it was. "While to a woman it involves a frightful strain." Mr. Clifford again agreed. "Very well, then; a little consideration surely should be shown; Mr. Oldfield's conduct is absurd."

"He certainly is placing me in a very awkward position."

"I should think he was; considering that the bridesmaids' dresses are practically finished, and that two of them have to go away on the day after the one we fixed, how are we going to postpone the wedding?"

"I'm sure I don't know; but what am I to do? His conduct's most mysterious."

"My dear Frank, his conduct's not only mysterious, it's monstrous; and I don't care what you say. He knows you are going to be married."

"Of course he does; he's known about it all along."

"He knows when you are going to be married."

"Certainly, I asked him to be present; he gave me to understand that probably he would be."

"Then probably he will be."

"But suppose I see or hear nothing of him in the meanwhile?"

"He is a most exasperating man. How long is it since you have heard anything of him?"

"About two months; rather over than under."

"Something must have happened to him."

"You know his ways; I've told you about them often enough. When he leaves the office, unless he volunteers the information, I never know when I shall see him again, and unless I've some pressing reason for wanting to know I never ask; I've more sense. He dislikes being questioned about anything, and he's always shown what I've felt is really a morbid objection to being questioned about his movements; it's only quite recently that I've known his private address. It isn't as if this sort of thing hadn't happened before; it has, again and again. One evening, about a couple of years ago, he left the office quite late, after being in regular daily attendance, early and late, for some weeks; I expected he would come on the following day in the ordinary course, but I never saw or heard anything of him for close upon four months; then one morning he walked in, and, without offering a word of explanation, took up the thread of affairs just where he had left it, and, what's more, showed quite a good knowledge of what had been going on during his absence."

"But what a state things would have got into if it hadn't been for you."

"Quite so; that's just the point, he trusts me. In the ordinary course of business I have complete control of everything. If anything unusual turns up, which is of importance, I hold it over for reference to him; but in the general way I run the entire show; which, after all, isn't saying so very much, because, when all is said and done, he's a first-rate man of business and a splendid organizer, so that it's quite easy for me to do. And you know, Daisy, he treats me very generously, and always has done; I've practically a share in the concern, which is a free gift from him."

"I suppose you're worth what he gives you."

"All the same, I never put in a penny—I never had one to put; and there are hundreds, I dare say thousands, of men who could do all I do, and who'd be only too glad to do it, for a tenth part of what he gives me."

"If I were you, I shouldn't tell him so."

"He knows, my dear, he knows. He's the same with everybody about the place; it's a principle of his to treat everybody generously who does honest work for him; he wouldn't be happy if he thought that a man wasn't getting a fair share of the fruits of his own labours. In spite of his little eccentricities he's a magnificent fellow, and I couldn't do anything to annoy or disappoint him—not—well, I wouldn't do it."

Miss Ross sighed.

"You hadn't arranged to be married during that four months' absence of his."

"I certainly hadn't."

"Suppose the wedding-day had been fixed for two months after he had gone, and he had known it, would you have postponed it indefinitely, till he condescended to turn up again?"

"I don't know what I should have done, I really don't; but I tell you what we might do—that is, if you wouldn't mind very much."

"Oh, never mind what I mind; my wishes aren't of the slightest consequence; I shall begin to wish that I wasn't going to be married!"

"Daisy! don't say that, even in jest. It's as hard upon me as it is upon you."

"Honestly, Frank, I don't see it. To a man, having his wedding-day postponed, and that indefinitely, is, of course, rather a nuisance; but to a woman, it's—it's quite a different thing."

"But I'm not going to suggest that it shall be postponed."

"Then what are you going to suggest? What have you been suggesting for the last—I don't know how long?"

"That's because the idea never occurred to me until just now; I don't know why; I suppose it's because I'm stupid."

"Now what idea have you got into your head?"

"I think I see a way out of the difficulty; that is, if you'll agree."

"Agree to what?"

"The great thing for us is to be married, isn't it?"

"I don't know that I'm prepared to admit it till I know what you're leading up to."

"Very well, then, as one of the parties I'll admit it; the one thing for which I'm living is to be married to you; when I am married I'll be happy."

"Thank you; that's very nice of you; but I'm not going to admit anything till I know what it is you've got at the back of your head."

"We're going to be married on Thursday—that is, this day week."

"We were to have been married on Thursday; I know my wedding dress is coming home on Wednesday."

"And after the wedding we're to start for a three months' tour on the continent, something like a honeymoon."

"We were to have started for a three months' tour."

"That's what I arranged with Mr. Oldfield. I said to him, 'Mr. Oldfield, after my marriage—at which I trust you'll be present—I hope to go abroad with my wife for a month, if I can be spared from the office.' He said to me, 'Clifford, why not make it three months?' I stared; he went on: 'A man isn't married often!'"

"Frank!"

"That's what he said; and it's true. 'Therefore there's no reason why he shouldn't make the most of it when he is; you take your wife abroad for three months, I'll see you're spared from the office.' And that's how it was arranged."

"Yes, and then he goes and disappears, and I'm not to be married at all, and that's how it's disarranged."

"Not a bit of it; the wedding needn't be postponed; the more I think of it the less reason do I see why it should."

"Frank! Then what ever have you been talking to me about ever since I don't know when!"

"Mr. Oldfield's continued absence needn't prevent my sparing a day to get away from the office to be married."

"Needn't it! I'm sure it's very nice of you to talk about sparing a whole day for a trifling thing like that."

"In any case, all that need suffer is the three months' tour. If Mr. Oldfield hasn't turned up by Thursday, after we're married we'll go for a weekend honeymoon. I'll return to the office on Monday. The house is ready, all it needs is its mistress; you'll be installed a little sooner than you thought, and when Mr. Oldfield does appear we'll go for our three months' tour."

Miss Ross sat looking at him with rather a complicated expression on her pretty face, as if she did not quite know what to make of his proposition.

"Frank, why didn't you think of it before? instead of worrying me, and making my hair come out by handfuls, by keeping on saying that if Mr. Oldfield didn't return in time, you couldn't possibly desert Peter Piper's Popular Pills, and that therefore the wedding would have to be postponed till you didn't know when."

"I don't know; but I didn't. I fancy, sweetheart, that it's because I was so looking forward to that scamper through Europe. It's so long since I had a real holiday—and such a holiday—with you! If you only knew how often I have dreamed of it!"

"And do you think I haven't dreamed of it too?" They were sitting very close together; she looked at him with almost comic wistfulness as she added, "A week-end honeymoon will be rather a comedown, won't it?"

"Compared to that elaborate tour, which we have so carefully planned, in which we were to go to so many delightful places, and do so many delicious things, rather! But it won't spoil by being kept; we'll have it; and in the meanwhile a week-end will be better than nothing."

"Frank, I'll tell you something. Rather than that the wedding should be put off I'd go straight home with you to our home, from the church doors; or I'd return with you to the office, and sit on a stool, till your day's work was done."

"Sweetheart!"

There was an interval, during which more was done than said. Then she observed—

"Now let me clearly understand; even if Mr. Oldfield returns on Wednesday we go for our tour."

"Even if he puts in an appearance in the church."

"Well, let's hope he won't put it off till quite so late as that; because, though perhaps you mayn't be aware of it, there is such a thing as packing; one doesn't pack for a week-end just as one packs for three months on the Continent. But, in any case, the wedding is not to be postponed."

"It is not to be postponed. Let me put it like this. You talk it over with your father—"

"Frank! don't be absurd! I fancy I see myself talking it over with papa. Why, do you know what he says? He says he can't see why a girl need make such a fuss about such a little thing as being married; he wonders why she can't go in a 'bus to the nearest registrar's, and then go, in a spirit of meek thankfulness, to her new home in another 'bus, and start darning the old socks which her husband has been storing up against her coming."

"Well, there's something in it."

"Is there? At any rate, I'm not going to talk it over with papa; he wouldn't talk it over with me if I wanted him to."

"Then talk it over with your mother, and—and the rest of the family."

"It is a matter for my decision, not for theirs."

"Precisely; only there's no harm in observing certain forms. And I'll make another effort to see if I can find out something which will point to Oldfield's whereabouts. I'll go round to his flat in Bloomsbury Mansions; they sometimes do hear something of him there; then I'll try every other place I can think of—there aren't many places, but there are some—then I'll come round to-morrow and tell you the result of my efforts, and you'll tell me the result of the family consultation."

"I can tell you that before you go; the wedding is not to be postponed."

"Of course the wedding is not to be postponed; but still there are things you'll like to talk over with them—they'll expect it; and then they can talk them over with me—you know the sort of thing. And anyhow I hope you don't object to my coming again to-morrow, if only to be told once more that the wedding is not to be postponed."

"Of course I don't object to your coming again to-morrow; you'll hear of it if you don't."

"But in case I should be prevented, don't you think you'd better give me an extra kiss or two?"

"Frank! I'm always kissing you."

"Not always; sometimes I'm kissing you."

"You'll soon grow tired."

"Shall I? Be careful what you say! you'll be punished if you say it."

"I hope you never will grow tired."

"Sweetheart, you mustn't even say it in jest!"

The rest was that sort of talk which we have most of us talked once; those of us who haven't are to be pitied; it is a kind of talk which is well worth talking. Then Mr. Clifford went on to Bloomsbury Mansions, which was Joseph Oldfield's London address; indeed, so far as his manager knew, it was the proprietor of Peter Piper's Popular Pills' only address. As usual he found the porter in the entrance hall; of him he made inquiry.

"Well, Coles, any news of Mr. Oldfield?"

In the porter's manner, as he replied, there was a significance which Mr. Clifford did not understand.

"I can't say that there's any news of Mr. Oldfield exactly; but there's something going on."

"Going on? What do you mean?"

"In his flat."

"In his flat! What's going on in his flat?"

"That's more than I can tell you, sir; but there's some one in there; in fact, there's two people in there. One of them says he's Mr. Oldfield's solicitor; I don't know who the other is, but he may be another solicitor for all I can tell; he looks as if he might be something in that line."

Frank Clifford opened his eyes.

"His solicitor? What solicitor? What's his name?"

"Seemed to me he was shy about giving his name; but when I made it clear that he wasn't going up unless he did, he said his name was Nash—Herbert Nash. He's quite a young chap—younger than the other, though he's not old."

"Nash? Herbert Nash? I never heard Mr. Oldfield speak of a solicitor named Nash; but of course he may have a dozen solicitors of whom I know nothing. How did they get in? Did you let them in?"

"Not me; they brought Mr. Oldfield's own key; Mr. Nash had it."

"That looks as if they'd at least heard from Mr. Oldfield quite recently, which is more than I have. It's lucky I happened to come just now. Take me up, Coles; I should like to see Mr. Nash."

The porter said, as they were stepping into the lift—

"I hope, sir, there's nothing wrong with Mr. Oldfield—that he's not ill, or anything like that; but it looks odd his solicitor coming instead of him, and that without giving any notice."

"It doesn't necessarily follow, Coles, that there's anything wrong with him on that account; most probably Mr. Oldfield is abroad, and has sent his solicitor instructions, in order to carry out which Mr. Nash has to visit his flat."

The lift stopped; the porter pointed to a door.

"I hope you're right, sir; I should be sorry to hear that anything had happened to Mr. Oldfield; to my thinking he's the pleasantest gentleman we've got in the Mansions, and I don't care who hears me say so. That's his flat, sir. You'll find them in there now. Shall I ring, sir?"

"No; I'll ring."

Mr. Clifford rang.

CHAPTER XXIX

IN JOSEPH OLDFIELD'S FLAT

The idea was Morgan's.

"We're going to call at Bloomsbury Mansions to begin with; that's to be the first move in our plan of campaign." Herbert Nash looking a note of interrogation, Mr. Morgan condescended to explain. "How many times am I to tell you that Bloomsbury Mansions was where Mr. Joseph Oldfield lived when he was in town? When he was there he was Peter Piper's Popular Pills; when he wasn't there if you'd talked to him about pills I dare say he wouldn't have known what you meant."

"But why should we go to Bloomsbury Mansions?"

"Doesn't your own common-sense tell you, my dear Nash, that the more a man knows about the game he's going to play the better chance he has of winning? Certainly it does, because you're one of the cleverest men I know. Very well then; if you and I can manage to be alone together in that flat for, say, half-an-hour, there's very little about Joseph Oldfield which, at the end of that time, we shan't know. Unless I'm mistaken, that's where the key to the situation is; it must be somewhere, and I tell you it's there. That's where all his business papers are, which you and Baynard couldn't find at Cloverlea; his books, his accounts, the lists of his securities; perhaps some of the securities themselves; and, what's more, the whole financial history of those immortal pills. We shall be able to find out what exactly Mr. Frank Clifford's position is, and how we shall best be able to get at him. I'm no gamester; I object to gambling on principle; yet I'm willing to bet a trifle that after I've been there half-an-hour I'll be in a position—with the aid of what I know already—to squash Mr. Frank Clifford between my finger and thumb; and between us, my boy, we'll have Peter Piper's Popular Pills, and the pile they represent, lying at our feet."

"I tell you again, Morgan, what I've told you before, that I think you pitch your anticipations too high; there are all sorts of difficulties in the way which you don't seem to appreciate. Anyhow how do you intend to get into this flat? do you propose to commit burglary?"

"Am I a criminal? a felon? I've been an honest man all my life, and I mean to die an honest man. No, my dear Nash, we're going in through the front door, in broad daylight, before the eyes of the whole staff of the Mansions, if the whole staff chooses to look on, and, as about flats they're mostly a prying lot, they may do; we're going to let ourselves in with Mr. Joseph Oldfield's own private and particular latch-key, and a very private and particular latch-key it is. I lay—betting again! you see, Nash, how a bad habit, once indulged in, grows on one—that, knowing what kind of people they are about flats, he had both lock and key specially made for him; and here that key is."

He held out a small and curious-looking key, of the Bramah type. Mr. Nash eyed it dubiously, as if it were something which he would rather leave alone.

"How do you know it is the key? and where did you get it from?"

"Question No. 2 first, as to where I got it. When the late Donald Lindsay was seized with that most unfortunate stroke I assisted in undressing him; afterwards I folded up his clothes and put them away, and, in the ordinary course of my duty, I examined the pockets. In a small and ingeniously placed pocket inside his waistcoat—which the commonplace searcher would have overlooked—I found this key, secreted. That set me thinking. You will observe that on the tiny ring to which it is attached there is a number. When I learnt certain facts I caused inquiries to be made of a firm which I happen to know manufactures keys like this, asking how long it would take them to make Mr. Joseph Oldfield a duplicate key to his fiat in Bloomsbury Mansions, quoting this number. They replied to the effect that they could let him have another key in four-and-twenty hours; so that's how I know that this is the key to the flat in Bloomsbury Mansions."

"You've a roundabout way of your own of finding out things."

"Roundabout ways are sometimes the shortest, and the safest. Now, my dear Nash, you and I are going together to Bloomsbury Mansions; you will be the bearer of the key; you will show the key to the porter who we shall probably find there; you will tell him that you are Mr. Oldfield's solicitor—which you are; let us keep to the strict and literal truth; he will say 'Walk in!' and, when we have walked in, I think that the rest you can leave to me."

Herbert Nash did not like Mr. Morgan's little plan; he disliked it very much, and said so with considerable force of language, which the gentleman to whom it was addressed did not at all resent. He simply smiled, and persuaded Mr. Nash; having means of persuasion at his command which that person seemed most unwillingly to feel that he was not in a position to resist; the result being that, as we have heard, the pair did gain access to the flat in Bloomsbury Mansions; the porter, as Mr. Morgan had prophesied, looking on as they went in. When they had entered they found themselves in a fair-sized hall.

"I wonder," said Nash, as if struck by the silence of the place, "how he managed for servants."

"The flat people provided service, I expect; they cater, and do everything for tenants if they're wanted to."

"Do you mean to say that he lived here all alone?"

"Generally, I fancy; though when the humour took him he may have kept up any sort of an establishment for all I know; I'll be able to tell you more on that head when I've been over the place. Now let me see. From what I know of the arrangements of flats I should say that that room over there was his own particular apartment." He moved to the door to which he referred. "Locked; however, there's the key in the lock, and it turns quite easily." He threw it open. "Right I am! Nash, this is Joseph Oldfield's Ali Baba's treasure-cave; perhaps presently you'll be fingering some of his precious things. But before we start at that let's see what's behind these other doors; I always like to know the lay of the land before I commence actual operations." Mr. Morgan began opening door after door, glancing at what was behind each, then shutting it again; Herbert Nash stood in the hall and watched. "Looks like a drawing-room; what did he want with a drawing-room, a lone-lorn bachelor? Seem to be some nice things in it too. A bedroom, furnished up to the knocker. My word! that bed cost money; he lay well. Bathroom; spared nothing even over his bath. Dining-room; nothing cheap about that either; he spent money upon this place; I suppose he walked straight out of the bath to his food. Another bedroom; everything in the palest pink; that's meant for a woman's occupation I'll swear. I wonder who it was meant for? Looks as if it had never been lived in. What are those over the way? Domestic offices, I take it; kitchen; yes, and the rest of it, I know; we'll pay attention to you perhaps a trifle later. Now we'll return to Ali Baba's treasure-cave. Come along, Nash."

Mr. Nash followed him into the room; he entered with what seemed dragging footsteps, glancing round, when he was in, with a shame-faced air.

"Morgan," he protested, "I don't like this; I don't care what you say, I don't like it; if we're not committing burglary, we're doing something which is not far off."

"Don't talk nonsense; you a lawyer! and talking about burglary! stuff! If you imagine, Mr. Nash, that I'm the sort of person who would commit burglary you're mistaken. Haven't you got all your explanations pat? You've as much right to be here as any man on this side the grave. Very nice room I call this; very nice; well adapted for a gentleman's occupation. The late Oldfield had a pretty taste in bric-a-brac; like Mr. Donald Lindsay, he'd a good eye for a promising investment. I'm a bit of an authority on the subject myself, so I know. There's a pair of powder blue vases over there—both Oldfield and Lindsay seem to have had a liking for powder blue—which wouldn't be out of the way at a thousand. And unless I'm mistaken that cabinet in the corner is a genuine Boule; Oldfield wasn't likely to have anything imitation about his place; if it is I should like to have the coin it's worth in my pocket; perhaps we shall have it in both our pockets before very long, eh, Nash? What do you think? My dear boy, the contents of this room, the mere trimmings, so to speak, are worth a small fortune in themselves, you can take it from me; I was quite right in calling it Ali Baba's treasure-cave."

"Morgan, look at this!"

"Look at what? Hello! what's that?"

Nash was pointing to a large framed photograph, which stood upon a centre table.

"It's Miss Lindsay; it's his daughter."

"So it is; and a fine photograph too; and a good likeness."

"She—she was with him even when he was here."

There was an odd catch in his voice; Mr. Morgan was as unmoved as ever.

"You mean her effigy was."

"And—and look at that portrait over the mantel."

"Rather a fine bit of painting; quite decent; good colour; clever drawing; face seems alive."

"Can't you see who it is? It's his wife."

"Never saw the lady; but I shouldn't be surprised; there's no mistaking the likeness to the girl. So while he was living a double life he was living it with his wife and child; queer thing human nature."

"Morgan, I feel as if those women were looking at us."

"Looking at us? What do you mean?"

"I—I'm sure they can see us; look how they're staring!"

"Staring! Nash! Stop that! One would think you'd been drinking; or perhaps it's a nip of something you want; there ought to be a decanter somewhere about."

"I want nothing; it would make no difference."

"Then let's get to business. I've a theory; you listen, and tell me what you think of it. From what we know of the late Oldfield I rather infer that when he left the flat he left the keys of all these drawers, and cupboards, and things, behind him; that's the kind of thing he would do; and I know that they weren't at Cloverlea; I'm guessing that they're somewhere about the place at this moment. Now what's your idea of the kind of hiding-place he'd choose?"

"I don't know; and I don't care."

"What do you mean by you don't care? You seem to be in a nice mood, my lad."

"I'll not touch a thing here; nothing!"

"Won't you? Then don't! Who asked you? I'll do all the touching that's wanted; only—mind! if you shirk now you'll pay for it when the time for sharing comes."

"I'm not quite the scoundrel you take it for granted that I am."

"No, you're another and a worse kind, you're a white-livered cur. You do the sneak game, when you think it's safe, for pennies; but when it comes to the man's game, for something worth having, you whine. I can see that I shall have to talk to you as I haven't done yet before you really do begin to find out where you are; but I haven't time to do it now. Where's he likely to have put those keys? Anyhow we ought to be able to get at his writing-table drawers without them; I shouldn't say that there was anything very special about their locks." He took something out of his pocket which he inserted in the keyhole of the top drawer. "It only wants a little—a little management. I thought so; that's done it; drawer No. 1." He drew the top drawer open, and instantly pushed it back again. "What's that?"

There was the sound of an electric bell.

"It's—it's somebody ringing."

"I know it's somebody ringing; I'm not deaf, am I? I don't need you to tell me that it's somebody ringing; but who's ringing? Who knows that we're here?"

"Perhaps it's the porter; or somebody connected with the Mansions."

The two men stood staring at each other; Nash white-faced. The bell was heard again.

"You go and see who's there; if it's the porter, or any one of that sort, you bluff him off. And mind, if you make a mess of things through funk, it'll be you who'll pay."

"I'm not afraid, Mr. Morgan; at least, not in the sense you mean."

Herbert Nash went to the front door; Morgan remained in the room, listening. Without was a young man; behind him was the porter.

"I beg your pardon," said the young man; "but the porter tells me that Mr. Oldfield's solicitor, Mr. Nash, is here; are you Mr. Nash?"

"I am."

"Allow me to introduce myself. My name is Clifford—Frank Clifford; I am Mr. Oldfield's manager—at Marlborough Buildings; possibly he has mentioned my name to you."

A voice came from within—Morgan's.

"Certainly he has mentioned your name to us, Mr. Clifford; we know it very well, and all about you. Step in, you're the very man we want to see. Nash, let Mr. Clifford in."

After what seemed to be a moment's hesitation Mr. Nash drew the door wider open, so as to permit of Clifford's entering. When he was in the door was shut.

CHAPTER XXX

WHEN THIEVES FALL OUT

"Come in here, Mr. Clifford; it's a very fortunate chance your dropping in on us like this; you couldn't have arranged it better if you'd tried. I've no doubt Mr. Nash is glad to see you, and I'm quite sure I am."

As Clifford followed Morgan into the sitting-room he eyed him a little askance.

"To whom have I the pleasure of speaking?"

"I'm Mr. Oldfield's most intimate friend; I know more about his affairs than any man living."

"May I ask your name?"

"Morgan; Stephen Morgan."

"Are you also a solicitor?"

"Not yet, exactly; I think I may describe myself as Mr. Oldfield's confidential agent. Come in, Nash; don't stop out there; then we can have the door closed—it'll be snugger."

Mr. Nash had stayed in the hall, as if unwilling to associate himself with Morgan's reception of the new-comer; indeed from his bearing one might almost have suspected him of an inclination to march out of the flat, and leave Morgan to deal with Mr. Clifford; possibly he was deterred by the prosaic accident that his hat was in the sitting-room. When Morgan bade him go in he went in, and Morgan closed the door behind him. Clifford looked from one to the other, as if there was something in the attitude of the two men which he could not make out.

"May I ask what you gentlemen are doing here?"

"You may ask; but, so far as I can see, it's no business of yours."

"Quite so; still—at the same time—"

"Yes, Mr. Clifford; at the same time?"

"I wondered."

"There's no harm in your wondering, Mr. Clifford; none at all."

Mr. Clifford turned to Nash, as if he preferred his appearance to Morgan's.

"Can you tell me, Mr. Nash, where Mr. Oldfield is? or how I can place myself in communication with him? As you are possibly aware, he has not been at the office now for some time, and his continued absence—and I may add, silence, because I have heard nothing from him—is occasioning much inconvenience."

"To whom?"

This was Morgan. Clifford seemed to hesitate, then replied—"To me."

"To you? Mr. Oldfield hasn't been in the habit of studying your convenience, has he, Mr. Clifford?"

The new-comer flushed, as if he felt that the other's words were meant unpleasantly. When he answered he looked the speaker straight in the face.

"Mr. Oldfield has been in the habit of studying not only my convenience, but every one's convenience, Mr. Morgan; if you suppose the contrary, I know him better than you do. And, just now, the circumstances are peculiar. I am to be married next week, and I can hardly carry out in their entirety the arrangements I have made unless I know what Mr. Oldfield's movements are likely to be."

"I see; you are to be married next week?"

"Mr. Oldfield knows that I am to be married next week."

"Does he? What's the lady's name?"

"Mr. Oldfield also knows the lady's name; I told him."

"Did you? Then I fancy he's forgotten."

"I never knew Mr. Oldfield forget anything that was of importance to any one in whom he was interested; so I take leave to doubt your fancy, Mr. Morgan."

Mr. Morgan looked at the speaker, for some moments, in rather a peculiar way; then he thrust his hands deeper into his trousers pockets, leaned back his head, and laughed. Clifford flushed again.

"What is the jest, Mr. Morgan?"

"Jest? Clifford, you're a funny one! you're all the jest I want."

"Sir!"

"I give you my word, my dear fellow—" Morgan advanced, with the apparent intention of laying his hand upon the other's shoulder; Clifford retreated; Morgan stared. "What's the matter? Why do you draw back?"

Clifford's manner was courteously frigid.

"You will be able to say anything you wish to say to me from where you are."

"Oh yes, I'm quite able to say to you all I wish from where I am; or from anywhere. Don't you think, Mr. Clifford, you're cutting it a trifle fine?"

"I don't understand."

"No? Surely you're not dull. I beg you to believe I'm not. Haven't I told you I'm Mr. Oldfield's confidential agent?"

"You have, sir; though what especial interest that fact should have for me I still fail to understand; and yet I believe that I am not dull beyond the average man. Mr. Nash, while Mr. Morgan is endeavouring to find words with which to convey his meaning to my comprehension, may I again ask you how I can place myself in immediate communication with Mr. Oldfield?"

Before Nash could answer, Morgan made a hasty movement towards the speaker, crying—

"You miserable hypocrite! trying to play the innocent with us! asking how you can place yourself in communication with Mr. Oldfield, when you know he's dead!"

"Dead! Mr. Oldfield dead, Mr. Morgan!"

"Stop that game of pretending, or I shan't be able to keep my hands off you! Not only is Mr. Oldfield dead, and you know it, but you killed him!"

"Killed him! I! Mr. Nash, is your friend sane?"

"Did ever rogue play the hypocrite so brazenly? and actually I've one of the weapons with which he killed him on me! and here it is. You killed him, Mr. Clifford, with that."

Morgan held out a slip of blue paper on which there was some writing.

"With that? And what is that? It looks to me rather a singular weapon with which to commit murder."

"Does it? you sneering villain! When Brown does all in his power to make of Smith an honest man, and Smith turns out to be a blackguard and a thief, do you think that isn't a blow to Brown? It was that kind of blow killed Joseph Oldfield; it was the shock of learning that you were a forger."

"Learning that I was a forger! Mr. Morgan, you—you said just now that you found it difficult to keep your hands off me; now I'm finding it difficult to keep mine off you. What justification have you for the statement you have just made, that I am a forger?"

"Isn't that justification enough?"

Again Morgan held out the slip of paper.

"I repeat the question I put to you just now—what is that?"

"It's news to you that it's one of the bills you forged?"

"One? Do you charge me with forging others?"

"I don't know what you got for them, Mr. Clifford, but you forged bills to the face value of over forty thousand pounds. Are incidents of the kind of such frequent occurrence in your career that it is necessary to recall this one to your recollection?"

"And do you seriously accuse me of forging bills for more than forty thousand pounds? Was ever anything heard like it?"

"Often; there have been plenty of scoundrels before you, if you find that any consolation."

"Don't imagine that because I endeavour to retain my self-control in the midst of this—this sudden nightmare that I am incapable of showing resentment; if that is what you imagine, you are wrong, Mr. Morgan. What grounds have you for asserting that I forged that bill, or any bill?"

"Mr. Clifford, drop the mask; the time for bluff has gone; try to be candid. You see, Mr. Nash and I know all about it."

"Do you? It so happens that I don't. I ask you again, what grounds have you for asserting that I've committed forgery? Don't be vague; be specific."

"I happen to know the man to whom you gave the bills."

"Do you? What's his name?"

"Sir Henry Trevor."

"Sir Henry Trevor? Harry Trevor? Do you venture to affirm that Harry Trevor says he got forged bills from me, or any bills?"

"He took them to the discounters; when they asked where he got them from, he said they came from you. What he got for them, or what share you had of the plunder, I can't say; at present I'd rather not know; these are details which may come out at the Old Bailey."

Up to then Frank Clifford had kept his countenance to a wonderful degree; but when Mr. Morgan spoke of the Old Bailey his lips flickered, as they might have done had he been suddenly attacked by St. Vitus' Dance; the movement passed, he was calm again.

"Will you let me look at that bill you're holding? I'll not touch it; I merely want to look."

"I'll take care you don t touch it. You can look at an old friend."

"What is the signature it bears?"

"Don't know? I'll tell you. Donald Lindsay, of Cloverlea."

"Donald Lindsay, of Cloverlea? And who is Donald Lindsay, of Cloverlea?"

"Really, Mr. Clifford, when you didn't become an actor what the stage lost! and now-a-days there are so few actors who are to the manner born. It's the very gist of your offending, you sly scamp, that you made such use of the knowledge you had surreptitiously obtained that Joseph Oldfield, of Peter Piper's Popular Pills, was Donald Lindsay, of Cloverlea."

Clifford stared, as if the other had been speaking in a foreign language.

"What's that? Would you mind saying that again?"

"I'll not say it again; I'll not pipe to your dancing, you brazen vagabond!"

"Are you hinting that Joseph Oldfield is, or was, I don't know which it ought to be, a pseudonym? that he had, or has, another name?"

"Is that the trick you're trying to play? You wish it to be believed that you didn't know there was such a person as Donald Lindsay; that he and Joseph Oldfield were one and the same; and that in putting the name upon a bill stamp you did it innocently, in ignorance that was childlike and bland. The idea is ingenious; as, I fancy, Mr. Clifford, most of your ideas are; but you won't find a judge or jury quite so simple."

Ignoring Mr. Morgan, Frank Clifford, to the unprejudiced observer, seemed to be engaged in reflections of his own; to which he presently gave shape in disconnected words.

"Donald Lindsay? I seem to have heard the name."

"I shouldn't be surprised."

"Donald Lindsay? Why—it can't be!"

"That conscience is pricking you at last? No, it can't be that."

"Harry Trevor wouldn't—couldn't—he couldn't do a thing like that; and yet—"

"And yet? So it's Harry Trevor now; as usual, everybody's guilty except the man who did it."

"Mr. Morgan, I'm willing to believe that you don't realize what a confused nightmare I seem all at once to be moving in, and that that explains your attitude. If you did realize how wholly you have taken me by surprise—"

"I do realize that; I quite think that you're altogether the most surprised man I've lately met. I don't know what you did expect when you rang that bell, but I don't suppose that you expected this."

"I did not; though you speak in one sense, and I in another. With reference to what you say about those bills, a horrible—I can only call it fear, has come into my mind, of which I scarcely dare to think, lest I should be guilty of heinous injustice; and before I speak of it—"

"You would like to have time to think it over?"

"I should."

"Then you shall have it; that's what I'm coming to. You will be at the office to-morrow morning at eleven o'clock."

"I will."

"You had better."

"You need not tell me that."

"Needn't I? I think I need. Mr. Nash and I are administering Mr. Oldfield's estate."

"Are you an executor?"

"I am; the only executor. I do not know that I ought to say so, but you will understand that I am not committing myself, and that I speak without prejudice; but, at present, it is our wish—Mr. Nash's and mine—not to prosecute."

"Prosecute!"

"Prosecute. Do you wish me to believe that you were unaware that forgers are occasionally prosecuted? Our first consideration is, and must be, the business; we fear that it may do the business no good to have the manager sent to penal servitude for forgery. These bills have been taken up, in the first place under a misapprehension, at a very heavy cost; we will tell you all about that to-morrow; you will have to make that loss good."

"I shall!"

"You will; do you imagine that you are to escape scathless? You are a truly remarkable person. But, as I have said, we will discuss that in the morning. I only trust that no further irregularities may be brought to light."

"Mr. Morgan!"

"Please drop that tone; it makes me sick; nothing is so nauseous as a futile hypocrite. My advice to you is, think things over, carefully, seriously; in the morning make a clean breast of everything; the more candid we find you the better it will be. Now, as Mr. Nash and I have much to attend to, I must ask you to leave us."

"That I am willing to do; but so far you have done all the talking; but, before I go, there are some remarks which I wish to make."

"We wish to hear nothing now—nothing; think first, Mr. Clifford, think."

"It is not necessary to think before making simple statements dealing with plain facts, and you will have to listen, willingly or not; I have had to listen, now it is your turn. What I have to say is this; that I did not know Mr. Oldfield was dead; that I did not know that he had any name but Oldfield; that I had no knowledge of his connection with Donald Lindsay, of Cloverlea; that this is the first time I have been made aware that there ever was such a person as Donald Lindsay; that I never before saw the bill of exchange which you showed me just now."

"I have proof to the contrary."

"That's impossible. That there may be a mystery about that bill, and about the others of which you have spoken, I admit; between this and to-morrow I may be able to institute inquiries which will throw light on it; but I assure you, Mr. Morgan, I am as incapable of forgery as you are. If Mr. Oldfield really did believe that I was capable of such conduct he was a much worse judge of character than I believed he was. Now, Mr. Morgan, I will go."

"With a lie upon your lips."

"No, sir, not with a lie upon my lips. You will either give your authorities for the statements you have made, or, in the morning, you will apologize. You will find that you will have to make many apologies, Mr. Morgan. I notice, Mr. Nash, that you have not associated yourself with the charges Mr. Morgan has made, nor with the language he has used; when I lay the facts before you in the morning, as I hope to be in a position to do, you will have no cause to regret your attitude."

With that Mr. Clifford marched out of the room, and through the front door. When he had gone Mr. Morgan leaned against a corner of a table, with his hands in his trousers pockets, and whistled; then he looked at Mr. Nash, and smiled.

"Got a face, hasn't he? He can bluff. We may find him rather a harder nut to crack than I imagined; it's just possible that we may have to change our plan of operations; the line he has taken up is a little unexpected. What do you think?"

"I don't think, Mr. Morgan; I know."

Mr. Morgan purposely ignored the peculiarity of the other's tone.

"What do you know, my dear Nash?"

"I know one thing; that if you do go to Mr. Clifford's office in the morning you will go alone."

"Shall I? How's that? Got a previous engagement?"

"Here, and now, you and I part company; you go your way, I go mine; under no circumstances will I associate myself with you again."

"Steady, Nash, steady; do you know where talk like that will lead you?"

"It will lead to honesty."

"It will lead you to jail, and pretty soon."

"Will it? I'll take the risk. It is not necessary for you to remind me that on a certain occasion I behaved like a blackguard, and perhaps worse; I have only regretted it once, and that's been ever since."

"Regrets, in a case like yours, are useless; they simply mean that you regret that you're found out. Of course you do."

"You'll find that my regrets mean more than that. I've behaved badly since; I've acted like a coward in allowing you to use your guilty knowledge."

"Guilty knowledge?"

"Yes, your guilty knowledge, as you'll discover if you're not careful; I've let you use it as a lever to drive me into further misdoing. You've threatened me with the consequences of my misconduct; I've been afraid to face them. That's over now; I'm going to face them, if only as the lesser of two evils."

"Tell me, Nash, what's started you in this conversational strain?"

"What's brought me to the sticking-point is your conduct to Mr. Clifford. He's an innocent man; of that I'm absolutely certain; every insult you flung at him stung me; it shamed me to feel that I was your associate. I'll be your associate no longer. I'll have no part or parcel in your attempts to entangle Mr. Clifford as you've entangled me. I believe they'll fail; but if they do or don't, I'll have no share in them. Henceforward you and I are strangers; I'm going; if you stay, you stay alone."

"Going, are you? Oh no, you're not!"

Morgan moved between Nash and the door. The two men confronted each other; there was something on Herbert Nash's face which made of him a new man.

"Mr. Morgan"—even in his voice there was a new tone—"more than once my fingers have itched to take you by the throat, and choke the life half out of you. If you are wise, you will not attempt to detain me, or I may find the temptation too strong."

Possibly Mr. Morgan was conscious that there was something unusual about Herbert Nash; his manner continued to be so conciliatory.

"Come, my dear fellow, don't let us fall out about nothing at all. I'm quite ready to listen to anything you have to say; only, before you take a step there's no retracing, do listen to reason."

"No, thank you; I've heard too much of what you call reason already; I'll hear no more. Stand out of my way."

"Nash, Nash, don't be hasty! If you'll only let me speak a dozen words, you'll view the situation in quite a different light."

"Shall I? Then I'll not let you speak them. I see the situation now in the only light I mean to see it. Stand out of my way."

Nash, moving forward, gripped Morgan by the shoulders; either the assault was unexpected, or he used great force. Swinging Morgan round, he sent him reeling backwards half across the room; until, coming into unlooked-for contact with a chair, he fell heavily on to the floor. Before he could recover Nash had gone from the room, and was out of the flat. Picking himself up, although he seemed a trifle dazed, Morgan went rushing after him. When he reached the landing he heard Nash's voice come up the well of the staircase, from the floor below.

"Porter, the man Morgan, whom I have left in Mr. Oldfield's flat, has no right whatever to be there."

"Hasn't he, sir? How's that? He seems to have done something to upset Mr. Clifford."

"When he comes down, if you find that he has anything on him belonging to the flat—papers, letters, anything—they have been stolen. If you allow him to leave the building with them on him, possibly you will be held responsible."

"Shall I? He shan't leave here with anything on him that doesn't belong to him, I promise you; there are two or three people about the place who'll see to that."

Mr. Morgan waited to hear no more. He slunk back into the flat and shut the door.

CHAPTER XXXI

HUSBAND AND WIFE

When Herbert Nash quitted Bloomsbury Mansions he went straight back to Littlehampton, by the last train of the day to reach that primitive place. When he arrived at Ocean Villas it was past ten o'clock. His wife had gone to bed; or, at least, she had retired to her bedroom. As a matter of fact, she felt as if she never wanted to go to bed again; unless going to bed was synonymous with eternal sleep. If only she could go to sleep and never wake! She was of opinion that she was the most miserable woman; many women think themselves that with less cause than she had. She was half-undressed, and, crouching on the floor, rested her head against the bed. In her hands was a telegram, which she had read again, and again, and again, until it seemed to have branded itself upon her throbbing brain so that she could not get it out of her sight even for a second. It had come to her earlier in the day, and, as telegrams are apt to be, was curt.

"Send another five hundred immediately. No excuses will be accepted.

"MORGAN."

Only a day or two ago she had given him a hundred pounds; then sent him another four hundred, and here already he was demanding five hundred more. The inference was plain; he would persist in his demands until he had wrung from her all that she had found on Donald Lindsay's table. Though he stripped her of every penny she would still be at his mercy; what would he demand from her then? Whatever it might be, how would she dare refuse him then, if she dare not refuse him now?

In a sense, indeed, she had refused him, as it was. He had bade her send the cash "immediately." That she had not done; she had purposely not sent it by the night's post; and now was racked by fears of the measures he might take to show her his resentment. Suppose he told her husband, as he had threatened to do? If he did! if he did! Had she not better hide in the sea before Herbert came back again?

His opportunities for telling were so numerous; he and Herbert were away together at that moment. That was another of her burdens. What was the meaning of this sudden, ill-omened connection which had sprung up between them? Why, all at once, had her husband become the inseparable companion of the man who had been wont to stand behind her chair? He had resented, so hotly, the fellow's presumption in even venturing to write to him; yet now they might be bosom friends; he even expected her to receive him as an equal. What did it mean?

Nothing kindles the imagination like a coward conscience. All sorts of hideous surmises had tormented her. A dozen explanations had occurred to her; every fresh one more unsavoury than the last. She could see that her husband had changed; in himself, as well as to her. He was not the same man; he was always brooding, irritable, depressed. Of late, not only had he not spoken to her a tender word, he had only addressed her when compelled, and then with scant civility. What did such conduct on his part portend? All kinds of doubts afflicted her; yet among them one was foremost. Was it not possible that Morgan had poisoned her husband's mind against her? He, perhaps, had not told him everything, she did not believe he had; but, with diabolical ingenuity, he might have hinted just enough to make Herbert afraid of hearing more. In that case her husband might be working Morgan's will under the delusion that, by so doing, he was protecting her; and all the while the man was wresting from her all that she had risked so much to gain—for Herbert's sake.

As, on the floor in the bedroom there, she wrestled with wild beasts of her own creation, on a sudden she heard the front door open, and a familiar step come into the house. It was her husband. She sprang to her feet, not with joy, but with terror. Why had he come back? He had told her that he would not return that night; perhaps not on the morrow. Why had he returned—when he had said that he would not return—without notice, at that hour of the night? for it seemed to her that she had been in her bedroom hours.

She heard him go into the sitting-room; finding it in darkness, no one there, he came towards where she was. As she heard him take the half-dozen steps which divided the two rooms, she stood by the bedstead, trembling from head to foot; it might have been her executioner, not her husband, who was coming. A wild, frenzied impulse came to her to turn the key in the lock, and so gain time; but before she could do it he had opened the door, and was standing in the room.

It did not need such a rarefied vision as hers was then to perceive that with him all was not well. She seemed to see him in a blaze of lightning, phantom-haunted, as she was. It was borne in on her that he saw her as the hideous thing she saw herself to be, and that that was why he stood there, white and terrible. If she could she would have dropped to the floor, and crawled to him, and hung about his knees, and cried for mercy; but she could not; she had to stand there, straight and rigid, waiting for him to speak. When he spoke his voice sounded strange in her ears, as indeed, though she was not aware of it, it did in his own.

"I see you guess why I am here!"

"Guess? How—how can I guess?"

"Has Morgan told you nothing?"

"Morgan? What—what could Morgan tell me?"

"Hasn't he told you that I'm a blackguard and a thief?"

The words were so wholly different from any she had expected him to utter that, in the stress of her agitation, they conveyed no meaning to her mind; she stared at him like one bereft of her senses, as, in fact, for the moment she was. He misconstrued her look entirely.

"Elaine," he cried, "don't look at me like that, don't! If you only knew what I have suffered, what I've gone through, you'd pity me, you wouldn't look at me as if I was something wholly outside the pale. I know you've guessed that there was something wrong ever since that—that brute came; you knew I wouldn't breathe the same air with him if I could help it; but it mayn't be, Elaine, it mayn't be so bad as you suppose. I don't ask you to forgive me; I don't even ask you to continue to regard me as your husband; I know I've forfeited all claims I may have had on you. All I ask of you is to believe that, at last, I'm going to try to be a man. I've come to tell you that, and to tell you that chiefly. I'm not going to stay; you need not fear that I'll contaminate the house which shelters you; but before I go I think I ought to tell you just what I've done, and what the temptation was; not to excuse myself, but so that, whatever happens, you, at least, may know the truth. I felt that I could not let the night pass without telling you the truth, if only because I have kept it from you so long, and in the morning it may be too late; I may not have the chance of telling it to you, face to face, again."

The longer he spoke, the more her bewilderment grew.

"I—I—don't understand," she stammered.

He made her understand, telling his tale as straightforwardly, as clearly, as it could be told; as it might have been told even by an impartial witness; the man that was in him was coming to the front at last.

"You see," he said, "I was at Morgan's mercy, or he thought I was; and, for a time, I thought so too; I was such a coward! And before long I should have been wholly at his mercy, had not the sight of that man, Clifford, roused me to a consciousness of what a coward I really was; then I knew that the only way to be free was to tell the truth, and let Morgan do what he likes. I've come to tell you the truth, first of all; and to-morrow I'm going to tell Frank Clifford the truth; and when I've found Miss Lindsay, I'll tell her the truth. If I have to suffer for it, I'll suffer; but at any rate I've escaped from Morgan. What a weight would have been off my mind if I'd escaped from him before!"

As she began to grasp the drift of what it was that he was telling her, she had sunk on to the edge of the bed, and, with distended eyes and gaping mouth, sat staring at him as if at some thing of horror. He mistook the meaning of her attitude.

"I don't wonder you look at me as if I were some repulsive object; I couldn't be more repulsive to you than I am to myself; I understand what you feel, what you think; I know I deserve it. I know you never would have married me if you had known me to be the thing I am; I have wronged you more than any one. I can't undo the bonds which bind us, that is not in my power, and I'm afraid the law will not help you. But this I can do, and I will; I'll take myself out of your life as completely as I can. Your aunt left you enough to live on; I think you had better sink it in an annuity; you'll be safer that way; and when I can I'll contribute what I can. I don't wish to be released from any of my obligations; on the contrary, I wish to fulfil them both in the letter and the spirit, and I will. So soon as I am earning money you shall have your proper share; but in any case it will be a comfort to me to feel that, in any case, you are provided for. And, in time, when I've done something towards regaining my self-respect, and—and you send for me, I'll come to you again, if only for just long enough to show that I am still alive. But you're rid of me till then. Good-bye."

He moved towards the door, as if the whole thing was at an end; as if husband and wife could be sundered quite so easily. She stopped him as he was going.

"Herbert!" She spoke in the queerest whisper, as if something had gone wrong with her vocal chords, the effect of which was to leave her partially strangled. She held out the telegram she had still in her hand. "Look at that."

He took it reluctantly, as if he feared it was a weapon which she aimed at him. Glancing at it, he read it aloud.

"'Send another five hundred immediately. No excuses will be accepted.

'MORGAN.'

What—what does this mean?"

"It means that I'm worse than you; much worse than you."

"Elaine!" She tried to speak, but could not; her voice was strangled in her throat; it was not nice to watch her struggles to regain the use of it. He moved towards her, startled. "Elaine! what's the matter?"

"I'm—I'm—I'm going to tell you, only I—I— Give me—something—to drink—there's some water—in the bottle." She pointed to the washstand. He brought her some water; but she could not drink it. She could not hold the glass in her own hand; she could not swallow when he raised it to her lips. He put the glass down on the floor. Her condition frightened him. Although he had just been speaking of leaving her for an indefinite period, now he knelt beside her on the floor, and, putting his arms about her, held her close, soothing her as best he could. It was while he held her that she told him; she confessed in her agony; the words being wrung from her as if they had been gouts of blood. He continued to hold her all the time. When, in his turn, he began to understand her story, he was man enough to realize that it was only his support which gave her the strength she needed; that but for his encircling arms, and the consciousness that they were his arms, she would collapse. As, by degrees, her meaning was borne in on his understanding, the fashion of his countenance was changed, and he kept his face averted, but he never moved. When, in disconnected sentences, the root of the matter had been told, she did what he had not done; she began, in a manner, to excuse herself. "It was—because you said that you wanted money, and—that we couldn't be married without it, that I went back and took the money—which was on the table. And Morgan saw me."

"Morgan saw you!"

It was the first time he had spoken; there was a curious contrast between his voice and hers.

"He was in the room all the time—but in the darkness—I never knew it."

"So Morgan has held us in the hollow of his hand; both of us!"

"I gave him five hundred pounds the other day, and now he's telegraphed for more."

"Poor Elaine! It seems, after all, that we're a well-matched pair, both thieves and cowards."

"Herbert!"

She spoke as if she shrieked.

"My dear, do let us look facts in the face now that we are trying to make ourselves known to each other."

"I—shouldn't have taken the money—if I hadn't thought—Nora was rich—and it would make no difference."

"I'm afraid that the question of Miss Lindsay's wealth or poverty could make no difference to the thing you did."

"I know that—now."

"When it seemed that Miss Lindsay was a pauper did you give her back any of the money you had taken under a misconception?"

"I meant to—but I never did—I meant to give her a thousand pounds."

"It's a pity you didn't; it might have caused the residue to appear a little less dingy. We're a pair of beauties! God help us both; we need His help!"

"I—haven't dared to ask for it."

But she did dare that night; they both of them dared. Already, since they had been married, they had had some strange days and nights; but that was the strangest night of their strange honeymoon.

CHAPTER XXXII

A FORGOTTEN COAT

Lady Jane Carruthers was one of those elderly ladies who are never quite well, yet seldom actually ill. She was a great believer in what she called "air."

"If you breathe the right air you're all right; and if you breathe the wrong air you're all wrong, and there's the whole science of medicine in a nutshell; believe me, my dear, because I know; mine's the teaching of actual experience. So long as I'm well in a place I stay there; I know the air's right; but so soon as I begin to feel a little out of sorts I know the air has ceased to be right, I go away at once; the consequence is that there are very few people who move about as much as I do."

It chanced that, in one of her pursuits after the right air, Lady Jane went to Littlehampton; and, being there, with nothing to do except breathe the right air, by way of doing something she sent for her nephew, the Hon. Robert Spencer. She dispatched to him this telegram—

"Come down to me this afternoon. I wish to speak to you."

When he received the telegram the Honourable Robert pulled a face; he happened to have a good deal to do. His impulse was to wire back—

"Can't come. Speak on."

However, he felt that the result of such a message might be disastrous; so, instead of sending it, he obeyed his aunt's commands, and went down to Littlehampton.

On his arrival, in response to his inquiries, Lady Jane informed him that the local air was still on its trial; she was not yet quite sure if it was, or was not, all right. It was true that she had had a touch of indigestion; but she was not certain if that had anything to do with the lobster salad she had had for luncheon three days running, or with some peculiarity in the neighbouring atmosphere. It was true that too much ozone was a disturbing influence; on the other hand she admitted that yesterday she had eaten rather more of the salad than she had meant to eat. Certainly the local lobsters were delicious; she had determined so much; but, for the present, the question of the quality of the local air was in suspense. The nephew knew his aunt. He was aware that if he asked her if there actually was anything which she wished to speak to him about she would look at him with chilly gaze, and inquire if she had not been speaking to him on matters of the most serious import already. Was he a Christian? Was he void of all human feeling? Did he take no interest in her health? Then what did he mean? As he did not wish to be asked what he meant in a tone of voice he had heard before, he listened to her ladyship doubting, now the lobsters, now the air, with the best grace in the world; for the Honourable Robert Spencer really was an excellent fellow. And, in course of time, his virtue was rewarded.

After dinner—at which there was no fish at all, as if it had been he who had suffered from the lobsters— she assumed a portentous air, and requested him to bring a dispatch-box, which stood on a side table, and place it in front of her; which he did.

"Robert," she began, "I regret to have to tell you that you are one of the most careless persons I have ever encountered." He admitted it; inwardly wondering of what act of carelessness he had been guilty this time, and what the dispatch-box had to do with it anyhow. Her ladyship went on. "When you were staying with me in Cairo, after you left me, you lost a suit-case; or, at least, you said you lost a suit-case."

"My dear aunt, I not only said, I actually did lose a suit-case; and a most important loss it was; for all I can tell it may have transformed the whole course of my life; and—and somebody else's life as well. By some stroke of good fortune you haven't come across it, have you?"

"No, Robert, I have not; nor do I imagine that anybody ever will, in this world." Whether she thought it likely that somebody would in another world was not quite clear. "I do not know if you are aware that, apart from your suit-case, you lost something else when you were staying with me at Cairo. I imagine, from your manner, that you have not discovered your loss even yet."

"It's very possible; I seem to have such a genius for losing things that sometimes I don't know what I do lose."

"I am grieved to hear you say so; it amazes me. It only shows how incapable a man is of looking after his own belongings; as I have always maintained. I never lost anything in my life, except a pair of house-shoes, which I left at Horsham House, and which have never been returned to me to this hour."

"I hope it was nothing very important I left."

"It depends upon what you call important. There are different standards in such matters; though you appear to have none. I should call it important; but then my wardrobe is limited. You left a coat and waistcoat."

"Well, I rather fancy that my wardrobe is more limited than yours; but—I don't recall that coat and waistcoat."

"I am not surprised; after what you have just said, nothing would surprise me. Baker brought them to me after you had gone; an admirable servant, Baker. Were I to repeat to her what you have admitted she would credit it with difficulty; she knows my ways. In the inside pocket of the coat were some papers."

"Papers? Aunt! What papers?"

Lady Jane unlocked the dispatch-box; took from it a small packet; and, placing her glasses on her nose, proceeded to read what was written on half-a-sheet of note-paper.

"This is an inventory of what was contained in the pockets of your two garments. Unlike you, fortunately, or I don't know where I should be, I am a creature of method; I do everything by rule. I drew up this list after Baker had searched the garments in my presence. In the waistcoat were three pockets; which contained, one penknife; two toothpicks—which I threw away; one pencil, or, rather, part of a pencil; three wax matches, loose, which were most dangerous, and which I had destroyed; a cigar-cutter, or, rather, what I presume is a cigar-cutter, Baker didn't know what it was; four visiting-cards, three of them your own, and the fourth somebody else's, and all of them shockingly untidy; and the return half of a ticket from Brighton to London, which was then more than three months old. In the coat were five pockets; it has always been a mystery to me what men want with so many pockets; judging from what was in yours I am inclined to think that they use them merely as receptacles for rubbish. Some of the things which were in yours I had thrown away; the following are what I have kept. One pocket-handkerchief; one pair of gloves; one tobacco-pouch; one pipe, a horrid, smelling thing which I had boiled in soapy water, but which still smells; one matchbox—empty. I suppose it was meant to contain the matches which were loose in your waistcoat; a cigar-case; a golf ball; while in the inside pocket were the papers of which I have told you."

"I don't suppose they're anything very serious, after what you've just been reading."

"Don't you? Then you must have your own ideas of what is serious; if I had thought they were of no interest I shouldn't have troubled you to come to Littlehampton."

"But, my dear aunt, what are they? You—you do keep a man on tenter-hooks."

"I don't know why you say that. I am going to tell you what they are; but, as you are of opinion that they are not serious, I should have imagined that you were in no hurry. There are letters written to you by Miss Lindsay; there are nine of them; some men would have thought them serious."

As he took the packet which she held out to him his countenance changed in a manner which was almost comically sudden.

"Letters written by—Why, they're Nora's! But—I thought—"

"Never mind what you thought, Robert; you see what they are. As this envelope is sealed, and is inscribed that it is not to be opened till after the writer's death, some persons might have thought that that was of interest also."

He regarded the envelope she offered as if he found it difficult to believe that his eyes were not playing him a trick. "Aunt, it's—it's the envelope which Donald Lindsay sent me, and— But I don't understand; it's incredible! Aunt, why didn't you let me know this before?"

"Why should I? It was in a coat of which you thought so little that you didn't even know you'd lost it; the natural inference was that you were hardly likely to leave anything of the least importance in the pocket of a coat which you valued at nothing."

"But—I thought I put it in my suit-case—I've chased the case half round the world. Aunt, what have you done?"

"What have I done? You mean, what have you done? If anything has been done I trust it is something from which you will learn a lesson. I said to myself, if these are of the least consequence, he will ask for them; since he has been guilty of such culpable carelessness I'll wait till he does ask. But I waited, and I waited, and you never asked, you never once alluded to them. What could I conclude? At last they slipped my memory, as sometimes trifles will do; I came upon them, by mere accident, as I was looking through this dispatch-box last night; so I sent for you that I might give them to you in person, though, naturally, I had long ago come to the conclusion that they were not of the slightest importance."

He drew a long breath.

"Well, this is the most extraordinary thing that ever has happened to me!"

"If that is the case I can only hope that it will teach you not to leave papers in the pockets of a coat which you fling down anywhere, anyhow, and instantly forget."

"I—I hope it will teach me something of the kind. As this envelope may contain a communication of much consequence, may I ask you to excuse me while I go to examine it at once?

"Why is it necessary that you should leave me? Why can't you examine it here? You know what an interest I take in all that concerns you. Sit down; open your envelope; see what's inside; you need fear no interruption from me."

"Then—if you don't mind—I will." Inside the envelope were two sheets of large letter paper, closely covered, on all eight sides, with Donald Lindsay's fine handwriting. Robert Spencer had not read far before he broke into exclamation. "What the—I beg your pardon, aunt—I didn't quite—but this is most extraordinary." As he read on, more than once he punctuated his reading with interjectional remarks; evidently what he read occasioned him profound surprise. When he had finished he looked about him as if he was not quite sure where he was. When he perceived Lady Jane he started from his chair in evident perturbation; as good as her word, she had not interrupted him by so much as a movement, and now sat eyeing him grimly. He turned to her with a laugh which did not sound very natural. "Well, aunt, we've done it, you and I, between us!"

"Pray attribute nothing to me; I decline to accept any responsibility for your criminal carelessness."

"I can only say that while Nora Lindsay has been treated like a fraudulent pauper, turned out of house and home, sent out into the world to earn her bread, she may be starving for all I know; I've left no stone unturned, but I've been able to find no trace of her; all the time the letter has been lying in your desk which shows that she is one of the richest women in England, and I verily believe that her father owed no man anything."

"If that is so, Robert, then I don't envy you your feelings when you reflect that Miss Lindsay's sufferings are solely and entirely the result of your own misconduct."

"If you had only let me know you had the letter!"

"Are you attempting to fasten blame on me? For your monstrous and incredible negligence in doing nothing, and less than nothing, to safeguard a document which you now assert is of such importance!"

"Well, what's done's done! And Nora has had her home taken from her, and the things she cared for scattered to the four winds; it's been one of the greatest steals on record! and she's been shamed in the face of all the world, and she may be eating out her heart in some last refuge of the destitute, and all the while—It's a pretty story, on my word!"

"It all comes from your mother and father taking it for granted that the girl was a beggar; I nearly had a serious quarrel with your mother because I told her I shouldn't be surprised if, after all, she was mistaken; but your mother's like her son."

"Thank you, aunt; my mother only took for granted what others took for granted. I've heard you say some severe things about Miss Lindsay."

"I've simply said that you're not in a position to marry a penniless girl; and you're not."

"If I could only have found her I'd have made her marry me, though she hadn't a shoe to her foot, nor a penny in her pocket; I'd not have let her go until she did. Thank God, she knew it, and that's why she's hidden herself. Poor Nora! Will she—will she ever forgive any of us! It's a tragedy I've never heard the like of; and all through some one's blundering. But, as I've said, talk's no healer. I can't go to-night, there's no train; but I shall go up to town in the morning to investigate some of the statements which are contained in this letter; and now, if you don't mind, aunt, I must get out of doors; I must have what you're so fond of—air."

He wanted something more than air; he wanted a vent for the feelings which filled his breast, as it seemed to him, to bursting point. He tore up and down the front; he had it to himself at that hour, so that the unusual pace at which he strode along did not attract inconvenient attention. The promenade at Littlehampton is not a very long one, but he walked ever so many miles before he had done with it. It was easy enough to blame Lady Jane; he felt strongly that that lady had not behaved so well as she might have done; keeping a letter from him while the weeks stretched out into months seemed to him to be a course of action for which there was no excuse; but, all the same, he was perfectly well aware that the fault was originally his. The parable of the grain of mustard-seed came into his mind as he thought of the Upas-tree of disaster which had sprung from a beginning which was apparently so insignificant; he thought he had put the letter in his suit-case and he had left it in one of his pockets instead; because of that slight misadventure ruin had come to Nora; such ruin! His aunt had punished him severely. He could not recall the coat even then; the only explanation of which he could think was that he had supposed he had packed the coat itself in his suitcase. If Lady Jane had but dropped so much as a hint! He did not know how much cause he had to rejoice because the letter was not where he had believed it to be; if Mr. Morgan had only found it when he reclaimed the suit-case it might have provided him with the means of keeping Nora Lindsay out of her own for an indefinite length of time; the tragedy might have become a tragedy indeed.

In the morning, when Mr. Spencer reached the station, on the platform were two familiar figures. He advanced to greet them.

"Why, Mr. Nash, and Miss Harding! this is an unexpected pleasure; I didn't expect to find such pleasant memories of Cloverlea at Littlehampton."

"Miss Harding," exclaimed the gentleman, "is now my wife; she is Mrs. Nash. We"—he hesitated, and then went on—"we are just finishing our honeymoon."

Mr. Spencer's face expressed astonishment which was hardly flattering to either of the parties concerned.

"You—don't say so; then—that's another unexpected pleasure. Mrs. Nash, you must allow me to offer you my congratulations."

He was about to go with some of the banal remarks which are made on such occasions when he was struck by the look which was on the young wife's face, and by the singularity of her attitude. She seemed to be in mortal terror. Shrinking back, cowering, she clung to her husband's arm, as if she was afraid that Spencer would have struck her. Nor did Herbert Nash wear the expression of beatitude which is supposed to be proper to a bridegroom who is returning from his honeymoon. It was apparently with an effort that he said to Robert Spencer—

"If you are going up by this train, Mr. Spencer, will you allow my wife and me to travel with you? If—if we can get a compartment to ourselves we have something to tell you, touching Miss Lindsay's affairs, which—which I think we ought to tell you."

The separate compartment was found; and, as a consequence, between Littlehampton and London, Robert Spencer read human nature, as it were, by flashes of lightning. Both husband and wife laid bare their breasts to him; and what they left unsaid he saw between the lines. It was a journey neither of the trio ever forgot. By the time the train entered the terminus his soul shuddered at the thought of the mountain of wrong which had been laid upon the woman he loved; who, after all, was the merest girl.

Yet, acutely though he felt for her, he felt also for the miserable pair who were in front of him; already they had probably suffered even more than Nora; and the worst of their sufferings were still to come.

The three got into a four-wheeled cab and drove to Memorial Buildings. Mr. Clifford was out. Then, the clerk who received them asked if they were Messrs. Morgan and Nash.

"This is Mr. Nash," explained the Honourable Robert, "but my name's Spencer. Has Mr. Morgan been here?"

No, he had not. Mr. Clifford had been at the office till eleven o'clock; and had then left word that if Messrs. Nash and Morgan called in his absence they were to be informed that he had gone to Mr. Hooper, of Fountain Court, Temple, where they would find him if they liked to follow.

CHAPTER XXXIII

THE AUTOGRAPH ALBUM

Mr. Hooper, leaning back in his chair, surveyed his cousin as if he were some strange animal.

"Although your conduct strikes me as—shall I say?—abnormal, I don't wish to insinuate anything disagreeable, my dear Frank; still, if you are sane I wish you'd prove it."

Mr. Clifford passed his handkerchief across his brow, as if he found the temperature trying.

"It's all very well to laugh—if you're supposed to be laughing—but, if you were in my position, you'd find it no laughing matter. I'm to be married next week."

"That is a prospect calculated to turn the strongest brain; granted!"

"Look here, Jack, I'll throw something at you if you talk like that; I've come for sense, not idiocy. Under the circumstances Mr. Oldfield's continued absence—and silence—was pretty bad to bear; and now to be told he's dead—"

"Dead? you don't mean to say that Oldfield's dead!"

"So I was informed last night by two men, one named Nash, and the other Morgan. Nash introduced himself as Oldfield's solicitor, and Morgan said he was his sole executor. A more unclubable man than Morgan I never met; he's not even a good imitation of a gentleman; how Oldfield came to appoint him as his sole executor is beyond my comprehension."

"What can you expect from a pill-man? I should take anything as a matter of course from the proprietor of Peter Piper's Popular Pills."

"They're a sound, wholesome medicine."

"Of course; we won't flog a dead donkey. And when did Oldfield die? and what of? did you know that he was ill?"

"I hadn't the ghost of a notion. And the best—or rather the worst—of it is that Messrs. Nash and Morgan seem to take it for granted that I knew all about it; especially the man Morgan."

"Why should he do that? And what's the harm if he does?"

Clifford was drumming on the table with his finger-tips, nervously; as a rule he was one of the coolest and most collected of men; now his embarrassment was obvious.

"That's one of the charms of the position; showing that one man may know another for a long time, and yet know nothing at all about him. According to the two gentlemen Joseph Oldfield lived a double life, and his name wasn't Oldfield at all."

"There you are again, the pill-man! It at least looks as if he had the saving grace of being ashamed to have it known that he was connected with his own pills."

"I admit it does make it look as if he were ashamed, though I don't see why he should have been; since, as I say, they are a sound and wholesome medicine."

"No doubt; the elixir of life; cure all ills; see advertisements."

"There is no reason why a man should be more ashamed of being associated with an honest medicine than with the profession of the law, which is not all honesty."

"True, O king! Still, however, let's pass on. If his name wasn't Oldfield, what was it?"

"Can't you guess?"

"Can't I—would you mind saying that again; only let me warn you that if you've come here to ask riddles there'll be ructions."

"Don't be an ass, if you can help it! I saw the girl who's in the next room in his room, yesterday."

"You saw her? I don't believe it."

"At least I saw her likeness; it was on his writing-table. She seemed to be looking at me during the whole of a very unpleasant scene; it was odd how the feeling that she was looking at me affected me; the excellence of the likeness is proved by the fact that I recognized her as the original the moment I saw her."

"Then do you mean—"

"I mean that, according to Messrs. Nash and Morgan, Oldfield's real name was Lindsay, Donald Lindsay, of Cloverlea. What's Miss Lindsay doing here?"

It was Mr. Hooper's turn to look surprised. As was his custom, when at all moved, getting up from his chair, he began to wander about the room.

"Why—she's typing, very badly, some absolutely worthless rubbish, for the magnificent payment of two guineas a week, which I can't afford to pay her."

"That sounds involved. Do you mean that she acts as your typewriter?"

"No, sir; she's my jobbing secretary; though I don't know what that is; nor does she. And in that position she's earning two guineas a week; which is more than I am."

"What's the idea?"

"The idea is that she's a lady; and that she wanted to earn her daily bread, desperately badly. Mind, you're not to breathe a word of this to her, or she'll go away at once, and probably never forgive me into the bargain."

"It strikes me that you've been entertaining an angel unawares. She says she's the daughter of Donald Lindsay, of Cloverlea."

"What she says goes. That girl wouldn't tell a lie—well, she wouldn't."

"Then in that case she must be worth piles of money. I don't understand why she's here; unless—Is it possible that she doesn't know of the connection between Lindsay and Oldfield?"

"Frank, there's a mystery about that girl; I've suspected it all along; now suspicion's growing to certainty. Let's ask her to come in, and we'll put her in the box. I'd give—more than I am ever likely to have, to be to her a bearer of good tidings."

"Jack! Is it like that?"

"You idiot! I've only known her about two minutes; besides, she'd never look at the likes of me; I feel it in the marrow of my bones. But that's no reason why, if you have good news for her, she shouldn't know them."

"One moment! The point on which I've come to consult you I haven't yet reached; and a very nasty one it is; all the same, my dear Jack, we must leave Miss Lindsay till we've discussed it. I'm accused of having committed forgery."

"Frank! you're jesting!"

"It would be a grim jest if I were; but I'm not. Yesterday Mr. Morgan charged me, point-blank, with having forged—and uttered—bills, for over forty thousand pounds; more, he seemed amazed because I did not at once confess my guilt and throw myself upon his mercy."

"The man's a lunatic!"

"Mr. Nash did not directly associate himself with Mr. Morgan's charges; on the other hand, he did not dissociate himself. His attitude puzzled me. I fancy that he had no doubt about my guilt until he met me, and that, afterwards, his judgment was in suspense."

"But what foundation had either of these men for such a monstrous accusation?"

"That's the difficulty; Morgan professes to believe he has a sound one."

"Whose name are you supposed to have forged?"

"Donald Lindsay's."

"But you never heard it till yesterday."

"That is so; but Morgan called me a liar, right out, when I said so; and appearances may be against me. Jack, I'm in an awkward position."

"I don't see why; you can bring Mr. Morgan to book, and there's an end of him."

"There's more in it than you suppose; it's not so simple. Let me explain; or at least try to. You've heard me speak of a man named Trevor, Harry Trevor?"

"I know! Sir Henry Trevor! He's a blackguard!"

"I'm afraid he's not all that he might be, but that has only begun to dawn upon me lately. At one time he and I were intimate. When I was last in Paris I met him one day on the Boulevard. Although, somehow, we'd drifted apart; our paths in life lay in different directions; still I was very glad to see him, and we chummed up at once. He was living in Paris; had an apartment on the Champs Elysée, at the top there, near the Arch. He knew everybody; took me about; I had a royal time. One night I dined with him in his rooms, he and I alone together. Now I'm reluctant to make a direct charge, because I've no proof to offer, but I wondered then, and I've wondered still more since, if he hadn't done something to his wine."

"How—done something?"

"You know I'm an abstemious man, I don't care for wine; as a rule I drink nothing at meals, not even water. But on an occasion like that it was different. I had one glass of champagne, one of those small tumblers; when the servant began to fill it up I stopped him; not that there was anything wrong with the champagne, I feel sure there wasn't. After dinner, with our fruit, we had some port; I wanted neither the port nor the fruit, but Trevor insisted. The servant had left the room; he himself took a bottle out of a cupboard; he laid it in a cradle; he drew the cork; you know the fuss some men make about drawing a cork of what they allege is a remarkable bottle of wine. He made all that fuss, he insisted upon my sampling it; of course after all the business he had gone through, I had no option; he poured me out a glassful. Now I believe that wine was not all he pretended."

"What makes you think it?"

"As soon as I tasted it I didn't like it, I told him so. He said I should change my opinion by the time I'd finished the glass; so—merely to get rid of it—I finished the glass in a hurry, and I liked it less than ever."

"How did it affect you?"

"It upset me; I was conscious that I was not in a condition in which I should care to do business."

"Did you say anything?"

"I told him that I thought the wine had a very funny taste; but he only laughed and said it was evident that I was no judge of port."

"You only had one glass?"

"One only; nothing short of physical force would have induced me to touch another drop."

"Then what did you do?"

"We went into the other room, his sitting-room. He took out an autograph album, it seemed that he collected autographs; though that was the first I'd heard of it. He began to talk about imitating people's handwriting, how good some were at it. Now it's a fact that I've always had an unfortunate facility for imitating handwriting."

"It is, as you say, an unfortunate facility; one not overmuch to be desired."

"When I was at school I used to imitate the masters' writing, the other fellows' writing, anybody's writing; it used to give me a sort of importance in the eyes of the other boys, and I'm afraid I sometimes used my gift in ways which weren't altogether to my credit; you haven't forgotten what boys are. Trevor was at school with me, so he knew all about it. As he turned over page after page of his album, he kept saying that I couldn't imitate this writing, and I couldn't imitate that; I hadn't tried my hand since I had left school; I didn't know if he was right or wrong, and I didn't care. Finally he came to a signature which, so far as I remember, was on a scrap of paper which might have been torn off the bottom of a letter; the name itself was recalled to my memory with unpleasant vividness yesterday—it was Donald Lindsay."

"Frank!"

"We are fearfully and wonderfully made. It had gone clean out of my mind till Mr. Morgan showed it to me yesterday on a bill of exchange; then it came back with a rush of recollection which frightened me. Wasn't that an extraordinary thing?"

"Go on; I don't see yet what you are coming to."

"Trevor made a special point of this signature. He sat down and imitated it himself, and then challenged me to do better. His imitation was a bad one; and—I did better."

"What did you write on?"

"I have a vague impression that it was on a blank sheet of paper; but I was in such a state of muddle that I couldn't positively affirm. Had I been myself I should have changed the conversation before, but I was in such a condition that I could only sit and listen, with but a dim appreciation of his meaning."

"But you do remember copying Donald Lindsay's signature on what you believe was a blank sheet of paper?"

"Unfortunately I do; the name meant nothing to me; I had never heard of such a person; I acted on Trevor's persistent suggestion practically like a man might do who was in a mesmeric trance. When I had finished, Trevor, taking it up, declared it wasn't a bit like, and, if I couldn't do better than that, he'd beaten me. So I tried again."

"You mean that you copied Donald Lindsay's signature a second time?"

"I did."

"On the same sheet of paper?"

"I couldn't positively say, but it wouldn't surprise me to be told that it was on a fresh sheet. I've a hazy notion that I copied it a third and fourth time; Trevor each time declaring that it was not a bit like. By that time my brain was torpid, all I could do was move my fingers; presently I could no longer move those. I lost consciousness. The next thing I can recollect is waking up in bed at my hotel feeling very ill. I rang for the waiter. When he appeared he told me, with a grin, that I had been brought to the hotel in a cab; that I had had to be carried out, borne up-stairs, undressed, and put to bed; the inference being that I was drunk. But I knew better. There happened to be staying in the hotel a doctor who practises at Karlsbad, with whom I had some acquaintance, Dr. Adler, a man of cosmopolitan reputation. I sent for him, and when he came he at once pronounced that I had been poisoned."

"Poisoned? Actually poisoned?"

"Actually poisoned. Adler saved my life; I believe that without him I should have died. It was three days before I could get out of bed; and then I was so weak that I had to be helped across the room."

"What did you do?"

"I sent a note to Trevor, by hand. The messenger returned with it, saying Trevor had left Paris the day after I had dined with him, and his apartment was shut up."

"And then?"

"I returned to London. I had already overstayed my time; I was wanted at the office; I resumed my duties, and forgot all about it; or, at least, I tried to. What could I do? The conclusion to which I came was that there had been something wrong with the wine. I had known Trevor the greater part of his life; I had never known him to be guilty of a disreputable action; I could conceive of no motive which might induce him to play tricks with an old friend, at his own table; I resolved that, when occasion offered, I would tell him the tragic tale of how his port had affected me; until yesterday I supposed that it was by sheer accident that so far an opportunity had not arisen, and that I had heard and seen nothing of Trevor from that day to this; and there you are!"

"That's not all the story."

"So far as I've actual knowledge it is; the rest is mere surmise, based on what Mr. Morgan told me yesterday. He says that bills for over forty thousand pounds, purporting to be signed by Donald Lindsay, have been discounted by Trevor, who asserted that he had them from me. If that's true it looks as if those pieces of paper on which I copied Lindsay's signature were bill stamps."

"Have you no recollection of them whatever?"

"None. If that is so then the possibility is that Trevor knew of the connection between Lindsay and Oldfield; and that that is why he hocussed me—Oldfield's managing man—into copying Lindsay's name; which points to a plot, on Trevor's part, of the most iniquitous kind."

"Where is Sir Henry Trevor now?"

"That I don't know. After leaving Morgan last night I hunted for him everywhere; wired to Paris, searched all over London. Nothing has been heard of him at any of his old haunts for at any rate the last three or four months; he seems to have vanished."

"Who discounted the bills?"

"That, also, I can't tell you; we shall probably hear all about that from Mr. Morgan. What I want to learn is, legally, in what position do I stand?"

"It's not easy to say. To begin with they'll have to prove that the bills were forged."

"And then?"

"Then they'll have to produce Trevor. A man who is capable of behaving as he has done is quite likely to be willing to swear that he received the bills in their completed state from you."

"Which means?"

"Your word against his; to clear yourself you'll have to convict him, which mayn't be easy, or agreeable for you."

"Sounds cheerful; especially as I'm to be married next week!"

"There's one hope for you."

"Only one? Let's have it."

"The fact that Miss Lindsay is in the next room. If she has anything to do with it she'll even forgive you for allowing yourself to get mixed up with such a scamp as Trevor; I know more about him than it seems you do. That girl could forgive anybody anything, she's a saint in embryo. I suggest that we invite her to come in here, and that we then put to her some leading questions."

CHAPTER XXXIV

When Nora entered she looked from one man to the other, as if she wondered by which of them her presence was desired. She declined the chair which Mr. Hooper offered. On his persisting in his request to her to be seated she observed, with the naïve mixture of humility and pride which became her so well, that she would rather not sit, as she was engaged in copying a passage which was more than usually involved, and to which she would like to return as soon as she could. Mr. Hooper, at her back, directed a glance at Mr. Clifford, of which, had she intercepted it, she would probably have required a prompt explanation.

"I think, Miss Lindsay," he said, "that it is possible that you will do no more copying for me, and that the passage of which you speak may remain unfinished."

She turned quickly round to him, alarm on her face.

"Mr. Hooper! Why do you say that? What have I done?"

"Everything you have done, Miss Lindsay, you have done excellently; if you will permit me to ask you a few questions, you will understand why I say it. Please sit down."

"Thank you; I much prefer to stand."

"You, of course, are at liberty to please yourself; but, in that case, Mr. Clifford and I must also continue to stand, and that may be inconvenient." Thereupon she subsided on to the chair which he had placed for her, glancing as she did so at the two men in front of her as if she suspected them of having conspired together to compel her to seat herself against her will. Mr. Hooper assumed an air which was almost judicial. "I beg you to believe, Miss Lindsay, that in putting to you the questions I am about to put I am actuated only by considerations of your own interests. If they seem at all impertinent, I assure you that it is in appearance only; as, if you will answer them frankly, you will immediately perceive. To begin with, how many children had your father beside yourself?"

It is possible that she looked as surprised as she felt; she could hardly have felt more surprised than she looked. She hesitated; then briefly answered—

"None."

"Then—pardon me if I pain you—were you not on good terms with your father when he died?"

Her eyes opened wider; it seemed that her amazement grew.

"Of course I was; what do you mean? If you had ever known my father you wouldn't have dreamt of asking such a—such a silly question; I don't wish to be rude, but you wouldn't. My father never said an angry word to me in the whole of his life."

"But, in that case, to whom did he leave his money?"

"To me."

"To you?"

"He left everything he had in the world to me absolutely; I don't know quite what it means, but I know that's what they said, absolutely."

"Then now it's my turn not to understand you. Your father was an immensely wealthy man. If you are his heiress, how is it I have the honour, and happiness, of seeing you here, in receipt of a modest weekly salary?"

"Every one thought papa was rich; I did; I understood him to tell me himself that he was; but it seemed, after all, that he wasn't. Indeed, as soon as he was dead, some man said he owed him a great deal of money, for bills."

"Bills!"

The interruption came from Clifford.

"I don't know what kind of bills they were; but I know they were bills of some kind, because I was told so; then they came and sold everything to get money to pay the bills, and I was left with nothing."

The two men eyed each other as if the significance of what the girl said surpassed their comprehension. Mr. Clifford continued his interposition.

"Miss Lindsay, Mr. Hooper has told you my name; it is Clifford—Frank Clifford. I believe I knew your father for many years, and am indebted to him for many kindnesses. Did he never mention my name to you?"

"Clifford? No, I don't remember his ever having done so."

"I saw your portrait in his rooms yesterday, and when I saw you this morning I recognized you at once."

"His rooms? What rooms?"

"His rooms in town."

"I didn't know he had any; we couldn't find out that he had an address in town."

"You couldn't find out that he had an address in town? I don't understand; there is something very strange here. Do you know a Mr. Nash?"

"Herbert Nash? He acted as my solicitor after my father was dead."

"Your solicitor, or your father's?"

"Mine. He went through my father's papers with a friend, and it was he who discovered that he had left no money."

"This is stranger and stranger. How many executors did your father appoint?"

"Executors?"

"How many executors did your father appoint in his will?"

"I never heard that he appointed any."

"Then did you ever hear of a Mr. Morgan?"

"Morgan? Stephen Morgan? Stephen Morgan was our butler at Cloverlea."

Mr. Clifford gave what seemed like a gasp of astonishment.

"Your butler! Miss Lindsay, would you mind describing your butler?" She did it so minutely that he identified his visitor of yesterday beyond a doubt. "I have had the pleasure of meeting Mr. Morgan, Miss Lindsay; but he did not introduce himself as your father's butler. Would it be asking too much to ask you to describe your father?"

"I can do better than that. He never would be photographed by a professional, but I managed to snap him two or three times with my own camera; I have a print of the very last snapshot I took of him here. It's not much as a photograph, but it's not a bad likeness." She took an old-fashioned gold locket from the bosom of her dress, and, opening it, held it out for Mr. Clifford to see. On one side was the portrait of her father; on the other was the portrait of some one else. "That," she explained, rather lamely, "is a portrait of—of some one I used to know."

"This," declared Mr. Clifford, looking at the likeness on the other side, "is the portrait of the man I have known for many years as Joseph Oldfield."

"As who? That's my father!"

"Do you not know he had a business in town?"

"I did not know he had a business anywhere."

"He had; he carried on that business under a pseudonym; I have always known him as Joseph Oldfield; for the first time yesterday I heard the name of Donald Lindsay. It seems to have been his wish that his commercial and his private lives should be wholly distinct, overlapping at no point; he appears to have succeeded in carrying out that wish almost too well."

"How—how extraordinary; and yet I'm not surprised. That is what he has been trying to tell me all the time."

"All what time?"

There was something in her tone and manner which struck the two men as curious; a sort of exaltation.

"He has been coming to me, night after night, in my dreams, always in such trouble; always trying so hard to tell me something; but he never could. Now I know what it was. If he comes again he'll understand that I know, and his trouble will have gone. You mustn't laugh at me; in my dreams his coming has been so real." Judging from their faces neither of her hearers was inclined for laughter. She turned to Mr. Clifford. "What was my father's business?"

"He was the proprietor of Peter Piper's Popular Pills, of which you have probably heard."

"Why"—her face was illumined by a smile—"he always had a stock of them in the house; it was a standing joke. He used to give a box to nearly every one who came, declaring that they were a simple, safe medicine for what he called 'common complaints.'"

Mr. Clifford bestowed on Mr. Hooper what might be described as a glare of triumph.

"So they are, Miss Lindsay; it is only ignorant people who doubt it. No one was in a better position to know than your father was, and he was their sole proprietor. If he left you all his property, then I am fortunate in being the first to tell you that, of my own knowledge, you are the owner of at least a million."

"A million! Mr. Clifford! Then—then—"

She had the locket still open, and was looking at the likeness which she had described as the portrait of some one she used to know; as she looked her sentence came to a premature end, and her face was dyed with blushes. Mr. Clifford went on, a little heatedly.

"You have been badly used, Miss Lindsay; monstrously used; and by those who should have made it their first aim to use you well."

Her radiant face contrasted oddly with his warmth.

"What does it matter? It has done me no harm. All the while I've felt that God was leading me through the darkness unto the light; and that's what He has done. So see how much I have to thank Him for."

The door was opened by Mr. Gibb.

"Two gentlemen and a lady to see Mr. Frank Clifford."

Without waiting for further announcement the visitors came in; in front Robert Spencer; behind him Herbert Nash, with Elaine at his side. When the lovers saw each other, each stood gazing as if fearful that the other was some entrancing vision which might resolve itself into air and vanish. Both cried, as if it was the most delightful and wonderful thing in the world that it should be so—

"You!"

They advanced, and only just in the nick of time remembered that there were others there; they could not have got closer and kept out of each other's arms. Mr. Spencer spoke as if in an ecstasy.

"You queen of dear women, I've ransacked all the stray corners of the world for you! Where have you been hiding?"

"Why," she replied, "I've been trying to earn my living."

"My Lady Quixote! all the while you've been a millionaire!"

"So Mr. Clifford has just told me. I haven't had time to realize it yet; but I think I'm glad."

"You only think?"

"I'm sure." She added—they were so close!—these words, which reached his ear only, "For your sake!" As she whispered her face crimsoned. Before he could answer she had moved forward. "Elaine!" When she advanced the other shrank back. "Why, Elaine, what's the matter?"

Mr. Spencer spoke.

"Miss Harding is now Mrs. Nash. If you will go with her into the next room I think you will find that she has something which she wishes to say to you."

So Nora went with Elaine into the adjoining chamber. The four men, left to themselves, began, with each other's aid, to piece together, into a comprehensible whole, the scattered parts of Donald Lindsay's strange history. While in the little room, where she had had such struggles with the typewriter, in the hour of her happiness, Nora had to listen to a tale of sin; and even while she listened, her one thought was how to comfort the sinner, to lead her, through the darkness, unto the light.

CHAPTER XXXV

BREAD UPON THE WATERS

Although so recently returned to the House of Commons, Robert Spencer has already made his mark; discerning judges on both sides of the House prophesy that ere long he will become a power in the State. If he does he will owe his success in no slight measure to his wife. Few things help a man more than a happy marriage; about the happiness of his marriage there can be no question. His wife is one of the loveliest women in London; one of the most charming, in the best sense of the word. All decent folk are proud to know she is their friend; the other sort know she is not their enemy. She has help and sympathy for all.

Peter Piper's Popular Pills still belong to Nora. Mr. Clifford not only continues to manage them; he has a share in the fruits of their prosperity. He was married on the appointed day, to Miss Ross's relief. Nora and Mr. Spencer were both present at the wedding, and Mr. Hooper was the groom's best man. The honeymoon tour was carried out on the lines originally planned. Nothing was done in the business of the forged bills. When matters were explained to Nora she insisted that nothing should be done. Probably hers was the part of wisdom; it is difficult to see how good would have resulted. Sir Henry Trevor still continues vanished; but it seems not unlikely that he is flourishing somewhere on the other side of the world. Occasionally remittances are received, sometimes for considerable sums, posted from different towns on the American continent, in envelopes which contain, beside the remittances, nothing but a half-sheet of paper, on which is always the same line, "Towards the discharge of a debt due to Donald Lindsay's estate." The inference is that these amounts come from Sir Henry Trevor, who has chosen this method of salving an obligation of which he alone knows the precise history.

Mr. and Mrs. Herbert Nash are in Canada, where they have not done badly. Nash is an honest and hard-working man; if anything, a trifle hard and stern. His wife is a good mistress of his home. She is the mother of three children. It is her continual prayer that they may not be led into temptation, but delivered from evil.

Stephen Morgan died in a London hospital on the day before Frank Clifford was married. He was knocked down by a motor omnibus. When he was taken to the hospital he was already unconscious, and already dying. On his return to consciousness, he was plainly near the end. With what seemed to be almost his last breath he begged that they would send for Mr. Clifford. Before, however, Mr. Clifford reached the hospital, he was dead. His ill deeds died with him.

Mr. and Mrs. Spencer have a house in the country, but not at Cloverlea. Nora had no desire to renew associations which had suffered so severe an interruption. The lodge at the gate of the new house is in the occupation of Mrs. Gibb and Miss Gibb—Angel Gibb. Miss Gibb is engaged to the second gardener. A question has lately arisen as to whether, on the occasion of their approaching marriage, he shall go and live with his wife and her mother, or whether his wife and her mother shall come and live with him. The point has been referred by both parties to Mrs. Spencer, who finds it rather a difficult one to decide.

Mr. Gibb is still with Mr. Hooper. He reports that business is looking up. It is a fact that of late several briefs have found their way into Mr. Hooper's hands. It is whispered that he is indebted for them to influence in certain quarters. However that may be, it is beyond doubt that he has handled them as well as could possibly be desired.

Richard Marsh – A Short Biography

Richard Bernard Heldmann was born on 12th October 1857, in St Johns Wood, North London, to parents Joseph Heldmann and Emma Marsh.

Shortly after his birth his father became ensnared in a bankruptcy proceedings which enforced the abandonment of a career as a merchant for that of a schoolmaster at a school in Hammersmith, West London.

By his early 20's the young Heldmann, showing a talent for writing, began publishing fiction. In 1880, he began to publish works of boys' school and adventure stories for the myriad magazine publications all eager for good well-written content. The most important of these was Union Jack, one of the better quality boys' weekly magazine associated with the popular authors G. A. Henty and W.H.G. Kingston.

Heldmann was promoted to co-editor in October 1882, but his association with the publication ended suddenly in June 1883. After this, Heldmann published no further fiction under that name.

The reason at the time was not immediately apparent but in April 1884 Heldmann was sentenced to 18 months of hard labour for issuing a series of cheques, all forged, in France and Britain the year before.

In order to be well away from the scandal and damage this had caused to his reputation Heldmann adopted a pseudonym on his release from jail. Shortly thereafter the name 'Richard Marsh' began to appear in the literary periodicals. The use of his mother's maiden name seems both a release from the criminal record now associated with his given name and a lifeline to a fresh beginning.

A stroke of very good fortune arrived when his novel The Beetle was published in 1897. There had been more than a few previous publications of his works but The Beetle would turn out to be his greatest commercial success and added some much-needed gravitas to his literary reputation. The story concerns a mysterious oriental person who follows a British politician to London, and then wreaks havoc with his powers of hypnosis and shape-shifting. The Beetle has some similar aspects to certain other novels of the period, including those such as Bram Stoker's Dracula, George du Maurier's Trilby, and Sax Rohmer's many Fu Manchu novels. Like Dracula, and also the sensation novels written by Wilkie Collins and others during the 1860s, The Beetle is narrated from the various viewpoints of multiple characters to create suspense. The novel is also layered with many themes and issues of the Victorian era including women's rights, unemployment, urban poverty, radical politics, homosexuality, science, and Britain's imperial adventures, particularly in regard to Egypt and the Sudan. The Beetle sold out upon its initial print run and thereafter sold well for the next several decades. After Marsh's early death the novel's story was made into a film and adapted for the London stage, both in the 1920's.

It should also be noted that in the year of its first publication it outsold Dracula, then also in its first year of publication. In hindsight a remarkable achievement.

Marsh was a prolific writer and wrote almost 80 volumes of fiction as well as many short stories, across several genres from horror and crime to romance and humour.

However, at horror he was particularly adept. Works such as The Goddess: A Demon (1900), in which an Indian sacrificial idol comes to life with murderous resolve, and The Joss: A Reversion (1901), whose central premise is that of an Englishman who transforms himself into a hideous oriental idol are prime examples.

An important element of many of Marsh's novels is the investigation of the mystery. Several of his novels are centered on the crime and its subsequent detection. In the novel Philip Bennion's Death (1897) a bachelor is discovered dead the day after discussing Thomas De Quincey's essay on murder as a fine art, and his neighbour and friend begin efforts to solve his death. In The Datchet Diamonds (1898) a young man who has lost a fortune on the stock market mistakenly swaps bags with a diamond thief, and then find himself pursued by both the thieves and police. In A Spoiler of Men (1905), Marsh puts together crime and science-fiction; the gentleman-criminal villain renders people slaves to his will by a chemical injection.

As with many authors success with popular fiction was never quite enough. He also wanted to be regarded as a serious author. His novel A Second Coming (1900) imagines Christ's return to an early-20th century London and is his most well-handled attempt in that pursuit.

His prolific output of short stories ensured his being published in a plethora of magazines including Household Words, Cornhill Magazine, The Strand Magazine, and Belgravia, as well as in a number of short story book collections. These collections; The Seen and the Unseen (1900), Marvels and Mysteries (1900), Both Sides of the Veil (1901) and Between the Dark and the Daylight (1902) all feature an eclectic mix of humour, crime, romance and the occult.

He also published several serial short stories. Here he was able to develop characters whose adventures could be related in discrete stories across numerous editions of a magazine. An example is Mr. Pugh and Mr. Tress of Curios (1898). They are rival collectors between whom pass a series of bizarre and disturbing objects—poisoned rings, pipes which seem to come to life, a phonograph record on which a murdered woman seems to speak from the dead, and the severed hand of a 13th-century aristocrat.

During his career he sometimes came up with characters or stories ahead of their time. His character Miss Judith Lee, a young teacher of deaf pupils whose lip-reading ability involves her with mysteries that she solves by acting as a detective was very pro-active in this regard.

Richard Marsh died from heart disease in Haywards Heath in Sussex on 9th August 1915.

Several of his novels were published posthumously.

Richard Marsh – A Concise Bibliography

As Bernard Heldmann
Boxall School: A Tale of Schoolboy Life (1881)
Dorrincourt [Union Jack, April-September 1881]
Expelled: Being the Story of a Young Gentleman (1882)
Daintree (1883)

As Richard Marsh
Capturing a Convict (Strand Magazine 1893)
The Devil's Diamond (1893)
The Mahatma's Pupil (1893)
The Strange Wooing of Mary Bowler (1895)
Mrs Musgrave—and her Husband (1895)
The Mystery of Philip Bennion's Death (1897)
The Crime and the Criminal (1897)
The Duke and the Damsel (1897)
The Beetle: A Mystery (1897)
The House of Mystery (1898)
Under One Cover: Eleven Stories by S. Baring-Gould, Richard Marsh, Ernest G. Henham, Fergus Hume, Andrew Merry and A. St John Adcock (1898)
Curios: Some Strange Adventures of Two Bachelors (1898)
Tom Ossington's Ghost (1898)
The Datchet Diamonds (1898)
The Woman with One Hand and Mr Ely's Engagement (1899)
In Full Cry (1899)
Frivolities: Especially Addressed to Those Who Are Tired of Being Serious (1899)
The Purse Which Was Found

The Girl and the Miracle (1907)
The Surprising Husband (1908)
The Coward behind the Curtain (1908)
That Master of Ours (1908)
A Royal Indiscretion (1909)
The Interrupted Kiss (1909)
The Girl in the Blue Dress (1909)
The Lovely Mrs Blake (1910)
Live Men's Shoes (1910)
The Twin Sisters (1911)
A Drama of the Telephone (1911)
Violet Forster's Lover (1912)
Sam Briggs: His Book (1912)
Judith Lee: Some Pages from her Life (1912)
The Master of Deception (1913)
Justice—Suspended (1913)
If It Please You (1913)
The Woman in the Car (1914)
Molly's Husband (1914)
Margot—and her Judges (1914)
The Man with Nine Lives (1915)
Love in Fetters (1915)
His Love or his Life (1915)
The Flying Girl (1915)
Violet Forster's Lover (1916)
The Adventures of Judith Lee (1916)
Sam Briggs, V.C. (1916)
Coming of Age (1916)
The Great Temptation (1916)
The Deacon's Daughter (1917)
On the Jury (1918)
Orders to Marry ([1918)
Outwitted (1919)
Apron-Strings (1920)

Periodicals

For Debt, Windsor Magazine (January 1902)
Returning a Verdict, Cornhill Magazine (January 1896)
The Lost Duchess, Cornhill Magazine (January 1895)
Mrs Riddles Daughter, All the Year Round (17 March 1894)
An Episcopal Scandal, Cornhill Magazine (February 1894)
A Rubber or Two, All the Year Round (16 September 1893)
A First Night, Cornhill Magazine (April 1893)
The Mystery of Philip Bennion's Death, Household Words (3/10/17/24/31 December 1892)
The Princess Margaretta, Household Words (3 December 1892)

The Puzzle, Cornhill Magazine (November 1892)

A Victim to Art, All the Year Round (2 July 1892)

The Burglar's Blunder, Derby Mercury (24 June 1891)

Pourquoipas, All the Year Round (9/16 May 1891)

The Pipe, Cornhill Magazine (March 1891)

When Greek Joined Greek, Household Words (6 September 1890)

His First Experiment, Cornhill Magazine (September 1890)

"Mignonette", All the Year Round (9 August 1890)

The Long Arm of Coincidence, Household Words (24 May 1890)

The Match of the Season, Cornhill Magazine (May 1890)

A Set of Chessmen, Cornhill Magazine (April 1890)

A Dream of Diamonds, Household Words (7 December 1889)

My Uncle's Flirtation, Household Words (16 November 1889)

"Em", Household Words (2 November 1889)

The Barnes Mystery: An Adventure of Judith Lee, Strand Magazine (October 1916)

"Scandalous!", Strand Magazine (August 1916)

What Fell on her Hat, Strand Magazine (April 1916)

The Adventures of Sam Briggs: On the Film, Strand Magazine (March 1916)

A Set of Chessmen, Cassell's Magazine of Fiction and Popular Literature (Dec 1915)

Sam Briggs Becomes a Soldier: A Fighting Man, Strand Magazine (December 1915)

Sam Briggs Becomes a Soldier: On the Way Home, Strand Magazine (November 1915)

Sam Briggs Becomes a Soldier: An Official Mistake, Strand Magazine (October 1915)

Sam Briggs Becomes a Soldier: In their Own Gas, Strand Magazine (September 1915)

Sam Briggs Becomes a Soldier: Sanctuary, Strand Magazine (August 1915)

Sam Briggs Becomes a Soldier: In the Nick of Time, Strand Magazine (July 1915)

Sam Briggs Becomes a Soldier: A Night Surprise for the Germans, Strand Magazine (June 1915)

Sam Briggs Becomes a Soldier: In the Trenches, Strand Magazine (May 1915)

Sam Briggs Becomes a Soldier: Baptism of Fire, Strand Magazine (April 1915)

Sam Briggs Becomes a Soldier: Two Stripes, Strand Magazine (March 1915)

Life in the King's New Army: Jack Carpenter's True Story, VI: Career for our Boys, Daily Mail (27 February 1915)

Life in the King's New Army: Jack Carpenter's True Story, V: The Tailor and the Man, Daily Mail (26 February 1915)

Life in the King's New Army: Jack Carpenter's True Story, IV: Hutments', Daily Mail (25 February 1915)

Life in the King's New Army: Jack Carpenter's True Story, III: First-Rate Fighting Men', Daily Mail (24 February 1915)

Life in the King's New Army: Jack Carpenter's True Story, II: The Berwick Borderers, Daily Mail (23 February 1915)

Life in the King's New Army: Jack Carpenter's True Story, I: Crossed Swords, Daily Mail (22 February 1915)

Sam Briggs Becomes a Soldier: A Man in the Making, Strand Magazine (February 1915)

Sam Briggs Becomes a Soldier: Sam Briggs Becomes a Soldier, Strand Magazine (January 1915)

The Amazing Visitor, Strand Magazine (December 1914)

Looping the Loop: An Adventure of Sam Briggs, Strand Magazine (August 1914)

The Torch, Strand Magazine (October 1913)

"Gaiety" Abroad, Strand Magazine (September 1913), 274-82

A Self-Appointed Guardian, English Illustrated Magazine (August 1913)

For the Cause, Strand Magazine (April 1913)

The Adventures of Judith Lee: The Affair of the Montagu Diamonds, Strand Magazine (February 1913)

The Adventures of Judith Lee: Mandragora, Strand Magazine (August 1912)

The Adventures of Judith Lee: "8 Elm Grove—Back Entrance", Strand Magazine (July 1912)

The Adventures of Judith Lee: The Restaurant Napolitain, Strand Magazine (June 1912)

The Adventures of Judith Lee: Uncle Jack, Strand Magazine (May 1912)

The Adventures of Judith Lee: Was It by Chance Only? Strand Magazine (April 1912)

The Adventures of Judith Lee: Isolda, Strand Magazine (March 1912)

The Adventures of Judith Lee: "Auld Lang Syne", Strand Magazine (January 1912)

The Adventures of Judith Lee: The Miracle, Strand Magazine (December 1911)

The Adventures of Judith Lee: Matched

The Burglary in Berkeley Square, Pearson's Magazine (December 1908)

The River of Light, Strand Magazine (December 1908)

The Girl in the Light Blue Dress, Strand Magazine (October 1908)

O'Rourke of the Saucy Sixth, Grand Magazine (June 1908)

The Adventures of Sam Briggs: The Limerick, Strand Magazine (February 1908)

The Adventures of Sam Briggs: The Star of Romance, Strand Magazine (July 1907)

The Adventures of Sam Briggs: A Social Evening, Strand Magazine (April 1907)

My Best Story and Why I Think So No. 21: The Strange Occurrences in Canterstone Gaol, Grand Magazine (October 1906)

The Adventures of Sam Briggs: That Hansom, Strand Magazine (May 1906)

The Adventures of Sam Briggs: Her Fourth, Strand Magazine (December 1905)

The Adventures of Sam Briggs: A Modest Half-Crown, Strand Magazine (November 1905)

The Adventures of Sam Briggs: The Gift Horse, Strand Magazine (March 1905)

My Wedding Day, Strand Magazine (January 1905)

The Adventures of Sam Briggs: The Girl on the Sands, Strand Magazine (October 1904)

The Parson, the Soldier, and the Child, London Magazine (November 1903)

The Girl and the Boy, London Magazine (October 1903)

By Whose Hand? New Short Novel by Richard Marsh, Answers (1 August – 31 October 1903)

A Girl Who Couldn't, Strand Magazine (January 1903)

The Kit-Bag, Windsor Magazine, 17 (January 1903), 298-309

Their Reasons: Two Hitherto Unreported Conversations, House Annual (1902)

At Large: Being the Strange Perils and Experiences of George Otway, Suspect, Answers (12 July - 27 December 1902)

The Handwriting, Strand Magazine (June 1902)

La Haute Finance, Windsor Magazine (March 1902)

A Wonderful Girl, Strand Magazine (March 1902)

Skittles, English Illustrated Magazine, (February/March 1902)

Breaking the Ice, Strand Magazine (February 1902)

My Aunt's Excursion, Windsor Magazine (January 1902)

The Haunted Chair: The Story of a Strange Mystery, Harmsworth London Magazine (January 1902)

Miss Donne's Great Gamble, Strand Magazine (November 1901)

The Man in the Glass Cage; or The Strange Story of the Twickenham Peerage, Manchester Times, (6 September – 27 December 1901

The Adventures of Augustus Short: Things Which I Have Done for Others, and Wish I Hadn't: The Address Which I Gave for Rudman, Cassell's Magazine (November 1901)

The Adventures of Augustus Short: Things Which I Have Done for Others, and Wish I Hadn't: Jones's Love Affair, Cassell's Magazine (October 1901)

The Adventures of Augustus Short: Things Which I Have Done for Others, and Wish I Hadn't: The Duel I Fought of Jarvis, Cassell's Magazine (September 1901)

The Adventures of Augustus Short: Things Which I Have Done for Others, and Wish I Hadn't: Griffin's Offspring, Cassell's Magazine (August 1901)

The Adventures of Augustus Short: Things Which I Have Done for Others, and Wish I Hadn't: McCulloch's Shoes, Cassell's Magazine (July 1901)

The Adventures of Augustus Short: Things Which I Have Done for Others, and Wish I Hadn't: The Fitzroy-Jenkinsons' Rooms, Cassell's Magazine (June 1901)

Staggers, Windsor Magazine (April 1901)

How I Drove a Motor Car for Randal, Strand Magazine (April 1901)

The Disappearance of Mrs Macrecham: The Amazing Story of a Strange Cat, Harmsworth Monthly Pictorial Magazine (March 1901)

The Irregularity of the Juryman, Strand Magazine (December 1900)

The Strange Fortune of Pollie Blythe: The Story of a Chinese "God", Manchester Times (12 October 1900 – 8 February 1901)

Pugh's Poisoned Ring, Harmsworth Monthly Pictorial Magazine (October 1900)

Willyum, Penny Illustrated Paper and Illustrated Times, (26 May 1900)

Willyum, Hampshire Telegraph and Naval Chronicle (26 May 1900)

The Goddess: A Demon, Manchester Times (12 January – 30 March 1900)

The Stolen Treaty, Manchester Times (27 October 1899)

For One Night Only, Answers (8 April 1899)

In Full Cry, Manchester Times (3 March – 9 June 1899)

The Colonel's Cane, Cassell's Magazine (February 1899)

The Burglary at Azalea Villa, Manchester Times, (13 January 1899)

The Burglary at Azalea Villa, Newcastle Weekly Courant (14 January 1899)

Our Christmas Burglar, Answers (17 December 1898)

Something to his Advantage, Manchester Times (7 October – 4 November 1898)

A Lesson in Sculling, Newcastle Weekly Courant (October 1898)

That Five Hundred Pound Price, Harmsworth Monthly Pictorial Magazine (September 1898)

The Chancellor's Ward, Harmsworth Monthly Pictorial Magazine (August 1898)

The Ossington Mystery, Ipswich Journal (1 April – 17 June 1898)

The Duchess of Datchet's Diamonds, New Zealand Graphic and Ladies' Journal (New Zealand) (7 May – 25 June 1898)

The Peril of Paul Lessingham: The Story of a Haunted Man, Answers (13 March – 19 June 1897)

The Purse Which Was Found, Answers (17 April 1897)

The Rector and the Curate, Answers (19 December 1896)

An Illustration of Modern Science, Pall Mall Magazine (November 1896)

A Battlefield Up-to-Date, Idler Magazine (August 1896)

Twins, Idler Magazine (January 1896)

Lady Wishaw's Hand, Leeds Mercury (January 1895)

Young George, St Nicholas (March 1894)

Exchange Is Robbery, Idler Magazine (December 1893 - January 1894)

The Tipster: An Impossible Story, Home Chimes (December 1893)

The Influence of Women, Home Chimes (November 1893)

By Deputy: A Reminiscence of Travel, Home Chimes (October 1893)

Rivals, Home Chimes (September 1893)

Capturing a Convict, Strand Magazine (August 1893)

A Burglar Alarm, Home Chimes (June 1893)

Music Halls and Theatres, Home Chimes (March 1893)

A Strange Bride, Manchester Times (6/13 January 1893)

The Mask, Gentleman's Magazine (December 1892)

A Vision of the Night, Strand Magazine (December 1892)

Nelly, Home Chimes (November 1892)

A Prophet: A Story, New England Magazine (October - November 1892)

Mr Harland's Pupils, Home Chimes (August 1892)

The Brothers in Grey, Home Chimes (April 1892)

The Half-Back, Derby Mercury (March 1892)

The Half-Back, Home Chimes (February 1892)

The Violin, Home Chimes (December 1891)

The Short Story, Home Chimes (August 1891)

Magical Music, Gentleman's Magazine (May 1891)

A Honeymoon Trip, Home Chimes (April 1891)

Mitwaterstraand, Time (September 1890)

A Pack of Cards, Longman's Magazine (August 1890)

The Burglar's Blunder, Ladies' Journal (Canada) (1 July 1890)

The Strange Occurrences in Canterstone Jail, Blackwood's Edinburgh Magazine (June 1890)

A Substitute: The Story of My Last Cricket-Match, Longman's Magazine (June 1890)

The Burglar's Blunder, Gentleman's Magazine (May 1890)

A Silent Witness, Belgravia (October 1889)

A Bed for the Night, Belgravia (Summer 1889)

Payment for a Life, Belgravia (Summer 1888)